Dedalus Original Fiction in Paperback

LE FANU'S ANGEL

Brian Keogh is an Irish writer, marketing consultant, speechwriter and journalist, and has collaborated on non-fiction books on economic and social subjects. He was previously editor of Irish business and public affairs magazines and headed Ireland's largest PR company. He has written a number of short stories.

Le Fanu's Angel is his first novel.

D0177071

Brian Keogh

LE FANU'S ANGEL

Dedalus

Supported using public funding by
**ARTS COUNCIL
ENGLAND**

Published in the UK by Dedalus Limited
24-26, St Judith's Lane, Sawtry, Cambs, PE28 5XE
email: info@dedalusbooks.com
www.dedalusbooks.com

ISBN printed book 978 1 912868 45 2
ISBN ebook 978 1 912868 47 6

Dedalus is distributed in the USA & Canada by SCB Distributors
15608 South New Century Drive, Gardena, CA 90248
email: info@scbdistributors.com   web: www.scbdistributors.com

Dedalus is distributed in Australia by Peribo Pty Ltd.
58, Beaumont Road, Mount Kuring-gai, N.S.W. 2080
email: info@peribo.com.au   web: www.peribo.com.au

First published by Dedalus in 2021

Printed and bound in the UK by Clays Elcograf S.p.A
Typeset by Marie Lane

CONTENTS

PART ONE

PART TWO

PART ONE

1

DE PROFUNDIS

I came to consciousness, or so I thought, in an abyss of nothingness, a world of black silence, bottomless, eternal. I had no corporeal existence, only a blank consciousness, with no memory of who I was or how I got here. It occurred to me that I was in a singularly vivid nightmare. I was locked into it and struggled in vain to pull myself awake.

Then the truth hit me: This was no nightmare. I was dead, in some kind of a temporary state, a fade-out from life to oblivion. The belief took root and blossomed, pricking and swirling in my consciousness. I knew that some medical experts believe that death wasn't always the complete end of things and even when body and brain shut down, some form of consciousness may remain for a time. Is this what it was, the final dying of cells in my body and synapses in my brain? How long before utter oblivion?

I remained in a state of terror and desolation, as timeless time passed until, in the farthest distance of the void, I thought I detected an infinitesimal glint of light, a pinprick in the fabric of my non-universe. Gently, unhurriedly, the light came nearer, expanding, now brighter, brilliant and intense. Its penetrating luminosity banished the void, a blazing, dancing radiance, of a whiteness beyond imagining. Abruptly the light was gone, and all was black void again. Then –

I jolted awake into a twilight existence, neither asleep nor fully awake, devoid of thought and emotion, hollowed out. I lay, gagged and trussed, in what appeared to be a four-poster bed, under a canopy of night sky, with stars flickering through slow-passing clouds. I tried to find an element of my identity and found a blank canvas, like one newly born, awaiting the imprint of experience.

I remained like this for what might have been minutes or hours, undergoing a form of catharsis, transmuting the horror of my death into a gauzy memory, a necessary preparation, perhaps, for returning to worldly existence. Because, some-where in that time, I began to make the transition from death to life.

My surroundings became clearer. I was alone in a room, a hospital ward, and on a raised hospital bed. It was a corner position, beside a high window that looked onto the night sky. In the ward, pale-hued plastic curtains on ceiling rails were pulled back. The ward held two other beds. One beside me was stripped to its shiny latex mattress and the second, catty-corner to me, by the door, held a stack of sheets, pillows and blankets.

Blades of pain were slicing through me and this awareness of my body told me I was, once more, in the world. I had been truly dead. Now, I was truly alive. The realisation came slowly but then with shock and astonishment and bafflement. How had I resurrected, like Lazarus and the daughter of Jairus, from that emptiness of death? My mind refused to compute the idea, shushed it, thrust it into a deep-down crevice of my mind to simmer awhile.

I was not gagged and bound, as I had imagined, but swathed in bandages around my forehead and my face. My left arm and leg were encased in heavy dressings and covered by a wire cage. I could not imagine what had caused this catastrophe. A plastic bag on an IV pole slowly dripped colourless liquid into needles in my arm and neck. A nose mask hissed oxygen. I had a pounding headache as if a garrotte was twisting into the back of my neck and my mouth tasted parched and tacky. I tried to call out but managed only a dry wheeze. I wanted desperately to remain conscious and not return to the blackness of that eternal amen, where, this time, I might be lost forever.

Time dragged its heels. The sky slipped from darkness to dull daylight as morning replaced night. Dim nicotine-yellow light illuminated the ward. Outside, the sodium glare of orange neons on the out-of-sight streets below threw a like tint on the slanted roofs and upper windows of buildings. The world was still, except for a distant church bell.

I moved my head and a further slash of sharp pain lacerated me. I was no longer alone in the ward. A doctor, I guessed, white coat, stethoscope, blue scrubs, was standing in the centre of the ward, staring at me, unmoving, hands in pockets. He was nondescript and scrawny, age indeterminate, lank hair, watery eyes, sallow face and a drooping bandit-style moustache. His words, when he spoke, seemed to come from an echo chamber.

'Think you got away with murder, eh?' His dull eyes blazed, and his mouth twisted into a lupine grin. 'Not that easy, you scummy vomitsucker. You made corpses of your betters. Now join them.'

I was stunned by the force of his fury. Who was he? What had I done?

With a visceral growl, the stranger, no doctor he, advanced on me. His hands, claw-like, emerged from his pockets and snatched a pillow from the near bed. As he came closer, I caught a pungent whiff of excrement from him. His yellow teeth bared in a fearsome grimace, he held the pillow in front of him with both hands, his intention frighteningly clear. My nerves twitched uncontrollably in terror. I tried to yell for help but choked. Pinioned and trapped, I pushed myself down into the bed, ignoring the pains shooting through me.

As the pillow touched my face, some survival instinct kicked in and, without thinking, I reached out with one hand, grabbed his crotch and squeezed, wincing as I pulled on a trocar needle in my arm. My grip had no strength and he easily shook me off. But I'd made him jump back a few steps with a grunt.

He came again, more slowly, and raised the pillow, then froze as he heard, we both heard, approaching footsteps and voices in the corridor outside. He glared at me, gave a snarl of frustration, pointed a menacing finger almost into one of my eyes, swung around and, in an instant, was out the door and gone.

A minute later, the same door opened to admit a female nurse followed by a male doctor, a genuine one this time, by the look of him. When the nurse saw I was awake, she favoured me with a mammy's beam of approval, apparently not noticing my mental disarray.

'Ah, you're back with us. That's a nice long rest you've

been having and I'm sure you're the better for it.'

Cork accent, posh Cork. The affluent Montenotte district, most likely. She was in her early forties, big-boned, with a prow of a nose and a prognathic jaw. The name badge on her button-front uniform read Celia Purcell.

'That man, he tried to kill me.' My tongue took a life of its own and all I got out was inarticulate croaking.

She poured some water from a bottle on the bedside table into a paper cone and held it to my lips. It tasted deliciously chilled, with a citrus tang. I sipped greedily. 'Enough for now,' she said, taking it away.

Still agitated, I stammered, 'Who, who that man…'

'This is Doctor Watson.' She indicated the doctor, misunderstanding.

'No, no. The one who attacked me,' I said thickly. Speaking was an effort, but I was finding the words. 'A doctor or witchdoctor. In the ward. Made off before you came in. You must have seen him.'

'When was this?'

'Seconds ago.'

She shook her head, tolerantly. 'Tut. No such person. A nightmare, likely.'

How could they not have seen him or passed him in the corridor? Did I dream it? In the presence of normality, my terror was fading, and I hadn't the energy to say more. Too much was happening, a succession of the increasingly inexplicable. I needed to slow things down, gain some balance.

'How are you this morning?' This from Doctor Watson, who had listened to the exchange without comment. He was young, mid-thirties, in green hospital scrubs, rimless glasses, unruly ginger hair behind a high forehead.

'You tell me,' I said dully.

He touched a screen on a monitor over the bed and examined it as it beeped several times. He took a chair by my bed and did what doctors do, shone a torch in my eyes – 'Can I ask you to follow the movement of the light'– held my wrist for a pulse check, lifted the sheets to study me, gave a few probing jabs – 'Do you feel this? And this?'

He nodded. 'Pulse racing a bit. That would be your nightmare. Otherwise, so far, so good.'

He sat back, looking tired, removed his glasses, massaged his eyes and cleaned the lenses absently with a corner of his scrub top. He had shaved recently and nicked himself twice.

'Why am I here? What happened to me?' I was getting my voice and some of my senses back.

He arched an eyebrow. 'You were in a car accident. Serious enough, to be frank. You sustained fractures, cuts and bruises, as well as internal damage, and you lost blood. That said, we got you stabilised, and you've been in an induced coma to let your body mend. The good news is you're off the critical list and making excellent progress.'

He gave a chuckle. You've been extremely lucky, though it may not feel so.'

His words were mostly floating out of my mind before I properly absorbed them. The nurse was nodding encouragement, as if to a child.

'Something I need to know…' I stopped, unable to remember what it was.

He saw my confusion and put a finger to his lips. 'Enough for the present. We can talk again, okay?'

They both headed for the door.

'What I wanted to ask,' I said, remembering. 'Who am I?'

Watson hesitated gave the nurse an enquiring look and they came back.

'I don't even know my name,' I said, ridiculously embarrassed.

'It's Kieran –'

'Sheridan,' I completed, the name all at once lighting up in my mind. 'Kieran Sheridan. Guess I do know my name.'

I prodded my memory. 'That's my lot. I've no idea who…'

'I wouldn't get upset about it. You'll remember when you need. Temporary amnesia is common after concussion and the trauma of an accident. Don't strain yourself and you'll find it comes back, in its own time, if not at once, in increments.'

He was right. As soon as they were gone, recall came in a disorganised jumble: my apartment, my office in the agency, relaxing in a darkened cinema, striding along Dun Laoghaire pier, hammering out my blog. People, too. Shay Dempsey and Cronin Brenner, Jacinta in Zagreb, Saul and Simon in the Cusco hostel in the Andes, my late parents, Uncle Jasper. I even remembered my hidden name – I'll come to that in time.

I owned a car, a silver S-Type Jaguar, ten years old, a treasured possession, costly to run. Had I wrecked it, written it off? Maybe I was in legal trouble, drunk at the wheel, had injured, even killed someone? Later, I'd ask later.

As memories dribbled in, I had the sense of being removed from them, as if they had been dormant in the far reaches of my subconscious and I was coming to them for the first time. As if they were another's memories. More recent events were losing clarity. The lunatic who'd tried to kill me:

was his murderous assault real or something I'd read or seen in a film? What of my death and the black desolation? No, that had been real. If so...

I tried to get things straight in my head. Even allowing for the fact I was evidently recovering from a car crash, my mental processes weren't meshing. I had died. But now, incredibly, I was alive. And a doctor who wasn't a doctor had tried to murder me, which could have been a nightmare, except it wasn't. My memory was back – but not like it was my memory. Call that clarity? Jeezus. What was happening to me?

I wasn't going to get any answers. On the contrary, my life was already unfolding in a way that would challenge my every perception of reality. Among other things, I would eventually discover I was not at all who I thought I was.

2

AN ANGEL NEEDS NO WINGS

Slow forward a week. The bite of my various pains had become dull aches and I existed in a mental haze, perpetually fatigued, sleeping or dozing most of the time.

I had requested no visitors, afraid I might blurt about being dead and alive and the weird things happening to me. There was no phone by the bed and my smartphone had gone missing, which further confined me to the world of doctors, nurses and meal trolley ladies. There was no return visit from my mad assassin, though the memory of him still had me sweeping the ward with a nervous gaze whenever I woke.

The bedside table was crowded with assorted Get Well cards from colleagues and clients. Two former girlfriends had sent almost identical bouquets of red and white roses, as if they had ordered them together. I had been sent a pile of books: the latest John Sandford and Michael Connelly and, weirdly, Gustav Meyrink's classic, *The Golem*. No less intriguing was a lavishly illustrated *John Lavery: A Painter and his Time*, with no note or card to identify my benefactor. I'd never given Lavery, an Irish painter of bygone years, much thought.

A nurse I hadn't seen before assisted me to the bathroom, pre-breakfast. She had flat, olive- brown features and silk-black hair, with a narrow grey streak visible along the centre parting. Her name tag was extra wide to accommodate a lengthy Asian surname. With a neutral smile, she stripped me of my garments and, with cheerful competence, administered a thorough head to heel, front to back, washing with a handheld showerhead, soap and sponge. It was a mutually asexual exercise. She gave my body the once over, smacked her lips and said, 'Amazing.'

Alarmed, I thought she was coming on to me. Then she added, 'I've never seen injuries heal so fast. It's astonishing, a miracle. Even your face was a whole lot worse last week.'

A few minutes earlier, Nurse Purcell had remarked much the same when she removed the cages around my arm and leg, unwound most of my bandages and clipped the stitches. It was true. I felt the steady improvement, apart from constant exhaustion and weariness.

I had a nasty shock when I saw myself in the bathroom mirror. My face looked like it had been rammed to one side and was defaced, so to speak, with ugly bruising in black, puce, yellow and nausea green. A Karl Malden nose. Pitted cheeks. Heavy growth of stubble, with gaps showing scars not fully healed. I was a passable knock-off for one of Doctor Franken-stein's cast-offs, a badly stitched patchwork of several cadavers.

My nurse of the impossible name, and with an incongruous hint of a Scottish burr, heard me moan and assured me the bruises would be gone in another week or two. The scars would fade. I should count my blessings, she said, no permanent facial damage, eyes unaffected, nose unbroken, no teeth missing.

What really upset me was that, beneath the scars and

bruises, I didn't recognise myself. I mean, at all. It was the face of a stranger. I examined the image examining me, almost expecting it to give me a sardonic wink. I had a momentary recall of inspecting myself similarly in a mirror not too long ago and then, too, not liking what I saw.

My mind had been baiting me with a bizarre possibility: I was still dead, had been for the past week, and I was currently going through a new phase of death, in which my dying consciousness was fabricating an elaborate but illusory dramatisation of an alternative world, a projection of what my life would have been if I hadn't died. This illusion might prove to be a temporary scenario, which would end at any time, abruptly or in a slow fade, when I finally ceased to be. And, then I thought with a spasm of cold horror, I would return to the darkness again.

I'm a film buff, with a small reputation as an online film and TV blogger. I've sat through numerous films and TV shows in which the protagonist dies and is restored to life, usually to fulfil some purpose or other, such as learning how to become a nicer person or bringing a killer to justice. Not relevant in my case.

As an alternative storyline, Adrian Lyne's film *Jacob's Ladder* has a US Vietnam veteran, now a postal clerk, living a routine life, except for flashbacks and weird hallucinations. Spoiler alert: the film's final minute reveals he had expired in a war zone field hospital and his back-home experiences had been wholly imaginary flashes, his desperate mind trying to come to an acceptance of death. Could I be going through something of the kind? The idea tossed uneasily in my befuddled mind but I hadn't the mental strength to follow it.

The morning passed, the ward shifting from light to shadow as the sun played hide-and-seek among the clouds. I was listless and heavy, in and out of sleep. From somewhere in the hospital, a tinny transistor had Édith Piaf emoting *The Three Bells*. Curious and irking that the hospital allowed radios without headphones. Outside, the traffic rumbled by, with an occasional yap from a car horn. Far off, a church bell tolled.

Coming out of a semi-doze, I found a newly-installed patient in the bed by the door. I gave him a quick scan, unreasonably miffed at finally having to share my ward. He was thin and sharp-featured, with a small button nose, a jaundiced pallor and short-cut black hair that fell across his brow. When he saw I was awake, he gave me a wave and a wry grin. I wasn't in the humour for companionable conversation or an intimate exchange of illnesses and hospital experiences, and with a perfunctory acknowledgement, I closed my eyes.

I blinked open when I heard him push out of bed and pad across the floor to settle in my bedside chair. He wore faded, blue-dotted pyjamas under a heavy dressing gown and a brown silk scarf around his neck that partly covered a dressing at his throat. I put him in his early thirties, my age, but with an older man's face, creased and drawn, citrine skin stretched over his features. His dark eyes were feverish and watery and he looked as one shambling towards death's threshold. Several rust-coloured blotches on his pyjamas, which I took to be bloodstains, made me queasy.

'I can see you've surely been through the mill, and that's a fact,' he said, looking me over with a quiet intensity that was off-putting. 'But, good for you, they say you're doing well.'

He seemed to decide this was enough about me and

proceeded to unpack his own troubles. A captive, though not captivated, listener, I hid my vexation and feigned interest. His name was Martin Doherty, his hometown Mullingar, he was an accountant with a modest practice and had a wife and five children. And stage four cancer.

'Throat. One lunchtime, it felt like I'd swallowed a cork-screw. This was only six weeks ago, can you believe it.'

He'd been through exploratory surgery, had a potato-sized abscess removed and now feared the worst, convinced the doctors were offering him false comfort, would not admit he was a terminal case.

'They won't tell me the truth. What can I do? My family, they can't get by without me. My children, they're only little babies. You see how it is?'

How did I come to be in a ward with a cancer patient? Strange bedfellows. I didn't want his company nor had I any wish to be a confidant to his problems. But his nerves were raw and he needed to talk. Besides, I was getting better, while he was heading the other way. So I suffered him and threw out the occasional monosyllable, but after a short time, I couldn't hold back my tiredness, his voice became a monotonous blur of sound and I drifted off.

I woke on my side, looking through the window at a cloud-filled sky and the fading light of evening. Reflected in the glass was a curious luminous glow behind me. When I shifted about, the ward appeared unnaturally bright and centred at Doherty's bed. A young woman was with him, her back to me, speaking softly, one hand holding his. His wife, probably. Then I heard his woe-is-me about wife and children. A doctor, so. She called him Martin and I thought he called her

23

Eva. Doctor and friend? Her voice was low and soothing, and, it seemed, effective because he was soon quiet.

She turned and came over to my bed with an expression of pure happiness when she saw me that permeated the whole ward with sparkling, golden sunshine. I caught my breath and the world gave a shiver of delightful anticipation. She was the most bewitchingly beautiful girl I had ever seen. Late-twenties, I guessed, tall and slender, with raven black hair that fell to her shoulders. She wore a cream blouse open at the neck, an emerald green scarf and lilac skirt, colours vivid and bright. I breathed in a fragrance that conjured up an arbour of summer flowers and fruit trees, intoxicating. The French, who else, have the words for it: *coup de foudre*, like a thunderclap, love at first sight.

No physical description could fully describe her astonishing delicate beauty that overpowered me and instantly held me in thrall. A face almost devoid of make-up since her naturally flawless skin required none; a slender nose and high cheekbones set off her most striking feature: large, lustrous, almond-shaped hazel eyes, fringed with long lashes.

Those eyes held an impish gleam of amusement when I evidently failed to recognise her. Indeed, a strange familiarity teased me, as if I'd once come upon her, in person or in a photograph, that we had crossed paths at one time. Surely I'd never seen her before. I would not have forgotten her.

In days to come, I would retrieve that moment when I first saw her and instantly knew with total clarity that my entire life to then had been a pointless charade. Each mental reviewing of her entrancing entrance brought a delightful frisson of incredulity. I would recall it in a loop: play, rewind, play, rewind, play. Always fresh discoveries: the slow-motion of her electrifying smile, the way her glance fell upon me, how she had seemed to float across the ward with grace and supreme assurance, the glow that enfolded her.

I said the first thing that came into my head. 'Where are your wings?'

'Wings?' she asked.

'Don't angels have wings?'

She laughed. 'Don't you know? An angel needs no wings.'

'Of course not,' I agreed, struck by the truth of it and reflected that millennia of artists and sculptors may have been gifted with more imagination than accuracy.

'Are you real?' I asked. 'The truth is –' here I tried to pass it off insouciantly '– I've been having this crazy idea I'm dead. Do you think you might be part of it?'

It was not the most felicitous conversational opener and I immediately wished I could take it back.

She didn't reply but sat at the edge of my bed, sending an erotic shiver through me as her body touched my blanketed legs. I struggled to get myself under control. I'd brushed my teeth earlier but wished I had mouthwash or breath freshener – and a clearer head.

'You have the most wonderful autumn-brown eyes,' I said.

'And you have two whopping black eyes,' she replied, a smile playing on her face.

'I think I know you, but my memory cells are in the wind this week. May I ask your name?'

She regarded me with surprise, as though I should have known.

25

'Aoife.'

'An evocative name, Aoife. Princess Aoife of old, as in that marvellous panorama by Maclise in the National Gallery, you know it? Aoife. An altogether Irish name… yet I hear a distinctive English accent.'

'I am English. My great-grandmother came from Athlone.'

'And her name was Aoife?'

'It was Maud. She said the name Aoife was in the family line and it passed to me.'

I remembered I hadn't given my name.

'I'm Kieran Sheridan.' On an impulse I added, 'Le Fanu. My birth certificate names me as Kieran René Sheridan Le Fanu. Way back, my folks were Huguenot refugees. Arrived in the seventeenth century. We don't use Le Fanu in public. Something of a secret, don't know why. Could be a religious thing. Or to escape the inevitable: "Are you related to *the* Sheridan Le Fanu, the ghost writer?"'

'Are you?'

'I believe I am, indirectly. When I was abroad, I called myself Sheridan Le Fanu but reverted to plain Sheridan when I came home.'

This was dreadful, I thought. I'm babbling. I wasn't normally shaky with girls. But this was different.

'Just call me Rumpelstiltskin,' I finished with an apologetic grin.

She leaned forward and seemed to look inward in wistful remembrance, an elbow resting on the overtable at the end of the bed, the long, slender fingers of one hand touching her chin: La Penserosa.

'I met Sheridan Le Fanu once,' she murmured. 'We were

introduced in the foyer of the Shelbourne Hotel. He was perfectly civil, talked of Swedenborg, mostly. But he was clearly unhappy to be in social company. I knew nothing then of his repute as a writer of the supernatural.'

I was lost for a response. Sheridan Le Fanu had died in 1873. Were we talking at cross-purposes? I wanted to keep the conversation going but, baffled, I couldn't think how to get it onto a normal plane.

Distracted, I asked, 'Do you know you are surrounded by a fabulous sunshine? It seems to come from inside you.'

She nodded. 'You have an aura, too, the faintest glow at present. It is your life spark. It will become brighter, more intense, as you understand it more.'

'Aura? What wild and magical things you talk about, rare and radiant maiden.'

'"Rare and radiant"? If you like Poe, I'm sure you will find this, too, has things to say to you.'

She held out a book she'd been carrying, a slim volume bound in rich brown leather, with gilded pages and a cover of intricate foliage sprays in gold leaf. On the spine I read, *Selected Poems of Dante Gabriel Rossetti*. Not my usual fare but I was ready to devour whatever she might recommend.

She took a silver pencil from her skirt pocket and wrote a brief note on an inside page. She marked the page with its book ribbon and slipped the book into the drawer of the bedside locker.

I thanked her and, for something to say, blurted, 'Your friend Martin Doherty's convinced he's dying, and he may be right.'

'*Angor animi*. Martin is past that. He was lost and needed

guidance. He'll be at rest soon.'

I heard her without comprehending. Either she was perpetually enigmatic, or my mind was more sluggish than I thought.

Her tone became urgent, intense. 'I must tell you. Your defences are weak and vulnerable. You are in danger from a wicked being who will try to overrun your mind and prey on your weaknesses. Bad things may happen, nightmares that are more than nightmares. They cannot last, remember that. Don't yield to them. And I promise: I shall come to you when you need me.'

'Are you a doctor?' I asked, now completely bewildered, trying to catch up. Strangely, it never occurred to me she was other than perfectly sane. She reached out and held my hand and I quivered with pleasure at her touch.

'No. I am a guide, you might say.'

I had completely lost the sense of our conversation. I was hot all over, my face wet with perspiration. 'Enough,' she murmured. She removed a white cloth from her pocket and wiped my brow. It was delectable, cool and refreshing and I relaxed. Once more, drowsiness overtook me. I fought it and tried to hold back the fall of my leaden eyelids. 'Don't go yet,' I pleaded. 'We have much more to talk about. I want you to know –'

She leaned over and kissed my cheek and a surge of out-and-out sensuality coursed through me.

She sighed. 'The time is up and I must leave you now. It may be a while before we can be together again. I don't know when. But I'll be with you when you need me, Michael.'

Kieran, it's Kieran, I tried to tell her, but she had gone.

Distantly, I heard that improbable radio again, now playing a song over and over, a one-time favourite of my grandma's:

> *I remember you*
> *You're the one who made my dreams come true*
> *A few kisses ago.*

3

Spooked

In dreamless slumber, I stood on an unknown shore watching the sea rippling towards me in sinuous waves that spent themselves at my feet in rushes of frothing foam. Endlessly, the heaving, swelling tide rolled in, never changing, unremitting. My mind was devoid of all thought, emotionless except for a quiet tranquillity. This was rest in peace.

The trance-like sleep carried me through an afternoon and evening and into the night. In the early hours, I was awakened by the sound of murmuring voices in the ward. They were coming from Martin Doherty's bed, hidden now by a surround of plastic curtain. A faint mist hung in the air in that corner of the ward. I had an impression of many persons crowded there, but while the bedside area was lit, there were no shadows on the curtain and I heard only soft voices. I couldn't make out what they were saying but they were relaxed and kindly.

'Oh, you are getting close. It's lovely, splendid.' Doherty sounded upbeat, no longer oozing self-pity. 'Wait for me, I'm coming, please wait.'

I was blinded by a flash of phosphorescent light from

behind the curtain that lit up the ward. When I regained my sight, a blue-white light hovered above Doherty's bed. It slowly faded, and the ward returned to semi-darkness and silence. I could make no sense of it all and expected to be awake for the rest of the night. But inexplicably, I slid back to sleep again in minutes.

The sun had taken the morning off, leaving a dull gunmetal grey sky. How bland and flat my world seemed without Aoife. I was utterly, crazily smitten, beyond anything I could ever have imagined. I pondered her abrupt departure. What did she mean by 'Time is up and I must leave you'? Like Cinderella dashing barefoot from the ball. When was 'a while' before I would see her again? Why not a day or a time or even a phone number jotted tenderly on my palm? And why get my name wrong? So many questions, a profusion of confusion.

I recalled the queer happenings in the early hours. Another bad dream? Perhaps not. Across the ward, the curtain had partly opened, and the bed held a human shape completely swathed in a white winding sheet, on the chest a black crucifix with an ivory Christ. So, Martin Doherty had died when strength wanes and spirit gives way. I had a prick of irrational guilt at having slept through his last hour and not kept empathetic vigil – though what difference would it have made? – and because I'd offered him no solace when he'd tried to engage with me earlier. But his end had sounded mellow.

I had a more immediate concern. I was sharing an otherwise empty ward with a corpse and it utterly unnerved me. Beads of perspiration were trickling down my back and I was having difficulty breathing. A panic attack. It was my first time even to be near a dead body, a situation I had contrived to avoid all my life.

Because phobias are irrational, it is difficult for people to understand how deeply they can disorder the mind of those afflicted. An accountant who worked with one of my clients had a phobia about feathers – I believe it's called pteronophobia. Once, when he heard an exotic bird had escaped New York Zoo, he boarded up the windows of his house in Terenure, for fear the bird would fly across the Atlantic and invade his home. Amusing, but not to him.

My dread, my phobia, was of anything to do with death and dead bodies. If I inadvertently caught sight of a funeral cortege on the street, it took considerable willpower not to head in the opposite direction. The sight of a hearse carrying a coffin could send my stomach into a spasm of fear, often leaving me ill. Whenever anyone known to me, intimately or remotely, died, I'd shun mirrors for twenty-four hours, fearful of seeing their bloodless face looking back at me. I learned that this was an age-old superstition and not unique to me.

Now, I was keeping involuntary vigil with a corpse, one freshly deceased. In the rational part of my mind, I knew the late Martin Doherty's remains were an emptiness, an absence. At the same time, I sensed a presence across the ward, indefinably menacing. He had known me for a few hours, had spoken with me, maybe even now was aware of me, his spirit not yet fully departed but lingering close by, resenting, perhaps, that I had treated him with polite indifference. Worse still, might he not be sniffing out in me a fellow departed being masquerading as one alive?

I forced myself to stop my involuntary shaking, lie still and switch my focus from the bed opposite to the pattern of the white matt tiles in the ceiling and at a crooked imperfection between two of them that might be a dead spider.

From the edge of my vision, I saw that the black and ivory crucifix had somehow become inverted on the sheet. To my horror, the sheet stirred and the crucifix slid across the swaddled body and fell to the floor with a soft thump. Ice whipped through me, crown to toes, and I heard myself groan. But when I looked directly across, I realised I had imagined it: the crucifix was in position. It wasn't inverted, nor had it moved.

I stared for a time at the motionless symbol on the dead man's covering and at the shape beneath and turned away once more, having no wish to contemplate that white-enveloped thing. It happened again. From the corner of my eye, the sheet quivered and jerked, as though the late Martin Doherty was attempting to free himself of his wrapping. The crucifix dropped to the floor again and a bloodless hand slipped from the sheet. An arm followed, swinging inertly. With a scream, I looked across full on. Again, the crucifix had not moved. No arm dangled.

Terror grasped at my thumping heart. My chest tightened painfully, and I was breathing hard. I was shaking again uncontrollably. An emergency call bell was on the wall behind me, out of reach. But if I got to it, what? 'Help. Martin Doherty's corpse is alive and kicking.'

I closed my eyes tight to shut out any further illusions. I didn't open them, even when I detected a low sinister growl and the sound of bare feet scuttling across the floor towards me. Petrified, I expected at the next instant a chill hand to seize my arm. Nothing, another illusion.

The spell finally broke when two orderlies in brown hospital coats came into the ward. They took no notice of me and I was incapable of speech then. 'Running late, let's get on with it,' said the older one in a nasal voice. He handed the crucifix to the second orderly, and laid blankets over Doherty's body, in a reverent manner, as though in religious ritual. I half expected him to produce a vial of holy water and sprinkle it around. The other, late teens, played dutiful apprentice corpse mover in silence. Together, they manoeuvred the bed out of the ward. Its wheels rattled as it moved along a corridor, and into another. I stretched my hearing to follow it as it faded and merged with the noises of a busy hospital.

A few minutes later, Nurse Purcell bustled in, together with the nurse who had earlier hosed me down. As Purcell commenced the usual pulse and temperature routine, I said nothing about my recent phobic peril. I didn't want them questioning my sanity. I was distracted when I realised I hadn't seen the nurses nor anyone else since early the previous day and I'd not been fed or watered in that time. Highly irregular, surely.

'You're the first nurse I've seen in twenty-four hours,' I said. 'I thought you'd forgotten me.'

I tried to make it jocular, not wanting to sound a whiner.

Purcell raised an eyebrow. 'What are you talking about, twenty-four hours?'

I looked at her, puzzled. She looked at me, puzzled.

'Are you having me on?' she said. 'I was with you less than an hour ago, remember? Right after Decay gave you your shower.'

The other nurse, whose moniker, I reprocessed, was DK,

her initials, assented with the tiniest nod.

Her words flummoxed me. 'I've been awake and asleep for considerably more than an hour, nurse. I was awake yesterday when Martin Doherty arrived and we talked. I woke last night during his final, eh, crisis. And I was awake when they took his body away.'

'Martin Doherty?'

'Yes, the same Martin Doherty who died last night and whose body –'

I stopped. I couldn't say: the same Martin Doherty who moved about under his shroud.

Purcell gave a hesitant smile as if she expected me to break into a guffaw and declare a joke and was ready to tell me it was in poor taste. DK's eyes darted to the corner where Doherty had lain as if she might see his body.

'Listen to me, you're not making sense.' Purcell was no-nonsense, tight-lipped. 'You've had this ward to yourself. You can thank a typical admin *snafu* for that, beds being in such demand. No one died here last night. More to the point, it's still Monday morning, Kieran, and what's after happening is you've woken with a vivid dream still spinning around in your head. Not at all unusual and not the first for you.'

She spoke as though a hitherto passive patient was un-expectedly giving signs of unpredictable behaviour. There was more to it. Both she and DK were tense, spooked. And I was spooked because they were spooked. The suggestion that the past twenty-four hours never existed was beyond absurdity.

'The bed, Doherty's bed. It's gone, taken away, don't you see?' I protested, as though this was evidence enough.

'What bed is that?' Purcell's tone had become briskly

professional. 'Let's forget it for the while, shall we? We need you out of bed for a few minutes so we can make it up.'

Clearly, the matter was closed. They assisted me out of bed and I plopped myself onto the bedside chair. They stripped the bed and remade it with fresh linen as I sat silently, clutching a dressing gown around my shoulders, an idiot king on his plastic throne, while they talked of the merits of professional development courses, not ignoring me, not inviting me to open my mouth. Their conversation sounded forced and, after they had resettled me in bed, they left.

I was stunned by Purcell's calm insistence that everything that had happened since the previous morning had been fabrications of my overwrought imagination. Could she be right? Had Aoife and Martin Doherty and the moving corpse all been no more than a drawn-out trick of the mind, a hallucinatory fantasy? What was happening to me? Was it further confirmation I was dead and playing a part in a non-existent existence? I considered with dismay the alternative possibility that my mind was perceptibly deteriorating, and I was less than wholly sane.

An hour later, an answer presented itself. The door opened, and a well-upholstered gent in a wheelchair propelled himself into the ward, who was about to smoothly, and even insistently, impart to me his expert and emollient explanation of these very matters.

4

DEATH CENTRE STAGE

'Good day, Kieran, I'm so pleased to meet with you. I am Augustinus van Vliet. Do call me Gus.'

He gave out his greeting, equal parts chipper and solicitous, as he glided his wheelchair across the ward to my bedside and, beaming, enveloped my hand in a light clasp. His oiled black hair was combed back Dracula-style, more Bela Lugosi than Gary Oldman. Rimless spectacles were mounted on a Roman nose. Salt and pepper stubble formed a beard of sorts. His navy-blue velvet suit draped a barrel chest and spindly legs.

At first, I assumed he was another patient from a nearby ward. Then, with a flourish, he produced a card from his waistcoat pocket and placed it on the overtable for my inspection. It identified him as Dr Augustinus N. van Vliet MB, MRCPsych M.Med.Sc., Consultant, Blackrock Clinic, Dublin 4, followed by suite number, phone numbers and email address. We both examined it and I had the whimsical thought that, as with Japanese business etiquette, I should comment on the letters after his name or express admiration for the typography. I thought of mentioning we were not in the

Blackrock Clinic. But he knew that.

An image jumped at me: Dr. Strangelove, wheelchair and all. How had they got hold of a shrink so fast?

'You're a head man,' I said.

He didn't get it.

'Psychiatrist?'

'Ah yes. Indeed, I am.' He gave an approving bob of the head, as if to acknowledge both his status and my insight.

My friend Shay Dempsey once said you can devastate anyone's self-confidence by fixing them with a steely glare and pronouncing: 'I know your secret.' I had no great desire to be shrink-wrapped. On the other hand, I was intrigued to learn how a psychiatrist might explain, or explain away, my recent experiences.

I'd naively imagined the nurses had dismissed my apparent hallucination once they'd left the ward or, at most, had dropped it into canteen chatter as an amusing but harmless instance of patient eccentricity. I was wrong. My account of what I had supposedly witnessed had triggered a response.

Should I comment on his obvious disability? Would it be maladroit to draw attention to his condition or graceless not to? I compromised with, 'Nice ride.'

It was, in fact, an impressive, soft purring, red leather top-of-the-line luxury powerchair in burgundy leather with walnut armrests. A sort of mobile La-Z-Boy recliner, with a swing control panel to one side that featured a Star Trek display of buttons and lights.

He accepted my compliment with civil dismissal and said, 'How are you today, in yourself?'

What did that mean? I hoped he wasn't going to spout a

load of psychobabble at me.

'In general, confused and muddled by everything,' I said.

He gave an understanding nod. 'It usually follows trauma such as you have been through.'

'Haven't I heard somewhere that trauma heightens the senses and brings clarity?'

'Haven't I heard somewhere?' was a habitual preface of mine, the outcome of spending too much time watching The Discovery Channel, National Geographic and YouTube and hoarding a veneer of knowledge of many things.

'In a way,' he said agreeably and got down to business. 'I'm told you've been witness to unusual occurrences over the past... since you came out of your short coma. I would be most obliged, Kieran, if you have the time and inclination to share with me your first-hand account. If you are up to it.'

'It began when I was dead,' I said. 'At least, that's how I think of it.'

I told him of my death, of the black void. 'I'm not sure I can find the words to describe the terrifying nothingness, the absence of everything.'

He surprised me. 'Final scene in *The Sopranos*? Tony in the restaurant, the screen abruptly going blank?'

'Fade to Black,' I agreed.

I'd been thinking of something else and had hesitated to mention it, lest I came over as a bit chichi. In my art student days, I learned that when the avant-garde artist Kazimir Malevich died in 1935, his corpse was displayed in an open coffin alongside his best-known work, *Black Square*, an oil painting of a dense, unrelieved, monotonic black square. I'd seen reproductions. Malevich had termed his painting the end of representational art. To me, now, it resembled the black pit where I'd been at the end of representational existence.

I told van Vliet of how a crazy man in doctor's garb tried to kill me, then vanished. I spoke of my first encounter with Martin Doherty, his lamentations of despair, his death in the night and the removal of his body. How I was freaked out when I saw the moving corpse.

I held back little, except all that mattered to me. About Aoife, I said not a word. I didn't know how to communicate my emotions – or that I'd want to. It was a breach of intimacy to speak of her to this mind-prober.

He heard me in silence, leaning forward in his wheelchair, creases of attention between his eyes.

'There you have it, Doctor. Don't know why the nurses are telling me there was no Martin Doherty, no death. Maybe they saw it as their duty to shield me from knowing what goes on in a hospital, that a patient died in the bed across from me. A fatuous attempt, surely? Patients die in hospital every day.'

'True.' His interest was fixed on something else. 'I'm surprised you didn't tell the nurses that someone, possibly a member of staff, had made a shocking attempt on your life. I would have expected you to look for an explanation, demand protection, have the police called. But you said nothing?'

I shook my head. 'I hadn't fully woken and my mind was cotton wool. Plus, if I'd claimed a doctor had tried to kill me, I expect they would have regarded me as crazy and' – a quick laugh – 'sent for a psychiatrist, maybe?'

Something Aoife had said popped irrelevantly into my mind.

'What does *angor animi* mean?' I asked.

He gave me a searching look.

'*Angor animi*? Hm. It means a perception, a certainty if you will, that a person knows he or she is dying. Where did you happen on the expression?'

'Not sure.'

I thought he might take it up. Instead, he said, 'Let me suggest we review recent events together and see where it takes us, look for a satisfactory explanation. To give me a context, may I ask a couple of things. You're thirty-three?'

'Like Jesus.'

The crucifix on Doherty's corpse popped into mind.

'Just so. Unmarried?

'Ditto.'

When I didn't offer a defence of my bachelor status, he gave a nod, as if he found my silence held its own significance.

'Your father and mother are both deceased. I'm sorry for your loss. When did that occur?'

'I was five. Hot day in June and they were sunbathing on Howth beach. I'm told Mum swam out to rescue a little girl who had drifted too far. She got into difficulties herself. Dad, who'd been buying ice cream, rushed in after her, and found himself in trouble, too. By the time a lifeguard had brought the child to safety, Mum and Dad had drowned. Pointless heroics, you might think.'

If he did, he wasn't about to say it.

'Undoubtedly a deeply distressing experience for you at that age,'

'I don't remember it like that. They didn't tell me, straight out. I was told Mum and Dad had gone away for a while, later that they'd been called to God and were looking out for me

41

from above. In time, I understood what they were getting at. Any shock and distress, such as I remember it, had spread itself thinly by then.'

'Ah,' murmured van Vliet, as though I'd confirmed a surmise. 'What happened after your parents died?'

We had strayed from what I'd assumed was the purpose of his visit, reconciling what I'd seen over the past twenty-four hours with what the nurses said I couldn't have seen. I supposed that's how it was with psychiatrists: go straight to childhood, explains everything.

It occurred to me that this inquisition, benign though it was, might be confirmation I was really dead. I was going through a quick-step parade of my life's highlights, such as they were, held up for review and possible meaning, like it's supposed to happen at the end to give a kind of closure. I had the unpleasant thought that when this questioning stopped I might begin to fade away. I pushed the idea aside and scrambled to stay in the conversation.

'I had an uncle Jasper, Dad's older brother, rich businessman. He paid my school and college fees and got me a job with his agency and that kicked off my career.'

I was editing a great deal.

'You resided with him?'

'No. I lived with my grandparents, Mum's folks, Cathal and Emer Kerrigan. Later, when I was eighteen, they got an offer to make their home in the States, a ranch in Arizona. Luxury spread. Friends of the late Senator McCain. They sold up and moved there and I shared an apartment near the uni. Two years in, they both had strokes and died within weeks of each other. I don't think either would have wished to go on without the other.'

'That's often how it is with older couples who have lived together for a long time. Did you get to their funeral?'

'No.' I tried not to be defensive. 'I was on holiday in Italy when they died and didn't know until after the funeral. By the time I'd get to Phoenix... I had even less money in those days than I have now and couldn't afford the trip. Uncle Jasper went.'

'And is Uncle Jasper still with you?'

'Dead, too. Drowned.' Maybe true and as much as I was going to say.

'Drowned? Like your parents?'

'Different. Freshwater this time.'

He pursed his lips, opting not to delve into this.

'You've made your career in advertising, I believe.'

'Eventually.'

This was an opening for me to mention my pre-advertising days. A decade of laidback drift, bumming around Europe studying art for the book I planned to write and never began. Art classes in Ravenna. Teaching Irish literature to English language students in Ljubljana. Going native in South America, flitting between time-limited visas in Peru, Bolivia and Ecuador.

But he'd listened to sufficient biography and his tone indicated he'd heard all he needed about my life and was ready to render a verdict. He sat back into his wheelchair and idly brushed a hand over the controls.

'My first concern, Kieran, was to review your drugs regime. Post-operative medications are a common source of occasional hallucinogenic episodes. It has not, repeat not, been a factor here. Temporary post-operative depression might have come into play. Not significant. That being so, what can we say with assurance? Remember your Sherlock Holmes?'

First Dr Watson, now Sherlock Holmes.

He said, 'Holmes's famous dictum was: "When you have eliminated the impossible, whatever remains, however improbable, must be the truth".'

'I don't think –' I began.

'Today is Monday, one-thirty in the afternoon. You are in no doubt? Should we switch on the television and get the day and time on Sky News?'

He motioned to the remote from the bedside table. What I'd assumed to be a medical monitor screen was, in fact, a TV set. I shook my head.

'Let us proceed,' he continued. 'Fact incontrovertible: you first woke in the morning, were given a shower and spoke with a Nurse Purcell. It was today, Monday, 8.30 a.m. And unquestionably you spoke with Nurse Purcell at 10.25 a.m., two hours later. In fact, this is still Monday, a few more hours on. Fact inexorable: it is impossible you witnessed what you thought you did in the intervening time. Twenty-four hours cannot be compressed into two. That which remains, however improbable, is you've had an hallucination – usually of a vivid, lifelike character.'

'Occam's Razor?' I ventured. Given two explanations, ignore the complex one and put your money on the simpler.

He gave a nod that might have been sympathy. He could guess I didn't want to accept his reasoning and I might stubbornly insist, for as long as possible, the events of the previous day and night had really happened.

'A minor point you might also consider is the improbability of a person recovering from an accident, such as yourself, and a final stage cancer patient, being placed side by side in the same ward.'

'I'd wondered about that.'

I could hear the institutional noises of the hospital, the passing traffic outside and the occasional hee-har sirens and whoops of arriving ambulances.

'Your experience is called a hypnopompic state,' he went on. 'In medical terms, it is the effect of temporarily depressed frontal lobe function, which can lead to slow reaction time and confusion at the time of awakening and give rise to powerful images, most likely the remnants of a dream. It need not alarm you. You were concussed in the accident but you have had no brain damage. Temporary retrograde amnesia, illusions and fantasies are common post-trauma symptoms. And you've had serious trauma, with a major car accident, invasive surgery and pain.'

Major car accident? Doctor Watson had mentioned it in our brief exchange a week ago and, for some reason, I'd supressed any thought of it since. Why?

Van Vliet raised a hand as if to forestall my interrupting him.

'A related factor may have been at work, what is called sleep paralysis, where a person awakens from REM sleep after a bad dream, and especially an intense one and elements of the dream encroach on reality and give rise to hallucinatory visions.'

'All very well –'

He talked over me, with a deprecating gesture.

'Forgive me. False memory is a common phenomenon. Our memory can play tricks on us. However, as we sit here now, we cannot escape the fact that your memory of events appears to extend over a period that cannot be compacted into the short time that passed.'

Another ambulance approached in the distance. The now frequent and familiar whoop was one I couldn't recall hearing during the past day and night. My imagined day and night, if I were to accept what van Vliet was saying.

'Your experience is far from unique,' he continued. 'A recent survey states that, at one time or other, one individual in eight admits to experiencing as real what is a vivid delusion. One in eight. It occurs, in particular, when an unexpected or tragic death has taken place.'

'What are you saying, Doc? It was all a waking nightmare?'

He frowned, as though reluctant to accept such a simplified description, then waved agreement.

'Think of why you have had these experiences.' I caught a whiff of his aftershave as he moved closer to emphasise his words. 'Let me suggest you may have been projecting your fears. The sight of a dead body is no pleasant business when you may suffer from what is called necrophobia: a deep, irrational fear of any association with death or dying. People with this phobia have an instinctive aversion to matters thanatotic.'

I was acquainted with necrophobia and what it meant, of course I was, and how it applied to my recent encounter with Martin Doherty, the corpse that maybe never was. Thanatotic? To do with death, I guessed, recalling Aimée Thanatogenos in Waugh's *The Loved One*.

'Three times, important people in your life – your father

and mother, your well-loved grandparents, your uncle.' He ticked them off with his fingers. 'They were taken from you in ways that denied you the opportunity to grieve and find closure. And now, at a time when your mind is shaky, your subconscious confronts you with the long-repressed theme of death. A much-needed time for grieving.'

He watched me with friendly concern, waiting for a response.

I was thrown by van Vliet. He didn't conform to my image of a psychiatrist, limited as it was to fiction and TV programmes, as one who would naturally channel the same wavelength as patients and encourage them to do all the talking, dropping in an occasional incisive question to guide them towards self-discovery. That was not his style.

'It's possible, yes,' I said. 'I'm surprised at your instant analysis after such a brief review. Sorry. Sounds offensive and I don't mean to be. Doesn't a typical psychiatrist require no end of sessions, years even, to uncover a patient's inmost secrets and hang-ups? Yet, here you are, resolving everything in one brief encounter.'

He laughed. 'I would not regard myself as a typical psychiatrist. And, you are right. A chat like this can only skate the surface. Think of it as equivalent to qualitative research in your business. You don't expect a small sample discussion group to give you the answers you want. Its purpose is to help shape the right questions. Yet, much can be achieved in such an exercise. Remember how Freud helped Mahler better understand his conflicted mind in that one afternoon stroll through Leyden.'

I had no idea what he was referring to. Doubtless a high

spot in the history of psychiatry. We were quiet for a while.

He said, 'It is good, in a therapeutic way, that you can confront what you have repressed for so long. You can now move past this. There is more to life than death.'

He gave a quiet laugh. His next comment hit close to home.

'You may be affected, though slightly, by what is often referred to as a death equivalent. Those who survive a near-fatal injury may come to feel that they are going through an unreal waking death where nothing matters. There is also a medical condition called Cotard's Syndrome. This occurs when a patient becomes convinced he or she is dead or, in some manner, doesn't really exist. From what I have observed and from what you have been telling me, I don't believe you have any such notions.'

I made an effort not to look away. Was there even the trace of a question mark in what he had said? I couldn't detect it. I thought: whatever Cotard's Syndrome is, your credibility has just taken a big hit, Doc.

He said casually, 'I'm surprised you haven't mentioned your car accident.'

'You understand me.' I said, feeling absurdly like I'd been caught out. 'Fact is, I've been evading the subject, not wanting to know what happened and what damage I might have caused. So, have I injured others, or worse?'

He held up a hand, this time in reassurance. 'No, no. Not at all. You were a passenger in a car driven by your colleague, the head of your firm, Mr Brenner. His car collided with another vehicle. It is astonishing your injuries were not more critical.'

He gave me a concerned look. 'I regret to tell you Mr

Brenner did not survive. People also died in the other car. Perhaps you might have been informed before now. Be that as it may, let us move on. You were in a coma for a time. Is it possible, probable even, that your subconscious picked up a passing reference from a doctor or nurse that you were in a fatal accident and this was an additional factor in bringing death centre stage to your mind?'

My concentration was sagging. I was turning over the apparently unavoidable truth that he was right about the time factor. Sherlock bloody Holmes and his aphorism could not be denied. It was not possible for me to experience what I believed I had. Therefore, no Martin Doherty. I recalled him in detail, his blood-spattered pyjamas, his despairing voice pleading for life. How could I invent him in such comprehensive detail? Evidently, I had.

Then the realisation hit me like a physical blow. Aoife, too, must be a concoction of an overwrought and untrustworthy imagination. No way, absolutely not, I told myself desperately. But I couldn't deny it. When I had eliminated the impossible, I eliminated Aoife. The vitality drained out of my body and a terrible desolation took hold of me. The sense of loss made me want to howl out my despair.

I had to be rid of this pleasantly smooth man, and his insistent, apodictic reasoning. He was leaning back in his wheelchair, a smile playing on his lips, waiting for me to respond to what he had been saying, seemingly oblivious to my mental turbulence.

'You're right. I'm sorry.' To my surprise, my voice sounded normal, unruffled. 'Truth is, I'm fatigued, Doctor, and there is much for me to take in. I appreciate that you've given me your time.'

He got the message and nodded slowly, unoffended.

'You've had much to absorb, physically and mentally, Kieran. The more rest you get now, the quicker your recovery. I shall be happy to continue our conversation, should you wish.'

He fingered his controls and the wheelchair moved in reverse towards the door with a low hum of its motor. As he opened the door, I said, 'After you've closed the door behind you, how can I be sure you're not another false memory?'

He laughed and pointed to his card on the table.

'Hold onto that, it will tell you I'm not an illusion.'

Much of what he had said would turn out to be superficial and not especially useful diagnosis. This last, though, would unexpectedly prove to be most valuable advice.

5

Sudden Light

Van Vliet left me in a cantankerous mood, dissatisfied with the interrogation, for that's how I thought of it. I wished I'd been less passive in getting him to justify some of his comments. I'd have liked him to ask some other questions on my life to date. I let myself indulge in fanciful daydreaming and imagined him asking this: 'Tell me about your personal relationships, Kieran. Have you ever been in love?'

'In love?' I might have replied, possibly with a wry smile. 'I've been in like-very-much. I've been in lust. But no, I've never felt the flame of love ignite in my heart. "Ever, till now, when men were fond, I smiled and wondered how".'

He would undoubtedly recognise *Measure for Measure* and not ask what I meant by 'till now', since I hadn't told him about Aoife. The next question he would pose was, 'What would you see as your purpose in life? What are your ambitions?'

How would I have responded? 'Um. Don't think I've got an answer, Doc. To get by, day-to-day, year-to-year. No more than that. Like the poet said, "I shall pursue my ambition by not having one.'"

At this, my imagination taking over, van Vliet would unexpectedly jump out of his wheelchair, short but powerful body balanced on stick legs, á la Toulouse-Lautrec, point an accusing finger at me and snap out, 'Shakespeare. Yevtushenko. Can't you stop quoting and bloody well speak for yourself? It's time you did your own thinking. And, while we're at it, you're a young man of thirty-three, not someone in his twilight years, so what's all this nonsense of death and the dead you keep going on about?'

Of course, van Vliet wouldn't have said that. I was having a go at myself. I dropped the wool-gathering and forced myself to consider his extempore judgements seriously. He had given me little time, less than an hour, I surmised, because I wasn't his client. I expect he'd been asked by someone in the hospital to do no more than observe me and run a quick assessment checklist to see if I might need more extensive psychiatric evaluation and treatment. He was probably reporting I was not crazy, just muddled. Fair enough.

Cronin Brenner's death had come as a shock of the unexpected rather than of sorrow. He had been my boss, the agency's CEO, a few years older than me, highly regarded in the industry, palpably ambitious. For a time, I thought of him as a sort of mentor and rabbi, until someone told me his opinion of me, a throwaway comment: 'Kieran, now, is a curious amalgam of ability and naivety. Very erudite chap, yes, but completely lacking in street smarts. Too much culture, too little savvy to get to the top.'

I was relieved that I bore no responsibility for the car crash and thankful it had been Cronin behind the wheel and it was his BMW and not my Jaguar that was junkyard scrap. It was a cold reaction, sure, but I never said I was a sensitive guy.

I didn't give too much thought to van Vliet's analysis of my state of mind. It seemed to be standard textbook stuff. Was there much difference between a psychiatrist and a fairground fortune teller? Both used shrewd observation and well-honed techniques to produce well-targeted hits among the misses. Why had he mentioned Cotard's Syndrome, only to airily dismiss it? Was he subtly letting me know my fear that I was dead was not unique? I was surprised he hadn't put forward the obvious possibility that my phobia was not about the death of others but myself. Soon as I had access to a computer, I would google this Cotard business.

I was, with some effort, avoiding thoughts of Aoife. I would have to confront Occam's Razor, but not yet. Meantime, I felt the heavy weight of depression.

Nurse Purcell returned, sans DK, pleasant but reserved.

'We're going to take you for an X-ray. Won't take long. When they've finished, you'll be coming back to a nice single-bed private ward that's become available.'

She unhooked the few remaining wires and tubes to give me mobility, with an occasional sidelong glance to assure herself I was being good, like a sane person should. An orderly arrived, a cheerful young man named Wayne O'Callaghan in a white sweatshirt and jeans, pushing a squeaky plastic and canvas wheelchair.

We took the lift down to radiology in the bowels of the hospital, where I was duly X-rayed. Wayne took me back upstairs, telling me in broad Dublinese about a patient he had wheeled the previous day who had been hover-mowing the lawn in his bare feet and had accidentally excised his toes.

'And we think we know problems,' he said. I reckoned my near fatal car crash injuries trumped the loss of toes but had sufficient nous not to argue the point.

Purcell joined us along the way. We negotiated a maze of passages and wards, Purcell and Wayne gossiping of hospital affairs, Montenotte Cork to Liberties Dublin. I tuned out. We turned into a pleasant compact ward with a single bed and an en-suite bathroom. I sat beside the bed and looked out the window at a busy street below, one I couldn't identify.

Purcell did another pulse check and departed.

'All the comforts of home.' Wayne waved at a large television screen mounted on the wall. 'Enjoy while the going's good, y'know. Anything else I can do you for?'

'No, I'm fine thanks.'

I felt something in the pocket of my dressing gown: van Vliet's calling card.

Hold onto that, it will tell you I'm not an illusion.

I had a gush of hope.

'One thing you might do for me, Wayne, and I'd appreciate it. Back in the other ward, I had a book in the top drawer of the locker, a book of verse that had been loaned to me. Would you mind getting it for me?'

'No sooner said than done, my man.' He took off.

I waited for Wayne, taut with suspense and anticipation, steeling myself for his return, head shaking, empty-handed, confirmation of my fears. Instead, he returned with the brown leather volume. My heart did a series of emphatic celebratory thumps. I'd not imagined Aoife, after all. My colourless world blossomed into a lustrous rainbow once more.

'Wonderful,' I said, unable to hold back. 'Wonderful.'

He dropped the book on the bed and grinned at my elation. 'Must be damn fine poems, for sure.'

Wayne was in no hurry to go. 'You must be a right class of a VIP to get this ward.'

I laughed. 'This is my reward for having naughty visions in the other ward.'

'Yeah, and how's that?'

I gave him a carefully abbreviated account of my supposed time with Martin Doherty.

He became pensive as he took it in and when I'd finished murmured, 'Man, oh man.'

'What?'

He hesitated. 'I don't know as I should tell you this, pal. Mister Doherty's no imagination. He was in your ward back there, like, and him and me, we had the odd confab. Throat surgery, right? Nice bloke, always in a pother about who'd be taking care of the missus and kiddies.'

Another pause. 'Thing is, like, you couldn't have seen him today or yesterday because he died two weeks ago, before you came in, and that's a fact because I took him to the mortuary.'

After he'd gone, I firmly shut my mind to what he'd said. Yet another mystery. I reached for the book and riffled through the poems of Dante Gabriel Rossetti. I knew of Rossetti as an artist, a leader in the nineteenth-century Pre-Raphaelite movement, and I knew some of his better-known paintings, *Bocca Baciata*, *The Annunciation, Beata Beatrix* and such. When it came to poetry, though, I was more familiar with the works of his sister, Christina.

The book fell open to the page marked by the ribbon

and to a poem titled *Sudden Light*. I saw the words Aoife had pencilled above it, *Sic itur ad astra*. I regretted I was Latin illiterate.

I read:

> *I have been here before,*
> *But when or how I cannot tell:*
> *I know the grass beyond the door,*
> *The sweet keen smell,*
> *The sighing sound, the lights around the shore.*
> *You have been mine before, –*
> *How long ago I may not know:*
> *But just when at that swallow's soar*
> *Your neck turned so,*
> *Some veil did fall, – I knew it all of yore.'*

It was as though I was reciting the words to Aoife, or she was whispering them to me, in great intimacy, knowing we both understood. *Sudden Light*, indeed.

6

DEATHMARES

Time-out, I cautioned myself. I needed to get a grip on things and, if possible, make some sense of the reverses of the natural order of things that were hitting me in rapid succession. The message, for so I regarded it, in *Sudden Light*, was confirmation that Aoife was neither delusion nor false memory. And, if Aoife was real, so was the rest: Martin Doherty and his death in the night. But how could a timespan that encompassed an afternoon, a night and an early morning occur in two hours? How to explain that Doherty had died a fortnight earlier, according to Wayne, who has no reason to lie? Facts irreconcilable, as van Vliet might say. There had to be an explanation, however outré.

I read *Sudden Light* again, searching for added meaning. Then, another poem by another poet came to mind, one that suggested an unconventional answer to all this: the opening pages of T.S. Eliot's *Four Quartets*:

> *Time present and time past*
> *Are both perhaps present in time future,*

And time future contained in time past...
...Time past and time future
What might have been and what has been
Point to one end, which is always present.

Back in my college days, there had been a brief flurry of interest in dream interpretation, a fad promoted by a student friend, Tom Terry Ferry, who was a devotee of a 1920s book, *An Experiment with Time,* by a respected Irish aviation engineer, J. W. Dunne. The book proposed, and I oversimplify an elaborate thesis, that all time – past, present and future – exists as one time. Hardly a new idea, but Dunne claimed it could be proven. One of his supposed proofs was that, if we maintained a record of our dreams on awakening each morning, we would find that some were clearly based on future, not past or current, events and experiences.

I'd borrowed the tattered copy of the book from Ferry and was sufficiently interested to start on it. I found the reading tough going and never finished it. I kept no note of my dreams.

I knew the scientific community had vastly more sophisticated theories of time and space than Dunne's long-dated work. My knowledge of science was and is shallow. I'd once watched a popular science TV programme on quantum mechanicals and something called Heisenberg's Uncertainty Principle which stated, as near as I could make sense of it, that everything we think we know about the real world is undoubtedly wrong.

I was aware of a concept known as 'spacetime', which I took to be part of the theory of relativity. I'd read somewhere that Einstein described any distinction between past, present, and future as no more than a stubbornly persistent illusion. I didn't need the brain of an Einstein to accept that dimensions of time and space might co-exist.

If time was not an absolute, if it was in a manner flexible, well then, it might be possible for me to square the circle and have had a twenty-four-hour experience within the passage of two hours. A sort of temporary time warp. Voodoo science, no doubt, but the best I could come up with.

You may wonder that I found this a credible explanation. In retrospect, it baffles me, too, that I so readily accepted it. It was one thing to read about spacetime and take a layman's why-the-hell-not approach to the possibility that it could be a plausible hypothesis. It was something else to believe it to be what I was experiencing. I think I was affected by the weird events that were disarraying my balance of normality and conditioning me to consider that any solution might be right, however offbeat.

I soon found myself grappling with another species of mental disarrangement. One of the quickest ways to acquire a reputation as a pestilent bore is to insist on regaling friends and total strangers with detailed accounts of your dreams. Don't worry, this is not my kind of sin. The situations I'm going to describe took place as I slept but they were not dreams, nor even closely akin.

Hearing van Vliet expound on my necrophobia, or browsing *The Golem*, may have set them off. But that night I had the first of a series of what I was to dub my deathmares.

These were ostensibly nightmares, but, in fact, real occurrences. How did I know what were dreams and what was real? Good question, the kind that the big thinkers like

Descartes brooded upon. For me, the best I could figure it, most dreams seem real while we're asleep – but the important thing is we realise when we awaken that they were imaginings. Similarly, when we enter the world of a good film or TV series or book, or even a first-person video game, we suspend belief. Afterwards, and this is what matters, we take it as natural that we had allowed our imagination to counterfeit reality.

I admit I was having difficulty in determining what was real. I couldn't drop the possibility that I was dead and invoking a temporary afterlife scenario. Putting that aside, admittedly, a lot to put aside, I defined reality as what appeared to me, after the event, to be real, such as my time in the black desolation of death, the madman who tried to kill me, my meeting with Aoife, and the day and night of Martin Doherty, alive and dead.

On that basis, I believed that my deathmares were the stuff of reality. I came to accept, absent any better explanation, that, in my vulnerable mental state, my consciousness had been thrust out of my normal life and into some adjacent dimension, one where my necrophobia was let loose without restraint.

With each living deathmare, I was brought face-to-face with what I most dreaded, Cimmerian places of dark shades, charnel domains, and the company of cadavers. My nostrils would fill with the sickly odour of death and decay: a halitosis world. From a state of deep unease, I would move on to terror and panic, aghast and repelled by what I was witnessing, fearfully drawn in as participant.

The first of these deathmares went like this:

I awoke from a nap, slid out of bed and made my way through the silent, deserted hospital and out the front entrance. I was in flimsy, bare-arsed hospital attire and barefooted, and with the aid of a metal crutch, stumbled along a cobbled street, I don't know where, with grey, run-down buildings, barred doors and bricked-up windows. I moved as fast as I could because, glancing back, I saw I was being pursued by the malevolent non-doctor, the screamer of invective, who had attempted to murder me in the ward. He was the worse for wear since I last saw him: hairless skull, yellow-brown teeth, several missing, a stringy, downturned moustache, a sour lemon expression. He was shuffling stiffly as though forcing arthritic legs to move and grunting like a pig with the effort but he was keeping pace with me.

He reminded me of a character in an American underground comic-strip, Bum Farto, a barbarous but bumbling Mexican bandit. Nothing comical about this guy. He clutched a soiled white pillow in one hand and I knew he was intent on making another attempt to kill me.

I was already feeling exhausted and was painfully taking in air in short gulps. Hoping to escape him, I made for an open gateway and found myself in a vast cemetery, with mildewed grave markers of the long disremembered, plain and Celtic crosses in all sizes, weather-ravaged headstones, some fallen and broken, monuments in stone and marble, collapsed tombs with anguished angels and chipped cherubs.

I could not find a way out of this awful place and scrambled over mounds of slippery muddy earth, snatching at gravestones for purchase. Beneath my feet, the dead put forth tendrils of awareness, sensing me, invading me with their emotions. I heard their plangent weeping and groaning that I seemed alive while they were dead. They were consumed with a single overwhelming emotion: how bountiful a gift to walk the land, to have one more day, dawn to dusk, to savour and cherish every second. They grudged my apparent possession of life and sought to tear at my mind and soul as if I could effect for them a miracle of resurrection. I kept moving, aware my stalker was slowly gaining on me.

I was halted by a funeral procession in a nearby narrow pathway, wending towards me with much loud lamentation, the men in formal mourning suits, the women in face-covering black lace. They were led by six ashen-faced bearers in top hats with rippling crepe and shin-length black coats, struggling on the rutted path to keep a heavy oak coffin on their shoulders. I was discomfited by the lack of dignity of my rear-end nakedness.

I had to halt and let them go by, which enabled Bum Farto to get within a few yards of me. As the procession passed me, one of the bearers tripped on my crutch. He stumbled backwards with a curse, resulting in a domino effect of bearers and mourners losing their balance and tumbling to the ground like a scene from a slapstick comedy. But it was not amusing. The coffin shuddered, see-sawed and fell to the ground. The cortege halted and a giant of a priest came running along the pathway, face as purple as his swirling vestments, and swore at me in a foreign tongue. I was profuse in my apologies, desperate to get away.

To my horror, the coffin had burst open and the cerement-bound corpse within twisted to and fro, smoke rising from the winding sheet. The priest shouted at me: 'This man hanged himself. This shows he has gone straight to the hellfires of his eternal damnation. You've no right to expose him like this to his family.'

Bum Farto was leering at my humiliation. My skin tightened with fear as he pushed others aside and confronted me, sneering, 'What are you doing crawling out of your grave and passing yourself off as one of the living?'

He had dropped his pillow along the way and was now carrying a long, sharp-ended spade which he began swinging at me. There were mutterings of agreement, then cries of outrage directed at me by the mourners, who began shuffling towards me with threatening gestures.

Abruptly, the scene dissolved, and I was back in my hospital bed, pulling around me the womb-like comfort of the bedclothes. Weirdly, while my entire body was soaked in perspiration as though I'd stepped out of a shower, my pillow and bedclothes were dry.

Years ago, when I had spent a few months living in a hostel in the Peruvian village of Pisaq, I took part in an Ayahuasca ceremony, an all-night ritual, during which a local shaman fed his magic brew to a group of us foreigners. We drank the foul liquid and sat in a circle, awaiting a promised contact with divine beings and a spiritual rebirth, with mystical insights into the true nature of the universe.

Throughout the night, the other participants were in ecstasy, conversing with spirits, weeping, slow-dancing and gabbling nonsense. Me, I experienced zilch, apart from nausea. I concluded I was an unimaginative materialist, with no supernatural vibes whatever. Now, perhaps, I needed to think again.

7

AN INSPECTOR CALLS

Doctor Watson breezed into my ward and went about the usual checks: chart review, inspection of scars, pulse taking, stethoscope to chest.

'You're continuing to make excellent progress. It really is extraordinary. However,' with a downturn of the mouth, 'your blood pressure is elevated and your pulse is faster than it should be. Stress?'

'What you'd expect, nothing serious.'

'Possibly.' He frowned, not wholly convinced. 'We'll keep it under review. Talking of stress, two Garda officers are here and they'd like a word. I can put them off for another time if you're not up for it.'

Another interview, a further round of questions. I didn't get to decide if I was up for it or not because they were coming in the door.

'No problem,' I said. It would pass the time.

There were two of them, plainclothes. One had an air of easy authority, six-foot-plus, burly, black and grey hair in a tight back-and-sides cut. He had an open-neck blue shirt, tweed jacket and knife-sharp cavalry twill pants. The other seemed content to be a background shadow, a smaller man with an expressionless, saturnine face and a mustard-coloured suit.

Watson appeared ready to remonstrate, decided not to and gave me an encouraging thumbs-up as he left.

'How's it going, auld son?' With a jovial air, the tall one strode over to my bed and grasped my hand. He let go when he saw me wince.

'My apologies. You okay? I'm Detective Inspector Breen and this is Detective Sergeant O'Hanlon. You got time for a little chat, a Mhic?'

'It's Kieran, not Vic,' I said, deliberately misunderstanding. 'And I'm sorry. I didn't catch your first names.'

Auld son, a Mhic. It sounded like patronising familiarity, yet my frosty response took me aback. Hospital life was making me crabby.

He grinned, unfazed. 'Fair enough. I'm Dan Breen and this is Des O'Hanlon. The quiet man.'

He indicated his colleague, who paid him no attention, walked across the room and got a second chair, which he placed beside the bed. They both sat. O'Hanlon took a notebook and biro from an inside pocket and waited.

Breen gave me a quick look-over. 'You're still the worse for wear, I can see. However, a lot better than when you came in, I'm told.'

'You should see the other guy.' Then I remembered. 'Scrub that.'

'Ah, don't worry. Now, if you're able, I need to ask a few things. Run it up the flagpole, isn't that what you advertising

65

people say?'

'Once upon a time.'

He spoke rapidly, as if with a speech impediment, words tumbling over one another. Occasionally, his tongue hesitated on a word, finally bringing it out in a little explosion. I had to strain to understand him.

'How much do you remember of the accident? They tell me you've amnesia as to what happened.'

'Don't remember it at all.'

He raised an eyebrow. 'Yeah? Still a blank?'

'Not a thing. Zip. Bupkis.'

Breen glanced at O'Hanlon. '"Bupkis", meaning nowt. When you hear someone talk Yiddish, it means they work in advertising, nu?'

O'Hanlon raised his eyes from his notebook, wooden-faced. Why did I resent Breen's easygoing ribbing? A vague uneasiness, I concluded. I feared some unknown accusation was about to be tossed at me that I couldn't rebut because I couldn't remember.

He seemed oblivious to my nerviness.

'Anyways, to get to it: what is the last thing you do recall leading to the crash?'

'Like I say, Dan.' His lips twitched at the familiarity. 'I've no recollection whatever of Friday, the whole day.'

It seemed to stump him and his eyebrows came together, thick and shaggy enough to nest titmice. Did he doubt my amnesia?

'As for the crash itself, I know only what I've been told,' I added. 'Which is that my agency head and friend, Cronin Brenner, was driving, I was in the front seat, we crashed, he was killed, and I wasn't. Don't even know where the crash occurred.'

'On Raglan Road.' He pronounced it Rag-alan and went off at a tangent. *"On Raglan Road on an Autumn Day"*, as in Patrick Kavanagh's great poem.'

'Great, my arse,' I said. 'Kavanagh at his most pretentious. He tried to hit on a girl, got the cold shoulder and decided he should have expected no less: *"When the angel woos the clay he'd lose his wings at the dawn of day"*. Seeing as how he's an angel, he thinks he shouldn't be chasing dumb bimbos. Sour Grapes would have been a better title.'

Breen looked put out that anyone who knew the poem would disparage it. In fact, I loved the poem. I was being obtuse now, still edgy that some guilty secret, buried temporarily in my amnesia, was swimming below the surface, ready to rise, *Jaws*-like, to take a lump out of me.

He was saying, 'Ah, don't talk like the snobs that rubbished him in his lifetime, every chance they got. You know, Obama quoted *Raglan Road* that time in his eulogy to Joe Biden's son.'

'Guess that makes it right,' I said, with a twist of a smile to soften the sarcasm.

He shook his head and went into another verbal swerve.

'Raglan. Now he was the fella, the English general, that made a pig's bris of the Crimean War, ordered the charge of the Light Brigade by mistake, then died of depression. And the Irish thought he was a great man altogether, for we named one of our classiest roads in his honour.'

'We Irish are well-known for our delight in the absurd,' I offered, wondering if bringing out random thoughts was an interviewing technique intended to confuse.

He said amiably, 'Back to business, as we must. Here's what occurred, best we can tell. Friday evening, nine days ago, at half-past eight, thereabouts, you were a passenger in a BMW owned and driven by Mr Brenner.'

I observed an occasional flash of white between his teeth and surmised that part of his semi-incoherence might be chewing gum. Nicotine gum, I supposed, because occasionally he patted his jacket pocket, checking that a cigarette pack was close at hand, confused when it wasn't.

'You departed the Dubliner Bar of the Ballsbridge Hotel, where you'd both had a few drinks, drove into Pembroke Road, and took a left onto Raglan Road. It was raining heavily. A hundred yards on Raglan, beyond the roundabout, the BMW veered across the road and hit hard into a Mazda sports car that had come from the Clyde Road direction. The Mazda catapulted into a tree and the BMW flipped over. So the witnesses have it.'

He paused as if to tick a mental checklist.

'Mr Brenner died instantly, as did the man and woman in the Mazda. You are the only survivor. That's it in a nutshell. Now, does any of this help your recollection at all?'

'Who were the couple in the other car?'

He dropped his voice. 'A Mr Paul Scully and a Ms Ruth Vann, both English. On their way to Dublin Airport to return home after attending some function in Wicklow.'

'Sorry to hear that.' I meant it. 'I seem to have gotten off lightly. Puts injuries and pain in perspective. It doesn't trigger any memory, though. It's as if you're telling me what happened to another person, another time, another place.'

'Be thankful you survived. I think somebody up there was looking out for you.' He rolled his eyes upward.

I snorted. 'Somebody up there didn't give a damn for the other three who died.'

Stop, I told myself.

'Who can tell?' Breen gave theology the same short shrift as poetry criticism. 'In practical terms, your survival is likely because you had on your seatbelt and Mr Brenner didn't. On top of that, Mr Brenner's airbag didn't open and yours did, which protected you from the worst effects of the crash.'

'That can't be right,' I objected. 'The BMW was less than a year old. How could his airbag not inflate?'

'That's a fair one. The BMW had a previous accident. Minor stuff: clipped a wall but with enough force to deploy the airbags. For reasons of his own, he had the repairs done by a back-street garage. They didn't refit his airbag correctly.'

I was bemused to be made privy to this information.

'The other car? Didn't it have airbags and seatbelts?'

He ran a hand through his hair. 'Wasn't much use to them. Not in a side-on whack and on into a tree.' He changed tack. 'How did you get on with Cronin Brenner?'

Odd question and my anxiety level bubbled. I stared at him, trying to read where he was heading. 'Well enough. We have – we had – a good relationship. Worked together on several client accounts. Professional relationship. Outside the agency, we each had our own social circle. Why ask?'

'Covering the bases.' A meaningless phrase. 'You must have resented that he took the job you were groomed for, no?'

He'd been doing deeper background checking than I'd have assumed. I wanted to ask him snappishly what its relevance might be. I didn't. In films, the cops always go hood-eyed and respond, 'We'll be the judge of what's relevant.'

'No,' I echoed him. 'When the economy crashed, it put paid to a lot of high hopes, Inspector, ah, Dan. Cronin will be a huge loss to the agency. With us for three years, give or take. Important clients came into the agency through his networking and I can't be sure we'll hold onto all of them. Even in a selfish way, his death is a blow.'

O'Hanlon was taking an occasional note. Breen seemed to have lost interest. Abruptly, he said: 'One feature of the accident has us beat. Witnesses seem to think Cronin Brenner and you were acting in a funny manner in the car before the crash.'

He paused, inviting me to clarify "funny". When I didn't, he continued, 'What they reported – and I'm quoting loosely – is there was either a fight or a celebration going on: hands raised in the air, bumping together, high fives, that class of carry-on.'

It made no sense. I tried to dredge up a recollection of fun and games with Cronin in the car. I couldn't see it. We weren't buddies in that way.

'Unlikely. I imagine the witnesses were confused.'

'What do you think they may have seen?' I sensed a Lieutenant Columbo question: help me out here, sir.

'How would I know? I don't know them, or what they imagined they saw or may have seen. Dark night, heavy rain, all happening in a few seconds. Who knows?'

He leaned forward: 'You remember the heavy rain?'

'I remember you saying it a minute ago.'

I tried not to show my concern. Breen was pursuing angles

I didn't understand. He seemed to think something wasn't adding up. But if a share of blame was heading my way, he wasn't giving me an indication.

Best I could tell, I had no responsibility for the crash and saw no point in prolonging the interview. Besides, I needed to pee and was loath for dignity's sake to get out of bed and use the bathroom while they were there.

'Let's end on that note, Dan. I'm tired.'

He rose from the chair, as did O'Hanlon, still Trappist-mute.

'My apologies,' said Breen. 'We won't overstay our welcome. You'll understand it was necessary we had this chat once you were able for it.'

'While none of it was fresh in my mind.'

'Ha. Over the next few days, when you're out and about again, call into the Garda Station in Glenageary, if you would, and give a signed statement, whatever you remember. Who knows, you may get your memory back by then?'

Before I could control my mouth, I said, 'You don't think I'm shamming?'

He was surprised. 'Now, would I think that? Loss of memory is not unusual in serious accidents. Not surprising, in your case, seeing as how you literally came back from the dead.'

'Aren't you misusing "literally"?'

He hesitated, then said, 'Don't think so, a Mhic. I have it that when they got you to A&E, you'd actually passed on. You flatlined when they pulled you from the car and in the ambulance and, third time, in ER. Defibrillators and such brought you back. Be thankful to God.'

'Interesting that I died,' I heard myself say. 'And disappointing. I didn't have one of those spiritual experiences I've heard of, through the tunnel and into heaven, greetings from long-dead relatives, the voice of Morgan Freeman proclaiming my time had not yet come. I've been short-changed.'

'Kieran.' He waggled a finger. 'If you've got amnesia, how do you know what you did or didn't experience in the time you were out? Maybe there was more than you think.'

Was he right? The manner of my death, the sense of being dead and the darkness would be fixed forever in my mind. But might there have been more, other facets of the outermost afterlife, that my memory had no wish to retain and hence had allowed me to forget?

8

THE SEPULCHRAL MUSEUM

A dozen years previously, on a holiday in Italy with a group of friends from university, I visited the Church of Santa Croce in Florence, where I happened on the tomb of the Polish Countess Sofia Czartoryska. The countess, once celebrated as the most beautiful woman in Europe and a notable patron of the arts and artists, died of cancer in her fifties in 1837.

In cold white Carrara marble, the sculptor, Lorenzo Bartolini, depicted the weak and emaciated yet dignified countess in her nightdress on her deathbed, braced on cushions, bedclothes to her waist, the time of her passing frozen in stony perpetuity. The stark realism of the sculpture, together with my attraction-repulsion to this near-death portrayal, shook me. I contemplated it for a long time, finding it both wondrous and terrifying, unable to move, shaken with undefined emotions. My companions grew impatient and dragged me away to a *ristorante* they had spotted earlier.

The haunting memory of the unhappy memorial was the likely source of that night's deathmare when I made a preternatural visit to a sepulchral museum.

I had again slipped out of bed, found the hospital empty of life once more and left by a side door, intending to go home – though I couldn't remember where I lived. Wearing black Viet Cong-style pyjamas under a dressing gown and on loose-flopping slippers, I lumbered and lurched with the aid of my metal crutch along a narrow street, devoid of people, with leafless trees that appeared scorched by fire, cracked pavements and seedy buildings.

I entered a shabby grey doorway and ascended creaky, rotting, bare-board stairs, one floor after another, peering into uninhabited, musty Dickensian offices, with grimy windows, shabby furniture, dusty inkwells and mote flecks drifting in a cold late autumn sun.

At the top, I tugged open a heavy oak door and stumbled onto the flat concrete roof of an immense building that stretched in all directions, with, at intervals, open granite descending stairways. I was oppressed with a rising sense of unfocussed misery and fear.

A now familiar odour, the fetid putrescence of human decay and rot, assaulted me, so pervasive it seemed to be worming into my skin. I slowly descended the nearest set of rough steps and found myself in a vast mausoleum, a necropolis for displaying many thousands of the long departed.

Levels of soundless, darkened corridors held burial chambers, glass-fronted, or in open recesses, where the dead were embalmed. More than embalmed, preserved, as if in frozen wax, at the precise intersection between life and death.

Many lay alabaster-white on their deathbed in apparent resignation. Others were partway risen in disbelief at their end. Yet others shuddered and convulsed in their death throes. A few comprised the centrepiece of elaborate *tableaux vivants*, lying on biers and staring wide-eyed at blanched and sorrowing family and friends. Some of the about-to-die were young and healthy, but most were shrunken and emaciated with age or wasting disease. Perspiring heavily, my stomach heaving, I wanted fervently to be gone from this place.

In a side passage, I was abruptly confronted by my murderous hunter, the one I had mentally named Bum Farto, in a brown shroud-like monk's habit, sneering through the wispy remains of his moustache. He was visibly corrupting with each encounter. In his hands he held a length of thick hemp rope fastened at the end into a noose. I turned and staggered away, hearing his shambling footsteps in pursuit. Who was this malevolent pursuer, in life and deathmare, and why was he fixated on doing away with me? I tried to find a way out of this dreadful warren of the dead. I could not. The corridors were a maze in all directions with no detectable exit.

One chamber, where swaths of black drapes adorned the walls, was the final abode of one-time important and prosperous Dublin citizens – legal and medical notables, business owners and their wives – lying on pall-covered catafalques or in ornate marble sarcophaguses, denoted by their hatchments. Alpha dogs and bitches in the day, now long erased from common memory. Fusty viewing windows displayed their rotted remains and rag-strewn, ashy-grey bones in various stages of decay. Death in all its glory.

Especially dreadful to see were accident victims. A stocky man in a shredded blue suit lay on a stretcher, his torn-off limbs placed by his side, his misshapen body wrapped in white sheets through which dark red blood oozed into a widening crimson pool. Death in all its gory. I heard what might have been a hiss of breath when I accidentally touched the wrappings. There was bloody wetness on my palm and I pulled away, frantically trying to rub it away.

Further on, a darkened chamber filled with stagnant green water held a teenage girl in school uniform, her blonde soggy hair floating above her head, her eyes open with fright, bubbles trickling from her nose and mouth, as she forever drowned.

I jerked away from these loathsome displays of death, my skin drum-taut and nerves jumping. From depths below, male basses chanted a requiem dirge in a tongue unknown to me.

Dashing around a corner, I was confronted by Bum Farto. His black lips twisted in a leer 'No way out for you. This is the seat of the dead, the cadaver, the stinky-poo, and I am the corpse whisperer.'

He sniggered. A gob of black substance slipped from a nostril and he snuffled it back. 'You are with your own kind and must remain with them. And, you and me, we have unfinished business.'

As he moved towards me, the noose held out and ready to loop over me, I was pulled out of the deathmare and back in my bed, sobbing and moaning, wearing dressing gown and slippers I couldn't remember having put on. I saw faint rust-red blotches on my hands where I had failed to fully erase the blood of the mutilated man.

Every night brought another deathmare and, more often than not, encounters with the living dead. I've viewed my fair share of horror films and dawns and days and nights of the living and walking dead. The inhabitants of my deathmares were not of that kind, not the walking cannibal vampire zombies of ancient myth and modern schlock. My dead, apart from Bum Farto, intended me no harm, saw no difference between me and them. They didn't realise they were in various stages of decomposition, bones showing through garish green skin and remnants of clothing. Nor could they smell the stink of their rotting flesh that permeated the air like an invisible mist.

I yearned to escape this nightly *Danse Macabre* and became convinced a malign force was seizing control of me as I slept, heightening and distorting my necrophobic fears and pulling me into a bleak netherworld of death and the dead to torture my mind and, in time, drive me to mental breakdown. It seemed to validate the idea I was dead and enduring a diversity of alternative existences. And I did not know how I could break free of it.

9

WOULD YOU BELIEVE?

On the first day of October, eleven days after my admission to hospital, I was discharged. The surgeon who'd worked on me when I was brought in, Yousuf Salah, came by in the morning, trailed by his entourage of doctors and interns who gathered around my bed. Swarthy, with thick black hair and moustache, he bore a striking resemblance to Saddam Hussein except Salah was smiling, which was not how I last saw Saddam on TV when they were hanging him. Surgeon Salah didn't ask questions, nor did he examine me. He gave a short, formal bow when I thanked him for saving my life.

'You have a good fighting spirit and that's what pulled you through in most exemplary fashion.'

'I've heard a Chinese saying that if you save a man's life, you're responsible for him thereafter,' I said.

Salah chuckled, 'It's a Middle Eastern belief, as it happens. That's why I have attributed your recovery to your own efforts, not mine. The responsibility is yours.'

I had begun to think of the ward as a prison cell, solitary confinement. Now, perversely I was sorry to leave this cocoon and return to the world. I had no special enthusiasm for my job. It was undemanding, the salary was reasonably good and that was it. Yousuf Salah and those in his profession could take pride in their accomplishments, saving lives, mending broken bodies. What had I to show? Persuading a client to fatten the media budget? Writing a cogent client meeting report? I reflected gloomily that Salman Rushdie's fame does not rest on inventing 'irresistabubble' for Aero when he was an agency copywriter.

Nurse Purcell bustled in with my morning pills and daily injections and informed me I was signed into Saint Camillus.

'It's a congenial nursing home in Greystones that also cares for people recovering from surgery. You live alone, right? You could do with a fortnight's convalescence.'

It sounded fine. I was no longer a hospital case but was still weak and lethargic. In new surroundings, I hoped I would leave my deathmares and Bum Farto behind me. As I was getting dressed and packing my few belongings, I heard the far-off reedy transistor radio. Maybe it wasn't a radio but a smartphone or iPod. It was playing that song again:

I remember you
You're the one who said I love you, too,
I do
Didn't you know?

After lunch, Shay Dempsey collected me and drove me to Saint Camillus Home. He was my closest colleague in the agency. We were both of similar age and both had the title of account director, but he was a proper AD, with a pair of client service executives working for him while I had none. We got on fine, watched each other's back and I regarded him as a solid friend.

He dressed like a *GQ* fashion plate. Today, it was a pearl grey suit, pastel yellow shirt, technicolour tie, all topped with a wide-ribboned fedora. He had recently shaved his beard for a local charity, a mistake to my mind. His neatly trimmed beard had given him a distinguished appearance, with a resemblance to English King George V or his lookalike cousin, the ill-fated Czar Nicholas II in old photographs. Now, I saw a baby face atop an adult's body.

'Yo, Ciarán,' he greeted me using, as he did, the Irish version of my name. 'You're looking top of the pops, considering what you've been through. I expected a more devastating rearrangement of your person and here you are, looking as though you were merely sliced by a budget cut.'

As we drove out of the hospital car park, I said, making conversation, 'How did our people take Cronin's death?'

'As you'd expect. Doleful countenances all round. Distressing when someone you know well, still youngish, full of drive and pizzazz, dies violently. As for you, not too much gnashing of teeth and rending of garments around the shop. Not that we don't love you. But you're still alive, what else do you want?'

'Tell me about it.'

We took the Strand Road along the coast, passing through Blackrock, with Dublin Bay on our left. It was cold and overcast and a thin fog hung in the air. Howth Head across the Bay was mist-cloaked, barely visible. One of the car ferries was gliding ghost-like out of Dublin Port.

I had an urge to confide in Shay, tell him of my bizarre

hospital experiences, describe the day and night that wasn't. It might be good therapy to talk about it, get another's objective opinion or explanation. I hesitated. I'd have to be circumspect and not raise questions on my state of mind. Er, Shay, would you believe a poetic theory of spacetime, a beautiful girl who, on leaving a dying patient, in fact, dead and buried, fell in love with me, despite my still unsightly facial scars and bruises, then vanished? That someone tried to kill me?

And how could I possibly mention that I wasn't fully convinced that I was alive and that the world around me, Shay himself included, might be an hallucination?

Oblivious to my mental vacillation, Shay was saying, 'Just inside the hospital today, I saw a direction sign that read "Office of Bad Management". About time, I reckoned, for the Health Service Executive to tell it like it is. Alas. When I got closer, it was "Office of Bed Management".'

I smiled and said tentatively, 'Weird things happened to me when I came out of my coma.'

'Yeah?'

'At first, I was convinced I'd died and was acting out a part in a creepy version of the afterlife. I spoke with a patient who, I learned later, had died weeks earlier.'

I stopped, already regretting my impulse to mention it. Shay seemed unsurprised.

'It's what you can expect, trauma plus drugs. Remember I had my gallbladder out years back? Supposed to have been keyhole surgery. Hah. Didn't work out like that, I got the full Irish slice. Anyway, I was in recovery, all doped, Sky News was on the TV in the ward and the running story was Amy Winehouse had been found dead. Remember? It barely registered with me. Not my taste in music and I had her as one of those drink'n'drugs problem celebs.'

He braked as a car ahead turned right without signalling. Shay tapped the horn, muttered, 'Arsehole,' and continued.

'I was in and out of consciousness and, at one time, Amy Whitehouse was on the television, all in black, walking behind a hearse. Blew my mind. How could this be? She's on live television attending her own funeral, walking behind her hearse. It was off-the-wall scary. A nurse enlightened me that it wasn't supernatural TV but the video of one of her hit songs, *Back to Black*. How we roared.'

He waited for me to resume my story, but I'd changed my mind. When I stared at the passing scene, he said, 'Cronin's funeral was yesterday, in Mount Argus. They give class funerals there.'

Mount Argus in Harold's Cross was the Brenner family place of worship. Headquarters of the Passionist Order and a once majestic church but now decidedly down at heel.

'Impressive send-off. Requiem mass, bishops, priests, government ministers, captains of industry, door-busting congregation. Some bishop delivered an extravagant eulogy that went on and on.'

'A paean in the ass?' I suggested.

'It was that,' said Shay, missing it. 'But gratifying, of course, to Larry.'

Larry Brenner was Cronin's father, a successful Dublin businessman. He was also chairman and owner of the agency.

'How's he taking it?'

'Hard to tell. He managed to put aside his usual dyspeptic personality and gave us his genteel manner as though born to it: wan greeting and firm handshake, hand over hand, for all. Catered buffet back at the house, smoked salmon, grilled prawns, canapes, two colours of wine. I met the other son, Quinn. Heavyweight guy in a badly-fitting suit.'

'Glad I wasn't there.'

Another funeral fortuitously avoided, as van Vliet might have commented. I was thinking of Inspector Breen's remark about peculiar goings on in the car prior to the crash and hoped Larry hadn't heard of it. With his known mercurial temper, I might be the focus of an unpleasant scene, to say the least, if he came to fix on me as in any way responsible for his son's death.

'What of the couple in the other car?' I asked.

'Their funerals? Dunno. In England, I presume. Far as I know, the papers had nothing about their arrangements.'

I needed a change of subject.

'Who's going to be our new CEO?' I wasn't sure why I asked. I didn't care.

He growled. 'You know how it will play out. We'll have a board meeting, mull over names, maybe think of approaching a promising candidate, and Larry Brenner will step in, hand us our new CEO.'

He slowed the car. 'Well, we've reached our destination.'

We were in a secluded cul-de-sac in a middle-class residential area of Greystones near the seafront. A gleaming brass plate at the entrance announced we were at Saint Camillus Convalescence Nursing Home. It was a fusion of several Victorian houses, with a capacious two-story extension at the back, all surrounded by an immaculately tended lawn garden.

He turned into the driveway.

'Isn't it time we asserted our independence of Larry and named our own CEO?' I asked, faking interest.

He snorted. 'Fantasy talk. Think about it. Larry Brenner owns the agency, for all practical purposes. His actual shareholding is dodgy, maybe, but if we dispute the ownership, we'll force his hand. Time was, he'd send a few thugs around to break legs. Now, you can be damn sure he'd be unleashing his legal hounds on us. The bad publicity could sink the agency. We're stuck with him.'

He was quiet for a minute, then said, 'Bollocks to Jasper for leaving us in this position.' He added, 'Excuse my speaking ill of your uncle, Ciarán.'

'Bollocks to Jasper,' I agreed. 'He sure done us wrong in the end.'

10

THE VANISHMENT OF JASPER SHERIDAN

Now that my one and only uncle is making a brief appearance in the story, I should mention one thing we had in common: we might both be dead, then again maybe we were not. His vanishment had brought my hitherto meteoric advertising career to a juddering halt and it remains a dusty Cold Case on Garda files.

Three years previously, on a raw and overcast Saturday in late February, the way I heard it, Jeremiah Aston 'Jasper' Sheridan packed a weekend bag and, shortly before noon, fired up his seven-year-old silver S-Type Jaguar with the leaping cat emblem on the bonnet and took the two-hour drive via the M7 to Killaloe, where he owned a six-berth cruiser, the *K.S. Le Fanu*, which he kept moored on the Shannon. He'd often take it for a solo weekend of cruising, stopping at village pubs and restaurants along the way. In fine weather, he might invite along a couple of clients or business prospects.

Having stopped for an excellent lunch at Matt the Thresher's Inn in Birdhill, it was already darkening when he climbed on board. It had turned into a pleasant evening, with a light wind rippling across the otherwise placid Shannon waters and gently rocking the cruiser. A pair of local anglers he knew were tying an adjacent boat. As he brought his bag aboard, he announced his intention to stay put for the night. He must have changed his mind because, a few minutes later, they heard his engine start and saw the cruiser head out into the lake.

The following morning, the *K.S. Le Fanu* was found dragging anchor, engine off, near Holy Island in Lough Derg. There was no Jasper. He had unpacked and laid out toiletries and pyjamas. Nothing indicated a hurried departure and there was no apparent motive for one. The cruiser's wooden dinghy, oars missing, was later discovered capsized among rushes some distance away. An extensive search and rescue operation was mounted without success.

An abandoned cruiser and the disappearance of a prominent Irish businessman was, for a short time, a media wonder, a mini *Mary Celeste* on the Shannon. There was speculation that, for reasons unknown, Jasper had shut the engine, dropped anchor and left the cruiser for the dinghy, which had capsized, tossing him into the lough. He wasn't a good swimmer and his body was never found.

When I was a child, he was Uncle Jasper, a heavyset, solemn man in a hairy tweed suit and leather hat with a bright yellow feather, an abundance of silvery hair, a comb-like white moustache and a pungent aroma of tobacco on him. Whenever he visited my grandparents, he would greet me, 'How are ye, Kyrie?' He told me Kyrie was Greek for Lord, and I liked that.

Uncle Jasper was exceptionally generous with birthday and Christmas presents (computer, bicycle) and, from time to time, I went with Grandma for lavish afternoon teas prepared by a Danish housekeeper in his mansion of a house in Glenageary. He was a reserved man and I was in awe of him. I was told he was a millionaire, which seemed riches beyond the counting.

He had inherited his father's estate, which included a mid-sized advertising agency, Acton Sheridan & Co. The sixty-seven staff of Acton Sheridan were housed in two adjoining buildings on the north side of Merrion Square, as well as mews buildings at the rear, and had the benefit of a free large car park, also at the rear.

Jasper expanded the business and added new clients, some small, some heavyweight and some that grew with the times. The agency was in and out of the top twelve Irish agencies in size of billings and revenues, never above number ten. It tended to attract solid, well-established Irish-owned businesses that eschewed what he termed flashy creativity for its own sake and favoured straight-to-the-point advertising. The agency won few advertising awards but that didn't seem to bother the clientele.

Jasper was a lifelong bachelor, abstemious in his habits, lived well, though not extravagantly, put most of the agency's profits back into the business and made shrewd investments in property. By the turn of the century, as sole owner of the agency, he was a moderately wealthy man.

I was not the son Jasper never had. I doubt he ever wanted a son. I bore the Sheridan name (and the veiled Le Fanu one) and he seemed keen to keep the agency in the bloodline. On Jasper's shilling, I took a basic commercial degree at University College Dublin followed by two years at the

College of Marketing, and an arts diploma. I'd never planned advertising as a career and it took me a long time to realise he was discreetly steering me towards his agency.

Before joining, I told Jasper I wanted to take a few months off to explore the art galleries of Europe. If he was displeased, he made no criticism. And he uttered no reproach when I returned to Dublin more than ten years later, having run out of money. As though no time had passed, he brought me into the Sheridan Agency and supervised my whirlwind progress through Production and Media to account executive.

One afternoon, after he'd raised me another step to account director, Jasper called me into his office, a wood-panelled room on the second floor, with a huge oak desk and a scattering of leather chairs and sofas. He was gazing out the window, one hand rattling change in his pants pocket, a habit of his that always brought to my mind the phrase, "he's got balls of steel".

He turned. 'I'm giving thought to my retirement, Kyrie. After I'm gone…'

He looked pensive for a few seconds. He may have been struck by the unhappy thought that, before too long, he would indeed be gone, retired or dead, and the young man before him would be alive and active.

'I've been running former times through my mind. Your great-grandfather, Mister Richard, not alone founded this agency, you know, but masterminded many a celebrated campaign in this room right up to the week he died at age seventy-eight, the month before he had scheduled his active retirement, and the very year I was born. This is his desk and this is the chair he sat in when he passed away.'

I hid my disquiet as I conjured a remarkably vivid image of a dead man, a thinner, wrinkled version of Jasper, marble-eyed, mouth agape, slumped in the chair on which Jasper's hand rested. He patted the shiny leather armrest with affection. If it had been up to me, I'd have had the chair burned.

He resumed. 'I don't aim to die in harness like Gran'pa Richard or my own dear dad. My plan is to get out in three years' time, when I hit the Good Book's threescore and ten. Or thereabouts. I'll be handing over the reins to you. You'll be managing director and you'll have the majority shareholding. The management team will help you run the agency as you see fit. This was a Sheridan company when I came into it and I want it to go on and prosper with the Sheridan name and ownership.'

Jasper had signalled these intentions to me, and to one or two others, more than once. I thought it wise, each time, to show surprise and gratitude. Not that it made any difference, the way things came about.

After a lifetime of business caution, Jasper lost the run of himself in the collapse of Ireland's Celtic Tiger economy. It was Jasper's misfortune that he succeeded in avoiding temptation in the boom years, only to succumb as the bubble burst.

Among his agency clients was an old St Andrew's College pal, Larry Brenner, who offered Jasper and half a dozen other cronies an opportunity to share in the assured and mouth-watering profits to be achieved in a huge property development project planned for Dublin Bayside that would include hundreds of plush residential units, a hotel and conference centre, a recreation complex, a marina and yacht club and a swish shopping mall.

Jasper signed on as an investor, putting in his money and borrowing heavily both through Larry and from his own bank and breaking a lifetime's resolve by signing personal guarantees and putting up the agency as surety. Then the Irish property sector nosedived, collapsing the Irish economy like an uncontrolled high-rise demolition.

Larry Brenner saw it coming and managed to come out of it with insignificant damage. Jasper, less prescient, was financially wiped out, losing the savings he had built over forty years. He had kept the advertising agency out of the bank's line of fire and instead pledged it to Larry as collateral for his loans – except for a nominal five per cent, which went to me to preserve the family connection.

In the few weeks before he took his final cruise on the Shannon Jasper had been putting on a bold front to hide his desperate financial troubles. His last week in the agency, he emailed a manically optimistic memo to staff and clients headed, 'Reports of my Debt are Greatly Exaggerated.'

After Jasper's vanishment, Larry took charge of the agency, based on his collateral agreement with Jasper. For reasons of his own, he did not file the transfer of ownership forms with the Companies Office, preferring to act as shadow owner, with his son, Cronin, as his nominated CEO. No one in the agency objected to Larry's takeover because his financial and business reputation had apparently survived in good order from the economic collapse.

I held my five per cent share and retained the title of account director and remained on the agency board. But I was no longer Dauphin.

One of Cronin's first moves was to acquire a boutique agency, A. Aaron Aardvark, headed by a one-time GAA All-Ireland hurling star, George 'The Barreller' Healy, and merge it into the agency, using the Aardvark name as a replacement for Sheridan. That was his intention. After sniffy comments from clients who found the name infra dig, and vigorous representations from agency personnel, he settled for Aardvark-Sheridan..

As for Jasper's disappearance on Lough Derg, there were the obvious suspicions of suicide, though nobody voiced them. Shay and I hired a cruiser on the Shannon to see if we could do better than the Gardaí. We got nowhere. A local spiritualist offered to hold a séance on board that would reveal where his body was located. When he saw we were giving the proposal consideration, he doubled his suggested fee and was fortunate we didn't toss him overboard.

I was not surprised that Jasper had no money to leave me or anyone else. There was behind-the-scenes agitation from Larry Brenner's lawyers. Loan money to Jasper of several hundred thousand euros apparently went missing. I got wind of suspicions that he may have surreptitiously passed it to me. As if.

In the weeks that followed, when his body remained unfound, another speculation was in the air. Jasper would not be the first in financial trouble to fake his death. I couldn't help fantasising he was enjoying the good life in a swanky retirement villa in Spain or in a pleasant senior citizen's condo in Florida or California and wondered if I might one day find an anonymous postcard from some such place in my post-box.

11

TIME OF THE GNOSTICS

I was feeling jaunty as I entered Saint Camillus Home, having convinced myself, with no good justification, that I had left my deathmares and other hellish experiences behind me in the hospital. I would be disabused soon enough.

The Home was a semi-religious establishment, which I might have guessed from the name. It was run by nuns. The well-polished reception area had several pious-themed pictures, including a kitschy painting of Jesus and Mary and kneeling before them a seasoned, long-bearded grey-robed ascetic, doubtless the eponymous Camillus. Off reception, an archway opened to a small chapel with a row of purple cushioned pews, a blue and gold cloth altar, stained glass windows and, drifting out, a pleasant odour of furniture polish and candlewax.

A white-garbed nun in her fifties awaited me. I heard her name as Sister Asbestos and she welcomed me literally with open arms that happily didn't envelope me. Ignoring my protests, she insisted I place myself in a wheelchair, another basic model, and pushed me on rubber wheels that glided sibilantly on burnished timber floors, along a labyrinth of identical, brightly lit corridors, all pink pastel walls, neon lights, vases of flowers in niches and recesses, and numbered bedroom doors to left and right.

My room on the ground floor was of reasonable size, with a compact en-suite bathroom, in all what I'd expect to find in a value budget guesthouse. The room was clean and austere, with the same aroma of furniture polish that didn't quite mask a disinfectant. The room had a hospital bed, a stuffed armchair near the window, a wooden chair at the bottom of the bed, a bedside locker, a built-in wardrobe and a dressing table holding an outmoded television set. The window looked out on trees and shrubbery.

Two pictures decorated the room, a pair of curiosities. By the bed was a framed print of Turner's *Angel Standing in the Sun*. Did the nuns know that it was a morose imagining of the Last Day? The other painting, near the wardrobe, was a large, original oil, dark with age, and depicting, best I could tell, a group of creatures in a forest clearing at night, gathered at a bubbling pool, with a yawning cave mouth in the background. Some were winged, others horned, one carried a scythe. The artistry was poor, and the picture was unsuitably mounted behind glass in a modern plastic frame. It was unsettling and, like the Turner, ill-suited for a nursing home.

Sister Eusebia (not Asbestos, I discovered), small, roly-poly and bespectacled, and looking like a precocious twelve-year-old, took me through a lengthy life and medical questionnaire. The mere act of part-unpacking exhausted me. As I sat in the armchair to get my breath back, I glimpsed myself, pallid as the bust of Pallas, in the full mirror inside the open door of the wardrobe. As she left, Sister Eusebia informed me I was in time for afternoon tea in the dining room.

The large, bright dining room had tables for four. Most of the residents were women. A few were convalescing from surgery, others, I guessed, were on life without parole, living out their days in fair comfort, palliative care and, in theory, minimum stress. I was the youngest there by decades.

Sister Eusebia tinkled a bell for attention. Spectacles flashing in the light, she gushed, 'Friends, we have a double celebration this afternoon. Monsignor Flinter, doyen of Saint Camillus residents, is ninety years young, and his latest book is published today.'

Loud applause was followed by a croaking chorus of 'For he's a Jolly Good Fellow'. I was unable to spot this literary Methuselah. Abed, perhaps, resting from his labours.

Sister Eusebia burbled on, 'To mark the special occasion, Monsignor has generously sponsored this delightful birthday cake and invites us to share it with him.'

Further applause and twitterings as a nun wheeled in a trolley bearing a huge chocolate iced cake. Atop it was one red wax candle, purloined, perhaps, from the chapel.

'I won't spoil your digestion with a speech,' boomed a voice of remarkable vigour for a ninety-year-old. 'Except to thank you, all and singular, for your kind wishes and assure you that, in extinguishing the candle, I haven't blown all over your cake. Please enjoy.'

Later, I wandered in search of a tranquil corner of the Home with a new book about Michael Collins that Shay had given me. I found a cosy lounge, with comfortable furniture, a fake coal fire and, happily, no television. The single occupant was an elderly man deep in a well-cushioned armchair, head on chest, dozing in front of the fire, a book in his lap. I seated myself in a similarly restful lounger and opened my book.

'Ah, Michael Collins, the greatest Irishman who ever lived.'

He had not, after all, been sleeping.

'Though his death might have been termed a good career move, had the phrase been current at the time.'

He sat ramrod straight in the armchair. Ex-military, was my first impression. The skin stretched his face, his pale blue eyes huge behind bifocals. He had on a charcoal suit of an old-fashioned cut, a stiff-collared white shirt and what may have been a striped club tie. In a place where casual wear seemed to be the norm, he stood out. I would almost have expected him to don dinner jacket, bedizened with campaign medals, for the evening meal. I estimated he was in his late seventies and wearing his age lightly.

'Flinter's the name, Don Flinter.' He held out a frail hand and I took it gingerly.

He was the antique author lauded in the dining room. I expected, close up, to find evidence of his nonagenarian status. I saw none. The only concession to age was a plaid blanket covering his legs.

'I understand you're a Monsignor. Sounds a heavy hitter.'

He smiled. 'An honorific, no extra pay or perks, and it means even less now I'm retired.'

'Congratulations on the big nine-O.'

His smile widened. 'Hard to credit I've reached this extra-ordinary age. I'm a lively youngster in an oldie's body and I often ask myself if my birth certificate got it dreadfully wrong.'

I peered at the cover of the book he had been reading, *Did Jesus Exist?* by Bart D. Ehrman. I thought: two thousand years on, they're still asking.

He followed my glance. 'An excellent piece of scholarship. Have you read it?' he asked.

'Not really my class of reading. I've read a total of one book on religion in my life, *Divinity of Doubt* by Vince Bugliosi, the man who put Charles Manson away. It told me all I need to know on the subject. Or, I suppose, all I want to know.'

'At least you read a book on religion, more than most, and an outstanding one at that.'

I'd lied. I hadn't read the book but I'd once watched a compelling Bugliosi interview on religion on YouTube.

He closed his eyes. To break the silence, I said, 'Do tell me about your new book – not your first, I understand.'

'My seventh, but who's counting? I've been writing books since I hit my sixties.' He said it with pride. 'I write of the early years of Christianity, a life's study and captivation. My new book is *The Time of the Gnostics*. The publisher's title, not mine.'

He smacked his lips, whether from approval or dissatisfaction I couldn't tell.

'Do you know of the Gnostics?'

'Not that I recall.'

'Ah, few do, these days.' He settled himself in his armchair. 'A fascinating group who were around when Christianity began. They sought to take it over, superimpose Gnostic beliefs on it, and, if possible, synthesise the two.'

'What were their beliefs?' I prompted, letting the

conversation pass an otherwise tedious evening.

His eyes glittered. 'A complex religion. In a few words, the Gnostics emphasised knowledge. Who we are, where we came from, how we got here and how we could return to the spirit world where we belonged.'

He frowned, as though dissatisfied with the simplicity of his explanation.

'In the Gnostic view, this world, our material world, is merely an illusion, a vast mirage. They believed that within us, or within many of us, is a divine life spark, our eternal spirit, soul if you wish, that is imprisoned in our body and we must free it from the material world. Only when we gain knowledge of this divine spark can we be reunited with the eternal.'

He had my attention now. It was like recalling a lost truth, things I had learned a long time ago and couldn't remember when or where. I wanted to ask something, but my questions evaporated in my mind before I could frame them. Aoife had spoken of the life spark, hadn't she? Could the off-the-wall superstitions of a dead religious sect hold some relevance for me?

He seemed gratified to have an attentive listener.

'Gnostics believed the ultimate true God was beyond our ability to envision. Our world is the creation, not of this eternal God, but of a lesser and imperfect god, who could therefore create only an imperfect world, with its disasters, pain and death. It is why suffering and evil exist.'

He was as enthusiastic as any author who has immersed himself in his chosen topic. His courtly tone was soothing, hypnotic. I guessed he would still be charismatic as a preacher, despite his age.

'At least your Gnostics tried to explain the problem of evil.'

Another nod. 'True, true. What else? Sophia, the divinity of wisdom, brought into existence minor deities, or angels, called Aeons, who were divided into compatible pairs, male and female, and who lived in a region of light and knowledge. In a cosmic catastrophe, they became separated and trapped in this imperfect existence and they needed to search out their other half in order to reunite in the spiritual world.'

He closed his eyes for a moment. 'On occasion, an angel would come to love a human and traverse the spirit domain to create between them a new compatible unity. I see you smile at that. Well, it's not an exclusively Gnostic concept. Every Christian believes it. Or should do. Because it's right there in the Bible, see Genesis 6.'

I couldn't stop myself. 'You don't mind my saying, this is coming across as tenth-rate Ron Hubbard.'

He laughed, unruffled.

'Ah, yes. It's extraordinary the ease with which Hubbard persuaded millions that his science fiction novels were a religion. You might say Scientology is a bad parody of Gnosticism. Perhaps Hubbard was indulging in a private joke to see if people would catch on.'

He shook his head. 'Consider the strange Made-in-the-USA religions: Scientology, Mormonism, Christian Science, Jehovah's Witnesses, Seventh-day Adventists. And as for the Rapture…'

I thought of saying that, when it came to belief in weird things, it would be difficult to better the beliefs of ordinary Christians but decided to quit while I was behind. As far as I was concerned, all believers were Flat Earthers.

'You ever hear of Lee Atwater?' he asked.

I shook my head. 'Person or place?'

'He was an American political consultant back in the time of Ronald Reagan. Lee was the expert in dirty politics and smear campaigns in his day and was so good at it that, in his 30s, they made him head of the Republican National Committee. I met him once, a really nice guy in person, actually.

'Well, at the height of his success, he was diagnosed with a brain tumour and given a few months to live. Lee immediately called a meeting of his staff, and said, ' I'm going to be dead soon, and I need to know if there's really a God and an afterlife and, if so, which is the right religion? And re Jesus: Is he God or isn't he God? I want you guys to do the research and give me a report with the answers, asap.'

In time, they came back and told him, 'Lee, we've done the research and talked with the country's top religious. The word is that there's no definitive answers and no way to prove absolutely if God exists or not. Apparently, a person either decides to have faith or doesn't.'

'How did he take it?' I asked.

'Lee decided to do his own research: he rented DVDs of *The Ten Commandments* and *The Greatest Story Ever Told*. A friend gave him a Living Bible and this became the moment of truth for him. He said that reading it gave him the answers he needed and he died a born-again Christian.'

'Inspiring,' I said dryly.

'After his death, they found his Living Bible. Lee hadn't taken it out of its wrapper.'

He paused, engaged with his thoughts for a time,

then returned to his favourite topic. 'I expect my book will prove controversial because I've suggested Gnosticism was not another early Christian sect. It was, and is, a school of philosophy that can trace its origins to the religious followers of Isis, the Mithraic mysteries, the classical Greek philosophers and has been a major influence on great thinkers throughout the ages, right up to Carl Jung, modern Kabbalah and others.'

Like the Illuminati, I reflected. If not Ron Hubbard, then Dan Brown.

'Haven't you found yourself in hot water, holy or otherwise, with your Church about your views?'

He gave a hoarse chuckle. 'Oh, no. They assume they won't be bothered with me for much longer. My opinions, by and large, are neither heretical nor novel. The Gnostic idea of the divine spark, the life spark – what might be termed the spirit or the soul – seeking truth beyond our material world, is at the root of all religions.'

He stopped. 'You must forgive me for going on. I find such ideas of limitless appeal. For myself, I've discovered the best evidence of this divine life spark, not in philosophy or theology but in music – in Bach and Beethoven and Mozart. Have you ever listened to Mahler's Eighth Symphony or Bruckner's Ninth?'

'I'm not much for music, I have to admit.'

'I urge you to listen to them and I think you will understand.'

'May I ask you a personal question, Monsignor? In all your years of study, have you ever had doubts that life continued beyond death, that there was an afterlife?'

My question didn't seem to surprise him.

'No, I have never found a reason to doubt. Belief in an afterlife of some kind goes right back to the early Stone Age people, who, primitive though they were, and seeing their dead rot away, crumble into bones and into dust, nonetheless sensed that death was not the end but a stage in an onward journey. The ancient Greeks believed in the transmigration of the soul after death to its next incarnation. They had a word for it, metempsychosis.'

'Huh,' I said. I'd been about to blurt, 'All Greek to me,' but for once my brain got there ahead of my mouth.

He was speaking as though mentally drawing on prepared notes and I remembered he was probably accustomed to pulpit or rostrum.

'Socrates argued that the soul is immortal and undergoes a constant cycle of life, death and rebirth. He believed that, in the interval between death and rebirth, souls pass through a place called Limbo, where they drink of the River of Forgetfulness and so are reincarnated without past knowledge or memories.'

I recalled kneeling in a cold darkened church confessional many years ago, preparing to bare my secrets to the dimly seen figure in the grille.

'When the Gnostics describe the world as illusion – that resonates with me,' I said. 'This may come across as odd to you… since my accident, I've found myself now and then thinking I'm, ah, dead, that things around me exist in my imagination, that my day-to-day existence is illusory.'

His head to one side, he made no reply. I thought he was giving it consideration. Then, his steady breathing told me age had caught up with him and he was asleep.

12

THE NIKROMANTZER

In bed, drowsy but unable to find sleep, words and phrases from the Monsignor played in my mind, possible cyphers to decode. There was a late-night film on the television, Wim Wenders's *Der Himmel über Berlin*, about angels roaming the streets of Berlin, listening to people's thoughts. I'd seen it before. Subtitled and not lightweight viewing. After a time, I drifted off.

An insistent tap-tap-tap woke me. When I sat up in the bed, it stopped. Since I had come out of that black void in hospital, I'd taken to sleeping with a light on and had got used to it. I was disturbed now to find the room in shadowy gloom, with only a faint external night glow from the part-open curtains. I didn't remember switching off the light.

The digital alarm clock read 02:00. A dog was barking far off and occasional passing vehicles droned by. Otherwise, all was silent. The tapping may have been a tree branch blown at the window. Merely this and nothing more.

As soon as I dropped back on the pillow, the tapping resumed, this time sounding insistent, urgent. I reached out and clicked the bedside light several times but the room remained in darkness. With a cold rush of horror, I realised the sound was coming, not from outside, but within the room.

In horror films, when innocents are woken in the dark by a menacing noise, they go stupid and say in a tremulous voice, 'Hello, is anyone there?'

'Hello, is anyone there?' I failed to keep the tremor from my voice.

Silence, stillness.

As I peered into the dark, a shadow passed between me and the window. My body lurched in shock. I tried in vain to raise myself again. It seemed as if invisible hands were pressing me to the pillow and pinning my chest, making it difficult to breathe.

My eyes adjusted to the darkness as I scanned the room and picked out the pale bedsheets and bedspread, the wardrobe by the wall, a dressing gown hanging on the door, the television set on the far table... and, in silhouette, a man sitting on the chair at the foot of my bed. He had been present from the time I awoke and was so wholly devoid of movement that my gaze had moved over him several times without seeing him. The shock of seeing him rocked me back in the bed, petrified.

'How are you, Kyrie,' came the raspy voice of Jasper. It was not my uncle but belonged to a creature of the purest malevolence.

Despite the darkness, I saw him clearly and recognised the one who had tried to kill me, the tormentor of my deathmare peregrinations, Bum Farto. He was substantially decomposed. I could make out his vindictive expression, dishevelled moustache, sharp animal-like canines. A bloody bandage was wound about his head, apparently to hold his jaw in place. His thin, rodent face was ashen and gouged with deep blackened cuts. One side of his face had caved in. He wore his monk's habit, now torn and charred at the edges and stained with black, dried blood.

He sang a grotesque stage-Irish bass:

> *'Now, who'd be wantin' your soul, at all, at all?*
> *Yerra, Tis oul' black Nick his self, come to call!'*

and launched into a chilling cackling fit.

My mouth opened in a mute scream.

A miasma of oily black smoke swirled around the creature and a dreadful pong invaded my nostrils, a stench of pigsties, rotten flesh and stagnant sewers that seemed to take visible shape, nauseating and repellent. Tendrils of stench wafted across the room. Bile rose in my throat and, unable to control myself, I spewed violently, a gush of vomit pouring onto my chest and bedclothes.

Yellowy rays of hatred burst from the fiend's eyes into my brain with excruciating agony. He hurled venomous curses and obscenities at me, his mouth in a vicious twist, his jaw clicking and cracking.

'Damn your soul, see what you've done to me,' he said in an eldritch screech. 'This is on you. Take into your body my stink, my shit and vomit and decay.'

I tried to say something but no words came.

'Behold my friends,' he snarled. 'Behold, the Devil Lords of Asmodeus, as they welcome you to our domain.'

That's what the name sounded like. It held no meaning for me. He was pointing a withered finger at the eccentric painting by the wardrobe. It was no longer faded but alive and expanding to fill the entire wall. In darkness visible, the hideous creatures outside the cave were beckoning me with evil leers and barking noises and lewd gestures. Behind them, the cavern's blackness gaped like an obscene orifice that seemed to drag me towards it.

'Who are you?' I managed to choke out.

'I am the Nikromantzer,' he growled.

'Necromancer?' I blurted, bewildered. 'Like out of *The Hobbit*?'

He gave an infuriated screech of fury.

'Play the fool with me to your cost? I am Nithael the Nikromantzer, servant of the AngelBeest, and I damn you to eternal annihilation. I command you at this time and from this place to return to the void of your extinction. I command it'

'Wait. Wait,' I cried, horrified. Was this even happening?

'She is not for you, ever,' he howled in triumph. 'As you have been my end, I am yours. With pain and horror beyond your imaginings, I command you to fall into the feculence of death, and this time no escape. See: you are fading, fading into black again. Come, come into your own.'

He crooned this last over and over in a vicious monotone, relentlessly, like the beating of a tom-tom. I sensed the room shudder and lose shape, echoing with the raucous baying and shrieking of the monstrous creatures in the picture. The mist around the Nikromantzer fused with a murky cloud that emanated from the cave and became swirling masses of thick green sinuous maggots slithering through the air towards me. The putrid smell grew more hideous and again I vomited all over myself and my bowels and bladder expelled into the bed.

The blackness of the cave enveloped me and I was being tugged into it, sinking into its depth, resistance seeping. The maggots crawled over me, wriggling into my ears and my nostrils and into my anus. The pain in my chest grew in intensity. I was losing consciousness and, like a swimmer paralysed by cramp, the pull of the deep and the slide into oblivion was treacherously welcoming. Abruptly a particle of my mind or spirit rebelled. I couldn't go now, not before I was again with –

'Aoife,' I whispered.

A flash of golden light lit the room. I heard a furious collective screeching of frustrated rage and the Nikromantzer's venom-filled bellow: 'Near, oh so near. Do not think, do not believe, I am finished.'

Then he was no longer in the room.

I emerged from the blackness, and into the lesser gloom of the night, sitting in the bed, drenched in sweat, gasping for air, pain subsiding, free of that evil presence and those monstrous beasts he had brought into life. The unspeakable stink was gone. My vomit no longer covered me or the bedclothes and I had not soiled myself. Relief washed over me as I slid down the bed, drained of energy and spirit.

A figure was at my bedside, holding my arm, with power, without force. From the margin of my vision, I glimpsed the familiar golden radiance. I wanted to see her, to speak with her, hold her, gasp out my gratitude. But I was unable to move.

Her reassuring grasp tightened, then relaxed. Her essence spread through my body and into my mind and spirit and I knew I need have no fear now. As I sank into sleep, I saw the alarm clock change from 02:00 to 02:01. Once more, time had stretched and contracted.

13

DARLING SANDRA PARRY RIP

I woke to a chorus of birdsong. An agency colleague, Lucy Shaw, told me once that when birds sang out in the dawn, they were rejoicing that their brief lives had been given another glorious day. I didn't know if this was true, or indeed how anyone could know what birds were thinking. Lucy was, after all, a writer of popular fiction as well as the agency's top copywriter. But the idea appealed to me and the morning trill of the birds usually gave me a bounce of optimism as to how the day would unfold.

Maybe that's why I was in good spirits. Or it might have had something to do with my sense that Aoife had been with me, an amorphous but palpable presence. Stepping out of the shower, I noticed my facial and body scars and bruises were now barely visible. Over the past week, they had continued to fade. Hair had regrown on the section of my head that had been shaved and only a thin scar showed. Incredibly, there was almost no obvious sign I'd been in a dreadful accident in which my injuries had sent me to death's pit and back.

As I dressed, I asked myself, not for the first time, what

the hell was going on in my life. I was confronting one crazy situation after another, all beyond comprehension. I had awakened from my post-crash coma and entered a personal world where the order of things was cockeyed, with the weird and outlandish and death-freakish facing me at every turn. Plus, I could not be certain if I was alive in the real world in any normal sense.

By this time, I should have been a blathering booby in the throes of lunacy. Instead, each time, after an initial shock, I managed to revise my notions of reality to accommodate the latest excursion through the Looking Glass.

With the bravado of daylight and the knowledge I'd survived, my memory of the night's icy terror was already dimming. It exasperated me that I had succumbed so totally to unbridled panic and fear. Okay, it was natural for horror to paralyse my senses. But I admonished myself that I should have found the strength to make a fight of it and not fall back on a piteous plea of help to Aoife. Not good enough, Kieran.

As I left my room, I noticed the cave painting was now a burnt canvas under its glass. I lifted the frame and checked that it remained sealed. When I put it back, the residue dissolved into ashy particles that fell to the bottom of the frame. Let the good nuns work that out.

After breakfast, I wandered aimlessly through the Home. It was apparently not custom-built as a nursing home and comprised several adjoining buildings that had been renovated, adapted and extended. As a result, it was more spacious within than it looked from the outside. I lost my way in its maze-like narrow corridors, reminiscent of those I had traversed in my deathmares, where I'd sought a way out of the sepulchral museum. *I walk on, once again, down these corridors…* the haunting opening monologue in *Last Year at Marienbad.*

My random perambulations brought me to a glass-panelled door at the end of a cul-de-sac passage. The glass was fogged with condensation and, from the splashes of colour beyond, I surmised an interior courtyard garden. I opened the door and was hit with a blast of humid air so potent that I swayed with light-headedness and had to grab the door to stop myself falling. I eased onto a long wooden bench, perspiration already dripping down my face and body. I was reminded of Humphrey Bogart in the orchid hothouse scene from *The Big Sleep.*

The bench had a brass plaque, with washed-out red lettering within a black border: "In memory of my Darling Sandra Parry RIP. You were my heart's delight". The maudlin sentiment stirred a fleeting compassion for the unknown grieving donor.

I was in a lavender garden, laid out in a circular quartet of lavender beds, bordered by boxed hedging, each bed thick with shrubs of a different shade: purple, green, white, and red with lilac flecks. The air was charged with the heady fragrance of the plants. A central area held a raised iron and wooden gazebo, like an old-fashioned bandstand. Four white gravel paths ran from it to wrought iron benches along a low redbrick wall, behind which were more benches set in the wall, these of heavy timber, with dividing trelliswork and metal decoration. Far off, a handbell was ringing.

Aoife, enfolded in her golden glow, was on a swing in the centre of the gazebo, swaying back and forth. Her face lit up with that dazzling smile of hers when she saw I had noticed her. I rose, dizziness gone, all but ran up the path, hopped onto the timbered dais and into a haven of fresh cool air.

Without hesitation, needing no words, I took her in my arms and lifted her light body off the swing. Our lips met unhurriedly, with a passion that waltzed languorously through us both.

A long time passed before our bodies and spirits parted and Aoife slipped back on her swing and resumed her slow, hypnotic rocking, her bright eyes surveying me happily. A puff of air tousled her hair. Once more, I had that sense of ephemeral familiarity.

'"Rarely, rarely, comest thou, Spirit of Delight",' I said, sitting on the wooden floor of the gazebo, a quote never far from my lips. 'I'm delighted to see you, Aoife. Where have you been? How did you know I was here? Are you –?'

I interrupted myself. 'Press delete on that. Now we're together, it's of no importance.'

'You prefer a woman of mystery?' Her voice was mischievous, her eyes serious.

'You'll always be that. The way you floated into my life in the hospital, like a Wanderer butterfly, or an angel that, wings or not, flew in and away. You've returned, as you promised, and out of nowhere. I don't need to know who you are, nor what world you're from. Not this one, I think.'

This was asking without asking.

'Not my world: our world.' She touched my face. 'It always has been ours. As for the rest, much is new to me, too.'

'You know a great deal more than I do,' I protested. So much of what she said continued to be unfathomable to me, like a poor translation from another language.

'In time, you'll know as much as I do and I expect we shall both know more than we do now. The answers are in our memories and we must rediscover the life spark ourselves.'

There it was again: *the life spark.*

She closed her eyes briefly, as though searching her memory, then shook her head.

I resisted an urge to ask her, as I did the first time we met, if she thought I was in a dead dream state and she a part of it. Instead, I said, 'I've been reading the book you gave me,' and quoted:

'Has this been thus before?
And shall not thus time's eddying flight
Still with our lives our love restore
In death's despite,
And day and night yield one delight once more?

Her eyes shone with pleasure and she took up the verse:

Then, now, – perchance again!...
O round mine eyes your tresses shake!
Shall we not lie as we have lain
Thus for Love's sake,
And sleep, and wake, yet never break the chain?

'It is not in the book. It was Rossetti's alternative final stanza,' she said, noting my enquiring expression. 'You understand, don't you?'

'Yes,' I wasn't sure I did, but what matter?

'Aoife, allow me the world's oldest pick-up line: Don't I know you? We've been together before, haven't we? How? I wouldn't forget, surely. Is my amnesia as bad as that? Let me try to remember.'

I screwed my face in mock concentration and, to my surprise, an image came to me. 'Yes, I see it now, a distant vision. Yes. You gaze on me with those beautiful pensive eyes, and in the background, I see a fabulous setting of lakes and mountains.'

She laughed. 'You are thinking of Leonardo.'

'*La Gioconda*? No resemblance. You're far more inscrutable. Sphinx-like.'

I took her hand in mine and relished the slight tremor of her cool palm as I lightly massaged it.

'I wish I'd known you all my life and yours, that we were childhood playmates, youthful friends, teenage lovers, sharing every minute of our lives together. I mourn the loss of all the days and months and years that you've lived, and I've never known you.'

We held each other's gaze, wrapped in soft silence. I was happier than I could ever remember or imagine, and I would have been wholly fulfilled had the two of us remained like this forever. I hated breaking the spell by mentioning the previous night. It was unavoidable.

'Thank you for chasing away Bum Farto. You saved my life, certainly my sanity. It was a near run thing.'

'Bum who? Where did that come from?'

'That monstrous being who has been tormenting me night after night and who tried to do away with me. He resembles a cartoon character except he's not at all funny. I underestimated him. He had more devil juice than I supposed. You warned me last time and I should have listened.'

She ruffled my hair, sending small tremors of electric pleasure through me. There was a new intensity in her voice.

'This one is a demon. His body is dead but his evil spirit remains still potent. By sheer force of will, he can still slither in and out of this world for short spells. He has been able to enter your mind and fasten on your deepest fears and give them form. Fortunately, his force is waning and last night was an act of desperation. He failed and you will find he can no longer terrorise your nights.'

'What of my deathmares, as I call them? I'm free of them?'
She hesitated.

'He weakens while you grow stronger. He may try to attack you through others, plant in their minds splinters of his own warped spite. The danger is not over. Whenever I can, I shall be your protector.'

I wanted to ask more, ask why he was pursuing me but I sensed our time was short, and I didn't want to dwell further on the Nikromantzer. Aoife may have been of the same mind.

'We shall not be able to meet in this way again. But in good time, in a different way, we shall come together.'

I heard myself say, in a voice utterly unlike my own, 'Then, come with me, Aoife. Away from this place. Today. Now. I know of a grassy sloping dell near an ancient ruined keep in a valley park where, by a slow-flowing, white-pebbled river at the edge of a pine forest, there is a secluded glade covered in soft golden pine needles. We knew it of old, remember?

'With sunshine golden as your aura to warm the day, we shall discard our clothes and wade across the river and in the shade of the trees, spread goose feather cushions and a chequered picnic tablecloth and you can tell me all of your life as we eat iced lemon cake and sip chilled Chardonnay and we shall –'

I stopped, stunned at my own words.

'I can't believe I said that. How incredibly fantastically unlike me. I had such a clear picture of us together, a memory of a time and a place we shared.'

She said, 'I saw it as you did, *come un sogno*, like a dream.'

From around her neck, she lifted a long thin gold chain with what appeared to be a golden cross attached. When she held it out, I saw it was not a cross.

'An Ankh?'

'An Ankh,' she confirmed. 'Crux ansata, symbol of the afterlife and eternal life, of male and female Aeons united, an amulet of great potency that will protect you.'

I scarcely took in her words, mesmerised as I was by the golden Ankh that seemed to glow with eager life.

'Don't you –'

'I no longer have need of it except to make it yours and ours.'

She slipped it over my head and the Ankh slid inside my shirt. There was an unbelievably sensual tremor as the warmth from her body on the Ankh touched my chest.

'Wait for me.'

'Always.'

She pressed my hand, kissed me, and tilted back on her swing. A pleasant lassitude came over me as I sat on the floor beside her. In a state of tranquillity, I closed my eyes for a moment. It must have been much longer because, when I opened them, I saw only the empty swing, swaying slowly to and fro.

14

DEATH NOTICES

Next day, I checked out of Saint Camillus Home, figuring I could now take care of myself. I'd have welcomed a further conversation with Monsignor Flinter before I left and was disappointed when a nun at reception told me, with awe in her voice, that he was in Paris promoting his new book.

Sitting in the foyer waiting for my taxi, my ears pricked when, faintly in the background, I heard that song again:

> *I remember you,*
> *You're the one who said*
> *"I love you, too," yes, I do*
> *Didn't you know?*

How could it be following me from the hospital? Or was I really hearing it? Of all songs, those kitschy, cheesy lyrics had smuggled their way into my mind and formed, as it were, Aoife's theme.

Earlier, I had thought to make a final brief visit to the lavender garden in the hope I might see her again. After wandering the corridors without success, I queried a passing nun who looked long enough in the tooth to know the geography of the place. Dear Lord, she had been here for many's the year and knew of no such garden, more's the pity. It sounded such a pleasant haven.

It was a short drive from the Home to where I lived in Silchester Road. My taxi made its way slowly along the driveway, gravel crunching under tyres, a sheltered lane, tightly foliaged with a diversity of trees: oak, yew and mountain ash. Overhead, branches linked arms, some leafy, others bare, to form a tunnel: twilight by day, Stygian darkness by night.

As I paid the driver, he remarked, 'Class kip.'

Huntsman Hall was a once splendid, still outwardly imposing residence at the end of a quiet road of no less gracious nineteenth-century homes in Glenageary, a Southside suburb of the well-heeled, apart from myself. It stood in its own grounds, surrounded by a high wall of studded granite. Cut stone piers that had once held iron gates opened to the gravel drive. The piers were topped by a pair of sculptured lions who once vigilantly guarded the entrance – *hic sunt liones.* The erosion of time and weather had rendered the sentinels blind and mangy.

The Hall had been built in the 1860s, in Queen Anne style on a grand scale, to the eclectic specifications of its owner, Sir Charles St. Mark O'Connor, a wealthy wine importer and Tory Member of the Westminster Parliament. Originally termed a villa, it acquired its Huntsman Hall name before it was completed, for reasons unknown to me. A double set of balustraded stone steps fronted an elaborately carved Spanish walnut front door. The exterior was of limestone with granite quoins at the corners and it was on three floors plus a basement. Two large bay windows projected from the ground floor. The floors above had painted sash windows with iron trestle balconies. The hipped slate roof held a quartet of high chimney stacks.

On Christmas week 1887, Sir Charles, returning from a reception in the Kildare Street Club in Dublin, and much inebriated, took a tumble from the top of the grand staircase to the marble hall below and broke his neck. His assets were outweighed by a pile of gambling debts and his family sold Huntsman Hall, quickly and at a bargain price, to my great-great-grandfather, Kershaw Sheridan, and it had since remained in our family.

On one of my visits as a child, Uncle Jasper had whispered to me, with a fake shudder, that Huntsman Hall was haunted.

'Some nights, Kyrie, late, when the wind rattles the shutters and the floors creak and groan and the house grows fearsome cold, I hear Old Charlie roaring out the most devilish oaths as he goes bumpity, thumpity down the staircase and whumpity onto the marble hall. Wakes me, I can tell you.'

'Aren't you scared?' I had asked.

'Goodness, no. Why should I be? Old Charlie can't do me harm: his neck's broken. Not to speak ill of the dead, he hasn't much going for him as a ghost.'

I was relieved, nonetheless, that he never invited me to spend the night in one of the bedrooms off the first floor's dim and dusty corridors.

The entrance to my apartment was at the rear. Someone, Shay most like, had brought the Jaguar from where I'd left it in the agency car park on the day of the accident. Taking the trouble to drive it here had been a handsome gesture. The house key was in its usual place within a hollow bone in the kennel of the non-existent dog.

When he had money to burn, Jasper had the exterior of the Hall renovated to retain its period grandeur and outwardly it gave the appearance of a flourishing place of residence. Inside, it was steadily losing the fight with time and neglect.

The main house was damp, old and unlived in, floorboards starting to rot in places, wallpaper peeling, hanging in yellowed strips and twists. Original features remained in the high-ceilinged rooms – several gilt mirrors, pitch pine ceiling beams, pillars, wall panelling, cornicing, centre roses. Even these bore evidence of disrepair. The front door was barred from the inside and the entire basement was shuttered and abandoned. What had once been a lively family home was no more, the residue a symbol, I thought, of the fall of the House of Sheridan. I had occasional daydreams of acquiring the money to renovate the Hall and restoring it to its former glory. Not a hope.

I lived in a duplex apartment that was a pearl in the dungheap. Jasper had it converted for a friend and colleague of his, Fred O'Loughlin, who was retiring after forty years with the agency. What had been stables, and then a garage that could hold half a dozen limos, became a ground floor lounge and dining area, with a kitchen and WC. The storage space overhead was now a spacious bedroom, with bathroom en-suite and a sizeable dressing room.

Shortly after the builders got to work, Fred O'Loughlin dropped dead in the middle of one of several of his farewell parties. When the renovations were finished, Jasper closed room after room of the main Hall and took up residence himself in the converted apartment.

Later, he had admitted to me, 'We were good friends, Fred and me, and he was my right-hand man in the agency. I was most upset by his death because I felt dreadfully guilty. You see, as I cogitated long on the apartment, what a fine place it was and how it would suit me bloody well, I was sorry to be giving it to him. Not that he didn't deserve it, with his long service to the agency.

'I came to envy him the luxurious abode I had prepared for him and, God forgive me, wondered how many years must pass before he died and I could take it myself. When he passed, my distress was diluted with a furtively pleasurable realisation that the apartment was now mine.'

Now it was my residence, though only as a squatter. Jasper had offered Huntsman Hall in its entirety to Larry Brenner as loan collateral. He had also designated it separately, and illegally, to three banks as part of personal guarantees on loans. The banks had first call, or maybe Larry. Or maybe no one. To everyone's discomfiture, vital documents that secured the grounds on which the Hall stood were absent from the various filing papers, which rendered the guarantees moot.

I'd moved in shortly after Jasper's disappearance, ostensibly to tidy the place, and never left. This is where I now lived and I'd no cause for complaint. Jasper had sold off most of the furniture in the Hall, keeping the best of it for his new apartment. I lived well above my means amid deep pile carpets, Persian rugs, comfortable leather armchairs and settees and valuable antiques. I was not short of hedonistic conveniences, with central heating, recessed lighting, smart television and Bose stereo, a Jacuzzi off the main bedroom, a well-fitted kitchen. My only expenditure was on utilities and on a twice-a-month gardener, once a lawyer in Wroclaw, who kept the grounds from becoming an unkempt wilderness.

I'd have luxuriated in the lifestyle more were it not for the perpetual nagging worry that one of the banks, or perhaps Larry, might one day remember the apartment, take the issue to court, arrange my eviction and hold a fire sale of the Hall, the apartment and its contents.

There was little evidence Jasper had ever lived in the apartment, no personal mementos, no photographs on the walls, no books. Some music, though. There was the Bose stereo system and a collection of Jasper's CDs and LPs of Golden Oldie nostalgia from the '40s to the '80s, Ray Eberle, Glenn Miller and Vera Lynn on to Frank Sinatra, Andy Williams, Burt Bacharach and the like. I played the records occasionally.

General Ulysses Grant once declared, 'I know only two tunes: one is Yankee Doodle, the other isn't'. Kind of like me, where music was concerned. Apart from the fabulous Helene Fischer, whom I'd heard once in concert in Dresden, my musical interests consisted of the occasional playing of Jasper's Oldies. I mentioned them to no one. I didn't want to be thought of as a young fogey. I'll amend: I didn't want to broadcast that, in too many ways, I was a young fogey.

I went through the LP collection to see if it had *I Remember You*. It was there, not the popular Frank Ifield yodel-e-hey version, but one I didn't recall having heard before, a throaty sensual Dorothy Lamour original. Talk about oldie: she recorded the song in 1942, when Hitler was not only alive, he was winning the war, just about.

I dipped into the overnight bag of odds and ends I'd brought from St Camillus found the Rossetti book and paged through it. I stopped at the sonnet cycle, *The House of Life*:

> *At length their long kiss severed, with sweet smart:*
> *And as the last slow sudden drops are shed*
> *From sparkling eaves when all the storm has fled,*
> *So singly flagged the pulses of each heart.*
> *Their bosoms sundered, with the opening start*
> *Of married flowers to either side outspread*
> *From the knit stem; yet still their mouths, burnt red,*
> *Fawned on each other where they lay apart.*

I found myself responding, mind and body, to its open sensuality. As before, it was as though Aoife and I were conversing in soft whispers and she was sending me sibylline messages of love and passion. I gently closed the volume and touched it to my cheek as if it might bring her close and allow me to inhale her perfume.

I thought back to my recent meeting with Aoife, the way she had unexpectedly appeared to me, in a lavender garden seen only by me, to vanish as quickly. When added to our first encounter, in a time that wasn't linear time, she was beyond rational explanation. I had no wish to analyse. She was mysterious, inexplicable and fascinating. I desperately desired to see her again.

To check a threatened bout of gloom, I made a pot of coffee, Valhalla Java, a gift from a client, which promised to deliver a caffeine bounce equivalent to leaping about on a trampoline.

A cup of the stuff was enough to shake off my lassitude.

I opened my laptop and clicked through the accumulated mail. There were Get Well messages, promos and the usual spam, tips on shares that were ready to explode in value, sure-fire techniques for keeping my women in non-stop orgasmic stupor and the tireless solicitor from unknown parts telling me in several emails that this was my final chance to claim the €12.7 million due to me as sole beneficiary in an unspecified will, please rush full details of bank account.

When I finished deleting, I logged onto the Dublin-SouthSider.com events web, where I had a film and TV review blog, using the nom de plume Cloudesley Shovell – I'd taken a fancy to the name of that long-drowned English Admiral. My most recent column, posted the day before the car crash, a snarky piece on the inaccuracy of every history or war film ever made, had drawn sixty-two comments. I would read them another day.

I left the site and stared at the Windows screen for a time, fingers poised over the keyboard, procrastinating. I knew what I wanted to do: read the newspaper accounts of the crash. I was hesitating because I still had this floating anxiety about cracking the carapace of my amnesia and discovering something undesirable. As a delaying tactic, I did a web search on Cotard Syndrome, which Gus van Vliet had dismissed. I was more than curious to see if the term applied to my situation.

From what I gleaned, Cotard Syndrome or Cotard Delusion was a portmanteau term that covered a whole grab bag of mental illnesses. It was sometimes referred to (but not in front of the patient, I presumed) as the Walking Corpse Delusion. It applied to patients who came to believe they were dead, or didn't exist, or parts of their body didn't exist or were slowly putrefying. Other sufferers considered themselves immortal; since they were already dead, they could no longer die.

The syndrome took in a number of other broadly similar delusional permutations and variations that were of no relevance to me. I could find nothing that covered my situation: a person who knows he may have died and has either come back to life or is dead and imagining that he is alive. In other words, hallucinating while dead. If it wasn't Cotard, it surely merited a syndrome all to itself.

I decided to look up 'Nikromantzer'. As I expected, there was an abundance of material on Necromancers and Necromancy and words that meant the same thing, a class of medium who could interact with the dead. Nothing on AngelBeest. I confirmed 'thanatotic' referred to death, after Thanatos, god of that ilk.

There were other names I'd heard only once but were as clear in my mind as though newly uttered. The name Bum Farto had given himself, Nithael, was that of a legendary fallen angel or devil. He and Asmodeus, the creature who had come alive from the painting, were likewise fallen angels.

Could I really believe this hooey? In one part of my mind, I knew it was nonsense and berated myself for taking it seriously. But I couldn't dismiss it. Bum Farto, especially, was no imaginary Fury. He was, as I had learned the hard way, the real deal.

Eventually, I checked the media websites. The coverage of the crash was not anything like as extensive as I'd imagined. Since there were several fatal accidents every week on Irish roads, I should have realised the reports would be brief.

The *Irish Times* had it on page five, with an eye-catching

night-time flash photo of Cronin's BMW on its side in the roadway, a mangled pile of metal, unrecognisable as a car.

The story ran:

Three die in Ballsbridge car crash

Three people died and one was seriously injured in a horrific collision involving two cars on Raglan Road, Ballsbridge, Dublin at 8.30 pm last night.

The dead are Mr Cronin Brenner, 37, chief executive officer of the Dublin-based Aardvark-Sheridan advertising agency, who was the driver of a black BMW, and a man in his 30s and a woman in her 20s, believed to be from the South of England, who were in a red Mazda sports car. Their names are being withheld pending notification of next of kin.

The three were pronounced dead at the scene.

A passenger in the BMW, Mr. Kieran Sheridan, aged 34, an executive with Aardvark-Sheridan Advertising, was taken to hospital where his condition is described as critical.

Locals described the scene as 'total carnage' and 'absolutely horrific' with debris scattered over the roadside. Gardaí investigating the collision have spoken to a witness who reported seeing the BMW veering into the path of the sports car.

The BMW was seen to be 'shuddering' as it went over the broken white line and onto the wrong side of the road.

Gardaí are trying to determine if the car suffered a blowout puncture before impact.

It was raining heavily at the time following a three-day dry spell and this may have affected road conditions. Both cars hit parked vehicles and a tree.

Mr. Brenner was unmarried and is the son of Mr. Larry Brenner, the well-known businessman and property developer.

The road is currently closed, and this morning remained sealed off pending a forensic examination by Garda crash investigators who arrived early in the morning and surveyed the scene. They hope to determine the precise circumstances of the accident.

Local diversions are in place, according to a Garda spokesman.

Anyone with information concerning the incident has been asked to contact Donnybrook Garda Station, the 1800 Garda Confidential Line, or any Garda Station.

Tight reporting, what else? Nothing I didn't know. It was eerie seeing my name in print, first time in the national press. I was absurdly annoyed they had got my age wrong by a year and imagined the reaction in the *Times* if they got a letter from me demanding a correction. I thought morbidly of Cronin: what had it been like for him? Did he have a horrified realisation he was about to die, or was he in denial to the end, thinking he could pull out of it?

I moved on to the *Irish Independent*, which had a racier headline: *Three Killed in Horror Car Smash*. The story was much the same. It ran a sidebar potted biography of Cronin, from school in Blackrock College (captain of famed Cup-winning senior school rugby team), Trinity College, MBS from Smurfit Business School and stints with Heinz in Pittsburgh and ad agencies in New York and Chicago, before coming back to Ireland to head Aardvark-Sheridan. Named Irish Advertising Person of the Year in 2018. An accompanying photo showed him at a Marketing Society event in the Westbury Hotel a fortnight before, in black tie and a wide grin that said he owned the town.

I nearly missed the story in the *Irish Daily Mail*. It was in the Sunday paper and had additional information.

The two dead from the Mazda were not, as I heard Breen say it, Paul Scully and Ruth Vann. He was Todd Pole-Scully, aged 40, a freelance writer, elder son of Doctor Kenneth and Mavis Pole-Scully, a retired couple living in Hawkhurst village, near Tunbridge Wells in Kent. The girl was Aoife Ruthyn, aged 27, a post-graduate research student at Cambridge University and daughter of the late Rev Winston Burke Ruthyn, one-time Lecturer in Religious Literature at Anglia Ruskin University and the late Mrs Rebecca Ruthyn. Both deceased had been attending a seminar in Wicklow, and it was not clear from the story if they were together. *The Mail* had a photograph of the girl and had run it big because her extraordinary beauty underlined the tragedy of her death.

I looked for a long time, dazed, at the photograph on my laptop screen. There was no mistaking Aoife's celestial face and those great bewitching eyes.

A desolate inscription on an ancient Greek tombstone came to mind:

> *Pity me*
> *Who is so beautiful*
> *And is dead.*

15

ROAD RAGE IN MONKSTOWN

The blurry newspaper photograph captured with uncanny precision that wonder-filled freeze of time when Aoife sat on my bed in the hospital that day: dreamily pensive, chin touching a slender hand, contemplating I know not what. Now, as then, she was intriguingly familiar. Suddenly, it came to me where I had seen her likeness, with the background of mountain and lake: on old Irish bank notes that stopped being legal tender when I was a teenager.

'Hazel Lavery,' I murmured.

Soon after the Irish Free State was established in 1922, the new native Government decided that the nation's banknotes should depict an archetypical Irish girl, Kathleen Ni Houlihan, the mythical symbol of Ireland. The commission was given to the renowned Belfast artist of the day, Sir John Lavery, who presented a portrait of Lady Lavery, his American wife, against a Celtic landscape. Thus, it came about that a Chicago-born socialite and an English-titled Lady became Ireland's representative *Cailín*. We Irish are well-known for our delight in the absurd.

Hazel Lavery was one of the most celebrated beauties and social hostesses of the early decades of the twentieth century. Both Lloyd George and Michael Collins wrote love poems to her. That and more I gleaned from a quick web search, including her family's motto: *Sic itur ad astra*. This is the way to the stars. It was what Aoife had written in the Rossetti book.

I remembered that anonymously-gifted book on Sir John Lavery I had received in hospital and checked the contents of my overnight bag. It wasn't among the other books and cards and things. I must have left it behind when I switched wards and doubted I'd find it now.

Next day, to clear my mind, I decided to get out of the apartment for a few hours. I took one of Jasper's heavy walking sticks, as I was still a bit unsteady on my feet. Doctor Watson had advised me not to drive for a month but I deemed it an excess of caution. I slid behind the wheel of the Jaguar and, after a few seconds of steeling myself, switched on the engine and swung down the driveway.

I took it slowly. My objective was the well-stocked Hewetts newsagent in Monkstown village, where kerbside parking was occasionally available. Not on this day. There was a funeral service in the nearby Catholic Church and cars were parked bonnet to boot both sides of the road around the village. Fortunately, past the roundabout, a van pulled out ahead of me and I eased into the vacated space.

As I exited my car, I looked up, as I always did when in Monkstown, at the turrets of the gothic-style grey granite Anglican Church that dominates the village centre, with its elaborately adorned pinnacles and castellations, much admired by John Betjeman among others. It was local folklore that these embellishments represented a complete chess set, though I could never identify the pieces.

A horn blaring from a car on the road brought my gaze down. The driver of a two-tone black and silver SUV had been waiting for the van to depart and was furious to see me apparently gazumping the space. I hadn't noticed him, it wasn't his space, and I didn't intend to move out. I was already fatigued, and this may be why, instead of miming an apology, I ignored him and walked on.

It was a mistake, suggestive of contempt. The driver flung open his car door, hopped out and bellowed at me, 'That's my space you've snuck into, cock!'

He was big and muscled, in lumberjack shirt and jeans, with a broken nose and a head of reddish stubble. I waved a hand apologetically and called out, 'I really didn't see you.' He reacted with clenched fists and face mottled with fury. 'What you want is a boot in the arse and my fist down your throat, cock,' he roared and came towards me fast.

My mental reaction surprised me. I decided on the instant I would let him get close and, with the least possible warning, slash my walking stick across the bridge of his nose. As he would freeze with the unexpected pain, I'd scythe his shins, bringing him to the ground. I hadn't decided on my follow-up and, in the event, didn't need to.

I leaned forward on the stick to give an impression of a helpless cripple and surreptitiously altered my grip to let my hand more easily wield it as a club.

What appeared to be a large white plastic bag was drifting along the road, blown in a gust of wind, and, before my attacker reached the pavement, his feet became tangled in it and he lost his balance. He flailed his arms unavailingly and fell forward into the rear of the nearest parked car, which unluckily for him was an old model Mercedes with one of those sharp-edged fins at the back into which he slammed his face.

'Jeeeb-us Thrist,' he howled as he slid to the ground. His hands went to his face and bright blood poured between his fingers. He sat sprawled on the road, moaning, then let go with a high-pitched screech of agony as a passing lorry that had failed to see his outstretched legs drove over them. I distinctly heard the crunch of his bones. There were cries and screams from the nearby funeral crowd that was emerging from the Catholic Church and a rush to help the man who now lay unmoving on the road.

My own brutal intentions gone, I looked on with horror, then quickly changed direction and headed for the entrance to the Anglican Church. Inside, half a dozen elderly men and women sat in its semi-darkness and paid me no attention. I flopped into a pew, breathing hard and with a painful cramp in my legs from the burst of speed. Nothing like as painful as he of the pulped legs.

In a short time, I heard an ambulance siren in the distance, grow near and stop. A few of the people in the Church turned their heads as another siren arrived a few minutes later. Police, I supposed. It was quiet for a time, then the ambulance moved off with a renewed burst of siren. Were they taking him to A&E to get his legs amputated or saved by surgeon Salah?

I'd never previously encountered road rage and, as is the worse of its kind, it had ended badly. I didn't feel guilty. Okay, I'd taken what he regarded as his car space. His response had been over the top, with an intensity of anger, his face and body twisted in fury, out of proportion to its cause.

I remembered Aoife: *He may try to attack you through others, plant in their minds little splinters of his own warped spite.* Was that it?

I was confounded by my own combative response. I am a physical coward by nature, as you may have surmised, and I'd go to considerable lengths to avoid confrontation. Yet this time I had no fear at the imminence of an attack from a hard man getting ready to deliver on his threat to give me a kick up the arse – and the rest. I was, on the contrary, confident about taking him on. I couldn't figure it.

It was the first time I'd been inside this church and I wandered around, casually examining its quirky decorative plasterwork and manifold wall plaques that commemorated Monkstown men of the past who died in red or khaki uniform in various parts of the long-gone British Empire, their British Empire. When I left, the only sign anything untoward had occurred was a large watery patch on the road where someone had sluiced away the blood.

16

RETURN OF THE HEIR

After my Grandma on the Sheridan side died, I came upon a large collection of photo albums of her early and middle years and that of my Grandad, photos in sepia, muddy mono and faded colour, and in a variety of sizes. Only a handful were dated after I was born.

One was a small colour photograph, bleached and slightly out of focus, of me, aged two or thereabouts, toddling along a grassy lawn, in a dark blue romper suit and an orange sun hat. It had been taken in Merrion Square and in the background were the Sheridan Agency buildings and the second-floor window, glinting in the sun, where I would in time have my office. Coincidence? More likely whoever took the snap, possibly Gran, had, with more confidence than prescience, positioned me against the setting of the family firm I might expect, in due time, to inherit.

Speaking of coincidence, from my office window, and directly across the Square, I had direct sight of number 70, the one-time residence of Joseph Sheridan Le Fanu, famous Victorian writer of the macabre and, as I suggested earlier, my possible kinsman. I would visualise him, thin, sallow-faced, bearded, dark-garbed, gliding along streets and lanes as he passed under the gaslights on dusky winter evenings. Dubliners called him the Invisible Prince, as he ventured forth when the days darkened to visit dusty antiquarian bookshops to pore over rare black manuscripts of astrology or demonology.

It was time for me to face my life in advertising again. I returned to Aardvark-Sheridan on a Friday, selecting the end of the working week to ease myself back into things. I'd been away for a month or so and somehow expected to see great changes and was surprised and disappointed to find none.

I drifted around the offices to signal my reappearance, catching up, chatting, unctuously accepting sympathy and condolences. Most people had questions about the crash but were too polite or tongue-tied to press me, when I verbally sidestepped. At times, it made for stilted conversations, terminated to mutual relief.

'Poor Cronin' was phrase of the day and talk of his funeral was acceptable middle ground. I heard about the obsequies and how it was a beautiful affair, 'beautiful and solemn', 'sad and beautiful', 'beautifully done'. I couldn't help reflecting acerbically that a mangled corpse about to be blasted and hammered to ashes in a crematorium was not a thing of beauty, however chic the ceremony. I kept these dour thoughts to myself.

Growing tired of meaningless palaver, I slipped into Cronin's empty office, sat in his high-back ochre leather swivel chair, put my feet on his glass-topped desk and looked about to see what he had seen in his working day. His office was spacious, taking half the second floor and located at the back, with a bay window overlooking a narrow well-tended lawn and a crazy-tiled path leading to the mews offices and car park spaces, with, further out, a stretch of grey slated rooftops and a distant bird's eye view of green DART trains pulling in and out of Pearse Station. Cronin had forgone Jasper's office with its gentleman's club décor and scenic view of the Square, because, he said, the passing traffic was too noisy

On the wall facing me, in a heavy gilt frame, and with its own wall light, was an oil painting of a bearded seventeenth-century man garbed in black. Cronin had claimed it was an original and he may have believed it. No one pointed out that it was, in fact, a reproduction of a well-known Velázquez self-portrait. Years earlier, I'd seen the original in the Uffizi Gallery in Florence.

The only sound in the room was the steady tick-tock of Jasper's old-fashioned wall-mounted pendulum clock that Cronin had purloined. I wondered idly who was keeping it wound and if it might abruptly fall silent, like in an Ingmar Bergman film.

On the vanity wall, Cronin, in black tie and blue dinner jacket, grinned from an array of photographs, accepting various advertising awards. The agency had improved on its award-garnering since he had become CEO and he took pride in this. There were other photos of him at marketing and business meetings in the US and Ireland, including an early one with the skinny junior senator from Illinois, Barack Obama.

With shameless nosiness, I poked around the desk drawers. They held only items of stationery, an empty pocket diary, and a paperback, Eoghan Smith's dark rumination on death, *The Failing Heart*. The literary critics had spoken highly of it but it was not the kind of surreal novel I associated with Cronin. In the bottom drawer, a copy of *Hustler* was tucked under a ream of writing paper, an incongruous memento mori of a status-conscious person unthinking of impending mortality.

I had never resented Cronin coming into the agency as CEO and displacing my crumbling prospects of heirdom. If not Cronin, it would have been another. Besides, he proved to be shit hot, as we say in the business, far more experienced and able and credible than I was ever likely to be. I had long accepted that my once unthinking assumption that I was heir apparent of the agency had been illusory.

What was he like? Cronin was smaller than average in height but had been a big personality, effortlessly projecting authority, screw-you confidence and a vibrant enjoyment of life. I admired his style and tried not to show it and had to fight the temptation to imitate his spiel and mannerisms.

There had been an obverse side to him, an incredible rudeness. He often showed for appointments an hour or more late without apology. He could interrupt a conversation to talk about something else entirely, indicating he had been paying no attention or wasn't interested. His incivility was selective: with clients or important business contacts, his manners were impeccable.

I flicked through *Hustler* and replaced it, as Shay stuck his head around the door, his visage still disconcertingly smooth-faced.

'I thought you might be here, trying it out for size. I heard you've been roaming around the place, trading pleasantries. How does it feel to be back in the real world?'

'Unreal,' I said. 'It's laughable in a way. For the past

few weeks, in hospital, in the convalescence place and in my apartment, I was bored beyond words and couldn't wait to be back in the agency and now I'm here…'

I was about to say, 'I'm already bored beyond words.' For some reason, I switched to, 'I'm looking forward to getting back to the action.'

He gave me a critical inspection. 'I get a surprise every time I see you, these days. Tell me the secret of how you've recovered so quickly? Even last week, when I left you at Greystones, you were still one sick boy limping around on a stick, with much bruising and serious facial scarring. I didn't say anything, but I assumed your once-handsome profile was marred for life. Now, it's like you left all blemishes behind you in an attic in Dorian Greystones.'

I feigned a wince. 'Shay, I presume you're in charge of this place in the hiatus.'

He snorted. 'Not at all. As far as acting CEO, well, that would be you.'

'Me?' I hooted but he was serious.

'You don't know? Improbable but true. You are the temporary boss: the last has become first. It's another of your esteemed Uncle Jasper's inexplicable legacies. Long before he disappeared, he filed papers naming you as acting CEO in his absence. I imagine he had in mind a brief illness, a trip abroad or suchlike. It never arose, because once Cronin came in, Jasper's writ no longer applied. It seems, though, your putative appointment was never rescinded.'

I was taken aback. 'First I heard of this nutty idea.'

'Took me unawares, too, and our other seniors, when Mike Coyle mentioned it en passant, and he should know. I gather he'll be asking you to co-sign a bunch of cheques for him soon. Cronin always pre-signed a few and these have run out. Seems you are, for the present, the second signature on all agency cheques. A one-off opportunity for you and Mike to abscond with everything in the bank.'

I was amused and bemused. 'Whatever about that, I can't see anyone taking me seriously as acting CEO, however brief my tenure. I have no illusions. Jasper over-promoted me to keep the agency in the family and I'm on the board, well, because I'm an all-round agreeable guy and it's not worth anyone's time to take me off.'

I would have liked him to disagree with my self-abasement but he merely said, 'Enjoy your new status while it lasts and don't let it go to your head.'

'Let humility and modesty ever be my watchwords,' I said with mock solemnity.

Back in my office, I sat at my desk, doodling on a notepad, thinking over my chat with Shay, feeling disconnected and detached, asking myself if I really gave a damn about the job any more or about anything. I was more than ever inclined to believe that everything that had occurred in my life since the car crash was a prolonged hallucination of my departing consciousness. Often, I seemed to recognise the unreality around me, that I was a bit player in a plodding television drama who'd read the script in advance, had my lines off by rote, knew how things would play out.

"Nothing matters very much, and few things matter at all." Which notable had said that? Talleyrand? Balfour? Boris Johnson?

All at once, I reined myself in. I found myself thinking,

what the hell, I can't continue like this or I'll push myself over the edge and into the kind of serious depression I'd escaped so far. Maybe I was alive, maybe not. In practical terms, it didn't seem to affect things, one way or another. My attitude of languid boredom was self-indulgent and I was in urgent need of a bucket of cold water in the face to bring me to my senses.

To date, everything in my life had been a lazy drift. College had been undemanding. My half-formed intention to write had been casually abandoned. My aimless years abroad were a long postponement of deciding on my future. Finally, I had been handed an undemanding job with promotion without effort, and I had managed, at best, a ho-hum performance, enough to get by and no more.

Time for change. Ambition was stirring but to what end? Becoming wealthy, successful, influential? Well and good, but such plums of fortune didn't set my juices going. My objective, above all, to find my way to Aoife, to be with her again, talking and laughing together, sharing thoughts, in each other's arms, making love. Right away and somehow related to all this, I needed financial security and the resources to pursue whatever path I would take.

How would I begin? Well, my temporary status as acting CEO might be a gift from the Fates. Cronin's death was a tragedy for him, maybe not for me. If the car crash hadn't taken place, he would be CEO for many years and I would never become more than his lowly acolyte, nor aspire to be more. Now there had been a disturbance in the order of things and, for the first time, I considered the possibility, remote and in ways I couldn't yet fathom, of becoming heir again, and gaining control of the agency. I needed to recognise and grab opportunities when they came my way. And from those beginnings, all kinds of possibilities might open.

17

THE SCAM

A few days later, Barry Owens, managing director of BlastOff, bounced into my office, bouffant hair, smart three-piece suit, gaudy tie, Jo Malone cologne, beaming easy familiarity, hand stretched out.

'Kieran, how's it shakin', fella? Lovely to find you well into recovery mode. Fantastic.'

Barry had started out selling PVC windows door-to-door and had never shucked the manners of a spiv salesman. As usual, he had dropped by without appointment, and, as befitted a client that was a big spender with the agency, didn't bother announcing himself at reception.

BlastOff was a chain of money-spinning, barn-style, bargain electrical goods stores around Dublin, located mainly in working-class areas, C2DEs, as we marketeers say. Much of the stock came from South Korea, Malaysia, China and Eastern Europe, with unfamiliar brands that sold cheaply yet attracted surprisingly few customer complaints.

There was, nonetheless, something iffy and dodgy about the whole operation and there were unverified stories that the store chain was bankrolled by a notorious Northern drugs family: ex North of Ireland, now Dublin Northside. It was not a rumour anyone in the agency wished to think about. BlastOff's advertising and print budgets were manna and moolah for Aardvark. It was our third largest client, and the single most profitable, and they paid promptly with no nit-picking invoice queries, ever.

It had been one of Cronin's special clients and, with his death, the board had put it in my keeping for the present. I liked to think of this as a sign of confidence. More likely, servicing the account was felt to be undemanding to manage, despite its size, and I had an otherwise light portfolio.

'Happy to see you, Barry, I'm doing fine. Grab a seat.'

He had already pulled over a chair and was straddling it, hands hanging over the backrest. He put on a serious expression.

'Gotta tell you, K, I'm still in shock over Cronin's passing. Awful beyond words. Good mate, Cronin. Two of us were close buds, went way back. You know we shared an apartment for a while in the Windy City across the big pond?'

I hadn't known, though I was aware Barry had worked in the States from the accent he affected. With the appropriate sympathetic noises out of the way, he resumed his joviality:

'Hard to say it, K, but the show must go on. So, you're running the BlastOff account for me. Excellento. I'm sure we're in good hands. Cronin proclaimed you the true goods, said it often. Well. Yeah. So. Let me get you up-to-date on the sales front.'

Barry's perpetual cheery chappy mood made him easy company. Eilis O'Donnell, Cronin's former secretary and now mine, pro tem, brought in coffee and I listened while Owens delivered a panegyric to the continuing success of BlastOff. Sales were notching new records and our advertising had his full approval.

'Very copacetic,' he beamed, rubbing his hands, pleased at finding an opportunity to say it.

'The very word I was groping for,' I said as I poured the coffee.

He was not much interested in my responses. 'Keep up the good work and sock home the message: "Top quality, great range, killer price. Visit your nearest BlastOff store right now, folks, and buy". Crude and simple. And effective. Bam, bam, bam.' He punched the air, then snapped open his briefcase and tugged out a thick file of papers. 'Here's what we got coming in over the next three months, fine products new to market, need an eye-popping new campaign. Can you conjugate first thoughts together by early next week, plus budgets?'

He dumped the file on my desk.

'We need big, bold adverts that set the adrenalin pumping. How I picture it...' He frowned in concentration. 'Nothing held back. Trumpeting elephants, trunk to tail, parading up O'Connell Street, carrying belly dancers in their scanties.' He frowned again. 'Course, I don't literally mean elephants. And I don't mean belly dancers, natch. But it's the tone. You get me?'

Oddly enough, I understood him without difficulty. BlastOff was going to be comparatively easy to manage. I put on enthusiasm.

'No problemo,' I heard myself falling into his lingo. 'You'll have the same creative and support team. Continuity and results guaranteed. I'm confident you'll find that to be satisfactory.'

'Continuity and results, I buy it absolutely. Cool.' His enthusiasm was teasingly catching, and it was like I'd said something innovative. He paused.

'Yes, indeed. While we're on the subject of continuity, K, can you confirm for me Cronin briefed you on our management fee set-up?'

'Management fee? Uh, don't believe he did, Barry.'

'No? Saw no need, I guess. Not your account and he expected to be around for many years. *Sic transit*, as the French say.'

'True. As they say in France, we know not the day nor the hour.'

I instantly regretted my mouth but it sailed by him. He nodded unctuously, then put aside mortality with a grin.

'What should I be briefed about, Barry?' I asked.

'No worries, it's a doddle. Many moons ago, when I placed the BlastOff account with Aardvark, I garaged a deal with Cronin, a side split, if you insist, a special commission for giving you the business. Cost to Aardvark: bupkis.'

I hid a smile at the word.

'The deal is, you pad your charge-out to us – add ten per cent on media, fifteen on print, design and all else. We pay you the face value and you remit ninety-five per cent of the overcharge to partners in Northern Ireland. Simple as that, in and out, no paperwork. No cost to the agency. Sweet or what?'

He said this last with diffidence, as though seeking no thanks for his generosity.

I knew nothing of this. 'News to me, Barry, as you can

imagine. No need for paperwork at your end, fine. Our end: how are we covering off how the money goes out to Northern Ireland – am I wrong or are we talking about a few hundred thousand euro a year?'

'There or thereabouts. Cronin had it buttoned. He didn't tell me how and I don't give a damn. It's not like we're talking new here, boychik? Connect with your bean counter. Mike's been running this from the get-go.'

He was still happy-go-lucky Barry, but now with the slightest edge in his voice. I didn't want my first meeting with one of Aardvark's big three clients to go sour because I was missing an angle.

'Sorry, slow on the uptake today. Give me time to get up to speed. I'll talk to the board members.'

He didn't care for that. 'Why? No need, I'd say. You and me and Mike. That's it. Too many mouths stiff the action, right?'

I took the meaning.

He gave me a cool appraisal, still pleasant but his good humour had fallen a notch. 'Since Cronin's death, K, I've had approaches from more than one of your competitors. Sure, they'll make me a better deal. As you'd expect. Who needs the hassle, right? We've got a good, mutually beneficial relationship going here and I'd like for it to stay that way.'

'I get what you're saying, Barry,' I said, acknowledging the threat.

He continued to stare at me for a time, jumped up, and thrust out his hand. 'Good enough for me, K. No worries. See you when. See you then.'

With another air punch, he was out the door and thumping

down the stairs.

He was wrong about the worries. From what he had said, Aardvark seemed to be complicit in collaborating with Barry in an ongoing fraud, involving overcharging and possible money laundering. I had a general impression of the value of BlastOff to the agency and a ten-to-fifteen per cent kickback came to upward of a million euro a year over two years.

The BlastOff account had been handed to me, and I had the responsibility to sign off on this. A few months back, several mid-level Irish bankers had gone to prison for putting their names to a phoney gloss on the books. They did it for the good of the bank and likely never thought, as they routinely penned their signatures, they'd end as fall guys, doing time.

If the rumours were true, BlastOff was a laundry for drug money. I wondered briefly if Barry was himself the boss behind the operation. Nah, I couldn't visualise him as a hard-guy mobster. Which meant he might be skimming from the real owners of the business, a drug lord or family that wouldn't take kindly to being ripped off if they discovered it.

Yet, none of this was foremost in my thinking. I could, without too much thought, ignore it all. But could I use this to my advantage? Maybe the Fates were tossing an early opportunity my way. Offhand, I didn't know how. But it came to me that my recently formed ambition to get control of the agency might not prove as impossible as all that.

18

A TALK ON THE WILDE SIDE

Mike Coyle dropped by my office to collect a batch of cheques he had sent me for my signature, something that still felt unreal to me. I'd left one unsigned, a cheque for €120,000 made out to BJO Marketing Partners, Belfast.

'I need to know more about this one, Mike, before I put my name to it.' I said.

I usually had a good rapport with Mike, a big, cheerful guy, overweight, open face, unkempt curly black hair. He had been with one of the big four accountancy firms before he came to the agency. He was a competent accountant, more journeyman than highflyer. It was telling that no one ever suggested he join our board. Today, he was pale and seemed hungover, his good humour missing.

He eyed me askance. 'It's payment for market research we commissioned for BlastOff. Straightforward, okay? We've already been paid by the client so there's no problem. So sign the damn things.'

But it wasn't straightforward. When I spotted the cheque, I guessed it was part of Barry Owen's scam.

'I don't think so,' I said to him. 'We need to talk. Tell you what. It's probably the last of the warm days outside. Let's get out of the office and fill our lungs with fresh air?'

'There's a mountain of work on my desk,' he objected.

When I said nothing, he sighed and acquiesced with ill grace. We left the agency, walked across the road and entered the Square. Into autumn, its trees were bare of leaves and the flower beds barren. But I never failed to get a sense of the elegance of centuries-old Georgian Dublin in its tree-lined pathways, contoured lawns and old-style black-coated iron railings and lamp posts.

As we ambled around the recently renovated sandy-gravelled perimeter path, I summarised my meeting with Barry Owens.

'You knew of the BlastOff arrangement?' I queried, resisting the temptation to do 'arrangement' in finger quotes.

'Of course.' He tightened his mouth irritably. I matched him with a snort of exasperation and he added, 'These mark-ups are over and above what we load anyway. It's okay, they're good with it and there's never been a query on any invoice we've sent.'

He sounded indifferent but I thought I caught an underlying unease.

'Huh. How are we getting away with that? I mean, how is it that nobody in BlastOff has made a fuss? I can't believe we overload our bills by, what, up to fifty per cent on the top and nobody's noticed.'

He rolled his eyes. 'Not surprising. For a company with its turnover, BlastOff is weak on financial control. There's one controller, who happens to be Barry's nephew, a couple of accounting technicians and a basement of junior accounts clerks.'

'What about the auditors?'

'The same as ours, Maughan & Maughan. In fact, Charley Maughan handles the audit for both of us.'

I gave a three-cent smile. Charley Maughan was a legendary tax adviser or a notorious one. Depended on who was talking. I'd seen him a few times in the agency, a small grey man with a golf club tie and blazer, a perpetually wary expression on his weasel face. Charley Maughan was also Larry Brenner's personal accountant.

We passed a small group gazing at the statue of Oscar Wilde in jade green smoking jacket, trousers of Norwegian stone and black granite shoes, in a pose of languorous man-to-manspreading. Very Oscar. We walked on, until Mike, decidedly peaky, stopped at a wooden bench and, without a word sat down heavily. I dropped beside him. Across the lawn, Bernardo O'Higgins, Liberator of Chile, stared impassively from his plinth, a bronze bust presented by the Government of that strip of a country. Further off, another bust, an uncharacteristically chubby Michael Collins, peered through the bushes.

Mike glanced at his watch. 'Need to get back to the office. There's nothing more I can tell you.'

He wasn't hostile, not friendly either.

'You understand, Mike, this is criminal fraud and maybe laundering and, if it's ever exposed, someone could do time. And it may well include you.'

Did I sound plausible? I didn't care. I wanted to rattle him.

'Don't be an ass,' he snapped. 'Excuse me saying this,

Kieran, but you're becoming a real buttinsky. That accident has popped your brain cells. Criminal? Everything was cleared with Cronin as CEO and Barry as the client. Fraud? Crap and poppycock, to mention two piles of excrement.'

'No shit. Tell me about the paperwork that's signed off?'

He stared at me as though it had suddenly occurred to him that perhaps he was mistaken in taking me for an uppity junior.

'Listen, Kieran. This was always Cronin's set-up and his responsibility and, need I say it, no one expected him to die that way, least of all him. You know, if there's any question of legality, well, the scheme was Cronin's as CEO –'

'– and he's dead and we can dump on him? My big worry, Mike, is what happens when the owners of BlastOff rumble how they're being ripped off. We've a good idea who they are and how many bodies, and parts of bodies, they've left around the place, those that have been found.'

To my astonishment and mortification, Mike was crying, tears slipping down his cheeks.

'Hey. No need for that,' was all I could say.

He wiped his eyes with his sleeve. 'Oh, I don't give a tinker's balls about Barry Owens or BlastOff or you, for that matter. It's, you see, my dad died on Sunday. We were close. We buried him yesterday.'

I understood now why he appeared off-colour.

'Christ, I'm sorry, Mike. I hadn't heard.'

'Thanks, man.' His expression was doleful. 'I didn't mention it around. And it wasn't in the papers. Dad was weird in some ways. He used to study the obits in the *Times* over breakfast and became fixated on the notion that one day, inevitably, his name would be there. He made us promise when he died we wouldn't insert a death notice anywhere. Once we agreed, he said he could read the *Times* in contentment knowing his name wasn't ever going to be among the obits. It was like he'd never die.'

Across the way in Leinster House, the Dáil quorum bell was ringing.

'Forget Barry Owens and the whole business,' I said quietly. 'It's lunchtime. Let's grab a bite.'

He agreed without enthusiasm and suggested the nearby National Gallery restaurant. I hoped we'd finished with talk of death and obits. Now he'd brought it up, though, I suspected I was going to get a further earful.

19

HER PALE AND GHOSTLY IMAGE

Lunch at the National Gallery was semi self-service, where customers selected from a display of dishes, got their choice microwaved, and paid at a cash desk. Not gourmet, but reasonable food for the price. I ordered a lasagne and salad and Mike, preoccupied, went for the same.

At the cash desk, a man in front of me shouted, 'Balderdash,' the first time I heard someone use the word in real life. He was middle-aged, stout and florid-faced, in an overtight tweed suit and yellow waistcoat, and he was complaining about his meal loudly enough to raise heads around the restaurant. It contained meat, he objected, despite his having made it clear he was a vegetarian.

He possessed the bully attitude of the self-righteous, the kind used to raising his voice to get his way. He flustered the young woman at the cash desk, who apologised and offered to change the meal. This didn't appease him. He couldn't decide on an alternative and seemed more concerned to elaborate on the incompetence of the staff who had given him the wrong dish.

A manageress hastened over and offered to assist him personally if he stepped out of the growing queue. He took offence at the suggestion he was not entitled to stand there and bellyache, and he demanded a description of all vegetarian dishes.

Behind me, a voice said irascibly, 'Ah get on with it, Tweedy Pie.'

The man whirled around and, fixing on me, barked: 'I'll thank you to mind your own damn business.'

'Who are you talking to?' I retorted, nettled at being wrongly accused.

His eyes bulged and he drew back a clenched fist. I stiffened, realising he was about to swing hard at me. Before I could move, he pivoted, wobbled and collided with a woman leaving the nearby beverage counter with a tray of cups and a pot of boiling water. The pot slid off the tray and the water cascaded down the man's crotch. He roared in pain and let go of his own tray, the hot contents of which joined the water running down his front.

I dropped some notes on the cash desk, gestured to Mike and grabbed our tray. We took a table in the corner, where we watched the man, who had fallen onto the ground, clutching his groin, moaning and swearing, eyes shut tight in pain, his face a bright purple, being lifted to his feet by two Gallery security men and carried out of the restaurant, attended by a distraught manageress. With an effort, he twisted around, opened his eyes and blazed a look of impotent rage at me.

'You looking at me?' I said, doing a bad Travis Bickle as he was hauled off.

'Great balls of fire,' I said with satisfaction. 'Bigmouth

got what he deserved. Painful things, boiled balls. Not that I speak from experience.'

'Don't you know him?' asked Mike. 'He's Patrick McCrane, runs his own little design studio in Ranelagh. Freelances for us, on and off. Tried for a job last year, didn't get it. The way he glared at you, I thought it was personal. He was about to sucker punch you before the boiling water hit his groin. Gave him pause, the way that kind of thing does.'

We ate in silence for a few minutes. I was thinking of McCrane fixing on me and his expression as he had readied a lunge at me. Pure, unreasoning hatred, out of all proportion to any imagined grievance, like the motorist in Monkstown. Restaurant rage, this time.

The restaurant was filling up, almost all the tables were now occupied, the hum and thrum of chat steadily waxing. I recognised some well-known faces: here, former Government Minister Shane Ross, there, the writer Paul Howard, unerring satirist of South Dubliners' pretentions. In a far corner was the journalist Colm Keena, bestselling author of well-researched works on death and the afterlife. I could imagine a riveting conversation with him.

'He went like that.' Mike snapped his fingers, drawing me back to him.

'Yeah?' It took me a few seconds to twig he had switched back to his father.

'He was out walking the dog on Sandymount Strand. People saw him stop and bend over, wheezing. Then he flopped to the ground and died. The cigarettes did for him: three packs a day. Nearly a full-time job in itself, and a ridiculous amount of dinaro from a pensioner's income. He'd been out of breath a lot and thought it was emphysema. It was his heart. Arteries clogged.'

I took refuge in banality. 'Sounds as though he departed without too much pain.'

'He told me when he was a kid of four or five his parents couldn't get a house and they stayed in one room of a tenement slum in Bridge Street, you know the place? Near St Audoen's Church, oldest part of Dublin, dump land. The tenement had been condemned and the living was primitive. Exactly what they wanted. The word was anyone living in a place scheduled for demolition was guaranteed one of the new Corporation houses in Crumlin. That's how it worked out for them eventually.

'During the time they lived in the tenement, whenever my dad was brought shopping by his mam, they'd pass a funeral home on High Street and at that time, this was the late nineteen-forties, a great many hearses were still horse-drawn, so he told me, same as coal lorries, milk carts, bread vans.'

His mind seemed to drift in recollections that were not his. He had given up on his food. Eventually, he continued:

'Well, when Dad went past the undertakers, he could hear the horses snorting and stamping their iron shoes on the cobbles and there was a little old man in black with a top hat with black ribbon, hearse driver, I suppose, who'd wave to him, friendly-like. To a child, it was a wicked smirk. You see, his mam had told him the name of the undertakers, Coyle, was same as our own, and he'd gotten the notion that the undertaker did for people named Coyle and the old man was inviting him in to be coffined. At night in bed, when he heard the hooves and rumble of a passing horse and cart, he feared it was the old man coming for him.'

'Horse-drawn hearses? You sure this was the nineteen-forties and not the eighteen-forties?'

Mike looked surprised. 'You still see them occasionally in Dublin, usually in places like The Liberties. Also big among criminal families. The horses have ostrich plumes, black if the deceased was married, white otherwise. Anyhow, my dad had his seventy-fifth birthday a month back. At the weekend, he told me he'd been woken in the small hours by the clip-clop of horse's hooves and wheels on the hard-pebbled road outside. Except the road outside was smooth. He knew then he'd had his last birthday.'

I surmised his father's premonition owed more to his constant breathlessness than horses and hearses. *Angor animi.* A man obsessed with newspaper obituaries, he sounded as necrophobic as me. Death was tirelessly tipping me the wink of familiarity and continued to place itself in my path to remind me of its presence. I was almost getting used to it.

After unburdening himself of his father's recollections of mortality, Mike become morosely silent and was twitchily anxious to get back to the agency. I didn't hold him. After he left, I took an hour to wander alone through the Gallery. This was my first visit since it had reopened after a refurbishment that had closed the greater part of it for the past six years.

I sought out Daniel Maclise's *The Marriage of Strongbow and Aoife,* an epic painting depicting the nuptials of Norman conqueror and Irish princess in the presence of a panoply of victorious knights while the native Irish lamented their dead in a desolate landscape. The massive canvas, newly restored, dominated the Shaw Room.

Nearby was another monumental painting, Sir John Lavery's *The Artist's Studio*, featuring wife Hazel, her daughter Alice and his daughter Eileen in a setting that was an obvious homage to Velázquez's *Las Meninas*. Next to it on the wall was Lavery's *Portrait of Lady Lavery as Kathleen Ni Houlihan*, the original of the banknote portrait. I had forgotten it was there.

A small crowd of foreign students grouped in front of the painting, conversing in whispers as though in church. I waited for them to move on and leave me to make my solitary devotion.

The resemblance between Aoife and the portrait of Hazel Lavery was in what they shared: a beauty that was boundless, the graceful pose and delicacy of the features, an air of unaffected elegance and those large seraphic eyes, fringed with long lashes, surmounted with sweeping eyebrows. No wonder Lavery wrote of the first time he met her, 'She possessed the largest and most heavenly eyes I have ever seen. Such eyes have not been seen elsewhere.' Contemporaries spoke of Hazel's devastating beauty and a besotted Lavery portrayed her in hundreds of his paintings.

I was fascinated rather than obsessed, even, I had to admit, a touch disappointed. Because, in soul and substance, I realised there was no true resemblance after all between Hazel and Aoife. It was a false comparison, the portrait holding none of Aoife's personality, her distinctive, unique magic.

In the Blackrock Market on Saturday morning, in a poky coin dealer's booth, I bought a pre-euro Irish five pound note. James Joyce had now replaced Hazel Lavery on the front of the currency but, held to the light, she was still there, her pale and ghostly image in the watermark. It was as close as I could get to re-visualising that immortal afternoon by my hospital bedside.

20

Send for the Crusher

Aardvark-Sheridan held its first post-Cronin board meeting in what we termed the client presentation zone, which is to say, the principal front room on the first floor, formerly Jasper's office, and one floor directly below mine. In addition to me and Shay, the board comprised George The Barreller Healy, Lucy Shaw, chief copywriter, Tara Hogan, who headed PR, Parnell Bradley, head of media, Ross Scott, who ran digital media, Mary Keannt, an account director, currently on maternity leave, and Cormac Carew, an art director, who, for the time being, worked from home, where he tended to his wife, who was receiving treatment for breast cancer.

We referred to ourselves as the board but it was a misnomer. Our so-called board meetings were no more than get-togethers of senior staff, plus me. We made routine decisions. On matters of importance, we could only discuss. Cronin, as CEO, had always taken the chair and was the decider. Now he was gone, decision-making was moot.

Lucy and I were the first to arrive.

'Odd, a board meeting without Cronin,' she mused. 'Gone

without a trace. Businesswise, he's left a significant gap. We're going to need a CEO of his calibre, and he had good instincts on how the agency should evolve. I'll admit, though, I never took to him, found his personality off-putting. He didn't have the highest opinion of you, you know. He made a comment once – how did he put it? – that you were all braces and belt and no trousers.'

'Yeah? Sounds witty. What did he mean?'

She shrugged and was saved a response by the arrival of Shay and Parnell, followed by Tara.

Shay took a seat and forestalled any idle chat: 'To business, folks. Since Ciarán is acting CEO, let him take the chair.'

The others reacted politely to the most junior present, who, because of a nepotism that no longer held sway, was technically, if temporarily, in charge. I wasn't about to assert my questionable authority and I didn't take Cronin's place at the top, an empty space that seemed bigger than it was, like a missing front tooth.

'Where's The Barreller?' Parnell asked, owlish eyes peering out of bottle glasses.

'Entertaining one of his clients to a round of golf in Elm Park,' Tara answered. 'What's on the agenda today, acting chairman?'

She said it matter-of-factly. Dressed in her usual dark business pantsuit and pale blue shirt and cravat, her long flame-red hair in a mess, she seemed forever running through life several hours late. A former journalist with the Irish *Sunday Times*, she'd had her own PR outfit until Cronin had persuaded her to come under the Aardvark-Sheridan umbrella as a semi-autonomous company. She enjoyed the media sobriquet of

The Scarlet Spinmeister.

I threw the meeting open diffidently. 'I think we may need to review how Cronin's death is going to affect the agency. Might I suggest –'

Tara raised a hand and said apologetically, 'I have news. Yesterday, Larry had me at his house. As you know, I'm a kind of friend of the family. He figured we'd be talking about a new CEO and said none of us could handle it – his words not mine – and there wasn't time to go headhunting. He told me Quinn had agreed to take on the job. Son number two will take the helm.'

Parnell broke the long silence. 'Pardon me, but what does Quinn Brenner know about running an advertising shop? Flippin' heck, this is making a joke of the agency.' He banged both hands on the table, then looked discomfited at his dramatics.

Parnell had once studied for the priesthood at the Dominican novitiate in Tallaght, where novices had their own swearword euphemisms.

'Quinn knows fuck all,' agreed Shay, who hadn't attended a novitiate. 'I saw him at the funeral. Big brawny guy, salesman's smile and smarmy but looks as if he could turn mean if you crossed him.'

Ross Scott came in and slid into a seat with a cursory apology. He headed the agency's newish digital and social media services, the fastest-growing part of our business. He wore his usual uniform of black tee-shirt and black jeans. None of us knew his age and I suspected he was just out of his teens. An honorary member of the board, he didn't hide his boredom at these meetings, said little and was first to leave.

No one objected, given that Ross was bringing in a lot of new and profitable accounts.

'What do we know about Quinn?' I asked Tara. 'You handle the Brenner Group's PR. Have you had any contact?'

I thought she was ignoring me, but she was considering the question.

'Little enough. Quinn's the youngest by two years. Larry's only child, now. He's best-known from his rugby days – Blackrock, Leinster, one cap for Ireland – strength more than finesse. Had a reputation as a dirty player and then a dirtier player broke his leg. If the two brothers were in the boxing game, Cronin would have been a compact middleweight, Quinn a super heavyweight.'

She struck a boxing pose and mimicked an overarm jab.

'Known to friend and foe alike as the Crusher. No advertising background. Became a partner in a second-hand car dealership in Coolock before Larry sent him over to the North of England to manage the Brenner interests there – nightclubs, property. Doing well. Married Jillian Crisfield last year, stunning airhead, a runner-up in the Ms UK contest. No kids yet.'

Lucy jumped in.

'The way I've heard it, Quinn has a reputation,' she said with a trace of fastidious distaste. 'Prone to violence. I'm told he's got a fierce temper and narrowly escaped conviction twice, once involving a one-sided punch-up at a hotel dinner dance, when he decided a drunk was giving Jillian the eye, and another occasion in a brawl in a rugby club. Both victims, big guys like himself, never knew what hit them and they woke in hospital. Larry spread money to keep it out of court. Like they say, The Crusher.'

'True,' confirmed Tara, playing with a strand of her hair. 'Quinn's changed, though. He thought he'd killed the man in the club and it scared the bejaysus out of him. Did some expensive anger management course and works hard to keep his temper in check. Tough business, running the nightclubs, I understand. Usually, he can rely on his size alone to deter most people and he has a Medusa-like twenty-yard stare.'

Parnell showed his frustration. 'He sounds a flippin' one-man disaster for us. Are we forever going to go "yessir, nossir" and jump to it whenever Larry Brenner delivers his flippin' orders? We have to confront him and sort out who owns this company. So let's bite the bullet and do it now?'

Shay smiled placatingly. 'I hear you, Nell. In fairness to our esteemed chairman, while Larry takes his slice of the profits, he generally leaves us alone. He hasn't interfered except for naming one or other of his sons as CEO. Do we want to goad Larry into legally forcing the issue of who really owns the agency?'

Parnell drummed the table angrily. 'If we –'

He stopped, as though no longer sure what he wanted to say.

I hadn't planned to add to the discussion. Earlier, looking around the table, I had a jarring flashback to one of my deathmares that had featured a meeting in the agency with colleagues and clients who were dead and starting to decay and didn't know it. The recollection had kept me in a shaky silence until I surprised myself by saying casually, 'Well, why not Quinn Brenner?'

It got me a round of odd looks. Usually, I said little or

nothing at these meetings, recognising my presence was something of a courtesy. I almost expected someone to tell me brusquely to stay out of board business. Tara frowned as though not sure who had spoken.

'None of us wants the job,' I continued firmly. 'Quinn may know little or less about advertising. Is that important? We want a CEO to schmooze clients, meet and greet on the new business circuit and run the admin side. He can do that, plus Larry will surely steer new clients to Quinn. And there's also, to be cold about it, a sympathy factor with him stepping into the shoes of his only brother who died tragically.'

After a short silence, my point was taken up. If there was surprise at my intervention and tone of authority, no one commented, and I suspect they'd forgotten within five minutes who had made the case for Quinn.

I took no further part in the discussion and, after some desultory and unenthusiastic debate, it was Ross who broke in with an impatient, 'What the hell. Let's send for the Crusher.'

Once again it was one of the junior board members who had pushed the meeting towards a decision. Heads reluctantly nodded and Tara was deputed to wait upon Larry and convey our thanks and warm welcome at the prospect of Quinn as CEO.

My intervention in arguing for Quinn had a double purpose. I thought it was a useful opportunity to begin to show my colleagues a more confident and assertive side of me. But mainly I recognised that, however much we discussed it, there was no question Quinn Brenner was going to become the agency's new CEO. It would suit me to have him in this position because I had little doubt he would maintain the

BlastOff kick-back arrangement with Barry Owens. And therefore would be vulnerable to whatever way I would make use of my knowledge of the apparent illegality.

I had said nothing to my fellow board members about the scam and I wasn't sure when, if at all, I intended to confide in them and risk losing control over the issue. It intrigued me that I was thinking this way. I had little experience of playing Machiavelli and wondered if I was going to be any good at it.

21

A GIFT FROM THE GRAVE

'Kieran, how are you, m'boy. Sorry to learn of that dreadful crash. I was out of the country when I heard about it. Appalling what happened to poor Cronin but thank the heavens you made it. How are you bearing up?'

The phone call from Peter Reynolds was unexpected. I hadn't seen or heard from him in several years. He was in his mid-seventies, a successful now-semi-retired accountant who ran a tax and investment practice for a select few. His clientele had included the agency when it held the Sheridan name, and he had been Jasper's personal financial counsellor. I'd met him occasionally when he came by our offices and we'd exchanged polite verbals.

'Best advice I can give you,' Jasper said to me once. 'If ever you need business guidance, on or off the books, or have an intractable money problem, business or personal, talk to Rennie. He'll see you right.' He'd tapped his nose and looked solemn as he delivered this *obiter dictum*. Cronin, when he took over, dropped Reynolds in favour of Charlie Maughan.

I batted bland pleasantries with Reynolds, before pausing

to let him get to the point.

'Would you have time to meet with me, whenever convenient, eh? Something we might usefully discuss.'

I was intrigued. It flashed into my mind: BlastOff and Barry Owens. Maybe he'd been asked to have words with me, rein me in.

'I'm fairly free this week. Tomorrow morning around eleven – your place?'

Reynolds lived alone in a comfortable redbrick on the north side of the city, beside the National Botanic Gardens in Glasnevin and, for his sake, I was willing to make one of my rare forays over the Liffey, albeit with a deal of reluctance.

The previous summer, I'd visited the Botanic Gardens in Glasnevin one Sunday afternoon with a girl I was dating at the time. As we strolled through the arboretum, I heard, with a small thrill of horror, bugles in the distance, a swirl of drums, then a brass band playing stately funeral music. Military obsequies. A breath of wind wafted the music closer, then it faded, then came back. Along one side of the Gardens were the old watch-towers and high walls of next-door Glasnevin Cemetery, the Dun Roamin and Mon Repos of a million plus Dubliners. The memory was disturbing and I had no wish to return.

I was relieved when Reynolds proposed instead we meet at Trinity College. He was taking lunch with his daughter, who worked there in alumni relations, and suggested we have coffee afterwards.

Trinity College was established by Elizabeth I to offer Protestant students a safe space from Popery. Until 1970, Catholics were barred from studying there to protect them from

Protestant heresy. The campus was a ten-minute walk from the agency and next day I was ambling across the quadrangle of its Parliament Square, politely staying out of line of sight of a film crew setting up a shoot with actors in Regency costume.

The college is a favourite locale for filming history-based drama. With careful framing, the camera can focus wholly on its classical buildings – the Chapel, the Examination Hall, the Regent House, the Old Library – suitable backdrops for any period over the past few hundred years.

Reynolds was waiting for me, not as he had said by the Campanile, the high granite bell tower that dominates the square, but at the nearby statue of nineteenth-century Provost George Salmon, now remembered, if at all, for his vigorous and ultimately futile attempt to prevent women studying in Trinity. Deservedly, he's commemorated with one of the ugliest public statues in Dublin.

Reynolds grasped my hand warmly. He hadn't aged in appearance since last I'd seen him. His thin light brown hair was expertly tinted and bald on the crown, an unintended tonsure . His face was tanned from what he told me was much overseas travel and he was evidently enjoying the lifestyle of the semi-retired.

He guided me towards a nearby college café that was vibrating with students, noisy but good-humoured. We found a vacant table and he ordered coffee. When it came, he raised his mug in an appreciative salute and exclaimed, 'I have to say, if you'll pardon me, it's extraordinary that you're already out of hospital after that traumatic accident. Your recovery is gratifying, your appearance astonishing.'

I made some him banal remarks about the benefits of clean

living. He wasn't paying much attention and was evidently keen to get to his purpose.

'I thought you'd be interested to hear our mutual chum Larry Brenner is in the process of selling Aardvark-Sheridan to an international marketing group,' he said casually.

'I hadn't heard,' I admitted. 'I'm shocked, yes shocked, naturally, but guess I shouldn't be. We're almost the only Irish agency that's retained local ownership. Are you sure about this?'

'My intelligence, as always, is as infallible as the Pope defecating in the woods.'

The news alarmed me. A sale would undoubtedly mean the end of my embryonic intention to gain control of the agency. To mask my concern, I said, 'I wonder how much my five-per cent might be worth in a sale.'

He frowned. 'More than you may imagine. That's why I suggested this chat. You might think of me as your uncle Jasper's proxy or agent.'

He had my full attention.

'Before I say anything else, I must give you context.' It sounded as though he'd prepared carefully for our meeting. 'When Larry Brenner,' he said the name with a downturn of his mouth, 'invited Jasper to invest in Dublin Bayside, I advised him to pass. He didn't need the money. He had more than he could ever spend. Waste of my breath. I might as well have been asking a child to save its sweets for Sunday.'

There was remembered frustration in his eyes. Then he slapped his forehead theatrically.

'Ah, the flourishing years of the Celtic Tiger Era, or, better, the Celtic Wildcat Era, when we were awash in billions of cheap eurodosh, buoyed by our imagined wealth, the Shining Light of Europe, as *The Economist* described us. I can still hear our Pied Piper of a Taoiseach, Bertie Ahern: "the boom times are becoming boomier and anyone who thinks otherwise should commit suicide".'

'The same Bertie Ahern,' I interjected, 'who declared letting Lehman Brothers fall was the great mistake "because they had their testicles into everything."'

'That was our Bertie,' he agreed with a dry laugh. 'As I was saying about our days of Potemkin prosperity, bliss it was in that dawn to be alive, but to be a financial adviser touting projects requiring ludicrous funding was very heaven. But, alas, when the thrifty *mittelklasse* German savers asked for their Euromoney back, they discovered that the reckless Irish had squandered it.'

This was familiar stuff. The boom times were at their peak when I was sauntering my way through the university years and I had assumed, without giving it much thought, that I was set to enjoy a prosperous life with little effort. This was relevant to what?

He gave me an indulgent look. 'Don't worry, Kieran. As the lawyers say, I propose to connect it.'

I was disconcerted that he could read me with ease.

He continued: 'When the bottom fell out of the barrel, many of Ireland's wealthiest people found themselves significantly less wealthy and concentrated on hiding from the financial institutions whatever assets remained to them, some with more success than others.'

'As I've been told, Uncle Jasper lost his shirt and underpants.'

'Yes and no.' Reynolds made a rocking gesture with his hands. 'On paper, he lost his accumulated life savings, which were substantial. But he made sure creditors couldn't get their hands on the agency or on Huntsman Hall. Jasper had been willing to gamble, but without risking either of the two things that he cherished. He got three banks, each unknowing of the other two, to loan him ten million in total, using the Hall as collateral for each loan. Through creative accounting and legal legerdemain, the loan documentation was fudged, and the banks later discovered they didn't have crucial pieces of paper necessary to validate the guarantees.'

He gave a sly smile at the recollection and I guessed who had assisted Jasper in his financial three card tricks.

'When they tried to figure out which of them had title to the Hall, they discovered none had. They were not about to sue each other, so the matter rests for the present in no man's land. It's why you're living there rent-free, as you know well. The place is an embarrassment to the banks.'

'That's how I understand it. Who actually owns Huntsman Hall now?'

'Good question.' His hands did another rocking gesture. 'No one knows. Jasper's estate – which is you – could argue a case in court that the personal guarantees, being faulty, are null and void. If you pressed it, you'd face expensive litigation and, with the inevitable appeals, a modern *Jarndyce v Jarndyce*. The three banks are each out substantial sums, they can't sell on to a vulture fund and are understandably reluctant to write them off. More coffee?'

Without waiting for an answer, he went over to the counter and got two fresh mugs.

'To resume, and this is why I suggested this talk, Jasper's other personal guarantee was to Larry Brenner for his share in the Bay project and he offered the agency as collateral. A paper loan and no actual money was transacted.

'Again, he hedged his bets. Sometime before signing the guarantee to Larry, Jasper, in great secrecy, placed the agency in a Trust. The key provision of the Trust was that the entire shareholding of the agency and its properties would transfer to you in the event of his death.'

He looked gratified at my astonishment but held up a warning hand.

'The Trust is known only to a few. But don't celebrate too quickly. The legal standing is far from clear. In keeping with Jasper's instructions, I was to inform you at a time I decided was appropriate. In view of Cronin's death, and, eh, other developments, the time is now.'

I tried to take it in. 'Does Larry know he may not legally own the agency?'

'Oh, yes. He is aware of the Trust. He has sought the best legal advice available and, as expected, that advice has been ambiguous and ambivalent. His promissory note from Jasper may be valid. Or not. Jasper, having effected the Trust, had no legal right to pledge the agency. Or, having pledged the agency, had no legal right to set up the Trust. No one can be sure how a judgement would go. It might go Larry's way or your way or some other way. It's why he has never petitioned for an accelerated death certificate for Jasper.'

'I'm not clear what I can do with this information,' I said slowly. 'Larry runs the agency as a shadow owner and, you may have heard, he's putting in Quinn as Cronin's replacement.

I'm not sure if my five per cent could block a sale, even if I wanted to.'

Reynolds leaned forward and tapped my knee.

'Larry has an Achilles heel. Four years ago, he went through bankruptcy proceedings in the English courts, where the law is more lenient than in Ireland. He was out of it within a year. He failed to declare he owned the majority shareholding in the agency. That omission could be deemed criminal. It means, if there were ever a dispute, Larry can't press his claim to ownership.

'There is yet more,' he said, producing the punchline. 'Jasper left you more than the shares in the agency via the Trust. He assumed you might have to take legal action to enforce your ownership. He set aside money for you.'

It took me a few seconds to take that in and it set my mind gyrating.

"How much are we talking about?"

"A quarter of a million in pounds sterling four years ago, which, with interest, is about four hundred thousand euro now."

I sat back, staggered. I assumed the money was illegal and doubtless my accepting it without declaring it for tax would also be illegal. That wouldn't stop me for a second. It was ironic, to put it mildly, I was about to take illicit money while attempting to use the BlastOff scam to strike at the Brenners.

"I thought Jasper lost everything in the Dublin Bay fiasco," I said.

He smiled wryly. "Strictly, the money might be deemed as due to the bank or to Larry Brenner and, if they knew about it, they would put up a good fight to get their paws on it. It's one of Jasper's bank loans, money he was due to pay to Larry as part of his investment. He never did hand it over. It is yours."

'A gift from the grave, sort of,' I muttered. 'Assuming Jasper is dead.'

If he heard a question mark, he ignored it.

'There's something else,' I said. 'I wonder if Larry knows what's happening in the agency right now.'

I gave him the high points of what I knew of the BlastOff skim scam.

He whistled softly. 'Well, well, well.' He didn't seem too surprised. 'The real owners of BlastOff, as I expect you know, are the McGorrick family, based in Belfast and Finglas, who mostly keep out of the public gaze despite a grisly reputation. It's headed by Rory McGorrick, one-time Provisional IRA offshoot, now boss of a gang reputed to be as vicious as any Colombian cartel. Be very careful how you act.'

As I walked back to the agency, it hit me I was entangling myself with something altogether more dangerous than I'd imagined. It was one thing to challenge Barry and Larry, another to come between a brutal drugs lord and his money. Was I up for it? I was about to find out.

22

CARDS ON THE TABLE

'Love it to bits,' enthused Barry Owens, after viewing the new campaign ideas. He expressed himself thrilled with the visuals and copy that closely echoed BlastOff's existing advertising. For all his talk of elephants and dancing girls, he predictably went for the straight hard sell.

'I'm good to sign-off on this,' he said, after I'd run through the creative and media stuff and the proposed budget. 'Important to ring the changes but always stick with what gets the job done. Innovate without change, a winning formula every time.'

He appeared to be his usual ebullient self, slapping my desk and with appreciative lip-smacking for the artwork. Yet his enthusiasm sounded forced. At meeting's end, he stood and walked to the window.

'Fine view, K,' he said, gazing out. 'Guess what I have from my office window? A scrap metal yard. Noisy, too, most times. Right. Won't keep you. Just to confirm we're hunky dory on the invoicing set-up, as per last week's colloquy.'

His offhand manner didn't hide the tension. Maybe Mike

had dropped him a hint of my mindset.

'Hunky dory? Of course,' I lied. Though I doubted if I could now avoid an open breach. I'd give it a try. 'Re this, I'm going to tell you in confidence – we haven't officially announced it yet – Quinn Brenner will be our new CEO and –'

'Muchas gracias for the newsflash.' From his sham surprise, it wasn't news to him. He beamed and took a step towards me and for a startled moment I thought he was about to pump my hand in congratulations. 'I know Quinn personally and he's a class act. The original big swinging dick of a salesman, born with the razor's edge. Ginormous asset to your agency, believe me, and a damn good fit for our business.'

He parked his backside on the corner of my desk. 'True story involving Quinn, by the way. When he was in the used car trade, back in the day, he was driving to the showrooms after lunch when a cop stopped him on Rathmines Bridge for speeding, probably noticed he'd had a few snifters, too. He got the cop chatting and instead of getting a ticket, he sold him a car, took the deposit from him on the spot.'

'If you ask Quinn the time, he'll sell you a watch,' he chuckled, overegging it. He was watching me as he spoke and the humour didn't reach his eyes.

'Quite a character,' I agreed. 'And I'm sure you'll want him in charge of the BlastOff account. I'm only caretaking.'

'Right, right. Meantime, until you pass over the baton, you keep the existing arrangements in place.'

'No problem. As I said last time, I'll run it by the other board members. Cronin never got around to doing that, frankly.'

It didn't sound convincing even to me.

'And like I said last time: is that necessary?' he asked, affability dropping away by the second. 'We've been doing this nice and smooth for the past couple of years now. Since, as you say, you're only the caretaker, why bring in the other guys?'

'I'm on the page with you, absolutely.' I heard myself again slipping into Barry-speak. 'You can understand I don't want to place them in an... exposed position.'

'Exposed? What's with exposed?' He made it sound like an obscenity. 'I'm the client... am I right? I sign off your invoices, right? QED, what else do you need?'

'I'll be discreet,' I promised.

He considered me in silence before he spoke softly.

'Since doing business with this agency, I've dealt with the top man, the CEO' – he pronounced it Chew – 'our much-lamented mutual friend Cronin. No disrespect, Kieran, you're a fine guy. But not in Cronin's class. Not nearly. I've had a good professional relationship with Aardvark until now and I'm asking right now: do you want to put it at risk while we're waiting for Quinn?'

I made no reply. After a long silence, he nodded, no more Mister Nice Guy.

'Well, you've put your cards on the table, pal. A winning hand? I don't think so.'

He cocked a finger, pistol-like, said 'Pow', blew away imaginary smoke and, with his meaningless 'See you when. See you then,' walked out.

I was gambling Barry wasn't going to sack the agency and take his account elsewhere. He'd have to be confident he'd find another Chew like Cronin Brenner, who'd support him in his rip-off. Given the size of the BlastOff advertising and its high profitability that wasn't impossible. But it would carry its own risks. Besides, Quinn Brenner was soon to take charge and, between them, they could squelch me on this without breaking sweat. Meantime, though, Barry had the small difficulty of getting my name on a cheque.

I hadn't worked out how I was going to play this. My end game was to lever it to prise control of the agency from the Brenners. I wasn't sure how, precisely. Much depended on Larry being seriously alarmed at the idea of a whistleblower who was prepared to throw a bucket of ordure on Cronin's posthumous reputation and create a problem for Quinn before he even took his new job.

Until recently, I would have gone some distance to avoid conflict, especially with Barry, whose show of conviviality never fully masked an undercurrent of menace. Now, my personality and attitudes were undergoing change in ways I couldn't yet define or understand.

On Saturday, I finally got around to doing something I kept intending to do and then forgetting. I dropped into the Tower Records store in Dawson Street in search of the music Monsignor Flinter had mentioned.

'What's playing?' I asked the youth in the classical department, indicating the wistful string music coming from the store's hi-fi system. He pointed to a *Now Playing* sign on the counter with a CD cover of a symphony by a composer called Einojuhani Rautavaara.

'Thought as much,' I said.

I couldn't recall which Mahler symphony Flinter had recommended. The Bruckner was number nine and I decided on the Claudio Abbado version because his name was vaguely familiar: I'd seen a programme about him on television when he'd died not long ago.

'You'd recommend this?'

His face lit. 'Oh, the best. It was Abbado's last performance and one couldn't ask for a more impressive finale. Appropriate, when you consider Bruckner was composing it on his deathbed. Probably that's why conductors select this piece at the end of their career. It was Klemperer's last recording and Lenny's last session with the Vienna Phil.'

I scanned the notes on the back of the CD.

'An unfinished symphony, isn't it?'

'It is, alas.'

'Does it mean I get a discount?'

He looked flustered before he took in that I was joshing. He smiled without showing teeth.

'I'll buy the piece that's playing as well,' I said, indicating the Rautavaara. The music had a haunting quality, and I liked the symphony's title, *Angel of Light*. The CD blurb had a quote from the composer that caught my attention. "Music is great if, at some moment, the listener catches a glimpse of eternity through the window of time. All else is secondary."

Music to my ears.

I departed with the first classical music CDs I'd ever owned. This, I thought, could be the beginning of a beautiful friendship.

Sunday afternoon, I got around to playing the Bruckner and it was my fault it left me cold because I used it as background while I did some cleaning and tidying in the apartment. The music seemed to go on and on, straining to reach a climax, never getting there, falling back, then having another try. Sisyphus music.

23

...AND THEN YOU DIE

Satan sat in his 1997 red Ford Focus around the corner from the place he was going to break into, toking a cigarette and brooding on a variety of grievances. A toothache had been at him for the past week and was now throbbing, despite the painkillers he'd been swallowing all evening. The bitch Tracy was pregnant again and about to make him, at age twenty-two, a father for the third time, which he could do without. There was the €200 owed to Shivers O'Connor because of a stupid bet on the outcome of a Premier League match.

And now this job, he thought irritably, as he got out of the car and walked off, leaving it unlocked, knowing it wouldn't be nicked in this snooty corner of South Dublin. The late evening was cloudy, dark at 9.30, dry, with a strong chill wind. There was no one about. Satan wore a black hooded anorak, heavy dark sweater and woollen scarf, navy jeans and black Nikes, logo painted over. He'd been told the house would be empty. The sole occupant, the target, was not due home until after midnight.

Satan, aka John Paul Dundan, was six foot three and

225 lbs, with a face and close-shaven skull that showed the scars of one who relished a good scrap. He had spent, altogether, six of his teenage years doing time for random violence, shoplifting and car theft.

Two years ago, he'd taken a shiny new Porsche Panamera for a joyride, not knowing it belonged to the son of a major drugs dealer and crashed it into a wall. Three heavies tumbled him out of bed the following afternoon and took him naked to the Dublin Mountains where they gave him a vicious beating and made him kneel and say his prayers, with the cold metal of a shotgun on the back of his neck. Shakily defiant, he choked an apology and asked if he could work for the dealer.

They fell about laughing, then one talked on his mobile and they didn't kill him. Instead, they cut off the little finger of his left hand. A few days later, Dundan was told he had a day job in the BlastOff store in Finglas, where he carried pre-packs to customers' cars. He was soon getting paid more than the going rate because he doubled as an apprentice heavy and proved handy at convincing shoplifters in the store they had made a horrible mistake. He was used from time to time, usually with others, to warn off freelance pushers around Dublin with whatever persuasion seemed right and fitting and do bodyguard for the gang's street dealers. Occasionally, he got odd jobs like this.

One of his mates owned a scuzzy black Alsatian dog called Satan and Dundan thought the name canny and purloined it for himself, it being, he reckoned, much more cool than being named after a dead pope. Among hard men, though, it was streetwise to keep a handle like that to himself.

Now, he was vexed his bung of €350 for this job was

on the skinny side, seeing as how they'd given him specific instructions to wreck the place proper, smash furniture and furnishings, flood the kitchen and loo, spray the walls, piss and crap on the carpets, maybe light a small fire and generally have a good time doing serious damage. On no account should he lift things. It was intended to be a warning, not a burglary. It struck him that he'd been given the shitty end of the stick again, because there was surely tasty stuff for the taking in a house like this.

Sod it. He walked up the quiet street of snob houses and into a narrow unpaved lane with high hedges on either side. It had rained earlier, and the lane was a path of mud. He came out across the road from the house. With a quick glance around, he crossed over and made his way up a long driveway, avoiding the gravel, moving through trees and shrubbery.

The house appeared out of the darkness and was bigger than when he had looked it over earlier, given that only one person lived there. He thought it odd. A place as substantial as this needed butlers and maids, like the big boss's joint had. He did a circuit of the building. In addition to the main entrance, with its double steps to a large front door, there was a second entrance to an annexe at the rear.

Since the house was isolated and nobody was home, Satan didn't bother with the doors. He pulled a heavy-duty torch from his pocket, wrapped his scarf around it, walked over to a side window and smashed it with a single swipe. The muffled noise was lost in the wind blowing through the trees.

He located the window clasp, pushed the window open and climbed in. 'Satan's here, folks,' he said in a stage whisper. A flick of the torch showed a small room with white walls and a bare wooden floor, empty of furniture. He moved into a passageway, with doors either side. He ignored them and followed the passage into the main hallway. Another passage faced him across the hall and to the right, an inner porch led to the front door. On the left was a wide, carpeted staircase. Taking his bearings, he reckoned the passage opposite ran to the annexe. He stood in the hall, considering where to begin his night's work.

Suddenly, he became shockingly convinced that someone, silent and lethal, was standing directly behind him in the dark. Satan was transfixed with panic, hairs bristling on the small of his back and goosebumps on his arms. A burst of adrenaline sent an icy finger up his spine and into his skull. With a stifled scream, he broke out of his paralysis, turned and swung his torch wildly. His eyes followed its swinging beam as it bounced off the walls. Nothing. The hall was empty. 'Sacred Arse of Jesus,' he muttered, making an effort to calm himself.

He moved forward, still shaken and cursing with whatever had crawled into his imagination. The staircase attracted him, looking like it was from one of those TV shows on the lives of the rich and famous. He decided to start his trail of destruction upstairs and work down. As he took a few steps, his hairs bristled as once more he sensed someone was stealthily pacing behind him. He whirled – and found no one there. With a muttered profanity, he tried to shake it off. What was the matter with him? If some other was in the house, they should be in fear of him, not the other way around. The swinging fists of Satan would explode their face, yeah. The toothache was making him mean.

At the top, he heard a noise from below him, as though

someone was doing a fast tiptoe across the hallway. He peered into the gloom and angled his head and had an impression of a white blur as it vanished into the far corridor. A cat, he guessed, relieved. A dog would surely have barked. He'd sort it later, slit its belly and serve it on a plate on the kitchen table. You da man, Satan.

A gallery overlooked the hallway, with an open archway to gloomy corridors at each end. He took the left corridor at random and moseyed along it, taking his time, opening doors. He switched off the torch and kept it in his hand, in case. In case of what? This house was giving him the creeps.

The first door he opened showed a room bare of furniture, like the one below. Same with the other rooms, all murky in a dim light, stripped wooden floors and pale walls, peeling wallpaper, and nothing else. How was he supposed to mess a place with damn all in it? The whole house couldn't be like this, could it? Besides, despite his orders, he hadn't intended to leave empty-handed. Cash, if he came upon it, or a few negotiable items. That was looking to be a bust.

He had an eruption of resentment and rage at the unknown owner of this shithole of a house. Maybe he'd just wait for the dickhead to arrive home and beat the crap out of him. It meant ignoring his orders for a quick in-and-out but he'd take the consequences.

One last door faced him at the end of the corridor, a broom closet, he guessed. He tugged it open and entered the final minute of his life. Life's a bitch…

24

A BLOODY SIGHT

In Cronin's unavoidable absence due to death, I got to attend a few high-status advertising industry events by filching invitations addressed to him. Besides, I was, in a sense, acting CEO, wasn't I? That evening, it was a black-tie dinner in the classy setting of the Royal Hospital Kilmainham, for the annual Advertising Impact Awards, two of which had been won by Aardvark-Sheridan, to our surprise and satisfaction.

I assumed the air of one accustomed to the stylish company and the history-laden elegance of the venue, once a home for old soldiers along the lines of Les Invalides in Paris and now a setting favoured by ritzy corporate event organisers. At the pre-presentation reception in the wood-panelled Baroque Chapel, I had the goofy notion I might bump into Cronin, not dead after all, who would ask me curtly what the devil I was doing there.

The evening was a bore. Dinner was of the rubber chicken variety. I tuned out of the platitudinous speech by a Coalition Minister who had been spoken of in his early political life as an Irish Che Guevara but who now had the mentality of a vulture capitalist. He did the honours in handing out enough awards to devalue their worth. A creative director from a leading London advertising agency brought the formalities to an anodyne conclusion by opining that Irish creativity was never more… creative.

I drove home nodding agreement to a podcast by a Professor Donald D Hoffman. I understood him only intermittently but he seemed to be saying that reality existed only in our consciousness and the physical world around us had no reality and was no more than a magnificent illusion, created by our consciousness. Absorbed in the relevance of the idea to my own life, I had turned off Silchester Road and was halfway up my driveway when I heard a high-pitched scream, then another, like some animal in agony. At the Hall, I hopped out of the car and listened.

At first, all was silent except for the trees swishing and crackling in the wind. Then the night air was filled with a wave of ear-splitting shrieks and howls. Not an animal this but a human being at the outer extreme of pain and torture. The frightful screaming stopped briefly then resumed, if possible louder and more panic-stricken. It seemed to come from inside the Hall and I could also hear the sound of banging and smashing as though heavy objects were being dashed against the walls. I imagined I saw the whole building shudder.

As I stood, confused and scared, one foot on the short lawn in the front, the big ground-floor bay window suddenly exploded outward in a torrent of glass, timber and metal and a human figure flew through the cloud of debris and hit the grass a few feet from me with a sickening thud.

I managed a step forward and took a quick look at what

remained of a man. Hard to be sure because there was no face, just raw meat. He no longer looked human, coated top to bottom in blood, on his hair, over what remained of his face, on his exposed flesh and tattered clothing. His blood was bubbling, pouring, glistening bright crimson in the moonlight. His head was at an unnatural angle to his body and one leg faced backwards. I didn't need to touch him to know he was dead

I glanced up at the great hole in the front of the Hall where the bay window had been and my heart jumped when I thought I saw movement within. Something grey and shapeless, shifting within a swirl of mist.

I didn't hesitate but turned and dashed to my car, engine running, Hoffman still expounding. I sped down the driveway, rocketed onto Silchester Road, luckily devoid of traffic, and was off in an unthinking panic, I didn't care where, to put distance between me and the horror I'd just seen.

Several miles away, I stopped the car, jumped out and puked what I reckoned was the entire contents of my stomach onto a grassy kerbside. I was wrong because I immediately threw up again. For the best part of an hour, I was in shock, retching, shivering, mentally closed down.

In time, I began to get control of myself. I got into my car and, after a time, decided to turn back and act as if I'd not seen the horror.

When I got to Silchester Road, it had the appearance of a filmset. The roadway was blocked by a Garda car with front and rear lights flashing. A black and white sign was positioned in the centre of the road: *Garda. Bóthar Dúnta. Road Closed*.

More Garda cars, an ambulance and several large dark

SUVs lit the area with their whirling blue top lights. Gardaí in Day-Glo, Hi-Viz jackets over uniform were standing in small groups, stamping their feet against the cold. Startlingly, at least two I could see were carrying rifles. This being upper-class territory, there was no crowd of gawkers, only a few passersby discreetly speculating as to what was going on.

I stopped at the sign. Right away, a burly Garda bustled over and waved me off, giving me a scowl when I pressed down the window and called out, 'I live here.' My voice sounded shaky to me but he didn't seem to notice.

'Doesn't matter shit,' he snapped. 'You can't take a car here. Park around the corner somewhere and walk back. And stay this side of the tape.'

He pointed to strips of blue and white ribbon twirling in the wind that criss-crossed the road.

'What's the problem?' I asked, but he was away, shouting at a pair of youths who were attempting to slip under the ribbon. Grousing to myself, I turned back and parked along nearby Glenageary Road, ignoring the double yellow No Parking lines, and headed back.

I stopped by a middle-aged woman, well wrapped in coat, scarf and knitted cap, who stood watching avidly. 'It's a hostage situation,' she told me with relish. As good a supposition as any. As I waited, I heard other guesses from the few people standing behind the tape: a hit-and-run, a burglar disturbed by the family, a flasher.

The Garda who had stopped me must have passed the word because a detective in a gabardine raincoat and flat cap and with the bearing of authority strode up to me, in the company of a hard-faced woman I assumed was also a plainclothes detective.

'You live here?' he asked, giving me the once-over. 'Where, exactly?' He was tall and thin, with steel-grey hair under the cap, rimless glasses and a David Niven moustache

'Four houses on the left, it's called Huntsman Hall. Can I ask what's going on here?'

I decided to say nothing about what I had witnessed earlier. I was embarrassed that I had bolted the scene in an almighty blue funk without even alerting the police.

'I'm sorry for the inconvenience.' His tone was formally polite. 'I'd appreciate it if you'd be patient while I ask a few questions. May I have your name, please?'

I obliged and added my occupation, resisting an instinct to hand him a business card. I told him I was the sole resident of Huntsman Hall. 'Substantial residence for one person,' the woman remarked neutrally.

His next question was a surprise: 'What animals do you keep, here or elsewhere?'

'None – here or elsewhere.'

'Pets?'

'Not even a goldfish. Okay, will you tell me what's going on here and why I'm not allowed into my home?'

He took in my evening dress and the fact I resided in a fine house and concluded I was a respectable citizen. He murmured to the female detective who walked away and joined a knot of uniformed Gardaí.

'Are those Guards carrying guns?' I pointed to three Gardaí, dressed in black, a SWAT team of sorts, who were grouped in a nearby garden.

He ignored my query. 'I am Detective Superintendent

Patrick Coogan. There has been an incident. One or two more questions, please. Have you had any reason to expect you might have a visitor calling on you?'

'No.' I thought it would be appropriate for me to sound antsy. 'I'm not saying anything else until we get out of the cold.'

'Yes, it is nippy. My apologies. Let's sit in my car and I'll tell you what I can. Do you have the keys to the main house?'

'Not on me. They're on a key hook in the apartment.'

Without his asking, I took out my apartment keys and handed them to him, He whistled and tossed them across to a Garda. We crossed over to one of the SUVs and sat in the front.

'Shortly after eleven o'clock this evening,' he said, selecting his words carefully, 'we got a number of phone calls from people living in the neighbourhood who stated they heard loud screams from the direction of your house. When we checked, we came on the body of a man on your lawn. From what we can tell, he was savagely attacked by what might be a pack of animals. We've had to assume these animals may be on the loose and have now either gone to ground or are roaming the vicinity.'

'Animals?'

Coogan rubbed at the condensation on the windscreen with a leather-gloved hand. He peered out at the activity on the road, Gardaí moving about briskly, like nocturnal bumblebees.

'We're warning residents to stay indoors. The rifles are, mostly, tranquilliser guns.'

The car door behind me opened, someone dropped into the back seat. A hand clamped on my shoulder.

'A night for the long johns or letting the liathróidi freeze.'

I recognised the garbled voice of Inspector Dan Breen.

'Evening, Super. I see you've met my good friend, Kieran Sheridan. A young man worth the knowing.'

Despite his clumsy banter, I was relieved at Breen's arrival, a Garda officer who could vouch for my bona fides. I was deliberating the best way to shake his hand from my shoulder when he anticipated me and let go with a pat.

Coogan twisted to take us both in.

'Hello, Dan. So, you two know each other. Good. I'm going to leave you in the inspector's expert hands. If you'll excuse me…'

He exited the SUV and headed purposefully across the road. I said to Breen, 'You're beginning to resemble Lieutenant Kinderman.'

'Lieutenant who?'

'Kinderman, the homicide investigator in *The Exorcist* film, full of bonhomie and good fellowship, always turning up unexpectedly with a line of verbal jousting.'

Before he could respond I asked, 'The superintendent mentioned a man killed by animals. Wild dogs?'

He seemed to ponder how much to tell me, then gave a what-the-heck shrug.

'That's one possibility. The examiner thinks otherwise, and we've had a veterinary inspector do a preliminary on the dead man. Her view is the wounds were caused by a big cat or possibly cats.'

'Cats?' I echoed. 'You mean a zoo-type wildcat?'

Breen didn't answer. 'We have a blood trail leading back from the body to your home. He smashed through a bay window at the front getting out and sliced himself thoroughly from the glass – not that it made any difference. We've found another broken window around the side, which may be how he got into the house.'

'A burglar?'

'Fair deduction,' he conceded. 'Seems like the attack took place inside your home.'

The memory, never far from the surface, of a bloodied body hurtling out of the bay window sent a cold shiver through me.

'Any idea who the dead man is?' I astonished myself with my continued veneer of calmness.

'I expect we'll find out before long. In the circumstances, we won't ask if you knew him. He was a bloody sight.'

His voice cracked slightly. Viewing the body had evidently affected him, as it had me.

A uniformed Garda rapped on the car window. Breen stretched across from the back and let it down and the Garda handed him my keys. 'The Boss says to give you these. We don't need them. We've been through the house and it's clear.'

Breen grunted thanks and put the keys in his pocket, then took them out and handed them to me

'You can't go in until tomorrow sometime. For the present, it's part of a crime scene. I suggest you find an alternative bed, wake your nearest girlfriend, or failing that go to a hotel, while we investigate and you stay out of trouble. Can't rule out whatever killed that man is still in the vicinity.'

I almost blurted a confession to Breen that I had been at the Hall earlier and witnessed the bloody corpse being flung through the bay window. But it was too late for that. At best,

I could expect a session of sceptical, and maybe suspicious, questionings from him and others. Fingers crossed that a neighbour hadn't seen my car roar up the road like a bat from hell, arse ablaze.

Breen walked with me partway down the road. The wind had died down and a crescent moon offered intermittent light. 'Silchester Road is one of the most peaceable places in Dublin. You don't expect something like this to happen here. Yet two of the bloodiest killings in recent memory, and both took place on this road.'

I knew immediately what he referred to. Some years previously, a pretty and popular teenager, walking home in the early hours had been brutally and repeatedly stabbed with a butcher's knife and, after crawling a few yards, had bled to death. The Gardai surmised that she knew her killer but, after years of investigation, during which time her grave had been desecrated, they failed to find a viable suspect or even a motive for the slaying.

'We damn sure better solve this one,' said Breen.

I said nothing but I very much doubted it.

I passed the rest of the night in the Royal Marine Hotel by the seafront in Dun Laoghaire where the night manager was a friend. From the well-stocked miniature bar in the room I poured a double measure of Jameson and sat at the window staring aimlessly beyond the dark and silent hotel gardens, to the watery expanse of the Bay and, on the far side, the distant twinkling of the North City's lights that looked to be reflections of the twinkling stars above. I thought about the bloody end of the presumed burglar and what I had seen and tried to fit it into the puzzle of the many strange things occurring around me. Eventually, I gave up, dropped onto the bed without undressing and succumbed to a dreamless sleep, or at least no dreams I could remember.

Feeling scruffy in yesterday's ill-creased clothes, I scanned the newspapers in the office next morning. Major news had broken the previous evening. A helicopter had fallen out of the sky into Lough Erne, killing the pilot and two passengers, one an Irish billionaire businessman. The story dominated the media.

As a result, the violent death in Silchester Road was relegated to lesser coverage. It was reported that John Paul Dundan (23) of Finglas Road, Dublin, a customer service representative with the local BlastOff retail store, had died in yet unexplained circumstances. There was mention of a possible animal attack, with cautiously ambiguous hints of a burglar encountering a guard dog.

25

SEE SATAN DIE

Silchester Road was quiet when I returned. Several Gardaí in pairs were making slow street patrols. The gawkers were long gone. A Garda car was in the driveway, two uniforms inside, talking quietly. One threw me a relaxed salute and I waved back. The front bay window, which Desperate Dundan had smashed through, was now covered in a sheet of semi-transparent plastic. Fluttering *Do Not Enter* strips festooned the main door. The grass on the lawn was muddy from clods of earth and footmarks. Otherwise, there was no evidence of the activities of the previous night. As I walked to my apartment I examined the ground and could discern no animal tracks.

The forensics people had been in the apartment and had cleaned the place before they left. I saw no signs of intrusion except, as I poured a Jameson, I thought there might be less whiskey in the bottle than I remembered. Breen had told me to stay out of the main house and that was my intent. I spilt some of my drink when I became aware of an intermittent shuffling sound from the main house, as though an intruder was walking around, stopping, moving again.

I was tempted to run to the Gardaí outside. On second thought, I persuaded myself it must be a door or window that hadn't shut properly. I unlocked the door to the main house and took a few tentative steps into the hallway, resisting the inclination to call out. I grabbed one of Jasper's walking sticks for protection, should I need it.

I soon found the source of the noise. A corner of the plastic sheeting taped to the inside frame of the broken bay window had come loose and was flapping in tune with my nervous system. After fixing it back in place, curiosity got the better of me and I decided to survey the house.

There was a rank odour of what I took to be blood pushing through the stale air, along with noxious bodily stinks. In the dull light, gloopy dark bloodstains were everywhere. My stomach churned. So much blood and guts and membranes from one person. Thick pools and streaks of it mottled the top corridor, the stairs, in the hall and on the bare floor of the front room, with a splotchy trail going to the smashed bay window. Many of the purple-black spots had been circled in white chalk. I thought of the likely bill house cleaners might be handing me in due course. I wasn't sure if my insurance covered it and put aside the distasteful possibility I might have to do a deal of scrubbing myself.

Back in the apartment, I locked the door and belatedly showered and changed. I found my drink where I'd left it, and flopped into an armchair. The apartment was warm from the central heating and, in minutes, tiredness came over me like a duvet. I sipped my drink and let myself drop off and, in a minute –

I was wide awake and alert, standing beside the armchair,

seeing myself slouched in relative comfort, hands cosseting the tumbler of whiskey, my head lying awkwardly on the headrest, chest rising softly without a sound, asleep. I heard footsteps in the hallway outside the apartment and crossed over to the door. Before I could unlock it, I glided through it and into the short corridor leading to the main hallway and a different time.

A door opened and a man slipped into the corridor and moved his head, orienting himself. He flicked a heavy torch on and off and its beam hit me in the face, but he saw nothing, turned away and headed into the hall. Fascinated, I followed him a few paces behind, noiseless without trying.

Maybe I was not as quiet as I thought because the man stiffened, whirled with a cry of fright, slashing the air between us with his torch, missing my face by an inch. He stopped and stood still, gasping, peering into the darkness, his mouth twisted in a snarl as he cast about for someone he sensed was there. He saw no one, which seemed to make him uneasy. He was a big, thickset young man, dark-garbed, with the mug of a boxer – broken nose and scarring under the eyes, head shaved, bar a line of hair down the back. John Paul Dundan, I presumed.

He headed up the stairs, mumbling to himself. Partway, he stopped and went pole rigid, spun with a yell, torch flailing. He rubbed his forehead, baffled to find nothing once more, his expression bewildered, looking like he might cry. I took him for a person of little imagination and this, as he might say, was doing his head in. He uttered a low moan and gingerly touched a swollen cheek.

With an effort, he resumed his climb on the stairs. I continued to follow his dark shape, a few steps behind. At the top, he jumped as if startled by a noise below. He peered over the bannister. Whatever it might have been had him unworried and a scowl of satisfaction flicked across his face. He walked along the gallery at the top and along the left corridor, opening doors as he passed, glancing in, closing them, swearing with annoyance. He came to the door at the end that led to the attic stairs and pulled it open.

A white shape exploded from the darkness onto his chest, hissing and growling. It was without form or substance, an entity of mist and smoke, yet of immense strength because the big man was rocked back by the impact and emitted a scream of shock and pain. The thing seemed to crawl up his body and immediately great bloody gouges erupted on his forehead and cheeks. He screamed again and, dropping the torch, made a grab at the twisting, writhing whatever that was now enveloping his face, slashing and gouging him. Large bite marks and welling blood burst on his hands. Another screech as one of his ears detached from his head and slithered down his shoulder. Most of his nose vanished, creating a bloody void in the middle of his face. There was a foul smell in the air as he lost control of his bowels.

Dundan managed to pull whatever it was off him and flung it away at the cost of a great lump of flesh gouged from his cheek. Howling and screeching in agony, he staggered blindly, passing by me or through me, unaware of me, in a mist of blood, the white spectre following relentlessly in his wake in a dervish swirling motion, likewise ignoring me. Fumbling his way along the balcony to the stairs, he was struck again. The thing hurled itself into his back and pitched him flying into space. His body hit partway on the staircase and cartwheeled wildly to the bottom.

He lay still, Then, with a terrible moan, he made a feeble attempt to push himself upright. He managed to get his knees under him, shuddered and sank helplessly to the floor. The pain was too much, and he vomited loudly and violently. Without warning, the attack resumed: vivid red slash marks appeared on his shaven skull and on the back of his neck. An instant later, he gave a high-pitched screech and grabbed at his groin. He rose, pulling at the thing until it let go, again with an agonising tearing of flesh. He ran limping, in a crouching zigzag across the hall, the attacks following him, shredding his clothes. A door opened of itself and he fled unseeing into an empty room where he was lifted off his feet and propelled at speed across the floor to smash through the big bay window in an explosion of shattering wood and glass.

John Paul Dundan lay unmoving on the grass. I didn't need to touch him to know he was dead and…

I woke, spilling the whiskey that had been resting on my lap. I was in the armchair in my apartment in the dark, sweating and heart thumping. Nausea swept over me, my stomach lurched. I made a dash to the lavatory and threw up.

My mind whirled as I knelt at the porcelain bowl, face wet with tears and perspiration. It was as though, unseen throughout, I had been a disembodied spirit, a ghost. I'd no idea who or what had killed him or why with such ferocious savagery. The entity, unrelenting and merciless in its fury, bore me no ill-will, was, if anything, my protector. And, given its blazing rage, that was more frightening than comforting.

26

A FISTFUL OF TROUBLE

The following week, I was taking a lunchtime stroll by the Grand Canal with Shay, making the most of a cold but sunny day. We were both well-wrapped, me in a Navy-style Winter coat, he with a long yellow and black woollen scarf and a full-length vicuna overcoat of the kind I associate with Prince Charles. As we headed back by Mount Street Crescent, we passed the church of my namesake, the eighteenth-century St Kieran's, the so-called Pepper Canister Church due to its distinctive cupola. My grandma had once told me her mother told her when she was a child that anyone who ran three times around the church anticlockwise would meet the devil coming the other way. She did not say why anyone would want to do this.

'Something I need to tell you,' I said and gave Shay an abridged version of the BlastOff scam and my recent confrontation with Barry Owens. To my surprise, he was laidback about it, less concerned with the scam than with what I might be doing to put the agency at risk.

'Kickbacks are not uncommon in our business, you

know,' he said, stroking his beardless chin. 'If what you say is true, and it seems to be, it's doing the agency no harm and, if anything, it clamps BlastOff more tightly to our bosom and gives them every incentive to keep the business with us. I think if it were my client, I'd simply ignore it and let events take their course.' He gave me a quizzical look. 'You're not developing an unhealthy streak of moral scrupulosity, are you?'

I grinned. 'Nothing like that.'

'If you say so,' he said dubiously. Then he stopped. 'Does this have anything to do with the mutilated BlastOff employee found in your front garden?'

'I've wondered. It's hard to see a direct connection,' I said evasively, dropping the subject.

Next day, Barry Owens did a one-man stampede into my office. Confrontation time. I expected sound and fury, but he took a measured tone as he leaned against the wall in my office, hands hanging loosely, reminding me of a Wild West gunslinger in nonchalant pose, yet ready to slap leather at a moment's notice.

'Christ, K, I'm prepared to be sensitive that you've issues about the payment arrangements for our business. Dunno why but you do. So, I want you to know, yesterday I gave Quinn a bell in London to wish him the best as new Chew, and he confirmed when he gets to the agency next week he'll be taking charge of our account, hands-on, from day one.'

His smile was dishwater and there was no longer any banter.

'He told you he'd continue loading BlastOff invoices and rebating them to Belfast?' I asked.

He shook his head. 'No need for you to scrabble around

in the… small print. As I said, Quinn sees no difficulties. And there's only one cheque you'll ever need to autograph. Tide things over.'

Evidently, Quinn Brenner was going to have no difficulty in taking over the skim. That's what I'd hoped. I glanced at Barry's smiling expectant face. This might be the last time he'd be talking to me as though we were good buddies.

'It's not that simple, Barry.' I tried to sound like I wanted him to see that, regretfully, I had no choice. 'The arrangement is illegal on several fronts. You, an employee of BlastOff, are ripping off the company in spectacular fashion and, up to now, we've been aiding and abetting. If it came to light, and with the size of the rip-off that's a real possibility, Aardvark-Sheridan wouldn't survive and anyone associated with it could find themselves stamping out licence plates on behalf of the State.'

He was holding in his temper, fists clenched, still hoping to find a button to push.

'Bullshit. And it's not your business anymore, is it?'

'Barry, leave aside the fact we've got the annual audit next month and there's no way the auditor's gonna green light this –'

He waved it away.

'If that's what's worrying you, don't sweat it. Charley Maughan's firm are our auditors, same as yours, so it's guaranteed to come up roses.'

If Maughan was ready to fudge the accounts for an audit, Larry Brenner was aware of what was going on.

I said, 'We're both aware of who really owns BlastOff and what they'll do to an employee they catch skimming. Are you sure it's worth the risk?'

He looked nonplussed, then gave a whoop of derision.

'You think this is about me, I'm doing a rip-off? You don't know caviar from shit. I'm acting for the owners. You're right, I wouldn't dream of crossing them. Nor should you, fella.'

I was now perplexed.

'Makes no sense. Why would they rip off themselves?'

'If you put that brainbox of yours to work,' he snapped, 'you might come up with an answer. It might be the right answer or it might be the wrong answer. Either way, it's not for you to question or me to answer.'

I had no intention of yielding.

He exhaled noisily, beyond exasperation.

'I'm not one to threaten, K. But this idiotic attitude is how you blow the BlastOff account and lose your job – and possibly a lot more. Be careful you don't find yourself riding into Shitsville on a spiked wire saddle.'

Whatever that meant.

I said, 'Last guy came to threaten me, met with a bad end.'

If Barry had nothing to do with Dundan's visit, I'd have expected a baffled look, maybe asking what I meant. Instead, he blinked and turned away.

Eventually, he said, 'Not my doing,' softly and quickly. Changing tack, he snapped, 'You are one dumb cretin, fella. You've no idea what you're about to bring down on yourself. A fistful of trouble, that's what. It's out of my hands now and it's…'

His words tapered off, as though he'd run out of threats. He was working hard to keep his anger in check and I detected something else in his tone, concern for himself. I had sympathy for Barry. He was the front man for dangerous people and was finding himself outside his comfort zone, discovering he was possibly not as tough as he'd imagined, and the strain was showing.

On an impulse, I said, 'I'll walk you out.'

He regarded me with surprise and said nothing.

As we walked down the stairs, I said, 'Barry, nothing will happen to me. I'm not changing my mind and you're going to have to work with that.'

'Yeah, yeah. Right.' He had given up on me.

His white Lexus was parked across the street. As we waited for an oncoming bus to pass, he eyed me speculatively. 'Know something? You've changed since your accident. You've had a personality transplant and I don't think it's going to turn out well for you.'

He stepped off the pavement and into the path of the approaching bus, no more than a few feet away and coming on fast. Without a thought, I grabbed him by the scruff of his coat collar and jerked him back so quickly he tumbled onto the pavement. The bus driver slammed on the brakes. The vehicle shuddered and must have given a hard jolt to the passengers. Seeing no one had fallen under the bus, the driver blasted his horn angrily, mouthed several obscenities and drove on.

Barry got to his feet, white-faced. 'Jeezus, toooo godamn close. Dunno what I was doing, saw the bus, couldn't stop myself. If you hadn't grabbed me... you've saved my life, K, saved my sweet life.'

I left him standing on the pavement. Back in my office, I watched from my window. For a long time, he stood irresolute. After warily waiting for a traffic-free street, he scurried across and sat in his car. It was a good ten minutes before he finally drove off.

27

A FIERCE BURST OF RAGE

Quinn Brenner arrived in the agency with little fanfare on Monday morning, introduced himself to Molly Moore, our matronly, highly efficient receptionist, got directions to Cronin's office and installed himself. Over the next couple of days, he had the board members to his den, one by one, one to one: Shay, The Barreller, Lucy, Parnell, Tara, Ross.

He oozed affability as he told them, disarmingly, how honoured he was to be leading an agency that had grown in a few short years under Cronin's leadership and how he planned to build on that with unspecific innovations. He invited each of them to send him, by the end of the week, their ideas on where they visualised themselves in the agency now and in the future and their proposals for developing new business. Bullet points ideally and on a single sheet for preference.

'A thoroughly, home-made nice guy on first acquaintance,' Shay told me. 'Not at all the trigger-tempered bruiser we've been hearing about. On the other hand, he does tend to overdo the charm offensive. And he's not known as The Crusher for nothing.'

Quinn was no workaholic. He kept an erratic schedule, coming in sometime after ten am, breaking for lunch at noon, back after three and away by five. Sometimes, he didn't return after lunch and occasionally he reappeared in the evening for a few hours.

Tara Hogan told me later, 'I have it from a good source Quinn didn't want this job and took it only because Dad asked him. He'd been having too much fun managing his nightclubs in Britland, where they're raking in the cash and are about to expand into the main Spanish tourist hotspots. He'll continue to spend two days a week in the UK and I doubt he's overjoyed at the prospect of giving so much of his time to running a low-revenue agency in backwoods Dublin.'

I was the last board member to be summoned and I got my invitation through Eilis O'Donnell, who was now his PA and no longer mine, at the back end of one afternoon to be in his office at eleven the following morning. I arrived promptly and found his office empty. Half an hour on, he hadn't shown.

'It's not personal, this being late,' Eilis said. 'He's awfully disorganised when it comes to time, especially in the mornings. Often, he forgets meetings altogether.'

'Must run in the family. Cronin was never on time. We used to call him the late Cronin, remember?'

I recognised the gaffe even as I saw her expression.

'I do but jest, and poorly,' I said and went back to my office.

At five minutes past noon, Eilis buzzed that Quinn was ready for me. When I went into his office, he was sitting behind his late brother's desk, the one I had tried for size recently. The desktop was empty, same as with Cronin, but there were half a dozen little mountains of files and paperwork on the floor. Quinn had organised a new visitors' corner with comfortable red leather armchairs and a modish glass coffee table in a semi-circle of artificial ficus and bamboo trees.

He greeted me with an extended-arm Nazi salute, though not so intended, as he sprang from behind his desk. I observed his huge hands with calloused knuckles and, as one enfolded my hand and the other my wrist, I reckoned he could crush both with comparative ease. But his grip, while firm, was not, so to speak, heavy-handed. He waved me to his oasis, where he joined me.

He was in shirtsleeves, tie askew – a big man, button-straining muscular, a hint of running to fat, thick lips, bulbous nose, small watchful eyes. This mix of uninviting features was moulded by a forceful personality into a face that was striking, and even, when he made the effort, actually pleasant.

He saw me eye the Velázquez reproduction.

'Valuable art,' he said.

'Richer than all your tribe,' I agreed.

He became avuncular.

'Well, Kieran, how ye doing? Wanting to meet with you.'

'So I've heard. I presume you've been busy.'

'Yeah, you could say. Ploughing the paperwork. Well briefed before I take meetings, head-to-head, knowing it, getting feedback, leveraging opportunities.'

He talked like that, dropping words, chopping sentences, so it was often a strain to follow him.

Watching him, I experienced out of nowhere a fierce burst of silent rage, of envy, resentment and frustration, physical in its impact. He was occupying the office where I should be and usurping what I had already begun to think of as my place. Shocked by the intensity of my emotion, I pushed it away with an effort, hoping it didn't show. He was oblivious, fiddling with a black Mont Blanc pen, capping and uncapping it, as if unsure how it worked.

'You were in the car with Cronin, night he died?' he asked, sympathy in his voice.

'My condolences.' I had not expected the question, though I should have. 'A heavy loss for you and the family. Sorry to miss the funeral. I was still tube-pinned to a hospital bed.'

'Tube-pinned?'

'Glucose in, urine out.'

'Of course, of course. Not to be expected you'd be with us, in your condition. Surprised to see you fit and well, God's truth. Word I heard, terrible injuries in the crash, more dead than alive, and here you are, hardly a scratch.'

'So they tell me. Surface impressions can be deceptive. I'm told the medics brought me back…'

I stopped. It would be crass to mention coming back from the dead when his brother hadn't.

He didn't take notice. 'Cronin a huge loss for us, Dad specially. Still haven't figured what happened exactly, the crash.' He raised an eyebrow questioningly.

'I'm no help to you. I know nothing, recall nothing.'

'Amnesia, right? I've heard. Wondering if memory of the night had come back, yes, no?'

'Neither wisp nor whisper. I may never remember. Sometimes, that's how it goes.'

He had parted his thin and well-diminished yellow-brown hair and made the mistake of growing long strands to cover the baldness and instead drawing attention to the skin beneath. Donald Trump without the fulltime coiffeur. His hair has been painstakingly arranged and plastered and he unconsciously patted it every so often to make sure no movement of the head disarranged it.

He changed the subject. 'What's the story? Guy killed by a wild animal your place last week?'

He made it sound as though I'd done something dumb.

I waved it off. 'An idiot burglar tried to take on a Rottweiler, as I understand it.'

His tight smile came and went. How much did he know? From his reaction, nothing. To avoid any further meaningless nattering, I asked him, 'Have you decided yet what you'll handle personally? A few of Cronin's clients have enquired, now they've caught the scent you're here.'

'Oh, getting there. Right off, taking two or three accounts, ones Cronin handled. BlastOff, given its importance. Naturally. You've been keeping it warm, yes. Thanks. I've talked to Barry, long-time mate, him and me mesh.'

Quinn shifted in his chair and farted. 'Ah,' he sighed, in no way discomfited.

'That's good,' I said ambiguously. 'BlastOff is doing nicely, as I'm sure Barry has told you. There was a problem about invoicing. It's being sorted.'

'Problem?'

'Didn't Barry mention it?'

He pulled a face. 'He gave me backstory. Your side of the story is what?'

'There's no "my side" to it,' I retorted. 'It's quickly told: there's an off-the-books agreement between BlastOff and the agency, whereby we've been overloading our invoices and remitting the difference to a company specified by Barry in Northern Ireland. Cronin set it up, I understand.'

A non-committal 'Hmm' from Quinn.

'Whatever way you reckon it, though, it's illegal, at best a case of money laundering.'

He puckered his lips in a soundless whistle. 'Yeah? Watch out using legal terms unless you fully understand them. Pearl before swine, no offence. If it's serious, I take it serious. Charley Maughan can due diligence it. Keeps my nightclubs in proper financial. Anyhow, it's with me, of now, and I'd appreciate you pass all files to Eilis this pm.'

'No problem. You'll find a formal note from me in the file outlining the position. The account was mine for only – what's it been? – ten days on a caretaker basis and, once I became aware of the illegality, I took responsibility for it. I've sent a letter to Barry confirming we're regularising things and no more cheques are going to Northern Ireland or anywhere else.'

'The hell you say? Jumping ahead of ourselves?' His voice was cold but as yet held no hint of menace. 'Keep grip on your own portfolio and leave BlastOff to me. Don't forget, I'm big chief of tribe now, kemo sabe.'

Again, I had that flash of pique. I stood. 'And I suggest a meeting of directors soon to review the BlastOff situation.'

'Suggestion noted.'

'As the captain of the *Titanic* was told, "Watch out for the ice."'

I wasn't quite sure what I meant, nor was he. He raised an eyebrow in amusement, then grunted with a pained expression, as though trying to keep the conversation going.

That or constipation.

As I left him, we were both eyeing each other speculatively. I guessed he was contemplating the most effective and least troublesome way to put me in my place. He had made no attempt to intimidate me and wouldn't necessarily take that route. For my part, I was aware Quinn was a substantial barrier between me and my burgeoning ambition to take control of the agency. He wouldn't be easy to dislodge and, as yet, I had no specific idea of how to go about it.

28

EXIT, PURSUED BY BEERS

A few days later, I met with a client, Liss Meagher, in Searsons Pub in Upper Baggot Street. She ran the Davenish chain of upmarket bookstores and wanted our agency to promote a series of in-store evening readings by well-known Irish novelists and poets. We got through the business end quickly. An eye-catching blonde in her early forties, who had taken over and significantly expanded the family-run firm, Liss was easy company and an entertaining raconteur.

When I left the pub, a cloudy but dry evening had turned unpleasant with heavy, sleety rain and I regretted my earlier impulse to take a brisk, healthy walk to Searsons rather than drive.

I passed a group of five men sitting in a semi-circle on the pavement at the corner of Waterloo Road, partly sheltered from the rain by a plastic construction awning, oblivious to the runnels dropping on them and the watery gusts blowing into them. They were dirty and drunk, with the wrinkled mismatched clothes of rough living and they gave off a repellent, stale odour. Cans of Coors beer were piled in a pyramid and they were noisily squabbling. Passers-by gave them a wide berth.

One squinted at me as I hastened by and wheedled, 'Hey man, how's about the price of a bed for the night?'

He winked and stretched out an open hand and, in veering around him, I accidentally bumped him, sending him sprawling into the stack of beer cans, which tumbled and scattered on the pavement. The men scrambled to their feet, with obscenities, and furious faces. In their drunken state, they were slow and clumsy getting up. With a quick apology, I kept moving and turned into Waterloo Road and made the next turn into Burlington Road, taking the long way back to my car.

The white rain was coming down heavy. Midway on Burlington, an object whizzed by me, landing on the pavement ahead and bursting with a muted explosion and gush of foam. It was a can of Coors. When I looked back, the feral five, far from having forgotten me, were now following in my direction. A second can flew by my head.

I was both alarmed and puzzled. If they were tossing good beer at me, their anger was way out of proportion to my having accidentally knocked over their cans. In a deserted Burlington Road, I was alone in the rain-swept night. I stepped up my pace.

A beer can hit me on the shoulder, to the accompaniment of yells of triumph. There wasn't much force behind it, but it smarted. I broke into an awkward trot. I was roughly fifteen minutes from my car, which gave them more than enough time to catch me. I had a fleeting thought: another episode of unreasoning anger aimed at me. Was this Bum Farto's doing? Was I not protected by the Ankh? I wasn't going to stop and check.

The rain had become pellets of hail, falling in bright cascading sheets. I glanced back and was shocked to see my pursuers, running like demons, were closing fast. I dashed out across busy Mespil Road, dodging the traffic, making for the Grand Canal tow path. Cars flashed past, rain and sheets of hailstones illuminated in their headlights.

I ran to the narrow, wooden lock bridge across the canal, slowed and cautiously made my way across. The timber was wet and slippery, and I used the handrail for safety. Four of the men were now bunched twenty yards or so behind me. The fifth, the one I'd originally jolted, the biggest and beefiest, had more speed in him and was already on the bridge and a few feet away.

He shouted: 'Got ya now, pisser,' and reached out for me. I let loose a wild kick that connected with his shin. He yowled in pain, his hands going to his leg. His eyes widened as he realised he'd let go the handrail. He overreached for it, grabbed air, teetered and, with a loud porcine screech, tumbled over and into the deep water of the lock below with a huge splash.

As I moved off, I heard him screaming and splattering. The other four yobs had stopped and were peering into the lock. Then, with inarticulate howling, they resumed the chase. One down, four remained – all of them infected with unreasoned hate and, I assumed, well used to dirty street fighting, while I'd never been in a fist fight in my life. Abysmal odds.

I scuttled along the far canal bank, nearly blinded by the hail and the rain streaming through my hair and into my eyes. I was sent sprawling by the outstretched legs of Patrick Kavanagh. That is to say, my shins smacked painfully into the life-sized seated bronze of Kavanagh on a stone bench by the side of the canal. My desserts for mocking *On Raglan Road*. Poetic justice.

I reversed direction and limped as fast as I was able across the road, with the idea of hiding in the bushes of nearby Wilton Park. A quick look showed me the small park, enclosed by iron railings, had only leafless trees and small bushes around the perimeter that offered no haven.

My hunters had temporarily lost me. Thoroughly drenched as if I'd been swimming the canal, I stumbled towards Lower Baggot Street. On my left was a nondescript glass and concrete office building, long unoccupied and scheduled for demolition. To the side, behind a shoulder-high iron fence, concrete steps led to a sunken garden of sorts, all but invisible in the dark.

I was tiring, breathing in noisy gasps and with rubbery legs. My injuries, past and current, were taking their toll. Sheer panic enabled me to swing my body over the fence, something I wouldn't normally have been able to do. Unfortunately, my momentum carried me straight into a low cement wall, my head banged into it and the world exploded in a flash of light and agony. The pain was awful, like I'd been stabbed in the eyeballs. I staggered a few feet and panicked as I realised I might pass out and leave myself helpless to the fiends. I flung myself down the steps and onto a grass margin and burrowed deep into the thick greenery. For a while there was silence, then they were ominously close. I heard them cursing and jeering each other as they pulled themselves over the fence.

'There's the little prickser.'

I tried desperately to stay conscious as I lay stretched on the ground, wet grass and earth in my nostrils, rain-freezing and rain-soaked, nauseous with the running and the pain. Without warning, a flickering bright gleam expanded into a gash in the fabric of the darkness. It became a great open fissure and beyond it a different world to the one I was in. Without hesitation, I let myself into it as I passed out.

29

THE WRATH OF ANGELBEEST

Around me, a vast cemetery stretched across space and time, over hillsides and valleys and flatland as far as I could see. I was once more in the outlands of the dead, the netherworld of my deathmares, places I hoped had been forever banished from my consciousness.

A full moon cast a probing silvery light onto the grave-stones, like a feathery snowfall. Barren branches of black winter trees pointed upward in silhouette against the grey sky. The rain and sleet had gone and so had my headache, along with my other aches.

This was unlike any of my previous visits: the dead and their underworld were no longer repellent or unnerving. There was no pervading stench of rot and decay, no bite of sorrow and grief in the air. It was sterile and artificial, as though I'd stumbled onto an abandoned film set of Styrofoam tombstones and empty plaster sarcophagi.

Funereal trappings abounded: grave markers, plain and ornate, moss-bedecked, steel-doored vaults, monumental works of sorrowing angels, weeping children, prayerful mourners, depictions of the deceased in stone togas and funeral garb, rusted premature burial bells. Many gravestones were crumbled and broken, their metal rail surrounds corroded and in pieces, the inscriptions lost to time and the elements.

At my feet was a ruined statue of a prayerful angel, wings broken off when it had toppled from its pedestal. Fallen angel. Never mind, I thought mordantly: an angel needs no wings.

I had all but forgotten my nemeses in the physical world, so I was dumbfounded to hear a yell. 'There he is, the bastard.'

I swung about and the four remaining thugs were a hundred yards away, coming at me, as though out of a mist, slowing as they slithered around gravestones and debris, their faces distorted in malice. One of them, long and scrawny, a knife blade glinting in his hand, gabbled through blackened teeth: 'You did for Donny, ya bumhole, and I'm goin' open youze up good.'

I didn't fear them, not in this place. Their presence infuriated me and I shook with rage. In this place, they were not fiends anymore, merely wretches, and they had entered where they had no right to be. I was determined to punish them with awful severity.

On the ground was a scattering of iron bars with spike points, the remnants of railings from a vault entrance. I grabbed one and, with a maddened roar, rushed at them.

They slewed to a halt, stunned at this unexpected onslaught, a fleeing victim transmuted into a howling berserker. With all my strength, I blasted the iron bar into the face of the nearest scraggy thug. His scream became a gurgle as his nose exploded in blood. He tumbled back, knife flying. Before he could fall or even raise a hand, I lashed out again and slashed him across the mouth, creating another eruption of blood, mixed with splinters of teeth and bone.

Before he hit the ground, I had swivelled to confront a second attacker, using both my hands to smash the bar down on his skull. With a terrible crunch, he dropped, literally poleaxed. The other two, panicked, backpedalled awkwardly. One stumbled against a gravestone and I was on him, swinging a vicious blow into the side of his neck. He swayed choking and cawing before keeling over. The other was running when a thrust of my bar took him in the back of his neck, dropping him instantly.

I was alone with the four bodies. Not for long. Out of the night, Bum Farto, the *soi-disant* Nikromantzer materialised, his aura a purple-black vacancy against the night. Most of his flesh had rotted beyond emaciation and his head was no longer recognisably human, his once-conspicuous moustache now a few lank white hairs. His body, skeletal as a Giacometti figure, was wrapped in the tattered rags of a burial robe. His fetid stink blighted the air as he neared.

'You are in the world of Nikromantzer, of Shadow and Shade, and you are mine.' He inhaled noisily between broken teeth and each syllable seemed to be drawn in hurt. 'Finally, time to return to your death.' His voice rose to a screech: 'I now call forth the wrath of the AngelBeest, Queen of the Dark Side, Banshee of Hellfire, Goddess of Vengeance.'

A column of ash-grey smoke poured out of a crack in a tombstone slab and took on a wraith-like form, dim and unearthly. The shape gained substance and became an unholy thing, a woman, yet not a woman, with dull steel armour under a long swirling green cloak. Heavy, crow-black hair hung in dense strands to her waist, twisting with a life of their own. Copious chalk powder on the grotesque face could not conceal the many gashes and scars. Her thick obscene lips were dark puce, with the wide wound of her mouth distorted in a fierce grimace. Her eyes, yellow and wild, stared unblinking at me with deadly hatred.

'Behold your end.' The Nikromantzer, stood behind her, howling his triumph.

She glowered at him, turned to me, raised a clenched fist, opened it and a bright orange-white lightning bolt streaked from it and into me. A stunning blow pulverised my chest and hurled me to the ground, where I writhed in agony, gasping for breath as an intense wave of unbelievable pain rushed through me. I tried to stagger up but couldn't. I was hammered again with another brutally stabbing force. My iron bar was on the ground in front of me, far away and getting smaller as I reached for it.

My brain locked, frozen in terror. I sensed my strength leaving my body and leaching into the earth beneath me, where long-dead bones stirred. My eyes misted over, and I dimly saw her fist open again and another high voltage flash surge towards me.

I heard myself scream as a sharp searing explosion of agony, the worst so far, hit my chest. The agony burned through skin and muscle, as though a hot poker had been thrust into me. I could smell my burning flesh.

Then, in an instant, the pain evaporated, and pure energy streamed through my nerves and blood vessels. A mighty potency spread in ever-expanding ripples.

The evil one, whoever she was, hurled another of her

bolts at me. It was harmless as a snowball and I swatted it away easily.

I stooped, found my iron bar and, imbued with massive strength, hurled it at her. Before it reached her, she was gone, dissolved into the smoke from which she had come. The bar sped on and plunged into what remained of the Nikromantzer's chest. A huge fountain of pus and blood gushed out. He tried without success to wrench it free and sank to his knees, screaming and screeching, his eyes rolling wildly in agony and fury.

I stood over him. 'Remember your Nietzsche: "What does not kill me makes me stronger,"' I snarled. 'You're finished, Bum Farto, you poor goddam excuse for a Nikromantzer.'

He glared at me in impotent rage. I broke eye contact and took a few steps back, recalling another notorious Nietzsche quote: "Battle not with monsters, lest ye become a monster, and if you gaze into the abyss, the abyss gazes into you."

Yellow fluid dribbled out of his mouth and he rasped, 'She could have been mine.'

'Not a chance,' I scoffed.

'This is not finished.' The light in his eyes was fading. 'Not. You think you... I can... I can reach... and I will...'

He was finally no more, curled on the ground, malignant and vindictive, the iron bar buried in his chest, vibrating as he raged, a monster from Hell. Then, he was gone, leaving no trace in this world.

'Anyone else?' I threw out my challenge to the cemetery, semi-hysterical. There was a stinging, throbbing ache where one of the lightning bolts had hit me and I tore open my shirt, wincing at the pain and gasped at what I saw. The bolt had hit the Ankh, thrusting it against my skin, and burning its shape into me as if with a branding iron. The Ankh itself remained pristine and emitted a faint golden glow. It had done more than deflect a lethal blow. It had seared into my being an enormous force of energy that had enabled me to defeat both the Nikromantzer and his bitch of wrath.

I sobbed with relief as I fell to my knees. I was beyond mere exhaustion. An almighty, throbbing headache had my skull in a vice that forced my eyes closed.

Eyes open, I came to, wet, cold, fatigued, sore all over, head thumping – back in the sunken garden by the office building in Baggot Street. The hail had given way to a steady cold rain. I was kneeling on the sodden earth by the shrubbery, holding a rusty crowbar covered in dirt and crimson blotches. Around me, the foursome lay on the ground motionless. Their heads were a mess and the rain hadn't yet washed away the blood and gore. I assumed at least two were dead, maybe all four. Quite frankly, my dear, I didn't give a damn.

Gritting my teeth with the effort, I hauled them, one by one, along the slushy grass, by their arms and legs into the deepest part of the thicket where I left them.

I made my way back to the steps and, clumsily this time, clambered over the fence and fell into Baggot Street. With the cover of night and rain, I slunk into the shadows and, taking side streets and lanes to avoid being seen, hobbling and wobbling, made my way to the agency car park.

30

TIME FOR PLAN B

The following morning, to my immense surprise, I felt refreshed, physically and mentally, pain and soreness gone. It was as if an elixir had been injected into my veins. My body had one discernible mark from the previous night: the shape of the Ankh on my chest, like a purple-red birthmark, sharply delineated. It was this, I suspect, that had me in such good form, the still potent residue of the surge of energy that had spread through me as I was branded.

I checked the web news. It had bupkis, as you might say, about bodies found in Baggot Street or in the Canal. I gave little thought to the yahoos I had killed. Self-defence, though the police might take a different view. In any event, it was unlikely they'd discover my involvement. Even if there were CCTV cameras in the area, the dark, rain-filled night surely would have rendered them valueless.

It was a routine day at the office, as if those damn Fates were pulling levers to switch me from the bizarre to the ordinary with hardly a pause. I was closing down my computer at around six that evening when Quinn The Crusher got me on

223

the house phone, all buddiness.

'Busy, Kieran? 'Bout time we chewed on matters of mutual interest.'

Sure, I was free to chew with the Chew and his strangled syntax. Other than an exchange of short, civil greetings whenever our paths crossed in the agency, we'd been keeping our distance.

He was doing a careless swivel in his chair, relaxed, awaiting his prey, as I fancied it, and more than physically filling the space left by Cronin. He motioned me to the visitors' corner and I dropped into an armchair. He stayed behind his desk, making no move to join me, ready to speak across the room at me. Irritated at the power play, I hopped up and pushed a chair over to the side of his desk and sat facing him in profile. He made no comment but there was a hint of a smirk.

'How is your read-in progressing?' I asked.

His head went back as though sniffing for sarcasm, finding none. 'Mostly finished, yes. For the present. Useful exercise, fully expected. Aardvark performing well, better than well. Cronin did a brill job. Up to a point…'

I sat back and waited out his inviting pause.

'Complacency number one killer in any business,' he intoned. 'I drive that home all the time. Can't assume luck will always do right for us. Often not, and imperative we raise our game.'

He pointed a thick, manicured finger.

'Talking of which, you're not helping much, are you? As when you showed the door to a big-budget, make that huge-budget, new client.'

A few days previously, I'd taken a call from a Patricia

Rooney who announced herself as executive secretary of a recently established lobbying group, EnCompassAll, which was planning a national campaign, what they termed a national crusade, to restore Irish Christian values.

In a national referendum, the Irish electorate, by a two-to-one majority, had voted to drop the longstanding total ban on abortion. EnCompassAll, with an awkward name and ample funding from unspecified sources, was determined to force legislation for a new ballot to reverse the result.

Rooney, in a breathy, refined voice, told me that, on the recommendation of Mr Larry Brenner, EnCompassAll had decided to present its upcoming high six-figure advertising account to Aardvark. Without discussion, I declined on the spurious grounds we were not, at present, taking on new business, due to the death of our CEO. Her soft and pleasant tone gave way to astonishment and anger and her call ended abruptly.

Apart from my own distaste for what I saw as religious zealotry, I knew Lucy, Tara and Ross, among others, would have opposed taking the account. Later, I mentioned it to Shay, who agreed we shouldn't get involved. The Barreller and Parnell, on the other hand, had been dubious at my tossing away any big-spending client.

'Yes,' I said to Quinn. 'There was no enthusiasm on our side in taking an in-your-face controversial anti-abortion campaign. Jasper, y'know, had the faith of our fathers, as the saying goes. Daily mass-goer –'

'Nothing wrong there,' he broke in.

'– High Wizard or whatever in the Holy Knights of Columbanus. But he'd have not permitted a crowd of rabid fuckeroos like EnCompassAll in the front door. We can do better than that lot.'

Quinn gave me a considered appraisal. 'Jasper's long gone. Maybe it was his view. Not necessarily mine and I'm CEO. Not for you to go negative on a potential client, whether they appeal to you or don't, especially one with a million plus campaign chest for openers and no other agency in the pitch. Don't have to agree with a client, or what they produce, or how they do business, capiche?'

I didn't argue. He had a point. I'd gotten ahead of myself. In my brief and meaningless reign as acting CEO, I'd slipped into the error of believing I was in charge. His next comment showed he had read me.

'Your honorary interim stint was a doff of the cap to the last Sheridan connection to the agency. Harmless nepotism. Never intended nor expected you to call the shots.'

I grinned.

'Here's you telling me I owe my job to nepotism as you sit in this office because you're Larry's son. How much irony is that?'

He gave me a humourless grin and cracked his knuckles.

'Ain't life the crazy one? For you, that ship has gone to the bottom. Fact is, your portfolio rides high in the water, light on cargo. You need to carry more of what contributes to our net – especially now I've got BlastOff. On which, I decide how we do business with Barry.'

I nodded. 'Regarding the anti-abortion people, I took the call because you were too busy running your dad's UK business. This agency needs more than a part-time CEO, you know.'

Quinn's face flamed. I'd provoked him, as I'd intended and I waited to see how he'd respond. His eyes slitted, his nostrils flared, his lips opened to show bared teeth and it struck me that humans are never too far from their animal nature.

He jumped up, knocking his chair over, strode around the desk and towered over me, making white-knuckled fists of his big meaty hands. 'Where the hell you get off having a go at me?' he bellowed. 'You want a busted face, I'm your man.'

Easy to see why people called him The Crusher. He was angry, all right. But I could see, beneath the bully bluster, he had himself in control and his main purpose was to intimidate.

I remained calm. 'Quinn, you're big enough and fool enough to do what you say and I can't stop you belting me one. I trust you'll be ready to pay the price, which will be impressively expensive.'

He gave me his hard stare and I gave it back. After fighting demons and fiends in the cemetery, I was beyond his kind of petty threat.

'Don't try me,' he warned. But his temper had blown over, an anger management technique, I supposed, count to ten, dwell on pleasant things. He righted his chair and sat behind his desk again. He took a lungful of air and blew it through his pursed lips, did it again, probably another relaxation trick, patted his hair and waved his hand, dismissing the argument.

'Shit, forget it. Not why I wanted this chat. BlastOff not your concern. Apart from anything, Barry won't deal with you.'

'You planning to continue the scam?' I asked.

His brow furrowed. 'As the fella said, "Read my lips: not your concern."'

'On the contrary, Quinn. As a board member, however unreal, a shareholder, however small, and an employee, however junior, I've a direct interest in this. Take it how you please, as threat, promise or ultimatum. Unless we stop it right here, I'm going to expose the whole business.'

He pulled at his lips, unconvinced. I hadn't angered him this time.

'Ballsology. You won't, pal, risk losing BlastOff and exposing the agency to scandal. Your threat, whatever, is dud.'

'If you play chicken, be prepared –'

I was on the point of saying, 'prepared to crash into the other guy'. Mentioning car crashes would be graceless. Instead, I said, 'If the agency falls, your loss is greater by many multiples.' I cupped my hands, doing the measuring scales. 'The agency is not mine, so it's no loss to me. I'll need a new job. Might be tough in this market, but I'll get one. You and your father, on the other hand, stand to lose a multi-million euro asset, and become tangled in litigation for years, your family's reputation thrashed and even featured in a civil or criminal trial. I can take the risks with an easier mind than you.'

He had abandoned his anger, real or simulated, altogether. He seemed to give weight to the pros and cons of what I was saying.

'Not how I see it. But. Tell you this: we both mull over the weekend, get together Monday, I'll give you final decision.'

He produced one of his matey smiles.

'Right? See, Kieran, you can't be comfortable in a business you expected to inherit. Never will, with me as the guvnor. Try this. You resign Aardvark, take six months, okay, year's salary, glowing references, office here as base until you're fixed. Or, a good bloke, Harry Freeland, owns an agency in London and I can swing you a decent job there. We'll even buy your shares in Aardvark, premium deal. BlastOff not your issue, doesn't affect you. Your decision, no pressure.'

I wasn't remotely interested in his offer but was fascinated to hear him make it. I didn't imagine he was giving ground, or he was going to end the arrangement with Barry. He was buying time for some reason. He made it sound spontaneous, but an offer like that had to have been pre-planned and vetted with Larry. Offering to buy my shares was likely the real aim.

'As you say, Quinn, let's reflect on it.'

I left and returned to my office to check if any new emails needed attention. I responded to several queries and switched off. On my way down the stairs, a mobile phone jingled *Oranges and Lemons* and Quinn's voice, slightly muffled called out: 'Hi, Dad'.

He was in the first-floor lavatory. I stopped to listen.

'Yeah, he's left.' A pause. 'You called it right, waste of God's hour. No loss trying, though… yeah, dumb shit, not interested in deal… got his own agenda and I can't figure… no… no… um. Hate to say, time for Plan B, right? Who've you got?… they're good… when? …know my view, rough him, hospital case, no more… why? You can't prove… won't argue, get it over with… sure… bye.'

The lavatory flushed, and I scooted back to my office. I heard him tramp back to his and close his door. I counted to fifty and noiselessly took to the stairs again. I saw Danny Ryan, our odd-jobs guy and, outside his day job, a national amateur flyweight martial arts fighter, descend from above, a pair of large plastic sacks of refuse in each hand. I waved to him and kept moving, hoping to forestall him calling my name aloud. To my relief, he gave only a preoccupied 'Night'.

On the way home, I stopped off at Gleesons pub in Booterstown, where I sometimes met with acquaintances from other agencies to talk shop and share gossip. This evening, the pub was quiet. I sipped a Jameson and rolled over in my mind what I'd overheard.

I'd heard one side of the conversation and could fill in some of the blanks on the other. What precisely was Plan B? Evidently another physical attack on me and, ominously, Quinn advised his father not to go beyond putting me in hospital. Then what? They planned to kill me? Once, that would have had me in a cold sweat. Now, such a threat didn't bother me unduly, since I hadn't given up on the idea that I was already, in some sense, dead. Dead but won't lie down.

I finished my drink and was about to leave when my mobile vibrated. No ID and I didn't at first recognise the hesitant voice.

'Mr Sheridan? It's Danny from the office. Danny Ryan. You need to get back right away. It's Mr Quinn. There's been a dire accident.'

31

THE DEFENESTRATION OF QUINN BRENNER

I made it back to the office in twelve minutes, twice running red lights. As I raced past the fortress-like, circular American Embassy in Ballsbridge, an ambulance sped by in the opposite direction, klaxon blaring, its revolving strobe light flashing the street. Could it be related to the urgent summons from Danny? Something had happened to Mr Quinn. Something 'dire'. Referring to the boss obsequiously as Mister Forename had not disappeared with the times. I couldn't imagine anyone in Aardvark ever calling me Mister Kieran.

Outside the agency, three Garda cars were parked with blue lights blinking, a pair of motorcycle cops stood by their machines chatting and curious passers-by stood idly on the pavement. I was reminded of Silchester Road the night of Dundan's death.

Sliding into a parking space, I hastened to the open front door where I was blocked by two uniforms. I identified myself, and waited, catching my breath, as one went inside and, after a minute, came back and waved me in.

Half a dozen uniformed and plainclothes Gardaí were in the hallway. No rifles in sight this time. Danny stood in the open annexe off the hall talking earnestly to a detective who was taking notes. He pointed at me and the detective waved me over.

'Kieran Sheridan? Spelt with a K, right? You a director here, right?

'Right.'

'You were here earlier?'

'Earlier than what? Can you tell me what's going on?'

He looked up from his notebook. Ruddy-faced, untidy black hair, small band-aid across his nose.

'We're putting it together. Seems like your boss...' he checked his notes '...Mister Quinn Brenner, fell out the window of his office.' When I didn't do hysterical, he added, 'He fell three floors at the back. He's alive but unconscious and critical. He's been taken to A&E in St Vincent's.'

'I don't understand.' I felt dazed. 'We were talking less than an hour ago. How could he fall out the damn window? Did he go through it or what?'

'As I said, we're in the process of getting the full picture. What did you talk about?'

What's that got to do with anything? I kept the thought to myself and gave the detective, Frank Slavin by name, an edited version of my meeting with Quinn: casual chat, shop talk. Arguments? Disagreements? Pshaw.

'This was an accident?' I gestured at the strong Garda presence.

'That's what we're trying to resolve. Did he usually work this late?'

'On and off. It's not always nine-to-five here.'

He asked a few more questions about Quinn's working habits and how Quinn and I worked together, then left me for Shay, who had come from the car park. Nobody stopped me as I took the stairs and stood at Quinn's office, door wide open. Best I could tell, the room was as I'd last seen it, except the big window had been raised from the bottom and was open, white curtains rippling, letting in the chilly air. Garda technicians, on their knees, backs to me, were examining the window frame.

In the hallway, Shay, in casual tawny honeycomb cardigan and sweatpants, was talking with Danny and with Paul Walsh, a junior designer, who was presumably working late.

I said to them straight-faced, 'I looked in his office. The good news is nobody's stolen the Velázquez.'

Shay looked puzzled, then shook his head and ushered us into a small meeting room off the hall. Danny and Paul sat on chairs. I perched on the table and Shay leaned against the wall.

I said, 'Thanks for the call, Danny. How much do you know of what's happened? Must have been directly after I left.'

Danny was unperturbed by the whole business. 'As you know, Mr Sheridan, I was taking waste to the basement when I saw you leave. Soon as you were out the front door, a bag burst and scattered paper and stuff over the stairs. I was picking it up when I heard Mr Quinn in his office on the phone.'

'Any idea who he was talking to?' Paul Walsh asked. Danny frowned at the interruption and the irrelevance.

'Uh-uh. Not my business and I had my hands full getting the rubbish back in the bag. I heard him put the phone down and say, friendly like, "Hi there, where did you come from?" and "I don't think we've met yet." Funny, y'know, because I'd seen no one go in. I was on the stairs all the time with his door in my line of sight. Next thing, Paul here came down the stairs from above.'

Walsh, a talented designer and a study in scruffiness looked at us as if he was about to get a rebuke.

'I had –'

Danny spoke over him. 'I heard a bang as the window was shoved up and Mr Quinn, was shouting to her, kind of edgy, 'What you think you're doing?' and he lets out this awful yell that became a scream and nothing. What you heard, too, right?'

Walsh nodded.

'Her?' I queried. 'It was a woman?'

Danny rubbed his temple, uncertain. 'Er, no, maybe. I thought 'twas a woman, the way Mr Quinn had been talking, sorta flirty, y'know?'

'Go on,' said Shay.

'I knocked on his door and went in when I got no answer. Weird. Window wide open, curtains blown in, no sight of Mr Quinn – or anyone else. Paul came in with me and we went to the window and saw him lying below on the ground. We called out but he wasn't moving. Paul rang for an ambulance and I ran down. He was unconscious in a pool of blood, legs twisted, broken. I did what I could, which wasn't much, stayed with him until Paul let the medics in.'

He made as calm and articulate an exposition of the facts as if he had been an account executive making a presentation to a client. Danny was useful to have around in an emergency.

Paul said abruptly, 'I'd a short meeting with him a few hours ago, to get his okay on the visuals for the Smithfield IT commercial. Know what he said as I left? "If I don't see you through the week, I'll see you through the window." What do youse make of that?'

'He says that to everyone,' dismissed Shay and asked Danny, 'How critical do you reckon he is? Best vibe?'

'Serious, no doubt, must have internal damage, no telling. I heard a medic say to a cop, "He's bad but he'll pull through."'

He wiped his lips. 'Y'know the craziest thing? The window. Impossible to open it by hand. The frame's been painted so many times over the years that it's hardened and thickened and you'd need a hammer and chisel to cut it away. Yet, I heard the window open, whoosh, in one go. Who has that muscle, eh? And, come to that, who had the muscle to force Mister Quinn out in seconds?'

32

TRANSFORMED

Two days after the literal fall of Quinn, Tara Hogan proposed an emergency Aardvark board meeting at her apartment in Sandymount Green where she lived with her partner and quasi-fiancé, Stu Sweeney, a successful Goodbody stockbroker. Out of politeness, she asked Kieran Sheridan, who technically, if, to her mind, absurdly, was once more the agency's acting CEO, to make the calls. Then she did what came naturally to her and contacted everyone herself.

After tossing the idea back and forth for a few days, Shay Dempsey had finally decided not to make a bid for the CEO job, now apparently vacant for the second time in a few weeks.

It had been on his mind from when he got the call that Quinn Brenner was hors de combat. He surmised that Quinn, should he survive, was lost to the agency and this time his fellow board members might be able to take it on themselves to name a replacement, calculating that Larry, still grieving for Cronin and with his other son in critical condition, would have the agency at the bottom of his priorities.

Even assuming the other board members concurred, could

they identify and attract a new CEO? The ideal candidate, he or she, would likely be a senior account director in another agency or a respected marketing director, either way a high-flying, new business magnet. Candidates like this were not plentiful, but they existed.

The problem was a potential CEO of this calibre was bound to ask the obvious question: did the senior staff of Aardvark, the self-styled board, have the authority to make the appointment and sign off on the remuneration package? An honest answer would mean the interview grinding to a halt, followed by a short goodbye.

Was it to be an internal choice, then? Shay asked himself. It would be a process of elimination. Lucy Shaw would be ideal in many respects, including gender: women were increasingly proving themselves best suited for the top corporate job, particularly in marketing. She wouldn't want it, though, had no ambition in that direction and would prefer to hone her reputation as one of Dublin's top copywriters while working on the breakout novel.

The Barreller Healy would like the job, would like it very much. He had seniority, experience, networking skills and sufficient gravitas for the position. But The Barreller made it clear to Shay he would not be a candidate and, over a drink in Dwyer's pub, confided his reason: Harvey Weinstein.

A few years ago, related The Barreller, when he still ran his own shop, he had been guest speaker at an advertising students' diploma course in the Imperial Hotel in Cork and, in his usual fashion, had laced his speech with a few off-colour jokes. A young woman sitting in the front row had taken personal umbrage and, to The Barreller's astonishment, made a formal complaint of sexual harassment to the organisers, claiming he had been giving her the eye as he delivered his witticisms. To his even greater bewilderment, the organisers had, in part, upheld the complaint and suggested he make a written apology.

He did so with bad grace, regarding it as an excess of political correctness to placate a prudish female, and the matter was closed. But currently, #MeToo revelations of the sexual misdeeds of Weinstein, Kevin Spacey, Bill Cosby, Roger Ailes, Al Franken, The Duke of York for Chrissakes, and a monstrous regiment of men had multiplied geometrically into accusations of past 'inappropriate sexual behaviour'. It was long past time for sexists to be held to account, and collateral damage was inevitable.

The mere fact he had been accused and judged guilty of 'sexual harassment' marginal though it may have been, lay on The Barreller's mind as something that might surface at any time and damage his reputation, even, Christ, lose him his standing in the profession. He was going to keep a low profile.

With The Barreller a non-contender, who else was in the ring? Parnell was too specialised in media. Tara might be persuaded but had she the stature, the cred? Uh-huh. That left only Shay himself.

'Do I want to put my hat in the ring?' he asked Julie, the diminutive doll-like blonde who was ever, in his eyes, the same teenage girl he'd married a dozen years ago. 'I'd get it, for sure and I'd be good at it, acceptable to clients and the industry. We'd have more money and perks.'

She looked doubtful. 'Are you truly unsure or are you trying to rationalise a decision you've made?'

He laughed ruefully. 'The truth? I've no idea whether I want the job or not. The one downside is my track record of running a business into the ground.'

'You and half the country,' she retorted.

Shay had left school at fourteen to work behind the counter in his late father's DIY retail store in Rathmines. At nineteen, he owned a shop of his own, Chez Shay, which most of his customers facetiously pronounced 'cheesy'. By age twenty-five, his chain of Chez Shay DIY outlets had made him a millionaire. Then came the Celtic Tiger crash, the banks mugged him, the business went bust and his lavish nouveau riche-ness evaporated in the twinkling of a liquidator's eye.

At the peak of his success, he ran a substantial advertising account with Aardvark, and the agency was one of several suppliers he had contrived to have paid up to date as Chez Shay glugged down the drain. An appreciative Jasper Sheridan rewarded him with an account director's job in the agency.

There were psychic scars, a year of suspecting, then knowing the Chez Shay empire was going out of business, was going to hurt a lot of good people like employees and suppliers in their pockets.

'Do you really, really want the extra responsibility, the commitment?' Julie asked now and answered herself. 'You don't need the job, Shay. Those shops brought too much stress, even at the best of times. Towards the end, you were a wreck. I'm surprised we both didn't have his-and-her nervous breakdowns.'

More than that, reflected Shay, as he parked outside the apartment complex in Sandymount. He had come close to suicide, though he never mentioned it to Julie or to anyone.

He had survived, getting his career back on track, building a comfortable, if more modest, lifestyle. He and Julie had abandoned Dublin for the small town of Maynooth, an hour's drive to the agency, where the living was cheaper and the local community friendly. He had contested and won election to the Council as an independent, which he regarded as confirmation his reputation was intact.

With a general election ever on the horizon, a seat in the Dáil might be within reach, even a junior ministry. He'd talked about it with one of the newly-elected independent deputies, who led a slate of other independents in a loose alliance that had real power in the Dáil.

CEO of Aardvark was a potential ulcer-maker to no good purpose. So, he concluded, I rule myself out. Which brings us back to Doh, finding an outsider quickly. A lot of work was needed. Candidates needed to be identified, a shortlist prepared, soundings made, interviews, a package deal negotiated. And round again to the question, what if the right person requested, not unreasonably, Larry Brenner's imprimatur? What if Larry –

He had his finger on the apartment bell when a crazy, outlandish notion slipped under the radar of common sense and into his mind: Ciarán Sheridan as CEO. He pulled away from the bell and paused at the entrance, astounded at the audacity, the absurdity. Could it possibly make sense?

Shay liked Ciarán, regarded him as a friend as much as a colleague. But let's be real here, he chided himself. Ciarán, the underpowered heir of Jasper, the traditional weak successor to a forceful leader, shoved aside by the Brenners, a competent executive, no more, an eager to please personality, over-respectful of clients, in awe of Cronin. Get real.

But wait. That was before the car crash and since then, day by day, wacky though it sounded, Ciarán had changed, transformed. No other word for it. Even physically. One would expect the sole survivor of a horrific car crash to be still strung out a month later, hesitant, frail, being urged to take more time off. Ciarán, on the contrary, showed more vigour and vitality than he had ever previously shown.

He seemed to have grown an inch or two, had lost his flabbiness. His hair was no longer thinning. He'd stopped wearing those oversized glasses and his deep-set blue eyes could hold an eerie hypnotic quality that hadn't been there before. He'd even stopped smoking. Dammit, he reminded him of those novels where a man is switched with his previously unknown twin.

Ciarán's personality had undergone the most noticeable change. He had a new-found laidback confidence that replaced the former diffidence. Both Lucy and Tara had mentioned lately what a different person he was. Tough guy Quinn hadn't daunted him in the slightest. Ciarán nixed the anti-abortion bunch without hesitation. And more: the pre-accident Ciarán would not have dared relentlessly hound the supposed scam with BlastOff, and unhesitatingly taken on Barry Owens.

There was something else: Ciarán had an exploitable asset, the Sheridan name, that, in PR terms, might provide a legitimacy, kind of, as a counterpoint to the unsettling loss of three CEOs in recent times, two in the past month or so.

Shay heard Parnell arrive behind him, with Tara following. How would they and the others respond to the idea? Tap their foreheads, tell him he was out of his mind? Come to that, how would Ciarán himself react?

33

MENACE IN THE AIR

As I drove to Tara's Sandymount apartment, the Ankh, normally quiescent, began to vibrate softly, sending out slow warm pulses that gave me small shots of adrenaline and seemed to signal some indeterminate menace in the air. I knew better than to ignore the hint and scrutinised passing cars and their preoccupied drivers, looked ahead and in my rear mirror but could see nothing amiss. I remained wary.

At Tara's place, Shay was at the entrance and Parnell was pulling off his motorcycle duds and chatting with Tara. Shay gave me a casual glance that wasn't quite casual before turning away with a thoughtful expression. I recognised he was seeking confirmation and reassurance of something and, with an unexpected flash of insight, it occurred to me what he might be thinking. Surely not? Had I, without realising it, placed the possibility in his mind?

The meeting was informal. We sat, drinks before us, in a semi-circle of comfortable chairs and settees: Shay, Lucy, Tara, The Barreller, Parnell, Ross and me. The penthouse apartment featured a tasteful and expensive décor that reflected the lifestyle of a double-income, no-kids-yet-lots-of-time couple. The expansive lounge with floor-to-ceiling picture windows looked onto Sandymount Green and beyond a sweeping panorama of Dublin Bay.

Tara was saying, 'When you consider, it's amazing we haven't lost a single client, these past few weeks. A reporter from the *Business Post* was mulling over a Jinxed Agency story. I steered her off. Let's have no more incidents for a while, okay?'

That got dry smiles.

The Barreller lit a small black cheroot and tipped back comfortably in a well-cushioned armchair. He dressed as ever in the manner of a cartoon Mafia character, sharp double-breasted, wide-striped dark suit, midnight blue shirt and tie to match, tinted glasses, slicked hairstyle, heavy gold rings and wrist bracelet. A Leesider's concept of the look of a godfather's *consigliere*. Incongruous, but it worked for him.

'I've had my antennas out,' he drawled. 'We've all been talking with clients, no doubt. Mine are behaving themselves, no surprise there. All good fellows. But I hear rumours one or two other clients are sniffing the air. Mutterings of what in the name of the blessed saints is happening in this agency? As the phrase goes, "To lose two CEOs seems like carelessness."'

Shay took it up. 'We haven't lost Quinn yet, though I can't see him coming back anytime. There's another side to this. In a ghoulish way, Aardvark is an object of interest now and there's a perverse cachet in our clients being able to say: "Oh, yeah, that's my agency and I've been given the inside story."' He paused. 'Not that there is one.'

Tara was sitting on a window seat, tight jean-clad legs

swinging. 'Attitudes change. They may question whether we're too preoccupied with our own problems to give them the attention they're due. Let their thoughts flow in that direction –'

Parnell, perched on the edge of his chair: 'You can be bloomin' sure other agencies are sniffing for blood in the water and will circle us soon enough. What do we do?'

The Barreller tapped his glass. 'An agreeable Chablis, Tara.' He sipped it appreciatively. 'Let us to our purpose. We need a new CEO without delay. Shay is right about Quinn. I've got it from a reliable source he's destined for long-term rehab. I don't expect he'll even want to be in the environs of Aardvark at any time in the future.'

'We've seen the last of him,' Lucy agreed. 'We'll miss his shafts of wit.'

She added, 'Spoonerism.' She hadn't liked him much.

Ross glanced up from browsing The Barreller's copy of Jordan Peterson's *12 Rules for Life*. 'Some say good old Quinn. Others tell the truth.'

'Tut. Show at least a smidgen of compassion,' chided The Barreller half-heartedly.

Ross grinned. 'I can't help picturing Quinn going out the window, screaming as he fell, as he carefully smoothed down his hair.'

I wasn't the only one who had to work at keeping a straight face. There was surprisingly little sympathy for Quinn in the room.

Tara scowled. 'It's as well he didn't follow my recommendations to publicise his arrival. He'd have been promoted as the new master of Aardvark, the great helmsman steering the agency to even greater things, and he turns out to be captain of the *Titanic*.'

I remembered my parting shot to Quinn about the *Titanic*.

'I'd like to hear views on how we are to acquire a new CEO,' said Shay.

The discussion went on for an hour or more, down byroads of distraction. Round we go, I thought, fools in a circle, repeating arguments that could be delivered by rote. I kept sthum, waiting to see if I had read Shay aright. I could still sense an undefined floating menace. But it was distant, not in the room.

Ross asked, 'We're certain we don't need to check with Larry?'

'Forget Larry,' Shay snorted. There was no dissent. 'He's nursing Quinn and he doesn't have Aardvark in his sights right now. That gives us a once-only, time-limited opportunity to decide on a CEO and go public with it. Time to cut to the chase. We have neither time nor latitude to bring in an outsider and we'd be in the position of desperate suitor. The next CEO, he or she, is here in this room.'

A long silence followed as they considered the options and implications.

Tara spoke: 'Let's not beat about the George W. The obvious candidate is Shay.'

Shay gave her a mock inclination of the head.

'Thank you. I'll confess it's crossed my mind,' he admitted. 'For all sorts of reasons, business and personal, I'm going to decline the proffered chalice.'

He added diffidently, 'I recommend Ciarán.'

At first, no one seemed to take it in. Then, a collective explosion of air.

'What do you say?' exclaimed The Barreller in astonishment. He waited for one of the others to trash the idea. When there was only silence, he opened his mouth as though to comment, then shut it.

Lucy murmured, 'Interesting.' She meant 'farcical', I guessed.

Parnell swung from Shay to me, pop-eyed. In his astonishment, the words burst out of him. 'W-w-whatzat? Holy Shiite militia! Pardon my French. I mean, sheez…'

Shay gave a shrug. 'Eloquently expressed, Nell. But I understand your misgivings. A month ago, hell, a week ago, I doubt if I'd be saying this. I'm surprising myself now by proposing Ciarán as our best choice.'

He threw me a curious glance. 'I don't know what that accident did to you. You've changed in a short time, big time.'

'Helluva thing to say,' I remarked neutrally. 'I appreciate it, assuming it's a compliment.'

'But –' Parnell couldn't seem to decide if he was stupefied or outraged.

Ross, with a sardonic expression, said to Tara. 'You're the image guru. What's your opinion? You'll be the person who'd have to sell him publicly as CEO.'

Tara eyed me speculatively and hesitated, fully aware the outcome might hinge on her support or not. She spread her hands.

'Dunno. Apologies in advance, Kieran, but this is too important for glossing over. Until recent days, I wouldn't have taken you seriously, even as a board member. You didn't have the heft, the experience, or the qualities of what I'd expect in an account director, never mind CEO. I've always seen you as a competent junior, despite what Jasper may have thought. You know Cronin more than once referred to you as Kieran Wuss, and he meant it as a simple fact, no nastiness intended. Well, not much. I always reckoned nobody changes personality overnight. Then again, perhaps they do where you're concerned. I know what Shay is talking about. At the same time –'

'Is that yes or no?' asked Ross with a frown.

She ignored him.

'What you may have going for you, Kieran, and I emphasise may have, is a good storyline: you're the last Sheridan, reclaiming his place, that sort of idea. The heir comes into his own. The dynasty restored. Ring the bells, blow the trumpets, et cetera. A Jeffrey Archer novel come to life, rinky-dink, yet compelling. Ye-es, in theory you can be marketed as CEO. Chancy, of course, if you don't measure up, to be blunt. We'd want you to win us an impressive new account or two smartly and lose none of our existing clients. Don't know if you can do that. Since you asked, Ross, I vote a qualified "possibly".'

She seemed surprised at her conclusion.

'As ringing endorsements go...' The Barreller said acerbically. I supposed he'd been expecting his name might have come to the fore, so he could modestly decline.

No one else jumped in. I saw it was hanging in the balance. The next comment, positive or negative, could decide the outcome. Shay had made the opening and was going to leave it to me to see if I could follow through.

'I don't agree with Shay's proposal,' I said. 'It's a leap too far. But seeing as it's on the table, may I suggest a relatively risk-free approach? Like this: I hold onto my title of acting CEO, but we take it seriously and see what happens? Short trial. If I don't pan out, nothing is lost and we target someone else. If it does work, the acting part of the title can be dropped in due course. I'm on for it. No false humility, no harrumphing. Are we interested on that basis?'

Another long silence, followed by a slow, reluctant, nodding of heads. It was no Eureka moment. They couldn't think of a better option, given the complexities of trying to hire an outside talent. They were impressed by what I'd said but were far from sure it was the right decision. My compromise made it barely acceptable, a decision that was not a decision and, if it didn't come together, had deniability, could be rescinded. It was a default solution.

Shay was smiling broadly, more with relief than satisfaction. I'd expected The Barreller to at least remonstrate. He appeared stunned by the outcome. He regarded himself as the agency's number two. We were not close and, until this meeting, he'd have seen me as way junior to him. But not getting the position himself, he didn't greatly care who took it. I was no threat to him in any way he could envisage.

He threw me a critical once over. 'As Theresa May said to Hilary Clinton, "Will someone tell us what the fuck's just happened?"'

He sniffed, then held out his hand. 'Bloody good stuff, Kieran. Damn good stuff, in fact.'

Ross said, 'You're the man, and if you're prepared to become more active on the social and digital media side, it's all systems go. You need a better Smartphone to replace the clunker you use. You're not even on Facebook or Twitter or LinkedIn, to say nothing of a few dozen other absolute essentials. You'll need to be baptised digitally.' He laughed. 'I got to tell you, Kieran. A member of my staff, who shall be nameless, described you to me as a prima donna. He thought the phrase meant pre-Madonna, someone living in a world before Madonna became famous. Ancient, out of touch.'

I grinned. 'I'll fix that. Truth is, we're living in the past as an agency. We're the last of the old-style agencies in this country and we've been dangerously slow to catch up with changes in the business: social media specifically. There's more. Strong international linkages. We need more specialisation in design, media buying, below the line. Cronin was giving us new directions, sharpening our offering.'

My words were sounding eerily familiar to me, as though I was repeating verbatim what I'd heard someone else say recently.

'Enough for the present.' I wanted to wrap it. 'I'll need the active support of the whole agency, obviously from you, Tara, and you, Ross, on the digital front. Also, I want to tell Larry Brenner as soon as possible, my first test in the job.'

Shay ended the meeting before buyers' regret surfaced. Both Lucy and Parnell had an I've-done-what? look. On the way out, I thanked Shay. With a glint in his eye, he said, 'Think of Napoleon: "Give me a general who is lucky." Our CEOs have been accident prone so far. Anyone else, I'd worry about. You've had your accident and you're still standing.'

As I drove off, I got that indefinable sense of danger again, stronger now and close by this time. The Ankh next to its scar on my chest pulsed. I did a slow check, but nothing appeared threatening. I drove through Sandymount village and along the Strand Road, the lights of Dun Laoghaire and Killiney glittering ahead in the late evening dusk.

The commuter rush was over and traffic was light as I reached the DART rail level crossing. The signal lights began to flash Barriers Down for an oncoming train as I got across the tracks and took the Rock Road to Glenageary and home.

34

DEATH ON TRACK

'This is a bloody stupid way to be doin' it. Why don't we take him at the house?' said Flynn, making his point for the fourth time with slightly different words.

'And like I've told you,' responded Wyse tolerantly. 'This is how Larry wants it. The house is no go. Some yo-yo got himself mauled there last week by a rabid dog or something. The cops are still showing a presence and we don't want them stopping us and peering inside the van and asking, "Oi, what's this?" when they see the gear. We follow him home, bump him on the way, he gets out his car, quick grab and we're in business.'

'Why not here, quick lift and away?'

Wyse sighed. 'Too risky. He leaves same time as the others. Plus, you can see the car park is too well lit. All those windows.'

There were five of them in the blue Toyota Hiace van parked in shadow in a laneway at the rear of Merrion Square, close to the private car park they had in view. Four had flown in from London early that morning and had spent most of the day in reconnaissance, checking the place in Glenageary and the route from Merrion Square. They'd make the hit in the evening and, all going well, they'd be home next morning. A tidy job, the kind Wyse had done more than once, though first time in Ireland.

He wondered why Larry didn't have local muscle on tap for this. It didn't bother him, because the pay was sweet. Usually, they took orders from Quinn, but Quinn was out of action, and he assumed this operation was payback.

Wyse thought Larry had sounded odd, voice coarse and edgy, when he'd ordered him to drop what he was doing, pull together a team, fly to Dublin straightaway. Eliminate this guy and dispose of the body so it's never found. Larry's shadow, Jackie Ronayne, met them at the airport, gave them their instructions and introduced Mick O'Keane, an experienced local wheel-man.

Jason Wyse ran a small London-based company, Loks-Guard Security Services, that provided security and personnel to businesses, including those owned overtly and covertly by the Brenners. LoksGuard was itself in the latter category and, when Larry said 'straightaway', Wyse didn't wait around. He had picked three for the job. Maurice Cookle was reliable. The other two, Ed Flynn and T.J. Bell were the best he could lay hands on right away – not top drawer but adequate. In his view, it needed only himself and O'Keane, plus one other at most but Larry had insisted on a full team.

The hammers were in an open toolbox in the van with the manacles, heavy-duty builder's hammers, with which they would break a selection of bones in the target's body before killing him, preferably while he remained conscious. When

Wyse objected, Larry doubled the fee and added a bonus. No more arguing. Wyse thought he'd been watching too many episodes of *Mafiosa* and the like, but he kept that to himself.

After dropping the others at a commercial hotel in the city centre, Ronayne took Wyse to the Clayton Hotel in Ballsbridge for lunch. He showed him a photograph of the target – Kieran Sheridan, early thirties, in an off-the-peg shiny blue suit, dark blond, fresh-faced, hair falling over his forehead, flabby, glasses, pussy look to him. Ronayne apologised for the photo. 'It's fairly recent, but the mark had a car accident last month and got cut. I'm told his appearance may be a bit different.'

'It'll do,' said Wyse.

'He's single, works in Larry's advertising company. Lives in part of an old house in Glenageary, out in the suburbs. Drives an old Jag, S-type, silver.'

'He won't be a problem.'

Wyse figured him for a son or brother who was being taken out as a tit-for-tat. Not that it meant a flying fuckwit to him.

'Easy-peasy,' said Ronayne. 'He has no protection and isn't expecting anyone to go after him.'

Then why not do him yourselves, thought Wyse.

Cookle, who had been sitting in back, with a view out the front, murmured, 'Thar he blows.'

Three men emerged from the rear door of an office building and strolled into the car park. They shared a basic similarity that briefly confused Wyse for a moment. In their thirties, in business suits and busy in conversation. The one on the left resembled the mark in the photograph. Yet, he didn't quite match the picture, being taller, thinner, indefinably different. It was Kieran Sheridan, though, because he made for the Silver Jaguar, got inside and pulled away.

Wyse had no more than a brief glimpse of Sheridan but instantly experienced a burst of bitter animosity towards him, as though unexpectedly sighting a life-threatening enemy. It struck him forcibly that, for his own survival and, yes, satisfaction, this man had to die. As the thought swept over him, he was astonished at the sheer intensity of his reaction. Puzzled, he shrugged it off with an effort.

O'Keane, without a word, had shifted gears and was following the Jaguar as it drove out onto Holles Street, left at the Maternity Hospital, up Lower Mount Street, over the Canal and on to Ballsbridge, past the American Embassy. Traffic was moderately busy and O'Keane let a few cars get between him and Sheridan.

He said, in response to an unspoken question, 'We won't lose him, he's going straight home.' Then, 'Ah, bollocks, he's not,' as the Jaguar's indicator flashed and it took the inner lane past the sprawling new Facebook campus and onto Serpentine Avenue. O'Keane followed. There was one car between them at the rail level crossing, lights flashing and barriers down, while they waited for a DART commuter train to pass. Then they were behind the Jaguar and making for Sandymount.

'Know where he's going?' asked Wyse, without concern.

'Nope,' replied O'Keane. 'I'm with him, wherever he goes.' In the back, the others squatted on a pair of wooden benches, discussing an ongoing murder trial in the Old Bailey. Ten minutes later, they watched Sheridan park the Jag at an apartment block, get out and wave to an Audi that had pulled up, as well as a motorcyclist, and go inside the building.

'What are they up to?' asked Flynn from the back.

'A meeting, obviously,' replied Wyse, ever patient. 'We wait.'

'Good a place as any to finish the job,' groused Flynn. Anyone else, it might have been nerves, but Flynn was a natural born kvetch.

A second Audi arrived and a woman in blue jacket and jeans got out and went into the same apartment block. A minute later, another car, Merc, more people. Social get-together, it seemed.

The evening had darkened when they emerged ninety minutes later, talking, backslapping and handshaking. Sheridan drove off. O'Keane waited thirty seconds and followed. He knew the area well and figured where the Jaguar was going. They went through Sandymount Green and onto Strand Road, the sea on their left, heading south to Dun Laoghaire and Glenageary. Rush hour traffic had peaked and a small stream of cars was travelling in the opposite direction towards the city centre or the Northside. O'Keane kept a black Toyota between him and the Jaguar.

At the Martello Tower, the Toyota signalled a right and waited for an opening in the oncoming traffic. No one slowed and there wasn't room to pass. O'Keane swore under his breath as the Jaguar put distance between them. 'We'll catch up,' he murmured.

Finally, the Toyota got to make its turn and O'Keane hit the accelerator. As they got to the bend that led to the DART level crossing onto the Rock Road, he growled with annoyance as he was halted by the flashing lights. The barriers were already down.

'Still think you'll catch him?' Wyse asked quietly. He didn't want Flynn butting in with querulous remarks.

'Yeah. The DART comes through quick enough. We'll be on his tail by Temple Road.'

That meant nothing to Wyse, but he noticed O'Keane drumming impatiently on the wheel and was about to say something, when the Hiace started to move forward slowly.

O'Keane gave an exclamation, slammed a foot on the brake and grabbed the handbrake to find it already full on. He flashed a glance in the wing mirror, to see if another vehicle might be shunting them from behind. But the nearest car was only now turning into the bend.

In the corner of the mirror, he saw white smoke rising from the tyres as the car was propelled forward. O'Keane stood hard on the brake. It made no difference. The van continued to slither reluctantly, as if on an ice-covered incline, though the ground was dry and flat. The white and red timber barrier bent and smashed as the van slid forward until it was athwart the tracks. There, it stopped.

'What the hell?' said Wyse as he saw, across from O'Keane, looming large through the side window, the green bulk of a DART as it rushed towards them. Death was certain and before his mind took that in, the train hit the van broadside, tossed it into the air and exploded it into hundreds of pieces of metal, engine parts, glass and human beings.

The three in the back were trying to figure the juddering and the thunderous sound when their world ended. The truncated body of the Hiace, spraying chunks and fragments, hurtled onto the tracks in a great shower of debris and somersaulted several times before stopping.

The driver of a DART coming from the opposite direction got a spectacular show. He applied the emergency brake, bringing his train to a screeching, shuddering halt, giving a glancing blow to the van, a massive lump of crushed metal and sending it, shuttlecock-like, back along the tracks into the first train. He was in shock and his first thought was that this was going to mean a wretched time for commuters the following morning, with the track filled with debris, the trains off and the crossing closed for the day.

35

DÉJÀ VU TIME YET AGAIN

'It's *déjà vu* time,' proclaimed Inspector Breen cheerfully as he walked into my office, just as Molly buzzed that he was in reception asking for me. Never a man to sit and wait for an invitation.

'Yet again,' I said. I was tempted to add that '*déjà vu*' did not mean, as he seemed to think, 'here we go again'.

'Indeed, a Mhic, boredom rarely sets in when you feature among the leading dramatis personae.'

'I am but an extra in this play, a humble spear-carrier, Insp – Dan,'

He hooked his gabardine raincoat on the coat hanger and took a chair across from me.

'By the way, I found that flick, *The Exorcist*, on Netflix. It had its moments. So, you think I'm Lee J. Cobb?'

'Now that you push me on it, only in appearance.'

'Enough of this badinage. Congratulations are in order. I'm told you've been voted the big kahuna of this advertising company.'

I tried to act humble, wondering who had told him. 'Not

quite. I've been acting CEO since Cronin died. It's a hollow crown.'

He gave me a sceptical look.

'Any update on Quinn's condition?' I asked. 'He remains on the critical list, I gather. The hospital is like your Sergeant O'Hanlon, reticent to the point of taciturnity.'

'He remains in a coma. Quinn Brenner, that is. The prognosis is positive and he'll pull through, though he may be in wheels for the rest of his life. A hard penance for a big, active fellow. Still, it's God's own mercy he's survived at all.'

He steepled his hands as if in prayer. 'We do say the same about you, don't we? Anyway, what happened to Quinn is yet another mysterious accident. I'm a long time in this job and I've never been involved in an impossible event. Now there's two.'

'Two? Ah, you've still no idea who or what killed the burglar at my home. No lair of wild animals discovered?'

'Investigation is ongoing, though it's not my case, happily. Let's talk of what happened to Mr Brenner, which doesn't make sense either.'

I was puzzled. What did he mean, it was not his case? He seemed to be always only peripherally involved in any Garda matter related to me.

I said, 'As Sherlock Holmes observed, "When you have eliminated the impossible –"'

'Yes, I've heard that one,' he said shortly. 'Since you mention crime fiction, this has the flavour of one of those old locked-room mysteries I used to read, John Dickson Carr, Ellery Queen, that mob. Ever read them? No? They passed the time, though realism was never their forte.'

I resisted sharing the fact that the originator of the locked-room mystery story was none other than my putative kinsman, Sheridan Le Fanu.

Breen stood and crossed the room to examine a satellite map of Dublin on the wall, leaning in to study the detail. His back to me, he said, 'The stumper is this. You left Quinn Brenner alone in his office and young Danny Ryan, in his statement, says he saw you leave, and had the office door in sight the whole time, heard Quinn on the phone, conversing with someone in the room. Next thing, he hears the window flung open and Brenner's scream as he was thrown out of it.'

'Surely a fall?' I protested, though without conviction.

He snorted and faced me.

'No, we're certain he was hurled out and with considerable force. That's what likely saved his life: a fall, or even a jump, would have taken him into the concrete basement. As it was, he was launched with such force he sailed beyond the basement area and landed among a great pile of garbage bags and cardboard boxes by the railings. Still a heavy fall, though.'

I attempted a mental image of big Quinn being lifted aloft and flung out the window.

'Dan, I couldn't imagine anyone being able to do it. Did you ever meet Quinn?'

'I've seen him in the hospital.'

'Well, you'll know he is, or was, a heavyweight rugger bugger, capped for Ireland. He would have made one mother of a fight. Yet I saw his office that night. There were no signs of a struggle, no upturned furniture, broken glass, no blood.'

He sat heavily. 'And a bay window that couldn't be opened because it was caked in multiple coats of dried paint.

How do you account for that?'

'Me? I don't. Your job, not mine, I'm glad to say.'

He snorted again.

'A rhetorical question. I'll admit I'm disappointed, though. I'd expect more from advertising fellas such as yourself whose stock in trade is ideas and imagination. So be it. Leaving aside the supernatural, we've reviewed a few possibilities.'

He ticked them off on his fingers.

'One, there was an alternative means of entry and exit. We've checked and there's none. Two, when you left, another person or persons entered the room by the window, succeeded in overpowering Quinn while leaving no signs of a struggle, launched him into the night and exited the same way. Again, not remotely possible. Too high and how could a fastened window be opened from the outside?'

Now he was sounding like Hercule Poirot or Adam Dalgleish addressing the assembly of suspects in the drawing room.

'Three, a conspiracy involving you and Danny and the other chap, Paul Walsh – you're collectively lying and either threw out Quinn between you or you had an accomplice, a large accomplice, you let into the office.'

He shot me a mock questioning look.

I shook my head regretfully and offered, 'Four, someone slipped into Quinn's office before Danny came onto the stairs, an exceptionally strong person, as you say, who forced open the window and threw Quinn out, hid in the room until Danny and Paul had come and gone, and made his way out.'

Breen sighed. 'Nowhere to hide when the two boys opened Quinn's door.'

'Well,' I said. 'There's a story by Edgar Allen Poe about murders committed with superhuman violence. The murderer was a trained gorilla.'

'Another wild animal?' he sniffed.

'Absurd, of course,' I retorted. 'Apropos, did your men find the beast that mauled the burglar to death yet?'

His eyebrows came together in a frown. 'That's the other damn mystery, isn't it, a Mhic? The veterinary experts are in no doubt the wounds were inflicted with animal teeth and claws, by a single animal they can't readily classify.'

Again I asked myself, why was he telling me all this?

'A lynx, perhaps?' I asked, sardonically. 'It's on the news that a lynx escaped a wildlife park in Wales recently.'

'And what? Swam across the Irish Sea and set up home in your place?'

'Okay, another newsflash for you. An eighty-two-year-old woman in Japan was found bleeding profusely from numerous deep cuts all over her body. Police thought it was a sword-wielding lunatic before they realised it was a stray cat.'

He barked a laugh.

'Dundan wasn't killed by a stray cat. Or the cat on the hood of your Jag. Or one of the decrepit lions on your gatepost.' He became serious. 'The other inconsistency is that the killer, animal or human, left no evidence whatever and, in particular, no tracks, no scats, of any kind in the house, on the ground or walls where the attack occurred. You'd think it was impossible for an animal not to leave any trace.'

He waited, as though expecting an answer. I thought again he was being unusually confiding.

He said in an offhand tone, 'On a different subject, there's that dreadful tragedy at the Merrion Gates on Tuesday night. The transit van hit by a DART and five men killed instantly.'

'Yes, it's been a big news story. Shook me. I drove home by the Merrion Gates around the same time that evening.'

'We've examined CCTV footage of the accident. Can't tell why the van crashed the barrier and ended on the tracks in front of an oncoming DART. Yet another bloody mystery. Immediately prior to the accident, the final car that went through the crossing before the barriers dropped was a Silver Jaguar S-type.'

'That was me, I'd expect. I wasn't aware, naturally, that I was last to cross before the crash.'

'Did you know any of the men?'

'You mean those who died?' I was surprised. 'No.'

'Coincidence, huh. Again.'

'Now that you talk of coincidence, call me paranoid but how come you happen to be working cases where I make even a minimal appearance?'

'And a lot of them too, don't you think?' He rubbed his temple. 'Could be I've been asked to keep an eye on you. Bad luck and tragedy follow you around, don't they? You're front-seat passenger in a car crash where your boss is killed outright. You're the last person to meet with your new boss before he is thrown out his office window. A burglar enters your home and dies with great violence. Five men die when a DART hits their van, and yours is the last car over the crossing before it happens.'

And five more dead at Baggot Street Bridge, I thought. Jeezus, the bodies are piling up around me. When I said nothing, Breen sighed, stood and collected his gabardine.

'Always a pleasure talking to you, Kieran. Won't be the last time, I'm sure. I may even learn something one day. Go forth with care. Your company has been decidedly unlucky with its CEOs. First, your uncle, Jasper Sheridan, missing presumed drowned. Then Cronin killed in the car crash. Now Quinn. It's like that Agatha Christie story, *Ten Little Whatsits*. Remember how it ended: *And Then There Were None*.'

'You do relish tossing off the last word,' I said, but I was talking to the door.

A few days later, newspapers carried the discovery of the bodies of four men bludgeoned to death in the undergrowth of an office garden in Lower Baggot Street, where they had lain unnoticed for several days until the odour of death in the air brought them to notice. Their names were being withheld for the present.

One of the tabloid websites added some speculation about gang warfare or a drugs deal gone bad, an increasing cause of violent death in Dublin. A separate single-paragraph item reported that the body of an unidentified man had been taken from the Canal Lock at Baggot Street Bridge. The reports did not connect the two stories.

My mind went back to that freezing cold, rain-drenched heart-lurching night, slinking to my car through the lanes and shadows. There was nothing in those deaths that could point to me. It would have been no surprise, though, to get another courtesy call from Dan Breen on the basis I might be involved with any outlandish fatalities in his patch.

36

THE RAGE OF LARRY

Tara dropped into my office to let me know me that Larry Brenner had asked for, or more likely ordered, a meeting with me next day in the ground floor reception area of St Vincent's Private Hospital. Quinn had undergone further emergency surgery and remained on the critical list. Larry was spending most of his time at the hospital during the day and had taken a suite in the nearby InterContinental Hotel at nights.

'I fear I'm not a friend of the family anymore,' said Tara ruefully. 'I made a positive remark about you and got such a chilling glare. You really want to do this meeting? Larry's unpredictable at the best of times and he's under enormous strain. Hasn't been the same since Cronin's death. Serious advice, Kieran: don't stand too close to him.'

The public area of St Vincent's Private Hospital was big-hotel style, with a cavernous atrium reception area, snazzy restaurant and café, anodyne abstracts on the walls, lots of well-cushioned seating, calm efficiency, staff and patients going about without rush or fuss.

Larry sat alone in an armchair in a corner of the reception

area, looking worn and diminished, arms folded, gazing into space. When I reached him, he glared at me, and with an impatient bark of 'Sit', gestured to a seat opposite him. I stifled a biting rejoinder, reminding myself he was still physically and emotionally battered. Besides, I didn't have to offer my hand and get a rebuff. It was odd, my meeting him like this. For three years, he had owned the agency where I was account director, and we had never once met or communicated.

He was a small man, about five-six, with a rosacea red face and quiffed-up silvery hair. Known as a natty dresser, he was now unkempt, like he'd spent the night grappling in the ring with all-comers. His suit was creased and crumpled, he was tieless, and his shirt collar was undone and twisted. Spots of blood dotted his nostrils; he hadn't shaved or showered lately and I caught a whiff of body odour when he shifted in his seat. He was blinking a lot and badly needed sleep.

'How is Quinn?' I tried for a sympathetic tone. He brushed it aside.

'He's broken, he is. But don't celebrate yet. He'll be back on top soon enough.' Without a pause, 'You see yourself running my company, eh?'

'Sorry to intrude on your privacy at this time. I wanted to tell you personally rather than have you read it in the media.'

A raw rage came in his eyes, though exhaustion took away much of its strength. His cheeks clenched, and his hands shook, even as he kept his voice level. 'How bloody royal of you. And telling me, not asking me, eh? Well, let me tell you, boyo. Forget acting CEO. Acting my bollocks. Before you're a great deal older, you will learn you are not taking over my agency. As of this minute, in fact, you're fired. Out.'

This last with a shout.

I shook my head. 'You'd better accept it's a fait accompli and I'm the CEO. The board took a unanimous decision and we're announcing it Friday.'

'Board, is it? You dumbshit fucks, all of you,' he shouted.

Any thought of exercising delicacy towards an old man suffering through the possible loss of a second son vanished. I was confronting pure malice, quite possibly implanted by my late tormentor.

Spittle flew out of his mouth. He saw it and was embarrassed.

'Can I get you a spittoon?' I asked.

A cheap shot at an easy target. I wasn't focussed on Larry now but on the vindictiveness in him. He stood abruptly and leaned over me, invading my space. It took an effort for me not to slink down in my seat.

'Don't try that line with me, boyo, or you'll regret it. I've taken on far bigger men than you, real men, and you're not even in the ha'penny place. Listen: I own the company, I do the deciding and I'll be sending you all an official note that the so-called board is abolished. Charley Maughan is now CEO and Chairman.'

He stopped, breathing hard, hands scratching and scuffing the top of the leather seat.

'Larry, I know you've got things on your mind,' I said in a pleasant voice, knowing it would grate on him. 'I'm the CEO of Aardvark-Sheridan. If you interfere, the brown solids are going to hit you with an unsightly splosh. The financial skimming that goes on will damage the agency and damage you worse. It will create massive waves of humiliation for the

Brenner name and family, including Cronin's legacy, and ditto for your friends and you'll have to explain to Rory McGorrick how you put him in the public eye.'

Larry jerked back as though I'd thrown a karate chop. Tiredness slowed his response, and his face had a confused expression. Finally, he growled, 'None of that matters a damn. What does matter is you killed Cronin and crippled Quinn, you bastard. You don't get away with that.'

Exasperated, I snapped, 'I'm no more responsible for what happened to Cronin and Quinn than you are for Jasper Sheridan.'

I'm not sure why I said it. It wasn't even a shot in the dark. Larry's eyes bulged, and he lurched back again as though I'd slapped him hard.

'Don't talk twaddle.'

In a flash of understanding, I realised Larry Brenner may have had a hand in the vanishment of Jasper, who may not have accidentally fallen into the waters of the Shannon and was probably not leading a pampered life in an opulent condo in a sun-saturated haven.

'That's getting a public airing, too, and a cold case investigation,' I said, spur-of-the-moment bluffing.

His unpleasant odour became stronger and wafted at me in waves. I heard the grinding of his teeth as I stood.

'We can talk again when the pressure is off, Larry. Meantime, you take care of Quinn, he's going to need you.'

I intended it as a well-meaning parting comment. Larry took it as a threat. He jumped up. 'What do you mean? Screw you, what do you mean?' He was yelling now, spittle spraying his surrounds. People stopped to look. I moved away from him fast.

He screamed, 'You come around here threatening my boy? You want to take me on? You want –'

His face empurpled with rage, he was blowing hard. I thought he was about to have a stroke. I didn't wait to find out and headed downstairs to the car park, his curses following me. As I pushed a note into the parking meter at the entrance, I thought I heard footsteps coming down the stairs, but nobody appeared. I reckoned Larry was not going to abandon his hatred towards me. As soon as Quinn was off the critical list, his fevered mind would revert to thoughts of how best to take care of me in the worst possible way. I couldn't have cared less.

37

THE OCCULTIST

'"Chillax!" Can you believe it?' Lucy Shaw's indignation gave way to a chortle. 'Who could imagine that, in today's competitive marketplace, the managing director of a major advertiser, a supposedly sophisticated executive, an MBA no less, would invite his fourteen-year-old son to name a brand of tea? And he gives us "Chillax" and Dad loves it. "Enjoy a tasty, nourishing cup of hot Chillax". *Gott in Himmel!*'

'Doesn't quite hit the spot,' I agreed.

It was late afternoon and Lucy was driving us from a session with Noel Bracken, boss of OB Beverages Ireland, a thriving importer of teas, coffees and juices with headquarters in an industrial estate in North Dublin. The meeting had generally gone well. While we contrived polite enthusiasm for the name proposed by his son, we persuaded a reluctant Bracken to sign off on brand name testing.

'How can anyone work in these soulless factory-cum-office estates?' said Lucy, indicating the vista of concrete and glass identikit buildings we were passing. 'Remember when OB had that elegant place in Ranelagh and then unloaded it before the market began to slide. Now, they are in a brutal building, surrounded by brutal buildings. Soul shrivelling.'

OB Beverages was not my client and when Lucy had invited me to what was a routine meeting she was letting me know that, for the present, she was prepared to accept me as the agency's acting CEO and was introducing me to her key clients.

We drove in silence towards the city centre, past rundown offices and showrooms and takeaways that were dilapidated or tatty or both. It struck me how shabbily people dressed these days, shades of black to grey, and where there was colour it was dull and faded. It was like everyone dressed in jeans plus whatever they could find in a charity clothes shop. Dreary clothes, dreary buildings, dreary lives, dreary world.

Lucy was saying, 'So, what are you reading these days?'

'I'm re-reading the supernatural stories of Sheridan Le Fanu. I find we have a connection, an affinity of sorts. Haven't read them since I was a teenager and I'd forgotten how fascinating and morbidly gripping they are, especially those based in Dublin of old. I'm also indulging in the perfuméd literary delights of the Victorian romantics, Dante Gabriel Rossetti, for one.'

'How imprévu. I'd never have guessed your bookish inclinations leaned that way. Rossetti, huh? Did you know that, when his wife, Lizzie Siddal, died from an overdose, he was so overcome with grief he placed his unpublished poems in her coffin? And, later, when he had second thoughts, he had to get the Home Secretary's okay to dig her up and get his verses back so he could publish them.'

'Maybe he reckoned she'd had them to herself for long enough.'

'Here's another piece of trivia. When Michael Collins was killed in Bealnablath, they found a book of Rossetti's poetry in his pocket, given to him by Lady Lavery, his alleged lover.'

'You're a veritable Lucipedia. While we're on the subject of books, I see your new one is out.' Her latest novel, a romantic crime caper, was in bookshops. She hadn't yet hit the big time but expected it would happen soon.

'The launch party is next Friday. We're doing it in that colossal public library in Dun Laoghaire. the LexIcon. I've set a scene there.'

I thought she might feel obliged out of politeness to invite me to the opening but she didn't.

We went by the stretch of quayside modern corporate offices that make up the International Financial Services Centre and crossed over the Liffey to regain the Southside at Matt Talbot Bridge, named for the reformed alcoholic and devoutly religious workingman who was once accused of strike-breaking. Hence Scab Bridge, its popular name among Dubliners.

'What started you on your career as a novelist?' I asked, making an effort at conversation.

'Other bestselling authors, the likes of Ayn Rand, James Patterson and John Grisham. If such putrid writing could sell millions, I figured I was in with a chance."

'Sounds reasonable.'

She laughed. 'My aunt Maebeth is of the opinion that writers of fiction, with few exceptions, have one decent book in them and, once it's out of their system, they should quit.'

'That's assuming the first book happens to be the decent one.'

'Aunt Maebeth practises what she preaches. Years ago, she commenced *Enduring Passions*, which, I understand, from various hints, is a romantic novel of Ireland at the turn of the last century, from the time of the Boer War, through the Great War, the War of Independence and the Civil War.'

'An Irish *War and Peace*?' I hazarded.

'Or an Irish *Jalna*. You read any of the *Jalna* books? Mazo de la Roche, Canadian. Highly popular once, now out of print. It took Aunt Maebeth ten years to write her novel and, soon as it was finished, she began revising and polishing and has been at it ever since, burnishing the writing, changing scenes, giving characters more backstories and flashbacks and introducing new ones. She still works on it several hours most days and intends to continue until she dies, when it may be published posthumously.'

'How old is she?'

'Eighty-one. She has a delightful little rose cottage in Wexford by the sea, and lives mostly in the people and events she has created. Not the worst of ways in which to spend one's twilight years. Perhaps it will be her destiny to spend her afterlife in the world of *Enduring Passions* that she is creating in loving detail.'

As we reached Ringsend, Lucy said, 'You know Eoin Sullivan, sales manager for Matheson Cider?'

Offhand, I couldn't place him, though he was one of our clients. When I shook my head, she said, 'Surely you know him? Tall, thin, uncanny resemblance to Steven Seagal in his heyday, except he has one glass eye, skiing accident.'

'Still don't know him,' I said grinning.

'What's so amusing?' she asked.

'Don't you know what Sullivan is in Irish? One-eye.'

She smiled politely. 'Very droll, m'Lud. Anyway, Eoin goes horse riding in the Wicklow hills at weekends. Last Sunday, he saved a young girl's life. She took a fall off her horse and tumbled into a river and he came by in time to dive in and pull her out and give her CPR.'

'Good for him,' I said absently.

'I had a meeting with him yesterday,' she went on. 'He was telling me of a weekend think-in he organised for his sales team, about twenty of them last month. They stayed at a place called Churchward Manor, near Glendalough. It specialises in corporate getaways: top-notch accommodation, good food and drink, golf course not far away, classy meeting rooms, think-ins, rah-rah sessions. Pricey but worth it, I gather.'

'Hmm. Should we do something similar for the agency?'

She considered it. 'Possibly. But that's not why I mention it. Eoin had a conversation with the owner of the place, a Mr D'Auvencour. Multi-talented chap, successful business owner, management consultant, professional hypnotherapist, and an occultist no less.'

'An eye specialist?'

She gave a mock sigh. 'Not an oculist, dummy, occultist, a practitioner of the occult: the dark arts.'

'Dark arse, more likely,' I snorted. It was a subject that made me uneasy, given my encounters with the late unlamented Bum Farto, the wannabe Nikromantzer and his AngelBeest. 'Conjures up hooded figures dancing naked around a bonfire at midnight, looking forward to the sex orgy. One way for companies to build teamwork.'

'No, none of that carry-on. Very professional. Anyway, he

was having a glass of wine with D'Auvencour who remarked in passing how terrible it was that two young people, his guests at the Manor a few weeks back, had died in a horrific car crash in Ballsbridge.'

It was as if someone slammed a fist into my chest. Lucy slowed down. 'You okay, Kieran? How absolutely stupid of me. You've looking somewhat green around the gills. Sorry, I shouldn't have dropped a reminder of the crash on you so crudely. I didn't mean to –'

'I'm okay,' I said, though I wasn't. 'Not to cut across you, Lucy, what do you know about Churchward Manor?'

'Only what I've told you. Eoin was going on about the sales pep talks and the brainstorming and so forth, and then he mentioned the couple in the crash.'

'Was anything said about them? Who they were? What they were doing there?' I tried to keep it casual.

'I presume they were on a corporate confab. Come to think of it, Eoin told me D'Auvencour said one odd thing.'

She gave me another quick glance and hesitated.

'Go on,' I urged.

'He said that they should never have been together in the car that night. He didn't go into details or offer an explanation but he insisted it had all been his fault and a dreadful error of judgment.'

38

DIES IRAE

I'm the only person who truly knows how Cronin died, thought Larry Brenner. He'd heard it from Cronin's own lips, his last words heard on his Smartphone. Kieran Sheridan had killed Cronin, and a month later, in some diabolical manner, Sheridan had caught Quinn with his guard down and sent him plunging from his office window. Now, the slimy streak of piss had openly announced his ambition to seize Larry's agency for himself.

He pictured Sheridan, grinning with gleeful triumph at how he had brutalised his sons, killing one, mutilating the other. Did that not justify a father's wrath and righteous vengeance?

Early afternoon, his own snoring and snorting had brought Larry out of a sleepless doze with a jerk. The back of his head had been pressing on an uncomfortable visitor's chair in the private ward, his stockinged feet resting on Quinn's bed. He ignored a vicious ache in his neck and tears filled his eyes at the sight of his powerhouse son now wracked and vulnerable, bundled in bandages, both his mummified legs raised on wire contraptions. He was sleeping, unmoving, hardly making a sound, his face sickly pale and without expression.

Larry left the private ward with a curt nod to the paid security guard at the door. Back in his hotel suite, he showered, shaved and changed into fresh clothes for the first time in several days. In the mirror, he saw a new hardness in his grim features, hatred in his bloodshot eyes for that murderous shit bastard.

In another part of his mind, he sensed he was not thinking rationally. He asked himself if what happened to Cronin and Quinn, in such short order, hadn't made him a little crazy. Larry was not a hater by nature and considered it inefficient. If people got in his way, he bought them off and if that didn't do it, he'd have them taken out, though there was little of that nowadays. Strong personal emotions were indulgences that had no place in business. Sheridan was an exception.

Earlier in the week, he had been frustratingly close to making an end to him. Standing in the hospital's waiting area cursing him volubly, oblivious to people passing by, he watched impotently as the bastard turned his back on him and coolly walked off. It came to him that this was as good a time as any to act. He waited until Sheridan was out of sight on the stairwell to the car park a floor below and followed. As he made his way down the stairs, Larry reached in his pocket for the penknife he always carried. Not much of a stabbing weapon, but razor-sharp lethal in slitting a throat.

He glanced quickly into the vestibule. Sheridan was alone, oblivious, feeding the ticket machine. It was a sin against nature not to kill him as the chance presented itself. Larry slipped the penknife out of his pocket, took a step forward and a hand was on his shoulder, pulling him back, and a voice whispered, 'No.'

Jackie Ronayne, his man for all seasons and purposes, ever present and unobtrusive, had arrived at the hospital to visit Quinn and observed Larry and Sheridan from the far side of the waiting area. When he saw Larry follow Sheridan, hand inside his jacket, he figured his intention and followed. Now, he held him, murmuring, '*Beidh lá eile ag an bPaorach.*' There'll be another day, another opportunity.

Larry had turned on him, furious, clenching the knife. Then the energy drained out of him and he slumped dazed against Ronayne. 'It's not right, Jackie. It's not right he's free to –'

He'd pulled himself together and allowed Ronayne to lead him back to the stairway.

Larry thought of how close he had been to finishing it and he wished now that Ronayne had not intervened. Sure, he would have been caught in the aftermath, with Sheridan's blood spattered all over him as he stood over the convulsing body in the neon-lit vestibule. He wouldn't have run, wouldn't have given a damn what they did to him. Besides, no jury would find him guilty of murder for avenging what Sheridan had done to his sons.

He paged Ronayne to collect him with the Range Rover. They drove towards the city centre, along dilapidated Pearse Street, across the Liffey at Butt Bridge, across rundown Gardiner Street and through seedy Parnell Street.

Ronayne had the wheel and Larry sat alongside as usual and gave a running commentary on the dingy condition of the streets and shops and cafes they passed, how it was a disgrace seeing that they were around the corner from Dublin's main thoroughfare and the General Post Office, birthplace of Ireland's fight for independence.

'These shop signs,' he groused. 'Chinese, Paki, Indian, Nigerians, Viet Cong, who knows what. No end to them. And now the EU is pushing us into taking in thousands of refugees, ay-rabs.' He scowled. 'Am I right or what?'

He wasn't seeking a response. Ronayne murmured what might have been agreement.

They parked in the big ILAC Shopping Centre in Parnell Street and walked a few blocks to a side lane at the rear of nearby North King Street. A red and blue lorry went by, three men in green work jackets squatting on the flatbed, impassive, looked at them incuriously. Larry gave them a cold stare and he passed and muttered something to Ronayne.

They stopped at a bustling open warehouse, large vans and small pick-ups and SUVs disgorging and taking on merchandise, yellow-jacketed and white-hatted men loading and unloading, forklifts shunting and beeping. Inside, aisles of storage shelves reached to the roof packed with boxes, cartons, steel drums and plastic cases.

A sign over the open bay read *AllHomeway DIY. Distribution Point North. Strictly Trade Only*. AllHomeway was a business interest of the McGorrick family.

A side wall was plastered with printed and handwritten safety and warning notices: NO UNATTENDED VEHICLES, NO TRESPASSING, SIGN IN FIRST, HARD HAT AT ALL TIMES, WEAR GOGGLES, DON'T PISS ON THE WALL. There were steps to a steel door with a CCTV camera above it that swung back and forth with irregular jerks. Other cameras on the roof covered nearby lanes and alleys. A worker, big, shaven-skulled, acknowledged Brenner and Ronayne with a scowl and a lazy salute, pressed a bell once, twice, once again, and went back to the warehouse, leaving them to wait.

After a minute, there was a thud of automatic bars sliding across inside and the door opened. They walked into a small empty space with whitewashed walls, a flight of hard stone stairs and a still camera overhead. They left the mantrap and climbed stone stairs, where a further steel door opened and they were in a large grungy room, furniture cheap and broken, walls badly painted in olive green, streaked with brown tobacco stains. The floor was bare and well-trodden. On one side, wire mesh frosted glass windows gave a multicoloured pointillist impression of the warehouse interior below. A barred wooden door opened onto metal stairs that led to the warehouse floor.

There were eight men in the room. Two heavies in tee-shirt, leather jacket and jeans sat on a worn settee. One stood and gave a you-know-the-drill gesture to Larry and Ronayne, who raised their arms and were frisked. The others took no notice. Two were sitting at cheap school desks, talking into mobile phones. Three were at a long metal table that had seen better days, putting small white packages into cardboard boxes. Larry recognised two of them, red crew-cuts, late teens, as McGorrick kids, Diarmuid and Fionn.

A bantam of a man with a broken nose in a light grey pinstripe suit stood in front of a door at the rear, mobile phone in his hand. He waved Larry forward. Ronayne stayed and looked out the window onto a view of rooftops and cabinets of electrical equipment. This being where it was in Dublin, the windows were iron barred.

Larry was ushered into a more comfortable room, an office of sorts. Not the kind any self-respecting businessman would use to impress clients or hold court but there had been a half-hearted attempt to make it presentable. The wallpaper had an embossed flower pattern and there was an off-white shag carpet. Sophistication was blown by an old *Playboy* centrefold tacked onto the wall, on which someone had used an official rubber stamp: 'Examined. Opened. Entered.'

Rory McGorrick sprawled in an imitation leather executive chair behind an L-shaped pine desk with matching filing cabinet and side tables that probably came from a business liquidation sale. Two men sat hunched on a beat-up settee. Larry recognised Connell, McGorrick's eldest son, heavy-browed, knife scar across his left cheek. The other was a skinny teenager, probably another of Rory's kids. He had the McGorrick red hair and a fluffy orange moustache. McGorrick was smoking a thin cigar and drinking from a Starbucks paper cup. He was a large fat man, ruddy-faced, with a few pale clumps of red hair over each ear, small eyes, thin lips. A scary man, who knew it and made the most of it. He wore a crumpled linen suit. His shirt, open to the navel, showed an old-fashioned string vest.

'Sit, Larry, old sod,' he commanded genially. The Belfast accent was thick enough to bottle. 'You know Connell and Dathi.' He waved in their direction. Larry nodded to them but gave his attention to McGorrick.

McGorrick took a long pull of his cigar and coughed. 'Hard times, these. There's a war in progress in this town, as you'll have read in the papers, which get the facts wrong, as ever. It's not of my making. Some people have desired to meet their Maker because they won't listen to what's in their best interests. We've had casualties, yes. As of last night, the scoreline is seven-two in our favour. Regarding nothing important, have you had any word from our mutual colleague, Barry Owens?'

Larry frowned at the non sequitur. 'Wasn't expecting to. Haven't dealt direct with him personally for a while.'

'I thought he'd be in touch, like. You see, friend Barry has a heavy dose of the blahs. He sent word he needed a few days' leave, rented a holiday home in Odense, he says. That's in Denmark, of all places. Hasn't been seen there. See you soon, said he. He surely will, one way or t'other.'

When Larry made no comment, McGorrick forced his face into a brief facsimile of concern. 'Sorry re Quinn and doubly sorry to be dragging you from the hospital. How's he making out?'

He waved his question aside, not interested. 'We have to talk business. Here's the fucking thing, Larry, *a cara dilis*, my good friend, here's what I'm finding it hard to understand. That advertising company of yours has been holding a goodly sum of my cash – my cash, right? – that shoulda been paid out ten days ago, and only got to Belfast yesterday. You said you'd take care of the lad responsible and I believed you. What happened? Nothing happened. That wee Sheridan boy is still walking around, and I hear the latest instalment of money is running late. Am I telling it aright, so far?'

Few men frightened Larry. Rory McGorrick was one. He tried not to show it and answered without a tremor, 'To be honest, with Quinn being touch and go, and coming after Cronin's accident, I took my eye off the ball. As for Sheridan,

I had a reliable team, they usually gave satisfaction. You know what happened.'

'Aye, I heard they picked a fight with a DART. What I don't know is how it happened.'

'Not sure I do, Rory. No survivors. They were following him home, with the purpose of a snatch. May have lost him at the Merrion Gates as the barriers dropped. Could be they didn't want to lose him or got impatient and tried to cross ahead of the DART – and they didn't make it.'

McGorrick blew a raspberry. 'Tell you why I find that a quare thing. You had O'Keane at the wheel, cool head, doesn't panic easy. Now, when the gates drop at a DART level crossing, the train is close, no more than a minute or so. O'Keane sits on his arse, and when he must have known it was on top of him, and he'd surely have heard the noise of it, not till then does he take it into that wee head of his to smash the barrier and jump the crossing. Doesn't come together, does it?'

One of the sons sniggered and earned a glare from McGorrick.

'No, I don't suppose it does,' admitted Larry. 'I can't explain it. The *polis* are scratching their heads, too, I hear.'

'Here's another hokey thing: who pushed your Quinn through the window and into the night, so he's now at death's door, though God is good, they say?'

Larry nibbled his lip. 'Sheridan again, and, before you ask, I've no idea how he caught Quinn. The only possibility is Sheridan and a crew of hired goons managed to take him unawares, clocked him and got the window open and pushed him through.'

His fear of McGorrick gave way to a consuming rage

when his mind pictured it.

McGorrick scowled. 'Okay, Larry, never mind. To the point. I don't have to tell you this is not per our agreement. Tell me if I'm right. I loaned you big bucks at a time when you'd have gone under without them, and, in return, you channelled money out of BlastOff so I could fund a certain supplier of much-in-demand substances. Your cheque this month was two weeks late. That's fucking out of order. My supplier threw a shape and imposed a nasty penalty which, by the way, I'll be passing on to you. I need your word, here and now, on your balls or your life or both, there will never – by which I mean never – be a delay again and our little arrangement will continue like clockwork. And, by the by, *I'm* going to take care of the boy Sheridan now, today, not you. No mess, no fuss.'

'Yes, I give you my word. But, there's something else, Rory, with great respect, it's time for us to review this draw-off arrangement with the agency. Charley Maughan tells me –'

McGorrick held up a hand. 'When a man says to me "with great respect", it means he's got none. So, *dún du clob is póg mo thóin*,' he snapped: shut your mouth and kiss my arse.

The boom of a shotgun in the street outside stopped him. Immediately following, a concussive *whoomp, whoomp* of explosions shook the room.

Outside, the red and blue lorry had reappeared and stopped at the warehouse, the three men standing in the flatbed. As fast as one lit the fuse on bottles of petrol, another tossed them into the open bay. The third lifted a shotgun from the bed of the lorry and took out the two men who'd come roaring out with revolvers raised. At the double boom of the gun, the other yellow jackets dropped what they were doing and dashed into the warehouse for safety, as fatal a thing as they could have done.

The impact of the Molotov cocktails was immediate, with the carefully scored flaming bottles bursting among the shelving chock-a-block with explosive flammables – paints, solvents, paraffin, LPG and gas canisters. There was a devastating explosion and within seconds, the place was a firestorm.

As the lorry roared off, men and women were pouring out in even greater panic, many with their clothes on fire, living torches, screaming. More terrible screams came from those deep inside who were trapped by the flames.

At the echo of the shotgun, McGorrick had shot out of the chair, small eyes darting and snarled, 'It's them, the pox o' the hoors on 'em.'

Further explosive blasts rocked the building. The two sons had pulled guns from shoulder holsters and were running into the outer office. McGorrick and Larry followed and walked into full-blown panic. Heavy, oily black smoke was already billowing into the room. Some of the men were pushing and banging at the closed steel door, which was unyielding. Three were impeding each other trying to get the door open, which should have been easy but wasn't.

One raised a chair and smashed a window to the outside, ran over and grappled with the bars, trying vainly to loosen them. The building was a fire trap and any fire and safety inspector would have ordered immediate closure, not that any F&S inspector would consider entering premises owned by the McGorricks.

'I know who's behind this, the arseheads, and 'tis their

sorry day,' hollered McGorrick. His voice held menace, but also uncertainty.

'Who?' asked Larry.

'A bunch of thugs masquerading as something else, call themselves the New Freedom IRA.'

Dies Irae, day of wrath. The morbid pun came unbidden to Larry. McGorrick might think this was the work of a competitor, but he knew with blinding certitude that, yet again, in some inexplicable way, it showed the hand of Kieran Sheridan.

McGorrick tried to shout orders to his sons but took a fit of coughing that doubled him over. Larry tasted the acrid smoke that filled his mouth and nostrils, and he, too, bent over, staggering, coughing convulsively, his eyes burning, his throat on fire. Rage boiled again, coupled with something close to resignation. He heard Ronayne beside him gasp, 'Time for night prayers, Larry.'

'No, Jackie. I sacked the good Lord last week. He wasn't performing for me or mine.' Maybe he only thought he'd said it, because his throat had closed, robbing him of breath.

More thick smoke was pouring through the doors and wooden flooring and Larry felt heat through the soles of his shoes. McGorrick was slumped to the floor, heaving and twisting like an animal in a trap as he tried to find air. Men were gagging and spluttering, crawling on the ground. The frosted glass was lit by the menacing glow of flames that threw flickering shapes on the ceiling. Continuous screaming came from the warehouse floor and Larry caught the dreadful sickly-sweet odour of burning flesh.

He couldn't stop coughing and wheezing. Weakness and

agonising pain overcame him. He recognised there was no way out, that he was going to die. Too late for revenge, too late for anything. He dropped to the ground, gasping for breath. Despite what he'd said to Ronayne, he offered a quick prayer that Quinn, at least, would pull through.

A man, a shape in the smoke, banged on the frosted glass with the butt of a handgun. Someone else pulled at the wooden door, bloody fingernails broken. A McGorrick brother, behind him, threw a panicked punch to his face that dropped him, grabbed a chair and swung it at the door. Larry knew what was about to happen but had no voice to shout a warning. The door burst outward and a great fiery blast rushed in. In an instant, men were alight and screaming. In his agony, Larry was aware of a blinding flash of the brightest orange-white, a soundless explosion, and then the entire floor collapsed, throwing him and everyone else into the inferno beneath.

39

SURRENDER

Like everyone else, I avidly followed the developing news stories on what the *Irish Independent* would call the North King Street Massacre. Fire engines were at the scene in minutes and firefighters in breathing apparatus battled to contain the fire and stop it spreading to adjoining buildings. They were unable to prevent the warehouse from burning to the ground in a spectacular conflagration, punctuated by huge explosions, watched from nearby vantage points by vast crowds of horrified and enthralled Dubliners. Thick viscous smoke blanketed the surrounding area and much of the city centre, along with a steady fall of black and grey soot. By evening, hospitals and GP waiting rooms in North Dublin were crammed with dozens of panicky people complaining of smoke inhalation.

Over the next three days, twenty-six bodies were taken from the smouldering embers, most burnt beyond recognition. A few had shotgun wounds. Eight of the dead were girls who had worked in the back office.

It became known it was a gang hit, since the Gardaí and the media were aware the warehouse belonged to the

McGorricks. The day after the fire, newspapers speculated that Rory McGorrick himself was among the corpses. It was not until two days later his body was formally identified, as well as those of three of his sons and, subject to further tests, a fourth. A fifth son had been stabbed to death three months earlier outside a North City fast food shop. That was, as the papers noted, the end of the entire male McGorrick family and, most likely, the demise of that particular gang, with most of their heavies also being killed in the blaze.

A few days later came the stunning news that one of the bodies was that of respected businessman Larry Brenner, identified by dental records and confirmed by DNA. There was astonishment as to what he had been doing in that den of thieves. One report hinted at a kidnapping and rescue gone wrong. There was much play on the ill-luck that dogged the Brenners, with one son killed in a tragic car accident, another still critical after a fall from his office window, a daughter who had died of leukaemia as a child – news to me – a mother dead of cancer and now this.

A fortnight later, Tara sashayed into my office and propped herself on a corner of my desk. Her tartan mini-shirt didn't extend much beyond her thighs, forcing me, for propriety's sake, to keep my gaze on the window.

'Quinn told me he wants to meet with you.'

'In the hospital?'

'They discharged him yesterday, and he's convalescing in a rented house in Dalkey. Healthy seaside breezes and that. In bed for the most part, though he's learning to move around in a special medical contraption that was flown in from a Swiss clinic. I think you should visit. He seems, well, resigned to the life he's going to face, and I got no vibe of hostility towards us – or you.'

Dalkey is an old-fashioned South Dublin town, more English than Irish in tone, a place where many of Agatha Christie's characters might have lived before being cosily murdered in agreeable surroundings. In recent years, property prices in the town had skyrocketed as Irish and British celebrities moved in, and Dalkey became known as Bel Eire, or so one local estate agent claimed.

Quinn had taken a large, newly-built house, close by the sea. A pleasant woman in nurse's uniform answered the door and brought me to an open plan lounge that covered most of the ground floor, with an array of cushioned armchairs and sofas. An open archway led to the kitchen and bathroom areas.

A middle-aged priest, plump with rimless glasses, had installed himself on a high stool at the kitchen table and was sipping a mug of tea and browsing a copy of *Phoenix* magazine. He gave me what may have been a wave or a blessing and went back to his reading.

The lounge had panoramic windows looking out on boat-filled Bulloch Harbour and the Bay. The white sails and colourful pennants of a score of small yachts flapped and swayed in the wind as they tacked to and fro, dwarfed by the ferry heading into Dun Laoghaire terminal.

Not far away, the top of the James Joyce Tower was visible. Further back was Dun Laoghaire's promenade, harbour and lighthouse, its spires, the stegosaurian-style rooftop of the massive LexIcon library and the ersatz Venetian palace that was the town hall.

Quinn sat stiffly upright at the window in what looked

like an over-elaborate dentist's chair. A muscular man in white everything, tee-shirt, pants, shoes and housecoat, presumably a nurse or physiotherapist, was talking with him in a low tone. He moved away when he saw me and joined the priest. He left the door open and we were in sight, though they politely ignored us.

Quinn was The Crusher no more. The Crushed, more like. Both his legs and an arm were encased in plaster. He wore a neck brace and the left side of his face was heavily bandaged. What I could see of it was a riot of blue-black and sickly yellow. Been there, done that, I thought. A long woollen shawl covered his shoulders, and he had an orange blanket across his lap. A bedside table held a glass of water and a number of bottles and pill vials. He didn't invite me to take the chair near him, but I sat anyway.

'Still around, Kieran? Or Ciarán, as Shay says.' He drew out the final 'awn' mockingly. His voice slurred, but his eyes were alert. 'And what's with the Lay Fawnoo name you've started to give yourself?'

'You sound better than you look,' I said.

'You think? Right now, I've got a metal plate in my face, various broken bones and I'm in this wheelie, with my own portable shitter, for a long time to come. Think Stephen Hawking.' He tried for a downbeat smile and failed. 'I'm off to an overpriced rehab in Colorado at the weekend for a few weeks, months. Not that I'm complaining.'

'My commiserations on your father's death. I met him for the first time recently at the hospital.'

He said, matter of factly, 'You sent the Angel of Death after him. As you did with me and Cronin.'

I held back my annoyance.

'Don't, Quinn. That's stupid talk. If I sent the Angel of Death, you'd be dead. Could be I sent the lesser-known Angel of Serious Bodily Harm. It's claptrap.'

'Is it?' He rotated the chair by moving a small joystick, and I got his side view as he took in the seascape. 'May be claptrap or you've sold your soul, who can tell? Me, I'm not claiming amnesia, as you did. Know what I saw, and hope never to see her again.'

He had a crucifix around his neck, I noticed. Cronin, too, had been religious. Was Quinn wearing it on my account, to ward off evil? Perhaps that's why the priest was in the next room, ready to spring into action should the need arise, with bulbs of garlic, a silver crucifix upraised, splashing me with holy water and demanding I renounce the Devil.

Quinn used the joystick to swivel his chair so he faced me again.

'Why are you here?'

'Because you asked me to come.'

He stared at me. 'I mean, what's your price to go away forever and take your piseog with you.'

I'd never before heard someone seriously use the old Irish term for a curse. If Quinn believed I could dole out bad juju, it was going to be easier to get what I had come for.

'I'm afraid it's you who must go away. I want you to relinquish control of Aardvark-Sheridan.'

'To you?' he said with the trace of a sneer.

'In part, yes. Before he disappeared, Jasper had plans to retire and spread the shareholding to the agency directors. That's how I'll do it.'

'Directors?' he mocked, then grimaced with pain. 'No directors in the legal sense. Aardvark is a valuable business. If I put it on the market, fetch a good price. You got that dosh?'

I sighed. 'I'm not talking management buy-out. No money. You blame me for Cronin's death and your accident. I hold your father responsible for what happened to Jasper. Regardless, we neither of us can prove what we say. Nonetheless, it's what we believe. I want the agency.'

He let out a low groan. Pain or incredulity, I couldn't tell.

'Man, Aardvark's worth millions, property alone. But that's not news to you.'

He twisted in his chair. I was doing his recovery no good and I needed to end this meeting.

'Don't agitate yourself, Quinn. You'll only make it worse. From what I understand, you've inherited a sizeable portfolio without the agency, both here and across the water. You can afford to let it go. If you think there's a curse involved, this is how you get it off your back.'

'Subtly said. Hearing the threat, nonetheless. No, no. Don't waste time denying. Like an old-fashioned family feud isn't it: Hatfield and McCoy? The Sheridans versus the Brenners, agency the prize.'

I laughed. 'Shut up, Quinn.'

Illness and tiredness squashed the angry retort that had formed on his lips. He attempted to swing his chair back to the window, but it seemed stuck. He grunted, tugged at the joystick, failed again and gave up with a growl of irritation. I guessed he wouldn't welcome help from me. I glanced over. The priest and therapist were chatting, pointedly oblivious to my presence.

Quinn's voice was tired and without emotion, 'Okay, take your damn agency. It's been crappy luck to my family.'

'You can keep the Velázquez.' I offered.

He ignored that. 'Give you a laugh: never had much interest in Aardvark. Took the job for Dad's sake. I leave this country Friday and won't be back. We Irish are supine losers. Great future until the banks bamboozled idiot Government into signing blank cheques to cover the mess. Then the Eurocrats stomped us and we tugged the forelock. We should have our own Brexit, if any sense. Hell with it, who cares. I surrender. Get your solicitor to talk to mine, I'll sign.'

With a smile, or perhaps a sneer, he asked, 'BlastOff's rip-off your problem. Still gonna come clean?'

'Maybe. You may have heard that Barry is back and he's taking over BlastOff now the McGorrick clan are no more. We're going to work something out. He's under the impression he owes me.'

I rose to leave since I'd gotten what I came for, and because Quinn seemed to be fading. He took a coughing fit, which brought the male nurse out of the kitchen to stand in the archway.

Quinn waved him off, 'Before you go, Sheridan, one thing. Tell me about her.'

When he didn't continue, I sighed.

'OK, Quinn, I will. But are you sure you want to know?'

He hesitated. 'No. Forget it. If you've done a pact with the devil, live with the consequences. Really don't want to know.'

Which was as well because I wouldn't have been able to explain what I didn't myself understand.

That evening, I was on the social circuit. An agency client,

Sarsfield Deering, a technology recruitment consultancy, was sponsoring a European Cyber Security Conference in Dublin. Tara and Ross Scott between them, had organised a reception in their offices in Adelaide Road. As CEO, acting or otherwise, it was now mandatory for me to attend such events.

I passed the time there with Aisling Dunne, who was CEO Europe for an Australian-owned upmarket credit card company that had established its European headquarters in Dublin where, as with many other global businesses, it could decide what tax, if any, to pay.

She greeted me, 'Aardvark CEO, no less. Impressive.'

'Sounds classier than it is. I asked for a raise and they gave me the title instead.'

She acknowledged the bogus modesty with a grin. Aisling was good company. We were neither of us interested in talking shop. Aardvark didn't have a credit card client, but it would have been gauche right then to make a pitch for her business. She asked me what I did before I got into advertising. I told her of my days as a popular entertainer.

'A small family legacy kept me in frugal comfort. To stretch it, I taught English in language schools in Eastern Europe. Later, in South America, I taught myself to play guitar and downloaded Irish song lyrics, sentimental schmaltz and patriotic ballads, the more anti-British the better. Big hit with locals and tourists. The rumour was that I was an Irish freedom fighter on the run and I became a minor celebrity.'

She was big into astrology and star signs and told me, in a confidential tone, that she had a gift for interpreting the tarot. At parties, she told fortunes with cards or by reading palms and said she had divined astonishing things.

'Shall I tell yours?' She took my palm in her hand and studied it for a minute. She laughed, uneasily. 'Unusual. I can't find your lifeline. It means you're dead, I think.'

I took back my hand. 'Either that or I'm hard to read.'

It was a cloudy, windy night when I left and I was hit by a wave of tiredness and lassitude as I got to my car. I drove carefully, side windows down, radio blasting. Traffic was light. I had to make an effort to avoid drifting into the verge. I couldn't figure my overtiredness. Was it a late reaction to my earlier meeting with Quinn, followed by a busy day in the office? Whatever, my concentration slipped and I ran a red light, almost hitting a truck.

I was relieved when I finally swung into Silchester Road. As I zipped past the shabby leonine guardians of Huntsman Hall, I prematurely loosed my seatbelt clip. I was going a little fast and had just eased on the pedal when my windscreen filled with the brilliant headlight beams of an oncoming car directly in front of me. I stamped on the brake, felt myself lose control as the car went into a skid. I raised an arm to shield myself from the blinding light. My head hit my arm which hit the windscreen and I was out cold.

It took a minute for my wits to unscramble and make sense of what had just happened. As I sat in the car, unable to move and shivering with nerves, the lights, which were on a timer, went out, leaving me in darkness. I had not had a close encounter with another car. The intense white blaze was the new halogen outdoor lights that a security company had installed at my request following the burglary and the death of Dundan. I had a sore arm and a sore head but it could have been worse.

I switched off the engine. In the minutes of total silence that followed, I slowly realised that my lost memory had returned and I was remembering that night two months ago, as if through a high end virtual reality headset. I was about to return to Raglan Road.

40

RETURN TO RAGLAN ROAD

The Dubliner Pub in the Ballsbridge Hotel is always noisily busy and cheerful at half past eight on Friday as business executives slide into weekend mode, jackets off, shirts and blouses loosened. It is a likeable enough place, though to my mind devoid of distinctive character, too similar in design, décor and custom to designer-generated Irish pubs that undoubtedly attract similar hip custom in Boston and Berlin, Canberra and Ho Chi Min City.

That evening, Cronin Brenner sat across from me in a semi-alcove table and I waited to learn why he had asked me here. The place suited him. He was a regular, on first-name terms with other regulars and the bar staff. I tended to think of him as a semi-alcoholic who imbibed regularly, but not always. Occasionally, he was late back to the office after lunch and laidback, a mild haze of gin wafting around him post-prandially. He held his drink well, never slurring or losing concentration.

We did well to have a table. The bar was filling up quickly with blathering, laughing, occasionally boisterous patrons, standing room only for new arrivals. Behind Cronin, on the wall, were framed photos of Brendan Behan and Sean O'Casey and someone else famous in the literary world I couldn't offhand put a name to. I half-listened as he droned on with an account of a client meeting earlier that had gone well. He was drinking his usual Cork Gin and Schweppes, doubles with little tonic. I had a pint of Guinness and I sipped it carefully to stay clearheaded. He was well ahead of me drinkwise. I had another pint in front of me, its creamy head evaporating into the black. He had finished his drink, and his gaze casually swept the bar for a passing waiter.

We were discussing... well, it was more a monologue from Cronin. He was on about Ged Stoker of MetroElectronics, who apparently had an orgasm when he saw the agency's latest creative ideas. 'I was walking on air,' said Cronin, more interested in the telling than I was in the hearing, meaningless flimflam before he got to why he'd asked me here since we were never social mates. It was not, as I'd assumed, a once-off after-hours bonding between boss and mid-level executive. It had another purpose.

Finally, he came out with it and I was slow on the uptake because I didn't get it straight away that he was firing me. When I realised, I was devastated, like I'd been hit by a thundering rhino. And I was astonished to see that he hadn't twigged to how it was affecting me, or really didn't give a damn as he platituded on, bored, eyes again doing radar sweeps of the pub, checking who's who, before coming back to me.

'The agency,' he was saying, as though spelling it out with patience to an obtuse intern, 'is at a standstill in terms of growth and that's dangerous. The key is a more aggressive drive to pinpoint and capture high-spending new clients. We need big dogs with big thinking who deliver added value to the agency and our clients and who have the networking skills and the access and the drive to produce great winning ideas at the interface. Deep creative minds who like to work at the market coalface. That plus bigger net profits for us.'

He was literate and fluent when it came to the patter. 'Here comes another arseful of the ould jargle,' as Jasper would disdainfully say of a jargon waffler.

'And that's your problem's right there, Kieran,' Cronin said with an eyebrow shrug. 'You're diligent and good at what you do. Such as it is. But you're no heavyweight, never gonna set the heather blazing. New business development isn't in your repertory, you're not contact-rich, so you bring nothing to the table. Need I say more?'

I heard what he was saying, partly in denial. The Guinness was reversing course in my stomach and it took an effort to keep it down. What was putting me off was Cronin's brisk, impersonal tone. He was not even going through the motions of feigning reluctance or regret. It's as if we were meeting for the first time. Scary.

Finally, I found my voice, 'Hang on, man. Things are not all bad. We're one of the few agencies the recession hasn't hurt. No client has decamped or gone under owing us big bucks. And our profits are up this year –'

I was mortified to hear myself pleading, bleating. He cut through it.

'Three per cent net. I put more in the poor box on Sundays.' A favourite expression of his. 'Not the point, is it? By my reckoning, the economy's on the edge of a repeat recession.

Think Brexit, Trump's trade wars, China's debt overhang, et cetera, and how they'll affect us. The agency needs to get its act together better than we've been doing. Truth is, we're living in the past. We're the last of the old-style, wing collar, tiepin, double-breasted, full-service agencies and we've been dangerously slow to catch up with the changes impacting on our business space.'

Cronin was casually lobbing any argument that occurred to him. He caught a waiter's attention and gestured another round for the two of us. Didn't ask me and I was too agitated to refuse.

'Kieran,' he said, in an attempt at sympathy that didn't come off. 'I appreciate Jasper's disappearance has changed everything for you career-wise. You were destined to carry on the family name in the family firm. Fine, fine. That's not how it's worked out, right? You expected a big slice of the agency when he retired and instead it wasn't his to pass on when he passed on. Your uncle left you dangling, over-promoted and overpaid where you are. That's being blunt, but there it is.'

I burst out, 'Hey, where's this coming from, Cronin? You know what the market's like in our business. I could be out for weeks, months, before a decent job comes my way. Plus, it's the kiss of death to apply for a position while I'm outside looking in. You know that. At the least, give me time to find something.'

The full whine. I couldn't stop myself.

Cronin shook his head, man of decision. 'That's putting off the inevitable and it's bad for morale to have an employee around the place once they're on the bench. I've got a plan for the agency going forward and I want it in place by month's end. Better you go now. In the circumstances, right, I'm giving you a blue-ribbon deal – six months' salary up front. Plus, I'll have a word with Dad to give you a tasty price for your shares.'

All I could think of was, 'I don't deserve this.' Feeble.

I got up. I feared I might start crying and didn't want the shame of doing it in public. I headed into the gents. Inside, two rugby club types – thirties, red-faced, hundred-euro haircuts – were taking part in a farting contest and, after a glance in my direction, they continued. Hilarious. They were standing at either side of the sole vacant urinal. I had to go into a cubicle to piss.

I was dizzy, hyperventilating, sweating, a droning in my ears, and I was worried that I might be about to pass out. I had a flash of a news headline, *Adman drowns after collapsing into hotel lavatory bowl*. Not funny. I couldn't stop myself wallowing in self-pity. Workless, moneyless, homeless. I had no savings, a few debts. Cronin's proposed largesse wouldn't cover me for long.

I waited until the rugger morons left, came out, choked on their miasma, doused my face and looked at what the mirror showed me.

Nothing to be happy about, for sure. A pitiful *amadán*, stomach starting to tip over the belt. Cheap suit, jacket creased badly, too tight. Dull hair, retreating on top. Heavy framed specs. Skin with a couple of acne pimples, blotchy. I appeared to be years older than I was. Jeez, when had I let myself go? I didn't have the cut or the edge of a cutting-edge adman. Would I hire this sweaty, downbeat guy in the mirror? Would anyone?

I kept hoping I might survive the evening with my career intact. Vain hope. Cronin meant it and I was about to join the legion of the unemployed, trying to get by on the dole. I visualised taking orders from people I'd worked with, socialised with, from behind the counter in McDonald's or Burger King or as a barista with a clown-happy rictus in Starbucks or Costa. I didn't have the heart and the guts and the footwork to try living abroad again.

I went back to the bar, through the throng of merry folks back to my seat. Cronin wasn't there. He was with a party of men and girls at a far table, fresh G&T in his hand. They' were looking expectantly at Cronin who was telling a story, a joke, because in a minute they were laughing. Was he talking about me? No. I tamped down the paranoia. He glanced towards me and went back to his audience.

I sat alone, taking token swallows of my Guinness, the taste of bile in my mouth. I watched Cronin. The worst of it was his indifference, blanking me out as a person. What did his friends over there think of me sitting abandoned?

Shame and humiliation and mounting rage were flooding in. Among the confident, job-secure people in the bar, I was not much good at anything. No specialist skills, copywriter, artist, designer, whatever. No hot-shot salesman. Not even an exceptional client relations executive.

My mood was doing a shape change, if moods do that, from self-absorbed self-pity to a simmering fury. In another stream of my mind, I was near suicidal and, hypothetically, running through the ways I might do it.

Eventually, Cronin made his goodbyes to his cronies and weaved his way to our table, a cheerful grin on his face. 'Do you know them, they're –'

He stopped, realising that I wouldn't know them and there

was no point in talking about them. 'Well, time to move on,' he declared, downing a final swallow of his drink. I still had most of my pint and two full ones beside it, losing their heads. Cronin tapped his foot. He had done what he set out to do by bringing me here and giving me the word. I was out – fire and forget, mission accomplished, as the military say, and now Cronin would be glad to see the back of me.

'Yeah. Wimp fired, sorted, let's get outta here,' I wanted to say this to his face as he settled the tab at the bar. I didn't, of course.

We had come in his BMW and he was going to drive me to my Jag, in the agency carpark. I guess he'd have preferred for us to go our ways there and then and was about to ask if I'd mind walking to my car, some fifteen minutes away. But it was raining heavily. No choice, he had to drop me back. When I got in the front seat, I noticed a thick prayer book on the dashboard, the sign of a daily mass-goer. I never thought of Cronin as particularly religious. That and a hypocrite of the first order, I was getting madder at him by the second.

I made a final go to reach out. 'What shocks me the most, Cronin, I thought we were on the same team, you'd always have my back.'

It's as though I'd made a distasteful remark. Quick headshake. 'Not to sound like the mafia, nothing personal, Kieran, it's business.'

God's gonads, even a Mafioso would at least have pretended to be regretful. I was already old business.

We drove across to Pembroke Road. Rain filled the wind-screen. I had a thought, 'Cronin, you can't fire me this way. I mean legally. I mean, it shouldn't have to get to this. I mean, in all fairness, I'll have to consider an unfair dismissal action.'

I mean. I mean. I heard myself, with disgust, abjectly apologetic, not wanting to offend. He had the interior light on, checking in the glove compartment. When he took in what I'd said, he glared at me. 'I wouldn't play that game if I were you. I can take the six months' payout off the table and, as for the rest…' He fiddled around in the glove compartment, darting quick glances on the road.

I'd expected we'd go straight to Baggot Street and onto Merrion Square. Instead, we swung onto Raglan Road, not the direct way to my car. The wipers zipped to and fro, barely clearing the rain from the windscreen, blurring the trees on both sides. Raglan Road was empty of traffic except for a car behind us and the headlights of an oncoming one far ahead.

'Where are we going?' I asked.

He ignored me, still preoccupied, groping for whatever it was. His lack of interest set me off.

His mobile rang and he pulled it out of his jacket. 'Hi, Dad. I'm on the way. Nearly there –'

I didn't exist for him. Something snapped in my mind. My vision turned filter red. I astonished myself with what I did next. I swung towards him and drove my elbow hard into his ribs. It hurt him, I guess, because he let a shout into his mobile, turned my way and yelled, 'What the hell are you doing?'

'Nothing personal,' I screamed at him.

I was committed and had to follow through before he could do anything. The oncoming car was much nearer. Insanely, I wanted us to smash into it. With my full force, I lashed out with my fist and caught him on the neck below the ear. He dropped his phone and gave a weird howl of agony, dog-like – yowhooo.

'Nothing personal, Cronin,' I yelled again.

Unlike me, he was not wearing a seatbelt and the impact of my punch shoved him onto the side door. He bounced back, into me, his hands flew off the steering wheel and into the air. I was off-balance, too, and made a grab for the rear mirror above me. Blinding headlights were yards, feet, inches away, larger and larger. We collided with a sickening thump, and we were twisting and spinning and everything blacked out.

I was briefly conscious. Black night. Freezing rain. Swirling smoke and the heavy reek of petrol. Caterwauling car alarms. I was wedged deep in the wreckage of a car, pinned and squeezed by an immense weight, rigid with shock and confusion and surging panic, cold as an ice block. The rain sluiced onto me, over me and through me. Something else wet and runny. Blood, lots of blood, the salty taste filling my mouth, choking me, its sourness in my nostrils. No pain yet, but I could sense it coming and about to slam into me.

I wasn't sure what had happened. Car. Crash. How? Cronin wasn't there. I remembered how the big prayer book had flown from the dash and walloped me in the head. Hit by an unguided missal. Ha, ha. Nothing was important anymore. A lot of noise. Above me, the sky alive with a million glittering stars, the brightest, a brilliant celestial spark. Ambulance sirens wailed far off. Nearby, a church bell marked the time. It's as though I was listening to the tolling of the stars. And then all went dark.

41

STARRY, STARRY NIGHT

I'm the only person who truly knows how Cronin died. The random thought occurred to me as I sat slumped in my car outside the Hall. I closed my eyes and tried to confront what memory had served up to me. But I was asleep within minutes, a deep sleep of shock that gave my mind an opportunity to discover not just the right answers but the right questions. The first pale fingers of yellow dawn light crept through the trees and awakened me. It was only when I shifted in my car seat that I became aware that I was cold and painfully stiff. But my mind was sharp.

I remembered with crystal clarity hearing the church bell toll the knell of parting life and looking at the countless glistening stars, a Van Gogh *Starry Night*, the crescent moon and shimmering spangles of light covering the heavens. That now-familiar song came to me:

I remember, too, a distant bell
And stars that fell
Like rain out of the blue.

Hold on. That couldn't be right. The rain was pelting from an overcast night, a black cloud-filled sky. How could there be visible stars? Yet, I had seen them in their vivid brilliance.

I straightened, with a thrill of elation that perhaps I was close to finding the answer I had been seeking all this time, even if I hadn't fully identified the question. I thought again of my extraordinary recovery and transformation into someone else: changed, different. Isn't that what I had been hearing from many voices time and again?

The truth was in the stars in the clouded night sky. *Sic itur ad astra.* Heart thumping, I had my epiphany and I realised I was not Kieran Sheridan.

I'd been Kieran for all of the previous thirty-three years. I had been Kieran in the Dubliner Pub at his humiliation, in the crash and in the car wreck as his life seeped away, and as he lingered in great agitation in the void between existence and extinction and glimpsed far off his next dimension. But when I woke in hospital, I was not him. I was in his physical body, and – like ill-fitting, awkward, off-the-peg clothes – had his memories and attitudes and modes of behaviour. But I was not him and, without conscious awareness, I had begun to impose myself upon him, changing, discarding, adding, more often utterly confused by the transmutation.

But there was a further conundrum: *I* was… who?

As a teenager, I once went climbing in the Wicklow Mountains with some friends. After much effort, we reached what we expected to be the top, to find it was only a ridge, with the summit looming far above us. We continued upward to arrive at another false crest, with a further climb, then yet an-other, and we wondered if we were ever going to reach the top.

That's how I felt now. Every discovery I was making was just another layer of mystery, a further ridge, and the mountaintop continued to be hidden in the mists above. Journey's end required a further ascent.

PART TWO

42

THE LORD'S WALK

It took several days before my whirling, agitated confusion and the incessant questions began to ease and allowed my mental state to return in slow stages to something near equilibrium. In the end, my thought processes seemed to go into a kind of suspension as I waited for greater insight and understanding of my condition. In due course, clarity came.

On Sunday, I was leaving the apartment when my eye caught a flicker of white in the dense shrubbery at one side of the Hall. A large, long-haired snow-white Persian cat appeared and padded gracefully along the grass verge toward me.

I stood still, not wishing to frighten it off. When the cat saw me, it stopped, sat and seemed to regard me thoughtfully. I couldn't tell gender for certain, but it had a doll-like face and there was something essentially female about her. We scrutinised each other. She was the most attractive animal I'd ever seen, her fur impeccably groomed.

'Where have you come from?' I asked.

I was almost expecting a response. She continued to observe me as though I was a passably interesting specimen. A small redbreast flew from a tree and onto the ground a few feet away. It noticed the cat and hopped over for a closer view. The cat glanced at the bird, ignored it and returned to me.

'Don't you have a collar or anything to identify where you live? It's remiss of your owner to let such an exquisite creature like you wander. I should warn you there are reputed to be foxes about.'

I was speaking conversationally and was in no doubt the cat was listening and understood me. I took a step closer, at which she rose slowly, kept me in her sight for a minute, turned and moved back to the bushes and out of sight. Disappointed, I made no attempt to follow and called out as I departed, 'Goodbye for the present. Nice to chat with a *chatte*, pardon my French. Do come back, sometime.'

I took a stroll along Silchester Road, admiring, as I always did, the variety of imposing Victorian and Edwardian homes, seeing it, as I was seeing most things, as if for the first time and through different eyes. Nearby Glenageary Road was a busy thoroughfare, full of the bustle of passing traffic. Where I walked was without sound, empty of people and cars. Earlier, it had been a dry day, but, in a quick change, the louring sky had become a canopy of grey clouds turning black. I doubted if I would get through my walk before it rained.

Over the past few days, the temperature had been falling. Along the road, the leaves, forty shades of brown and orange and russet and gold, were twisting and spinning their dance of death in the wind and carpeting the pavements under the trees.

Unexpectedly, I thought I saw Aoife in the distance. It was no more than a momentary glimpse, a flash of tossing black hair and white raincoat as she vanished into a side path.

I called her name and hastened after her with hopeful heart thumping with excitement. It had been so long.

Two centuries back, in the year of Waterloo, workmen had built a pathway to carry stone from the nearby quarry at Dalkey to construct Dun Laoghaire harbour, four kilometres away. The pathway, known as The Metals, still exists and, at Silchester Road, there is a short spur where some of the stone was used to build houses. It is now a rarely traversed way, named, for obscure reasons, The Lord's Walk.

I'd gone no more than a hundred yards along this path, with no sign of Aoife or anyone else, when the world halted. The wind ceased, and the distant drone of ambient traffic receded and went silent. The only sound was the now familiar tolling of a distant church bell. I sensed a split-second disturbance in the atmosphere, as though time was undergoing a spasm. There was a perceptible shimmering in the air and all about brightened into vivid colours. It was as though a vast oil painting had interposed itself on the path in front of me. I even imagined I could see the vigorous brushstrokes of the artist, the matt of the canvas.

If I concentrate hard, I thought, I can project myself into this painting and into what seems an incredible place that has welcoming magic in the air. If I don't, it may vanish, and the opportunity lost forever.

Unmoving, hardly breathing, I tried to attune my mind to this fantastic dimension, seeking a way to connect with it. The path trembled. A soft swooshing whistled through the air and all at once I was out of my body, out of The Lord's Walk and into the most extraordinary world I could ever have believed possible.

I'm transported to a new and different existence, another reality, flooded with a brilliance that is more than light: a powerful force of living energy that transforms my consciousness. I vibrate with emotions that overwhelm me – euphoria, elation and an understanding that all manner of great wonders are here. My mind is in an elevated state of tranquillity, liberated from all worries, problems and responsibilities.

It is a mellow summer afternoon and I'm in the countryside, strolling along an unpaved loamy road, a boreen, with hedgerows on either side of wild shrubs ablaze with red and green and purple flowering and blossoming hawthorn, blackthorn and dogwood trees. Birds fly about, robins, great tits, blue tits, yellowhammers and whitethroats. Butterflies in fabulous colours flit by and bee-buzz fills the background. The air shimmers and vibrates in waves of faint tremulous light.

In nearby meadows, horses and cows raise their head in my direction with unconcern, before they resume their placid grazing. There is a pleasant aroma of burning turf, interspersed with the fragrance of lavender. The horizon quivers in a summery haze.

The golden sun in a heavenly blue sky beams agreeable warmth, tempered by the mildest puff of wind. I breathe air that is pure and clear, and the splendour of the light animates everything, intense, not overdominant, imparting a lustre that gives sharpness and richness to colours.

I am describing none of this with fidelity. There is no way to portray one dimension in words of another. When I speak of my emotions and the shapes and colours and atmosphere that fill the senses, I use only lame and inadequate words that give a spurious impression and bear only a grey and muted resemblance to what I experience.

To the right, some distance away, in the surrounds of a cluster of trees is a large Tudor manor house, with ivy-covered walls, windows blazing orange in the sun. The backdrop is of distant mountains and I can see with startling clarity, numerous green and purple and golden fields, dotted here and there with substantial country homes. On the side of the mountain, an old-style steam train, toy-like in the distance, chugs along, hardly audible, its engine emitting bursts of grey-white smoke as it hauls a dozen bright blue and yellow carriages along a threadlike track.

There is melody in the air, like background film music richer, haunting music, performed on instruments I've never heard before.

I'm not in any way unsettled. To find oneself in a strange and unknown land is surely cause for bewilderment, unease, even rising panic, with questions crowding each other: where is this place? What country? Where does this path lead? How did I get here? How do I get out?

On the contrary, I am deliriously enchanted here. I accept it wholeheartedly and am content to undertake a leisurely journey of discovery where there may or may not be answers.

From the summit of a rise, I make a long and easy descent into a wide valley of prosperous farmland, a quilt of verdant, yellow and golden harvest fields. The atmosphere is transfigured, glowing, shimmering. Scents of fresh fruit and cut corn immingle in the air. A verse from one of my schoolbooks, by the melancholic poet James Clarence Mangan comes to mind, his opium-induced fantasy of an earlier, mythical

Ireland, that may have given him solace even as he perished in the great Irish famine of the 1840s:

> *I walked entranced*
> *Through a land of morn;*
> *The sun, with wondrous excess of light,*
> *Shone down and glanced*
> *Over seas of corn*
> *And lustrous gardens aleft and right.*

Cheerful men and women walk by, others in the fields are gathering the harvest. They are not peasants or farmhands, for this is their land, too, and they are filled with the happy knowledge of it. They appear to me in a haze, as if I'm wearing the wrong spectacles. They have a faint glow about them and seem to know me and wave, occasionally calling a greeting.

There will be occasion enough to commune and share the wonder. For the present, I want to see this Shimmer Kingdom, as the name comes to me, for myself, by myself.

The sky is a vibrant azure, with, here and there, snow-white clouds drifting across. Birds singly, in pairs and in aerobic flocks, dart and wheel about. Can I, too, fly? I no sooner have the thought than I lift myself off the ground and float along at walking speed. I savour the sensation for a minute and take flight, into the blue and white sky until the valley is far below me. The experience is incredible. I streak through the air, rising and falling at will, with an even greater sense of perfect joy and freedom.

Unlike the flying super-beings of the films, I'm not flashing horizontally like a missile, arms thrust forward to cut through the ether. I'm vertical, the land beneath me, requiring only my wish to progress. There is the lightest kiss of wind on my face and my skin tingles with goosebumps, which prompts me to think about my substance. My body has a quasi-existence because I'm using my senses – to see, to smell, to hear, to feel. Yet there is no physical body. As I look, I'm an invisible man.

Seized with an impulse, I fly to the nearest cumulus and fulfil a childhood fantasy by walking on clouds as though they are snowscapes. I know well that clouds are insubstantial mists of suspended water droplets. Here, they are soft mountains of a dry fluff or cotton substance that hold me. It is an illusion: the clouds are incapable of bearing any weight and, having no body, I'm weightless, and can hover atop them.

Angels need no wings, Aoife had said. True. Over the ages, a million descriptions, paintings and statues of angels backed by massive aerodynamic fins had been mistaken. I imagine an overweight angel scampering along the ground, slowly making speed, great swanlike wings flapping furiously to achieve lift-off. Preposterous. I'm chortling as I position myself to sit on the edge of a cloud and survey the land below.

From this lofty eminence, what I think of as my realm is far below. I can discern no curvature of the horizon and the terrain spreads out for an infinite distance, with towns mere specks and the rise of mountains barely noticeable. It is a vista of never-ending scenic magnificence, of hills and valleys, rich pasturelands, parks and woodlands, dotted manor houses and villages, occasional windmills and, here and there, a city, everything extending in all directions into an eternity of space.

In the most remote distance, an odd blue-yellow light catches my eye: a tremulous glow, faint, glistening, quivering, emitting warm waves. It seems to be atop a stone tower and bathes a wide circle of the surrounding area. There is something about its radiance that is mysterious, sacred even. Far away though it is, it has a magnetic pull, urging me gently, seductively towards it. Not yet, I think, but, in time, I shall make my pilgrimage to this strange-lit spot. For now, I descend from my downy vantage to the ground, curious to see what else my new-found world can offer.

I am at a place altogether different from the previous bucolic setting. I've arrived, unheralded, into a vast circular, many-layered amphitheatre. In wooden walkways on rising tiers, under many-coloured parasols and large sun brollies, dozens of holidaymakers relax in colourfully striped deckchairs, talking, reading, dozing. Beyond the amphitheatre, I see the red and white top of a bandstand and hear the musicians – band or orchestra – playing marches, polkas, waltzes and whatnot with gusto.

The centre of the amphitheatre's ground level has a shallow circular swimming pool of pale blue water with a spouting Manneken Pis in the middle. Young men and girls, some in swimsuits, sit at the edge, legs dangling in the water, faces upraised to catch the cool spray of the fountain.

In shaded recesses and corridors around the pool, small kiosks and pavilions sell sweets from glass jars, lemonade, iced fairy cakes, gingerbread men and sandwiches, books and magazines – *The Strand, The Burlington, The Cornhill, Once a Week, Punch, Boy's Own Paper* and others. An ice cream shop features on its back wall a delightful gaudily coloured reproduction of portly Edward VII, red-lipped and rosy-cheeked, surrounded by crossed Union flags and redcoated soldiers with white pith helmets.

I'm in a seaside place in the first years of the twentieth century, somewhere in Ireland or Britain. The holidaymakers appear to have stepped out of gaily illustrated holiday posters of the period, men in boaters, open-necked shirts, striped blazers and baggy slacks, women like hourglasses, skirts trailing the ground.

I realise I'm viewing a mirage, though a solid one, filled with life. With the passage of time, all here are already dead and this amphitheatre is long gone, demolished or a deteriorated weed-covered ruin. But that's not what it's about. This is life that will not pass away, ever. In this part of the Shimmer Kingdom, I am witness to a summer's outing on a day that is more than a century past. The people are real and yet they are shades, ghostly presences living and reliving a perfect holiday afternoon, their world preserved in psychic amber.

The amphitheatre, the holidaymakers, the day – I'm here for a reason, I think, to learn something. What? In part, it is that all here are both mortal and immortal and own this afternoon to treasure again and again for eternity. There is an afterlife where people can, if they wish, and as they may choose, re-inhabit the good occasions and emotions of life from within their own Shimmer Kingdom. Time does not pass, nor does life.

Something else I know, and with absolute certainty, Aoife is here, and it is her invisible presence that gives it much of its magic and enchantment. I realise I've known this in some part of my consciousness from the time I turned into The Lord's Walk. My fleeting sight of her ensured that I would follow, as though she had led me to this place.

A middle-aged man passes, an elegant gent in a boater, striped blazer, sandy moustache, humming happily to himself.

'Pardon me,' I say. 'Have you by any chance seen –'

'Well, well, indeed,' he breaks in, giving me a wink of familiarity. 'She was here earlier, to be sure. Mentioned you, in fact...'

'Do you know where I might find her?'

He scratches his chin ruminatively. 'It's like this. To find your Aoife, you must continue to go across distance and times. You will see her again soon, then nevermore, then forever more.'

I'm about to query this mystifying piece of information when he says, left eye down in another wink, 'Time's up for you, I fear, old bean,' and I become aware that with great reluctance, I can no longer be here. The air quavers and trembles and the bright colours fade.

The Lord's Walk on a wet October day came into focus.

'Hello. Are you okay? D'you need assistance?'

A man stood before me, frowning, middle-aged, in a flat cap, shiny black raincoat and open black umbrella. His small brown-and-white Jack Russell on a leash sniffed me suspiciously.

I must have been an odd sight. It was raining heavily, soaking my hair, dripping down my face and drenching my clothes. I was standing unmoving like a shop dummy, gazing vacantly into space, oblivious of the downpour and without an overcoat.

'Thank you. I'm fine.'

My tone seemed to ease his mind. I glanced at my watch. By my reckoning, I'd spent many hours in this veiled world, yet it was less than ten minutes since leaving my driveway. Another spacetime aberration.

'You live around here?' the man persisted, with a broad gesture. This was the class of place where lifelong next-door neighbours would not necessarily know one another.

'Yes, indeed. Across the road, in fact. I came out for fresh air before the rain. I got, er, disquieting news in the post, a family matter.'

With a curt nod, he headed off, his dog looking back at me doubtfully.

'Thank you, thank you,' I shouted, and man and dog quickened their pace.

Shivering in my apartment, I stripped off my sodden clothes, towelled myself and ran a hot bath. I chucked in most of a bottle of Radox and sank in comforting warmth under a thick blanket of foam and bubbles. I had to ask myself if anyone, during a normal sane existence, had ever encountered anything like this, the latest and, by a long measure, the most astounding of the happenings to come at me.

What was indescribably otherworldly about the Shimmer Kingdom was the enchantment. I had no doubt that, for whatever reason, Aoife had guided me there. Every wink of time, blade of grass, pebble, building, every atom and molecule had been lovingly touched with her magic. And my emotional state of joy and serenity at being in this world was because it was her world also. Nirvana, as Buddhism has it. Or is it Hinduism? I'm not much for eastern religions.

I had no answer but, what was of greater importance to me, I had received one huge revelation. The inevitability of death and the accoutrements of death and the dead themselves were not to be viewed with terror. Dead bodies, whatever their condition, were but inanimate waxworks, or cast-off ragged overcoats of the spirit. Life existed both before and after death. Blissful, then, were the dead, and I had no cause to fear them. My necrophobia was irrational and I could toss it to the winds.

43

CHURCHWARD MANOR

The website for Churchward Manor billed it as an Executive Team Engagement Centre. It was described as 'amid pleasant woodlands and the spectacular natural scenery of County Wicklow, close to the famed early monastic site of Glendalough'. The Centre promised outstanding facilities for small corporate group meetings, seminars, sales meetings, reviews and strategy think-ins. Photographs showed spacious timber-panelled meeting rooms with antique furnishings and artwork and the usual high-tech business seminar equipment. Other photos showed period-style dining rooms, a cosy lounge bar, a spa and comfortable bedroom suites.

I googled D'Auvencour and found a single reference to Mr René D'Auvencour, who, a year earlier, had addressed Wicklow Junior Chamber of Commerce on the subject of managing executive stress. The blurb noted he was a visiting lecturer at Oxford University, the Boston Medical Center and the University of Paris 6. Other than that, the Web failed to net him. Peculiar.

Then I happened on a brief article on the Manor by the late

Mortimer Roche, a local amateur historian. Members of the Churchward family, originally from Norfolk, had relocated to Wicklow in the time of James I and built a manor on the ruins of a thirteenth-century Norman castle. Two hundred and fifty years on, in 1864, their descendants sold it to an order of nuns, the Sisters of Saint Philomena, newly arrived in Ireland who demolished the old manor and replaced it with a substantial convent.

It served as a novitiate and residence until the 1960s when the Vatican dropped St Philomena from the Liturgy, with the implication she probably never existed. The order never recovered from that. New entrant numbers collapsed, and the order dissolved. After years of lying empty, the convent was acquired in 2002 by the present owner, a Ray Davenport (close enough), who gutted the interior and renovated the Manor as a conference facility, with the Churchward Manor name revived.

No question, I needed to visit Churchward Manor and meet this D'Auvencour. He may have been the last to see Aoife alive, apart from Todd Scully, who drove the car that night. Apart from that tantalising possible glimpse on The Lord's Walk, I'd not seen Aoife since the lavender garden that was (and was not) in Saint Camillus Home. I was excited at the thought of at least speaking with someone who had known her.

I rescheduled several unimportant meetings, cleared my desk and email and headed for Churchward Manor. An hour out, I passed the early medieval ruins of Glendalough, glimpsing the round tower through the trees, an enchanted place of holy gloom, as an English poet described it. A dozen miles on, a signpost indicated a side road to Churchward

Village. I drove down a narrowing lane, barely wide enough to let two cars pass abreast, and reached a walled enclosure with an arched gateway. A discreet sign told me I'd arrived at the Churchward Manor Executive Team Engagement Centre. In front of a manicured lawn stood the Manor house itself.

There was no disguising that the exterior had once been an ecclesiastical establishment. It was evident in the Gothic Revival style, the cloister walk that took most of the frontage and the churchy arched doorways and mullioned windows. It was a large, three-storey building of red sandstone, with tooled limestone impost blocks, under a slate roof. A large limestone circular tower dominated the left end, with windows and crenels topped with merlons.

A car park sign directed me to a clearing in a wood close by that held a score of cars, one a high-end BMW, the others three to six-year-old medium-sized saloons and estates, salesman's models, the kind I'd have settled for if, *faute de mieux*, I hadn't inherited Jasper's Jaguar and acquired notions above my station. I parked and took the pathway to the front entrance of the Manor.

It opened into a spacious hallway, with leather seating, glass-topped coffee tables, the dark timber floor glossy. Vases of fresh-cut Christmas roses, camellias and witch hazel decked the hall.

A decorative medieval suit of steel armour, knight resting on a broadsword, stood in a recessed corner, with his companion or adversary in another. One wall featured a display of arms, swords, spears, axes, maces. No vestiges of a convent remained within and I observed no sign of cultish practices. It had the ambience of an old-fashioned Victorian big house – what my own Huntsman Hall might once have been on a smaller scale.

A young, pleasant horse-faced girl sat at a reception desk and gave me a friendly greeting, flashing white teeth and prominent gums. The badge on her blouse named her as Eadaoin Horsmough.

I produced my new business card. It named me as Kieran Sheridan Le Fanu, acting CEO, Aardvark-Sheridan Advertising. The Le Fanu part of my name had become who I was, a new this-is-me statement. When I ordered the cards from Oliver Foy, the agency's production manager, he said, 'Are you related to the famous –'

'Yes,' I replied. 'I'm descended from Richard Brinsley Sheridan.'

Which, to the best of my knowledge, may have been true.

I asked to speak with Mr D'Auvencour. 'Sorry I don't have an appointment. I happened to be, ah, in the area and thought I might visit.'

'No problem. I'll see if he's available. Please take a seat,' she gestured and spoke in a low murmur into her desk phone.

The lounge was bright in cream and lilac colours and furnished with comfortable armchairs and couches. I noticed a well-used hardback book on one table, blue cloth, no dust jacket. Idly, I picked it up. A. J. Ayer's *The Problem of Knowledge*. A Dublin Airport parking ticket stub marked a page that had a paragraph underlined in red pencil, with triple exclamation marks in the margin.

A view which I have not considered is that people are differentiated from one another not by the possession of any special properties but by being different spiritual substances or souls. And the reason why I have not considered it is that I do not find it intelligible. How are we to tell, for example, whether the same soul inhabits different bodies, simultaneously or successively? Does it ever happen that two souls get into a single body?

I replaced the book as a thin, handsome woman, impeccably groomed in a white business suit with pale brown bordering appeared and introduced herself as Jacinta Boudren. I was annoyed with myself that I'd given no thought to explaining a) why I was here and b) why I was really here.

I remembered D'Auvencour was a medical man of some sort. 'Is it Mr D'Auvencour or Doctor D'Auvencour?' I asked.

'Strictly, it's Doctor Doctor D'Auvencour. He holds doctorates from German universities, among others, where they use the double title. But Mr will do fine. He should be free in fifteen minutes or so.'

She had a busy face. A disconcerting squint winked every few seconds. She would finish sentences by clamping her mouth shut and jutting out her jaw in an unintended angry grimace, gone before I could be sure it had been there. That and her semaphore eyes were unsettling, and I wondered how she worked in proximity to a doctor without either of them doing something to alleviate things.

I apologised again for dropping by unexpectedly. 'Your signpost on the main road reminded me that I'd been recommended to visit the Hall and, well, here I am and I hope it's not inconvenient.'

My unlikely explanation tailed off, but she accepted it. It was not in any manner inconvenient, she assured me. She didn't ask who had recommended the Centre, and I assumed my status as acting CEO of an advertising agency gave me standing as a potential client. She led me to one of several connected smaller lounge areas off the hall and left me to await the master. The layout maintained the club atmosphere: deep carpet, soft white velvet-cushioned armchairs, polished tables, more magazines, coffee on the brew.

I inspected the paintings on the walls and found an eclectic gallery of Irish artists of the past – Jack Yeats, Louis le Brocquy, Walter Osborne, William Orpen. Minor works, suggestive of a conservative taste, yet an impressive collection. There was a John Lavery portrait, though not of Hazel.

In an alcove, not immediately visible, was a large oil painting, different from the rest. When I got close, my breath caught in astonishment and I actually staggered back a pace.

There it was, intense and vivid as my first experience of the glories of the Shimmer Kingdom: the country boreen, the brown and orange autumnal foliage, horses and cows in the field, the manse in the trees, grey smoke curling from the chimneys. Swallows crossing a blue and yellow sky. The steam train making its way across the distant hills.

Behind me, a voice said, 'Splendid, is it not? Don't you imagine you can walk right into it?'

I turned to meet Mr D'Auvencour.

44

MEETING MR D'AUVENCOUR

I had visualised D'Auvencour as a small, stout man, balding, goateed and bow-tied, with a phoney geniality that would fail to mask a creepy menace – resembling the Satanist portrayed by Niall McGinnis in Jacques Tourneur's *Night of the Demon*. I was wrong. D'Auvencour had a well-trimmed goatee. Otherwise, he was tall, six foot four, I estimated, powerfully built, with thick black hair swept back from his temples in a widow's peak that gave him a vaguely Mephistophelean appearance. But there was nothing disquieting about him. His green eyes, enlarged by wire-framed spectacles, were friendly and seemed to look at the world with good-natured amusement.

'I am René D'Auvencour and I'm pleased to meet you, Mr Le Fanu.' His voice, a bass cello, accent neutral, had the slightest hint of a question mark on my name. Or maybe I was self-conscious about it.

'And I you. Thank you for meeting me out of the blue like this.' I shook his proffered hand.

My gaze went back to the painting. 'An evocative scene. It's as though I knew the place. Are you familiar with it?'

'Not that I'm aware. It may even have been painted from the imagination.'

'No, no. I've walked along that country road. Are you acquainted with the artist?'

'I'm not that old.' He pointed to the artist's signature and date, bottom left: 'Sandra Parry 1876'. A shiver ran up my spine as I recalled: Darling Sandra Parry.

He said, 'Incredibly alive, is it not, with all those brilliant colours and shades of an autumn day in the country? With what deft touches the artist has brought nature to life – can't you sense the gentle rustle of the trees? The smoke from the chimney rises and dissolves and that distant train is about to steam slowly out of picture.'

As he spoke, the painting seemed indeed to awaken, and all I needed to do was step forward to enter the scene – much as I had done.

'Well, enough of that,' he said, breaking the spell. 'What can I do for you, Mr Le Fanu?' he asked with a glance at my card. Again, a hesitation at my name. He guided me to a deep leather armchair and sat opposite me.

'Thank you for seeing me,' I said. 'Eoin Sullivan, a business associate, speaks highly of your programmes. I wished to see for myself and I'm glad I did. Churchward Manor is an impressive establishment and might be a good venue for a staff bonding exercise our agency is planning. A dozen people or so, over a long weekend?'

'Or midweek? This is our busiest time of year and we have few weekends free. Jacinta manages the diary and has a better idea of what is available.'

I hedged, trying to think of a way to broach the real purpose of my visit and avoid being foisted onto Jacinta Boudren.

'I'm surprised I haven't heard of Churchward Manor before. How long has your Centre been doing business here?'

'Coming up to ten years.' He was cordial, patient and something else. He seemed to see through my dissembling and find me entertaining, like I was a curious and half-expected character. I had an absurd image of myself as a bird that had fallen down the chimney and was testing its wings in the fireplace, under his observation.

He gave me a look as though inviting me to finish my verbal throat clearing and talk about why I was here. Taking a gulping breath, I began. 'Truth is, Mr D'Auvencour, I've another reason for visiting, my main purpose, in fact. You had guests with you at the Centre last month –'

'Aoife Ruthyn and Thomas Scully.'

I stared at him, stunned into silence.

'Come, my dear Mr Le Fanu, we are in County Wicklow, not the far side of the moon. The news of the appalling car crash has been in the public domain, including your name as sole survivor, though as Sheridan, if I got it right. The national newspapers reach this part of the country, to say nothing of Wi-Fi internet. And I do have friends in Dublin, who keep an eye on things for me.'

I wondered about these friends. Someone on the staff of the hospital or at St Camillus Home?

'The reason I'm here,' I rushed on. 'I came here to discover more about Aoife and, er, Mr Scully.'

'It is natural you would. And what would you expect to learn from me?' His tone was considerate, forbearing.

'Whatever you might tell me. I presume they were part of

a group?'

'No, they were here separately and individually.'

'Patients? Or friends of yours?'

I tried not to sound as if I was pleading for crumbs of information. He considered me thoughtfully and said, 'Patients? That's not a term I would use. But why do you ask?'

I hesitated, not sure how to continue. 'I've been told that you are, among other things, a scholar of the, ah, occult sciences. Can I ask if Aoife and Scully came to see you in relation to, um, the occult?'

He pursed his lips and I thought he was going to start laughing.

'A curious question and not an idle one.' His eyes twinkled. 'Do you know what the term occult means?'

'Not much, and what I know is probably wildly erroneous, from books I read as a teenager – *The Devil Rides Out*, Black Masses, calling on Beelzebub, blood sacrifices, inverted crucifixes…'

He chuckled. 'No, none of that in my life, though it would add piquancy to it. You'll find no occult lodge of evil sorcerers hereabouts. The occult is no more nor less than the acquisition of knowledge beyond the natural. Hence the loose expression, the supernatural. It has been called secret knowledge because it explores a world hidden from most people, who are fully preoccupied with their day-to-day lives. That is all.'

I remembered Monsignor Flinter and his Gnostics, searching for their own secret knowledge.

'There are those, and among them I include myself, who progress our studies and research through the wisdom of the Light. Others, a small number, persuade themselves they can communicate with the Dark Side, black magic as the fanciful Wheatleys of fiction would have it.'

D'Auvencour was not the first person of late to disclose more than I'd been expecting. Was there some empathic aspect of my personality that invited confidences and explanations?

'Mr Scully was a case in point, one of those who looked to magic as a quick fix for life's problems. He associated with a set of amateur dabblers in black magic who conducted unsavoury experiments with dead animals and human bones at night within the husk of the Hellfire Club in the Dublin Mountains.'

Like all Dubliners, I was aware of the Hellfire Club, a burnt-out humpbacked ruin that looked down on Dublin from the heights of Montpelier Hill. I was familiar with the legends of evildoings and satanic apparitions at what was reputedly the site of a prehistoric burial ground and later the hunting lodge haunt of hedonistic Georgian bucks. I had read of a night-time Garda raid on the place a few months back.

'Mister Scully convinced himself that, in a previous life, he had been a member of the Club and had partaken of fantastic rituals there,' D'Auvencour said with asperity. 'He told me that, before their so-called coven dispersed, they had summoned demons of the underworld with the aid of a rare book of dark magic, *The Necronomicon*. I felt obliged to tell him that *The Necronomicon* was a fictional invention of the writer H. P. Lovecraft. Demons existed only in the imagination of his coven. They might as well have tried summoning Mickey Mouse or Ronald McDonald. I reminded him of the recent case of a woman who attributed her apparently miraculous recovery from illness to her prayers to a statue of the Virgin

Mary. No one dared tell her it was a *Lord of the Rings* evil figurine.'

My laugh was forced.

'I send him on his way,' he continued. 'A sadder though regrettably not a wiser man. With hindsight, I may have misjudged him. Scully had indeed developed strong and sinister abilities. The day of the car crash, I had a foreboding.'

He seemed to be talking to himself. 'That morning, Aoife, who was my guest, was going home for a short break. I was about to chair a business meeting, so we made our farewells and I left her at reception waiting for her taxi. Later, Jacinta informed me that Todd Scully, who had departed the previous evening, had returned to the Manor to leave me a note. He observed Aoife with her suitcase and offered her a lift to Dublin Airport. She accepted, and they departed in his car.'

'You were afraid he might harm her?'

'Heavens, no. Scully by himself was no threat. He could do her no harm. But when I heard the dreadful news of the crash, I realised I had not been sufficiently on guard when Aoife was here under my protection. I should have remained with her until she had left. If I had, I don't believe she would have died that night.'

I was no longer interested in Scully. 'And did Aoife represent the Light?'

He held my gaze.

'You already have the answer to that, Mr Le Fanu. You've met with her, talked with her. Is there not a special bond between you?'

I stared at him, stupefied.

'If this were a novel of the occult,' he laughed, 'you would now be saying, indignantly, "What vile sorcery is this?".'

He became serious. 'My apologies. I should not be flippant. I have been aware of your affinity with Aoife as soon as I saw you. You are both closely linked and your destinies entwined. Your aura has much in common with hers.'

'You can see my aura?' I asked. 'I must admit I can't. Aoife spoke of auras but I've never been altogether sure what they are.'

'Your aura reveals much about a person,' said D'Auvencour. 'It appears as a body halo, an aureole of luminous radiation that surrounds a person.'

He made a circular motion, indicating the outline of my body. It made me vaguely uncomfortable, like I was in the presence of a mind reader. I stole a quick glance, to see if there might be traces of a glowing light. I saw nothing. He followed my glance and shook his head.

'It is there, even if you don't yet see it. Everyone has an aura. Physically, it comprises particles of electromagnetic energy. It is a manifestation of a person's inner being: spirit, soul, eternal spark, whatever term you use. It is sometimes called charisma, a word much overused and misused. Your aura is faint, and not fully aligned to your physical form, which is unusual. Weak though it is, I recognised right away an aspect of Aoife's aura in you.'

He gave me a long look. 'I believe you are entitled to learn what I can tell you of Aoife. If you're free, you might join me for a light meal and we can talk further?'

45

THE LIVES OF AOIFE

We made our way to a small dining room on the first floor of the tower, which, I learned later, held his living accommodation. The room was brightly lit and furnished in Regency style – a polished extending dining table, chairs with sabre-shaped legs and rolled backrests, a walnut drinks cabinet, a marble-topped console, old hunting prints on the wall. A variation of the Manor's elite club décor. The table was laid for two, with a generous seafood salad, sauces and homemade breads. The wine was a Grüner Veltliner.

I raised my glass, 'Sláinte.'

'Lechaim.'

'Reincarnation and regression are not interchangeable terms,' D'Auvencour said abruptly, as if to clarify a comment I'd made, though I had said nothing. 'Reincarnation literally means entering a new body. When a person dies, their spirit, after an interval, begins life again in a newborn body at the moment of conception or, sometimes, taking over the body of a person who is at the moment of death.'

'At the moment of death? I haven't heard that before.' I

said. I realised guiltily that I had been lost in thought for the past few minutes and couldn't work out how our conversation had arrived at this point. I made an effort to focus. His remarks were interesting but I began waiting for an opportunity to bring us back to Aoife.

'In rare circumstances,' he replied. 'And only when destiny's stars are dancing in particular and uncommon alignment. Past life regression, on the other hand, is a technique that enables a person in a guided hypnotic trance ostensibly to recall details of one or several of their many past lives.'

He continued with his mini-lecture.

'Sceptics would argue there are no true past life regressions and what is apparently experienced during a trance may be any one of a number of things – information acquired at one time and not consciously assimilated. Or a fantasy intended to please the hypnotist. Or, as followers of Jung might suggest, inherited memory from past generations or a collective consciousness. Or a gene-borne memory.'

He dismissed them with a decided shake of the head. 'There are far too many instances of regression where none of these objections stands scrutiny. I've had patients who recalled past lives with the kind of specific information of period and place they could not have been aware of but which I was able later to verify.'

As I considered how to move our discussion towards the purpose of my visit, he got in first. 'I came to know Aoife Ruthyn only in recent months. Ruthyn is a Scottish name, I believe, though her family had their home in Surrey for several generations. She was orphaned as a child, like you. Both parents and her sister, her only sibling, died in an air crash outside Paris when returning from a holiday in Corfu. Aoife was due to be with them, but a fever kept her back with a nurse.

'She was well provided for financially and was raised by an aunt and uncle. They travelled widely and saw little of her, especially when she was in boarding school. She was an excellent student and went up to Cambridge to take Modern History.

'At age twenty-four, that's three years ago, Aoife slipped on an icy path on a winter morning, hit her head on the ground and was hospitalised with concussion. It was not regarded as serious and she soon recovered. But from that time, she experienced occasional daydream visions. They were fleeting glimpses, lasting no more than a minute or two. She was in a place of elation, yet suffused with a rare melancholy, a sense of having lost a close and intimate friend, a friend above all others, as she put it. She understood this person, never seen or identified, had died or gone away or was where she could not reach him. She would search for him through archaic streets and buildings, in cities unknown to her and empty of living people. Awake, her sensation was of overwhelming loss.

'These emotions became so draining and depressing that she was referred by her GP to a respected psychiatrist, Professor Jane Rawling Beddison. Professor Beddison's initial prognosis was that Aoife was clinically depressed because of unresolved issues around the family she had lost before she had properly known them. Soon, Beddison concluded there were deeper problems.'

He gave a slight nod of concurrence with Beddison's conclusions.

'With Aoife's agreement, she used hypnosis, taking her back to early childhood. To Beddison's immense surprise, Aoife, without prompting or suggestion, reverted beyond her own childhood to that of a ten-year-old girl – not Aoife Ruthyn but Marie Martyn, youngest of a large family of a craft tailor and his wife who lived in Oranmore, near Galway in the West of Ireland. She spoke in a mix of Gaelic and rough English and gave the date as 1821. She described her family, her home and the environs of Oranmore in much detail.'

He frowned. 'Not all practitioners of regression hypnosis believe reincarnation is involved, and Beddison considered Aoife's supposed regression was subconscious storytelling that disguised deep-seated problems.

'Beddison is a friend and one-time colleague of mine and we had both discussed regression therapies at length. I have a modest reputation in this field and have facilitated dozens of regression experiences. Given Aoife's continued interest in learning more of Marie Martyn, Jane recommended she consult me.'

He closed his eyes as though he had forgotten I was in the room.

'I first saw Aoife around Easter this year. As an aside, one of the first questions she asked me was if René was my real name. I said that it was. She said, "René means 'reborn', doesn't it?"'

He chuckled. As it happened, René was my middle name but I said nothing, not wanting to raise a distraction.

He continued. 'Aoife possessed an extremely attractive aura. She proved a good subject and slipped into a trance quickly. I took her back to times before her birth. Over several sessions, I failed to reconnect her to Marie Martyn, either as child or adult, whose single appearance remains a mystery. Instead, two other lives emerged.

'The first was Sandra Parry, only daughter of a widowed clergyman, who had a pleasant and comfortable living in Lucan, near Dublin, during the late nineteenth century. Sandra was in her mid-twenties, the same as Aoife, and they were of similar personality. She was well brought up and educated, a likeable and friendly young woman, in charge of her life. Her mother had died a few years before and she had a good relationship with her father, a respected New Testament scholar in his sixties, somewhat scatterminded, as she said.'

'Sandra Parry.'

'Yes, the painter of the garden scene in the lounge we both admire. I acquired it from an antique shop in Dublin. I had commissioned an agent to track it down for me.'

He resumed his story. 'Where was I? Yes. In one other crucial respect, Sandra was like Aoife – she had that same emotion of sadness and depression. For Sandra, there was an understandable reason: she had met a man, fallen in love with him and, within a week of first meeting him, he had been killed in a railway accident. She herself died less than a year later when her heart, never strong, gave out.'

'Perhaps she died of a broken heart, if that's not being theatrical.'

D'Auvencour inclined his head. 'That was Aoife's belief, and I don't discount it. Broken heart syndrome, stress-induced cardiomyopathy, is well recognised by the medical profession.

'I'll move on to the second life we encountered and I'll have much to say about her. This was Grace Delany, born at the beginning of the twentieth century. She lived in the family home in Lower Mount Street – not far from your offices in Merrion Square.'

'I've walked along Mount Street a hundred times.' I tried to visualise how it might have appeared, more than a century earlier. Apart from the motorised traffic, cars and double-decker buses in place of trams and horse-and-carts, not that different.

'I imagine you have. It is interesting her regressions were Irish. Aoife herself had never been to Ireland before coming to meet with me here. With a name like Aoife, I presume she had some Irish heritage.'

'Her great-grandmother introduced the name.' I remembered what Aoife had mentioned to me the first time we met.

If my knowledge surprised him, he gave no sign and went on.

'By the time she came of age, she was living with her only sister. Both her parents were dead, victims of the influenza epidemic and her brother had been killed in the Great War. She lived frugally, augmenting a modest inheritance by working in a solicitor's office in Harcourt Street. Aoife, as Grace Delany, relived an incident, a central juncture earlier in her life. I'm going to tell you about it.'

46

MARCHING THROUGH DUBLIN

We moved to his office study, directly above where we had just eaten. He pulled his chair from behind his desk and sat facing me as I perched comfortably in a cushioned window alcove. Oak bookcases lined the walls, crammed with every format of book, from heavy leather volumes darkened with age to new-looking dust covers and paperbacks. It was a working office, no pictures or framed certificates on the walls, no personal items, only a small desk with an Apple laptop.

D'Auvencour told me that Aoife was an excellent hypnosis subject, intelligent and perceptive, and described his method of inducing a deep trance.

She sat on the couch in this room, head well cushioned, a light blanket covering her body, at ease, eyes half-closed.

'…and you are completely relaxed. All is good. You have no weight in your body and you feel yourself floating. It is a most pleasant feeling. And as you relax even deeper, you will hear me count backwards from twenty to zero, and as you hear me count, you will begin once again to see your life to date pass before your eyes, twenty, nineteen, eighteen, moving slowly, moving back like the numbers I'm counting... now moving back more quickly, the days and the months and the years now slip by in front of you, and you are relaxing deeper and deeper... nine, eight, seven, you are now a child, now a baby, now, as you have easily done before, go back before that time, five... four... three...'

Grace was sitting at an open first-floor window in offices in College Green, the plaza in front of Trinity College. A large and enthusiastic crush of people lined the pavements and spilled onto the street. Boisterous youths had climbed onto the plinths of the statues of King William and Oliver Goldsmith and were exuberantly waving Union flags. Across the street, spectators packed the windows of Jury's Hotel.

The crowd was looking with anticipation up the long, wide Dame Street, the commercial hub of Dublin. In the distance and getting nearer by the minute they could hear the steady tramp of marching feet and military bands playing familiar marching airs – 'The British Grenadiers', 'Let Erin Remember', 'Garryowen'.

It was an afternoon at the end of April 1915 and the newly recruited soldiers of the 7th Division, Royal Dublin Fusiliers, having departed their temporary billet in the Royal Barracks, were now marching through the centre of Dublin to the Liffey Quays, where they would embark for further training in England and thence to the battlefield. There was a more direct line of march along the quays from barracks to ship, but the authorities had routed the march through Dame Street to give Dubliners an opportunity to bid a suitable farewell to their heroes and encourage other young men to enlist.

Dame Street and College Green were draped with bunting

and floral displays and Union flags in a variety of sizes. Earlier, as Grace walked along the street, colourful recruitment posters were on every available space. A glowering Lord Kitchener pointed a gloved forefinger almost in your eye, saying, 'Your Country Needs You.' A column of soldiers led by a kilted piper marched by a Celtic round tower: 'Irishmen! Won't You Join Them?' The Angels of Mons descended on the battlefield, a reminder of whose side the Almighty favoured.

Now the troops, fresh young men, came into sight and were marching along College Green, rifles shouldered, four abreast – peaked caps, khaki, puttees, gleaming bayonets fixed for the occasion – and were greeted with tumultuous shouting and cheering. It was a warm day and they were perspiring under their full pack plus blanket and oilsheet. Still, they were in fine spirits, belting out their Division song with gusto:

Left, right. Left, right. Here's the way we go,
Marching with fixed bayonets, the terror of every foe,

Grace laughed at the words and the enthusiasm. With a leap of her heart she saw brother Aidan, her junior by two years, in the second rank of D Company, the Pals Battalion, with his friends from Trinity College rugby club, in their late teens and early twenties. She waved her lace handkerchief frantically and shouted his name. It was lost in the hubbub. Aidan peered around from time to time but failed to see her in the window above him. He sang lustily with his fellows:

A credit to the nation, a thousand buccaneers,
A terror to creation are the Dublin Fusiliers.

Grace had a tremor of fear for Aidan and his pals: mere boys in uniform playing soldiers. When the time came, would they be able to stick their enemy with those shiny nasty bayonets? Or would the big Hun soldier brutes, who murdered babies and violated nuns, stick them first?

She wished she could be in the street below to say goodbye again to Aidan, make him feel dauntless and gallant, and regretted she had accepted the invitation of a family friend, Brice Richardson, to view the march from the vantage of his accountancy office. She would prefer to have been among the cheering thousands, the impeccably dressed gentlemen in bowlers and the lace-bonneted ladies, happily standing alongside the shabby cloth caps and shawlies of the tenements.

Students from Trinity and the College of Surgeons pressed boxes of cigarettes, chocolates and other gifts on the marchers. A steady stream of women young and old walked alongside, keeping pace with the marchers, having a last conversation with husbands, brothers and sweethearts.

'You relate it as if you were there yourself,' I interrupted.

'I don't have an eidetic memory,' D'Auvencour replied amiably. 'I can, though, tell you what Aoife as Grace recalled more or less verbatim. She was good on the small details and I did tape our sessions.'

He resumed: Now the crucial event. As Aidan moved from view, she noticed a motor car towards the rear of the Division, a Wolseley open phaeton tourer, with two junior officers, under a recruitment banner urging *Fight for Ireland* in large green lettering. As the car passed under her window, one of the officers caught her attention. He was lounging in the back seat, grinning as he took in the jolly atmosphere of the street.

He was the most incredibly handsome and dashing man Grace had ever seen, and she had the impression of having known him forever. Known him closely, indeed, intimately, and at the thought, she flushed from neck to breastbone. He happened at that instant to glance up and saw her, framed in the open window. Their eyes met, and it was as though lightning passed between them. Astounded, he gazed at her spellbound and, with an uncertain expression, mouthed *Sandra?* Seconds later, the tourer had driven past and out of sight.

D'Auvencour gazed beyond me as if his mind was in that long-ago teeming and noise-filled street.

"She desperately wanted to leave her place at the window, rush down, catch up with the parade and speak to him. It was not to be. She slowly lost her vision of that day and emerged unbidden from her trance.'

'Incredible,' was all I could think to say.

'You think so?' said D'Auvencour, 'My final session with Aoife was no less extraordinary.'

47

SUDDEN DEATH

By this time, Aoife had become conditioned to the hypnosis sessions and had quickly drifted into an increasingly deep trance as D'Auvencour went through his routine.

The first day of June 1920. The midday Angelus bells from churches nearby and far away pealed and chimed across Dublin. Grace stood at the open front door of the solicitors' offices in Harcourt Street, making a final check of the letters she was about to deposit in the red letterbox across the road. The sun came out from a cloudbank, brightening the street and glistening the tram rails, wet from a recent shower.

A steady flow of people were exiting the stone-colonnaded entrance of the railway terminus. A tram, with its brightly coloured advertisements for Lipton's Tea, Donnelly's Bacon and the Metropolitan Laundry, dropped off and took on passengers. Directly across the street from Grace, two British army officers paused to light cigarettes and her heart flipped a beat as it always did at the sight of officers' khaki, jodhpurs and polished leather boots. At a glance, though, she saw they were older men, heavily built. Not him. Never him, it seemed.

With a thunderous roar, two Crossly Tenders packed with steel-helmeted soldiers under anti-grenade cages sped up Harcourt Street from St Stephen's Green and screeched to a halt a dozen doors away, blocking the street. The Tommies disgorged fast and rushed into one of the houses, rifles at the ready, bayonets fitted, screaming orders and cursing volubly.

She sighed. The violence was worsening by the day. A month previously, Myles Mallin, a clerk in the office, had shakily described in vivid detail how he had been on a tram at Ballsbridge that morning when several thugs dragged an elderly man from his seat and onto the roadway. They had put a revolver to his head and shot him dead. He was, according to Mallin, a senior civil servant from Dublin Castle.

Another military truck hurtled around the corner from nearby Hatch Street and rumbled noisily past carrying a squad of the new special constables, nicknamed the Black and Tans for their mix of green police tunics and military khaki trousers. They had become an increasingly frequent sight around Dublin, tough, semi-disciplined, mostly demobbed officers, organised with the aim of eliminating Michael Collins's murder gang. 'Medicine more toxic than the cure,' old Mr Hanley, one of the firm's partners had muttered.

Without warning, Grace heard several loud craa-acks from nearby, like gunshots, though she wasn't sure. She watched, not fully taking in what was happening as, across from her, the two officers dropped to the ground. She thought they had been hit, but they spread-eagled themselves, pulled out revolvers, and fired in her general direction.

Surely, they couldn't be shooting at me, she thought, even as she was abruptly slammed by an invisible hand. The street and sky were bright pink and inverted and she blacked out. And then she was among a small, silent cluster at the doorway of her office with the two officers who had zigzagged across the street. They were kneeling by her body, as it lay on the ground in a widening pool of blood.

Grace gazed dispassionately at the body, a broken puppet in a heap of clothes, face bloodless and open-mouthed in surprise, eyes open, unseeing, like one of her dolls. It was the corpse of another, not hers, not her, not anymore. Her emotions froze and nothing mattered.

She noticed Hatch Street was no longer Hatch Street and had become instead a blank space, an absolute emptiness, as though a gigantic, uneven rectangular strip had been ripped from the fabric of reality, from ground to sky. She seemed to glimpse a world of sunshine and crystal pure air and great beauty. Then, to her immense disappointment, it faded and vanished. She remained for a short time, uncertain about what she was seeing, peering into a wavering nothingness, until, at an inner urging, she moved forward into the blackness and abandoned forever a world that was no longer hers.

'It was Aoife's final session with me,' said D'Auvencour. 'It took place two days before her death.'

I politely declined his offer of a room for the night and he walked out with me. In the hallway, I noticed, on a wall in a passageway, in a glass-fronted frame, a set of photographs of what I took to be corporate seminar participants. I paused to look at them. One jumped out at me: at the front entrance of the Manor, D'Auvencour was in company with two others, all three dressed casually. One was a Garda Chief Superintendent whom I had seen on television in connection with a major fraud case. The other was Inspector Dan Breen. He beamed out at me as though tickled that I could now make a fair guess at on whose behalf he had been keeping an informal eye on me.

48

LUX AETERNA

One morning a week later, as I left the apartment a flash of white within the gloom of the shrubbery caught my eye. I thought it might be the white cat and hoped to see that charming creature again.

I pushed my way cautiously through the thicket of rough shrubbery for some distance until I reached a seemingly impenetrable obstacle of low-lying thorn bushes and a rusted barbed wire fence that marked the property boundary. Before me was a sizeable uncultivated meadow, a wilderness of small trees and scrubs, slopes and hollows with shoulder-high grass and weeds and blackberry brambles at this time of year devoid of fruit. In a far corner, partly hidden by thick bushes, I saw the whitewashed walls of a small, ramshackle cottage. White lace curtains fluttered at an open window, which suggested it wasn't derelict. The meadow was uncannily quiet, except for a far-off mass bell.

It was unusual to find such a large overgrown field in this locality of premium land values. In the two years since I'd moved into Huntsman Hall, I'd never had cause to push my way into the shrubbery, nor had I seen this great meadow from the top windows. I was curious to explore it, though I was daunted by the abundance of spiky thorn bushes and the septicaemia potential of the rust-brown barbed wire.

As I stood, irresolute, seeking a break in the fence, the meadow began to flicker and shudder, as though hit with a mild quake. It blurred and dissolved into a different scene, and I knew my Shimmer Kingdom was going to open before me. Pressing gingerly against the barbed wire got me nowhere. Instead, I allowed my mind to relax, felt myself separate from my body and I passed across the divide.

My spirit is in dancing exultation. I am bodiless once more, yet I breathe in the strong, sensuous fragrance of smouldering turf and lavender, always the heady scent of lavender. All about is serene and tranquil, shimmering its soft vibrating light.

There is music in the air again. This time I recognise Bruckner's Ninth, not as I heard it in my apartment but now a musical metamorphosis, superbly crafted improvisations on the original and on instrumentation I've never heard before. How had I missed, on listening to the CD, the flowing, haunting beauty and throat-catching purity of love at the centre of this music? Its inherent melancholy is now a delicate and lovely hymn without end, in tune with my emotions.

I am in front of a small railway station, the doors and gate are now open wide in welcome. Within, the single platform is immaculately clean with well-tended grass verges, beds of huge yellow sunflowers and multi-hued flower baskets.

I'm the sole passenger, alone on the platform, save for a small, black-bearded guard in a Prussian blue uniform, with rows of shiny silver buttons. On seeing me, he offers a stiff shoulder bow and briskly signals with his emerald flag, until a gleaming blue and yellow train emerges from a tunnel mouth. It chugs around a bend, and into the station, to halt with a shrill and gleeful blast of whistle and exuberant release of steam. I open the door of the nearest carriage, climb in and stretch out on the mulberry velvet-cushioned bench seat.

As though this train has been arranged specially for me, the whistle blasts again, and I'm as excited as a four-year-old on my way to sea and sand, or wherever it will be, as the train puffs and clanks through the station and into the countryside, and rattles unhurriedly along the tracks. I take in the view, and realise I am a passenger in the train I observed on the mountainside when I first entered the Kingdom. In fact, I can see my boreen in the distance below, a tiny, twisting thread of gold amid the greenery.

The train clatters past forests and farmland and village clusters of miniature whitewashed, slate-roofed buildings, with occasional stately manors set in tended lawns and gardens. We chug across an old stone many-arched viaduct, with people below waving and running and hallooing, as if the sight of a train is still a novelty. Sometime later, with more blasts of steam and shrieks of whistle, we ease to a halt at a station with the name *Endover* in gold lettering on a sign.

I step out. The station has red and yellow brick offices, waiting rooms and luggage rooms, all enveloped in hazy, lazy summer warmth. I'm alone except for butterflies, bees and numerous cooing pigeons on the station roof. *Endover* is laid out with white-pebbled walls, a well-spruced station, with flower beds of geranium, lobelia, sweet alyssum, and a long, golden privet hedge on the far side. Enamelled-tin advertisements promote perfumed soap and deluxe writing paper, as used by Princess Olga. Rays of sunlight glance off the single metal track.

I leave through a short tunnel and come out onto a seafront and an extensive curving beach of pristine sand. The fresh tang of the sea permeates my senses, as I commence a stroll along the length of a timbered esplanade. A mild breeze tempers the heat of the sun in a glorious sapphire sky, with here and there a languid puff of white cloud.

I reach two high stone pillars set a few feet apart topped with gold pineapple finials, and beyond an expanse of golden-brown strand and miles of shallow seawater, dotted with dunes and knolls and hollows, flecked with grey-green tufts of marram grass. I cross the shallows to nearby dunes and enter a sheltered grove of chestnut trees and beyond them, at a timber-clad summerhouse, Aoife sits on a wooden bench in characteristic pose, leaning back, hand to her chin, lost in contemplation – Lavery's immortal Kathleen Ni Houlihan. The radiance of her golden aura wraps her in charismatic luminosity.

I'm overwhelmed. She is more lovely and graceful than the images in my memory. When she sees me, those wonderful hazel eyes sparkle and her smile of pleasure all but stops my heart and, surely, I must still have one, for what else is thumping so fiercely?

I could happily stand before her contemplating till the end of time her beauty and her spirit of kindness and pleasure, utterly without guile or artifice.

'Michael, can you believe this... magic world?' In her captivating English accent, exotic and erotic to my Irish ears, her words come in a rush as if they've been held back too long.

'Between us,' she says. 'We've made a world that is divinely marvellous. Once, I doubted we would ever find each other. Did you think the same? This time, I don't intend to lose you: we are together now and for eternity.'

'For eternity,' I repeat happily. What I need to express requires more than words. I take her in my arms to embrace the sweetness and pure love of her spirit, as our souls commune and infuse and know each other as we become one. I, she, we swim in waves and swells of pleasure beyond physical delight. I touch her aura with my mind's eye and trace its contours and sense how gently it beats. An unhurriedly building tremor courses through us. We enter each other's aura and are one, and I experience, as she experiences, a slow, sensation of stunning rapture that reaches a crescendo of fulfilment.

Gradually, I notice things, the musical chime of bells as though from the farthest distance, faintly heard, and a pleasant fragrant aroma in the air, like burning sweet grass.

With my arm around her waist, her head resting against my shoulder, we walk towards a bridge that spans a deep valley with a wide, leisurely flowing but shallow river below and together we cross over.

We are in a tunnel of overhanging trees. A winding sandy path directs our way, lit by shafts of light through gaps in the canopy of thick green and brown foliage. We come out into an immense parkland of rolling lawns, glades, hummocks and hollows.

We sit on a grass verge near the statue of a Pan-like figure. I breathe in the heady perfumes of a rainbow of many exotic flowers. Aoife reaches over and takes my hand, making invisible hieroglyphics on my palm with her forefinger.

'I have never been here before,' she says. 'I mean, to this part of Heaven. Oh, it's not Heaven, but I can imagine nothing more… celestial.'

She lazily stretches her arms and moves them back and forth, reminding me of an angel's wings. Though angels, as she once told me, don't have wings.

'How do I appear to you?' she asks. 'I'm ghostlike, a shade, unseen by me, as I guess you are to you. But we can see each other.'

I hold an imaginary lorgnette and she flashed me that smile.

'You're dressed in a stunning green and gold long dress, with a subtle blue-grey trim. A silver tasselled belt highlights the slimness of your waist and a wide-brimmed straw hat with a golden bow matches your magnificent aura. You have perfect hazel eyes deeper than the forest, perfect black velvet hair, perfect skin and an entirely perfect body.'

Again, that incredible smile.

'How do you see me?' I ask, curious.

'Much as when I saw you in Dame Street, as you went to war, just now, a century ago. Khaki uniform, stiff peaked cap, a jacket of pockets and pleats and straps. Green shirt and tie loosely knotted, riding breeches, leather boots, so polished that I might find my reflection. If I had one. Tall, impossibly good-looking, flashing blue eyes, pencil moustache, classy top-to-toe, brilliant golden aura. I never even knew your name.'

'Lieutenant the Hon. Audoen O'Brien, forever at your service.'

I gave a passable military salute.

'Edwin?'

'Pronounced that way, though the spelling is –' and I spelt it. 'As in Saint Audoen, Dublin's oldest church. In the mess, they called me Audience.' I grinned.

'I shall ever think of you as Michael.' She says it lightly, with an underlying seriousness in her voice.

'Let it be Michael because my Audoen persona is no more.'

'What happened to him, to you? Afterwards?'

The memory comes easily. 'I had a good war, insofar as there is good in war, and especially in that dreadful conflict: medals, promotion, mention in dispatches and so on. The girl in the window in College Green was in my thoughts every blessed day and night. I wrote letters to her regularly. Of course, I had no idea where to send them. I fully intended to find her again, if I had the luck to make it back.'

I expelled a deep breath. 'I survived battle for more than four years, with a single wound, minor scratches and occasional trench-sickness. Astonishing, really. I went all the way to the final month, dash it. First of November 1918, around noon, and Brevet Colonel Audoen O'Brien and his regiment have crossed the Sambre Canal. We're singing half-heartedly how we've got the Hun on the run, oh what fun, oh what fun, and the fighting was pretty well over, and like everyone on our side, I was weary and damnably careless.

'I was striding upright, at the head of a unit, now silent but unwary, going through a field of spectacular vivid blue and green lavender, and I was singing to myself that old folksong:

Lavender's blue, dilly dilly, lavender's green,
When I am king, dilly dilly, you'll be my queen.

'I thought I caught a flash of movement in the distant trees.

If I should die, dilly dilly, as it may be,
Let me be laid, dilly dilly –

'Out of the cold noonday sky, a large shell fragment took me, and I was dead before I heard the explosion.'

She tries to look grieved but can't hide her amusement at my drawled delivery, her laughter delicious, melodious, guileless in its absence of inhibition and I join in, tickled that vestiges of Audoen's personality survive.

We stroll by the stream. The music has changed. At one time, a great otherworld orchestra, at another a single melody, voice or instrument, I cannot tell, full of intense introspection – wistful and passionate, joyous and vaunting.

Aoife whispers in my ear, 'That's Elgar. For me, the loveliest music he has ever written. He composed it the year I first heard it. It's as though he knows this place, that his soul had made pilgrimage here.'

We have come into a magnificently landscaped domain of stately trees, shrubs, topiary, herbaceous borders, tree-lined avenues, terraces, trellis-work, sunken gardens and lily ponds. A gravel path bisects an elongated and sinuous lawn of luxuriant emerald green. We walk zigzag fashion, leaning into each other, and Aoife is saying, 'When René took me back to my lives as Sandra and Grace, I've since often wondered: what of earlier lives? Were we together, lovers, in different bodies, in different ages? Or have we passed each other across many generations without knowing or meeting even once?'

I shake my head. 'Perhaps with each lifetime it becomes more difficult to remember. Hard to imagine, though, I could ever pass you by. I never gave much credence to stories of lovers meeting through the ages, in different lives. Now I know.'

We continue our unhurried wandering along serpentine avenues, passing under pergolas of granite and oak beams, climbing roses, swathed in clematis and wisteria, and reach a set of moss-covered steps that take us to a vale of lily ponds and sunken gardens, blooming in greens and yellows and reds and blues encircled by yew hedges.

'Do you remember our first contact here?' she asks. 'If you no longer hold the memory, come into me and let my thoughts be ours.'

Her mind returns to a long-ago time when she stood at the entrance to that numinous distant tower, to which we are now close by, drawn by a strong magnetic attraction to its intense blue-yellow radiance. In her memory, the entrance dissolves and a warming, enveloping light envelops her. It is the portal to the Great Light, a higher dimension far beyond any imagining.

I share her thoughts, I am part of them as, through her, we remember. She has entered the tower. Small from the outside, the interior is colossal, with no walls or floor or ceiling, without limit. This cosmic chamber has an opening, a gateway to a slow-drifting universe, eternal in time and space, visible only as a kaleidoscope of evanescent shapes and iridescent colours. At its core, a brilliant white light blazes forth an incandescence of eternity.

Within this awesome radiance, she discerns many pleasing and sacred entities. One, singular from the rest, hardly even a shape, a presence, yet tangible, looks upon her with emotions of love and adoration. The presence reaches out from the light, and touches her with the gentlest exhalation, and she absorbs goodness and purity and sweet affection, and is engulfed with a passion greater than any sensation she had ever known.

As this memory sweeps over her, sweeps over us, in an explosion of blissful light, we unite and achieve again, as we will many times, a fusion of spirit that transfigures the experience of life, of love, and is full of irresistible energy and joy.

We are infolded in these ecstatic emotions and desires, and our auras intermingle and meld into a fulfilment of body and mind, knowledge and emotions. I am her and she is me, two entities and one Aeon. *Lux Aeterna*, the eternal light embodies and encompasses our love, entwined and entwinned in the exquisite harmony of the eternal.

EPILOGUE: I REMEMBER YOU

I have no memory of how I made the transition back to my physical world but it happened gently and imperceptibly. One moment, I was in the delicious enchantment of the Shimmer Kingdom; the next, it was a far off memory. Curiously, there were no withdrawal symptoms, even as I understood that I would not be returning for a very long time, just a long mental sigh as I accepted that this is how it was to be.

I had learned almost everything, but there was one final mystery to be resolved, a final tessera to fit into place and complete the mosaic. To be one in both spirit and body, Aoife and I must yet find a path through the different dimensions to be united, finally, in both the Shimmer Kingdom and this physical world. And so I waited.

In the days that followed, the original remnants of Kieran receded as I took control of the disoriented mind and body I had acquired, retaining his memories and some of his attitudes, preferences and prejudices. What I didn't care for or require, I was able to bury in a deep and inaccessible mind shaft.

At Tara Hogan's insistence, I had increased my presence at business-related social events, and so I found myself at a reception hosted by one of our newer clients, the Irish Arts & Culture Foundation to announce an arts sponsorship awards scheme. Tara had secured Dublin Castle as the prestige venue for the launch.

The Foundation was the child of some leading players in Ireland's financial services industry and the elite of Irish business were there in force, with spouses and partners, an occasion for much mutual preening and backslapping in the opulent surroundings of St Patrick's Hall, where once the elite of Anglo-Irish society held their ceremonials, balls and levees under the great triptych of Vincenzo Valdrè's ceiling frescos and walls bedecked with the flags of the Knights of St Patrick, Ireland's chivalric order of knights.

Tara had put together a semi-lavish, black-tie event, with three senior and junior Government Ministers attending. An all-female string quartet played classical favourites and I recognised Mozart's *Nachtmusik*, as well as a piece by Tchaikovsky.

I had come to accept what Monsignor Flinter had once said to me that some music held within it a dimension of the spirit that transcended the limitations of matter. I was in the early stage of discovering Bach, Beethoven, Vivaldi, Mahler and other composers, listening for those who seemed to draw their inspiration from beyond the material world. Rautavaara's *Angel of Light* symphony, for instance. I now listened to it often.

To my delight, I came on the source of the glorious music I had heard with Aoife as we walked in the garden. It was the slow movement of Elgar's violin concerto, that intensely romantic passage where I discovered, the composer had proclaimed, 'This is where two souls merge and melt into one another.'

Around the Hall, a tasteful set of display units illustrated the aims and members of the Foundation under a canopy of scalloped white silk hangings. Tara was scrutinising it with a wary eye. As I approached, the join of the scallops become detached from a central fastener, loosened and fell. I quickly pulled over a chair, jumped up, stretched out both hands and grasped and held both scallops. Tara hopped onto a chair beside me, tottered in her high heels, steadied herself, and we successfully re-pinned them. Our efforts garnered a round of playful applause from nearby guests and we responded with a bow.

'Damn these display people,' muttered Tara darkly. 'Heads will roll for this.'

'Forget it. This is the most fun for these people all evening. Besides –'

I never got to finish. I sensed a brief tremor around me and it was as if the lights in the hall dimmed momentarily then flared to life again. The conversational hum became an indistinct buzz and I thought I heard the music switch briefly from the classics to –

When my life is through
And the angels ask me to recall
The thrill of them all
Then I shall tell them
I remember you.

Still on the chair, I almost fell off when, looking across the room, I saw Aoife, sitting alone at a table in a far corner, her distinctive golden aura lighting the area around her. For no more than a second, though it seemed much longer, my world hung suspended and the room stopped in a freeze frame, before resuming in an explosion of animated chattering bodies.

I stepped nimbly off the chair and weaved my way towards her, waylaid several times by people I knew reasonably well, or in passing or not at all, who wanted to chat. The car crash still made me an interesting person, enhanced by stories of my status as upcoming wunderkind CEO and agency owner. At any other time, I'd have welcomed the opportunity to talk with such useful business contacts. Now, I halted only for as long as it was polite.

It flashed through my mind that the Fates had shaped me to their purpose and that my curious surge of ambition some weeks previously to head the agency had the consequence of bringing me to this evening's event and to this moment.

My heart was beating a tattoo, *vivace assai*, as I reached her table, breathless, lightheaded, striving for outward composure. Around me the room and its people were changing, and the Castle Hall seemed flooded with sparkling brightness, like sunlight emerging from a bank of clouds. The musicians were playing another piece I knew, Schubert's *Death and the Maiden*. How rollicking the Fates could be.

'Hello, Aoife.'

She smiled. 'I'm sorry, but I'm Ciara.'

It was Ciara and it was Aoife, and Sandra and Grace and maybe others. I should have anticipated a different name and a different body: Aoife's slender grace and beauty, but taller and younger, early twenties. Her hair was shoulder-length golden blonde, the colour of the harvest corn. But her eyes were the same, those enormous bewitching hazel eyes of my dreams. She wore a simple white dress with a yellow buckle belt. She reminded me of those marvellous girls in white in the seaside paintings of Louise Mansfield.

I took in her aura, her spirit, her spark – and an excitement she, too, tried to contain.

'Then, hello, Ciara. I'm Kieran, your counterpart in name and destiny. May I join you?'

'Please do.'

Her accent was affluent South Dublin in place of Surrey English. 'Obviously, I remind you of someone,' she said. 'Which is interesting, because I seem to know you also, though we haven't met before, or have we?'

I said:

> *'You have been mine before, –*
> *How long ago I may not know:*
> *But just when at that swallow's soar*
> *Your neck turned so,*
> *Some veil did fall – I knew it all of yore.'*

Her eyes widened, her neck turned so, the veil did fall. 'Wow. It sounds as if the words are yours. Are you a poet?'

We were both trying and failing to act casual.

'The words are Rossetti. The sentiments are mine.' To lighten the mood, I asked, 'How come you sit here alone? I'd expect you to be surrounded by admirers,.'

She laughed at the obvious flattery. 'I'm here with Mum and Dad. They're over there with the Minister for something or other.'

I glanced over at the tall, grey-haired, elegant man in animated conversation, leaning into the Minister, alpha male style, his willowy ash-blonde wife, a decade or two younger, by his side. Ciara's father was Bernard Russell, chairman of the Russell Holden Group of diversified technologies and one of the richest men in Ireland. No half measures in Aoife's return.

She dropped her gaze. 'I shouldn't come right out and say this but I'm glad I came tonight. I had to be persuaded. It's my first outing since I left hospital.'

'Oh. Nothing serious, I trust?'

She made a moue. 'Bad enough. I was riding near Blessington and Pumpkin threw me head over ass into a stream in flood after the rains, knocking me unconscious. Luckily, other riders were passing by, and one pulled me out and called the ambulance. They thought I was dead but got me breathing again, saved my life.'

'Well, thank heavens for that.'

She said shyly, 'When I first saw you standing on that chair with your hands out and those pillowy sheets behind you, I didn't realise what you were doing, and the oddest thought came into my head.'

'Oh?'

'I thought you were an angel, standing over us, spreading your great white wings.'

Bliss was dropping onto me like the first cool raindrops of a shower on a hot summer day. I had, we had, reached the end of a search across the ages to come together now and for eternity and all would be good and pure and joyous and beyond imagining.

I laughed happily. 'Don't you know, an angel needs no wings?'